BLOOD
of a
STONE

Jeanne Lyet Gassman

TUSCANY
PRESS LLC

WELLESLEY, MASSACHUSETTS
www.TuscanyPress.com

Tuscany Press, LLC
Wellesley, Massachusetts
www.TuscanyPress.com

The characters and events in this book are fictitious. Any similarity to real persons, living or dead, is coincidental and not intended by the author.

Publisher's Cataloging-In-Publication Data
(Prepared by The Donohue Group, Inc.)

Gassman, Jeanne Lyet.
  Blood of a stone / Jeanne Lyet Gassman.

    pages : map ; cm

    Issued also as an ebook.
    ISBN: 978-1-936855-30-8 (HB)
    ISBN: 978-1-936855-31-5 (PB)

    1. Slaves--Rome--Fiction. 2. Murder--Rome--Fiction. 3. Man-woman relationships--Rome--Fiction. 4. Betrayal--Fiction. 5. Redemption--Fiction. 6. Jesus Christ--Fiction. 7. Rome--Fiction. 8. Christian fiction. I. Title.

PS3607.A87 B56 2014
813/.6   2014951165

Printed and bound in the United State of America

10 9 8 7 6 5 4 3 2 1

Text design and layout by Peri Swan.
This book was typeset in Garamond Premier Pro with 1676 Morden Map as a display typeface.

In loving memory of my parents,
Henri and Zella Lyet,
who believed I could be anything
I wanted to be.

ACKNOWLEDGMENTS

Some say it takes a village to raise a child, but in my case, it took a village to create a book. I would like to recognize a few of those "villagers" who were so helpful during this process: the publisher, Tuscany Press, and more specifically, Peter J. Mongeau, who supported this book from the very first time it popped up in the slush pile for the Tuscany Prize; my editor at Tuscany, Eric Rickstad, whose patience and insight walked this book through multiple revisions; historical expert, Sean P. Burrus, Perilman Fellow and Ph.D. candidate in Jewish History and Religious Studies at Duke University, who researched and answered questions on topics ranging from New Testament names to ancient rituals of magic and divination; Annie Bomke, of Annie Bomke Literary Agency, whose early suggestions for revision led to the eventual publication of this book; the amazing faculty and advisors at Vermont College of Fine Arts, most particularly, Clint McCown, Diane Lefer, Abby Frucht, and Nance van Winckel, all of whom guided me to new levels and understanding of the writing craft; members of the Writer's Round Table Phoenix, who read some of the very first chapters of this book; the many members of the vast writing community at large, in person and online, for their support, encouragement, and high expectations; and last but certainly not least, I owe a deep gratitude to my family, who never stopped believing in me. Larry, Genevieve, and Greg, I promise you will never have to cook Thanksgiving Day dinner for me again.

For readers who would like to know more about life in first century Palestine, there are many excellent resources. *The Oxford Handbook of Jewish Daily Life in Roman Palestine,* editor, Catherine Hezser, is a comprehensive work of essays on Jewish daily life in Roman times and contains detailed bibliographies for expanding one's research. John Rogerson's *Atlas of the Bible* contains articles on lifestyle and Biblical events, topographical maps, and photographs of the region. The magazine, *Biblical Archaeology Review* is a wonderful resource for current archaeological research of biblical sites and includes fine photos and articles by research scholars. Richard M. Mackowski's book, *Jerusalem, City of Jesus,* is an authoritative guide to first century Jerusalem.

Readers who would like to know more about the Nabataean culture will find www.nabataea.net especially helpful.

These are just a few of the many resources available for anyone interested in learning more about the peoples, lands, and cultures of first century Palestine.

AUTHOR'S NOTE

This is a work of the author's imagination. The timeline of some events and the portrayal of some historical figures have been rearranged and altered to fit the needs of the story. This book should be read solely as a work of fiction, not as a version of history. The intent of this book was to depict the Jesus movement from the point of view of an outsider, from the perspective of someone who was neither Roman nor Jewish. We are all outsiders until we make a commitment to our faith.

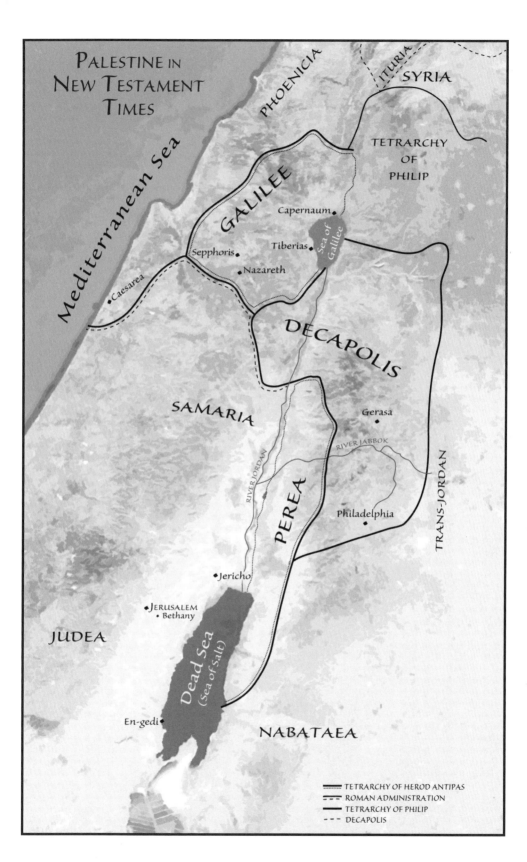

PALESTINE IN
NEW TESTAMENT
TIMES

Mediterranean Sea

PHOENICIA

ITURIA

SYRIA

TETRARCHY
OF
PHILIP

GALILEE

Capernaum

Tiberias
Sea of
Galilee

Sepphoris

Nazareth

Caesarea

DECAPOLIS

SAMARIA

Gerasa

RIVER JABBOK

RIVER JORDAN

TRANS-JORDAN

PEREA

Philadelphia

Jericho

Jerusalem
Bethany

JUDEA

Dead Sea
(Sea of Salt)

En-gedi

NABATAEA

TETRARCHY OF HEROD ANTIPAS
ROMAN ADMINISTRATION
TETRARCHY OF PHILIP
DECAPOLIS

BLOOD
of a
STONE

CHAPTER
ONE

The golden-brown scorpion crept out of a crevice in the mortar and picked her way over the rough-hewn stone blocks of the courtyard wall. This was her domain. She lived hidden within the shadows of the refuse trench gouged between the rural villa and the hillside, where she hunted among the trash and debris for her prey. Her small size intimated an innocence, but she had a sting that could kill a man. Those who encountered her wicked kiss called her the Death Stalker. On this late warm afternoon, she crawled perilously close to a thatch of tangled black locks belonging to a slave named Demetrios.

The scorpion dropped from the wall, landing in Demetrios's hair. Aware of something crawling on his scalp, Demetrios brushed it into the slime at his feet.

Intent on the activity on the other side of the wall, he remained oblivious to the danger lurking a step away. On any other day, Demetrios would have seen the Death Stalker while scavenging through the garbage, seeking out bits of discarded food that remained edible, but on this day, he pressed his eye closer to a crack between the limestone blocks, ignoring the decomposed

1

figs and vegetables that oozed between his bare toes and the biting flies that stung his ankles.

Demetrios's deformed leg gave way, and he slipped, falling flat on his chest. Inflamed by the sudden movement, the scorpion scuttled toward Demetrios's face, her tail arced, stinger poised to strike. Demetrios lay still, watching as she came closer. He dug his fingers into the muck where he found a chunk of rock. The Death Stalker crawled up the base of the wall, hovering just above his head, turning, seeking her prey.

Demetrios gripped the broken rock. He slammed the stone down upon the Death Stalker's back, crushing her with a single, forceful blow. Demetrios exhaled with relief; he would not be her victim today.

He clutched the wall to pull himself upright, then squeezed deeper into his hiding place where he could spy on the conversation between his master and the Jewish slave, Elazar. His master, Marcus, a retired Roman general, slouched on a bench drinking a cup of wine. "Twins are supposed to be good luck," he complained to Elazar, his voice rising to a shout, "but this boy has been nothing but trouble since the day he got here. He limps around, does little work, and eats too much. He can't even take care of the animals."

Marcus gulped wine and glared at Elazar. "Last week, one of my pigs died." He swiped his mouth with the back of his hand. "How do we know he's a twin at all? That story about the brother dying at birth? Probably a trick to bring a higher price."

Elazar's expression remained impassive, but his stiff posture betrayed his disapproval. "The pig suffered from bloat. And why would the father have lied about such a thing?"

"We should get rid of him."

It had been more than a year since Demetrios's father had sold him to the Roman. That day, they had trudged along a dusty road from their hovel in the Decapolis city of Gerasa through fields of wheat and rolling vineyards. Demetrios's father took in the scene with a sweep of his arm. "All of this land belongs to the Roman general," he said as his eyes followed his hand across the horizon. "Twenty hectares. He will have good-paying work for both of us."

But the farm showed signs of neglect: the wheat entangled with darnel weeds and the grapes shriveling in the heat. As Demetrios climbed the rutted trail, his father prodded him along, each ascending step shooting pain up Demetrios's twisted leg, broken during one of his father's violent rages. At the massive wooden double gate of Marcus's villa, Demetrios's father warned the young man not to speak. Demetrios stared at the two-headed image carved in profile on the gate: one face fierce, the other peaceful. His father knocked loudly, stepped back, and the two figures at the gate waited.

The doors swung open without warning, hinges squealing like an animal in pain, and a Jewish man—Elazar, in fact—dressed in the traditional striped robes, stood before them. With his dignified manner and flowing gray beard, he could have been easily mistaken for a pious teacher. He straightened to his full height and peered down at Demetrios and his father. "What do you want?" He was careful to balance the delicate tone of his voice between petulance and consideration.

"Who is at the gate, Elazar?" a more hostile voice growled from inside the house. With even less warning than the opening of the gate, a burly man charged into the vestibulum and shoved Elazar aside. A crisscross of scars sloped down the newcomer's left cheek, causing one brow to droop. As battered as his face was, he still stood strong, with a broad chest and muscled arms, solid as rock. "Who are you?" Nothing balanced or delicate about this voice.

"I've heard you were seeking a cheap slave," Demetrios's father

3

said with a brave face to help propel his words.

Startled, Demetrios turned to his father. "But—"

His father stomped on Demetrios's foot and spoke quickly from the side of his mouth. "Quiet."

The Roman laughed and circled Demetrios, jabbing Demetrios's ribs with his finger, the odor of sour wine on the Roman's breath burning Demetrios's eyes as he lifted Demetrios's thin cloak, studying his arms and chest. "What are these bruises?" The Roman scowled. "And what about that leg? Is he lame?"

"No," his father replied sharply. "He's strong. The limp doesn't interfere with work." He looked at Demetrios. "He's a twin," Demetrios's father added. "The brother died at birth, eighteen years ago, but a surviving twin will still bring good fortune to your house."

Demetrios wondered why his father was lying about such a thing. There was no twin brother, no other sibling. Demetrios's mother had died when Demetrios was born. And now, just he and his father remained.

Demetrios's father pulled Demetrios's shoulders back and forced him to stand up straight. "Let us speak of price," he said.

"Father—" Demetrios said, disorientated and feeling sick with sudden panic. His eyes began to fill with water.

Elazar grabbed Demetrios's arm. "Come, let me show you the animals."

Demetrios limped beside Elazar under an arch into a large atrium. In the center of the courtyard, long-legged insects flitted and danced across the stagnant green water in the rectangular impluvium. "Do you bathe in that?" he asked.

"It drains into a cistern. We use it during the dry season."

As Elazar guided him away, past square rooms open to the atrium, Demetrios caught glimpses of chambers furnished with couches and rugs, floors decorated with mosaic tile, yellowed frescoed walls painted with images of women frolicking naked in lush gardens; statues of men and women and beasts. "Are those the gods of the house?" Demetrios asked.

Elazar frowned. "They're graven images. Nothing else." Elazar paused, looking at Demetrios more closely. "What is wrong with your leg?"

"I do better when I have a stick to lean on."

"We will see to it later." Elazar steered Demetrios to the rear of the villa where he raised the latch on a locked gate and motioned for Demetrios to follow him down a graveled path through an overgrown garden. Beyond the garden, they entered the stables. A great roan horse whinnied as they walked past, and then they approached the donkeys' pen, a single, foul space reeking of feces, the beasts bumping against one another as they nuzzled for attention from their visitors.

Scooping up some fodder from the manger, Elazar dropped it into Demetrios's hand. "Keep your palm flat, they won't bite. Speak kindly, and they will do your bidding." The donkeys lapped up the food and licked Demetrios's fingers. Elazar smiled. "You have a gift for this. See how much they like you?"

The back gate suddenly slammed open and Marcus marched toward them. "Elazar! Bring me the spotted gray and the one with the weak eyes."

Demetrios waited, uncomfortable in the presence of the Roman, wondering where his father was, until Elazar returned with two donkeys. The first animal lurched, fighting to get free. Cataracts covered the poor beast's eyes, and its nostrils were caked with green pus. The donkey was completely blind. The second donkey's bony legs were so frail, the creature wobbled. Raw, bare skin shone through the rangy fur on its flanks.

5

"Keep him here," Marcus said as he hauled the animals out the rear exit.

"Where is my father?" Demetrios screamed, running after the master. But Marcus backhanded him to the ground and Elazar wrapped his arms around Demetrios, holding him tight. Demetrios squirmed, prying at the man's fingers, desperate to escape. "Be still."

Demetrios flailed. Freeing one arm at last, he elbowed Elazar in the stomach. Elazar doubled over in pain as Demetrios staggered to his feet, limping as fast as he could manage, back through the courtyard, past the impluvium, and into the vestibulum.

His father stood at the entrance gate with the two roped donkeys.

"Father! Wait!"

Demetrios's shrill cry reverberated off the mosaic floors.

But his father did not wait.

He left with the sickly donkeys he'd accepted in trade for his own nearly grown son; and he never looked back.

Marcus grasped Demetrios's arm, holding him in a firm grip. "Stop your bawling. You belong to me now." The front gates of the villa banged shut. For Demetrios, it was his last day of freedom and his first day as a slave.

Now, as Demetrios watched Marcus and Elazar through the cracks between the stone blocks, he realized danger was about to visit again.

"I can teach him to do more than care for the animals," Elazar said.

Marcus thumped his cup on the bench, wine sloshing over his fingers. "That's all he can do, and it's not enough! He's not worth the pittance I paid for him. Take him to Gerasa tomorrow and find a buyer. He's a man now; let him be someone else's problem." He leaned forward, the slanting sunlight deepening the battle scars that marked his face. "And don't think to cheat me, either. I expect the full payment."

"The Shabbat begins at sundown."

Marcus downed the rest of his wine. "You Jews." Part accusation, part warning, he let these words hang in the air as he bent forward and considered the dust between his feet. "The day after then." He rose and left for his sleeping chamber.

As Marcus walked out of view, Demetrios slumped against the wall and sucked in a deep breath. The slave market was no place for a slave with a limp. He would be beaten, starved, and worked until he died. He slammed his fist against the wall, blind to the pain. "I'm not going to Gerasa," he declared. "I will be a free man." He knew he could delay no longer. He would have to escape tonight.

CHAPTER
TWO

As the sun dipped behind the hillside and black shadows cloaked the atrium, the house fell quiet. Elazar retreated to his quarters near the animal pens where he began his weekly ritual of prayer to his mysterious god. Demetrios paced the small confines of his room, listening, waiting. Marcus was in his bedchamber drinking, but it would not be safe to leave until Demetrios heard the Roman's loud snores.

Demetrios wanted to run away before, but now he knew he had to act. Marcus's abuse had begun the day after his father had sold him. Demetrios had been instructed to follow Elazar around to learn the ways of both the household and the stables. That morning, when Elazar brought Marcus his morning meal, Demetrios stood next to Elazar's side, watching the Roman warily.

Marcus took a deep drink of the wine, then motioned for Elazar to place the platter of fresh bread on the table. He took one bite and spit it out. "Where did you get this?" he demanded. "It's stale." He flung the large plate at Elazar, striking him in the shoulder. Elazar slumped to the floor, grunting.

Demetrios rushed to Elazar's aid. "Are you hurt?"

Elazar shook his head. "I'm fine."

Demetrios could see that Elazar was not fine; a spot of blood stained his cloak where he had been cut. He turned to face Marcus and glared at him.

Elazar placed a restraining hand on Demetrios's arm, saying, "Demetrios, don't . . ." But Marcus was too quick for them. He leaped from his couch and punched Demetrios in the face, slamming him into Elazar. Demetrios reeled, as his vision blurred. He heard Elazar say, "Master, forgive the boy. He meant no harm." But the damage was done.

When the Roman was dissatisfied with Demetrios's work, when Demetrios moved too slowly, Marcus pounded him with his fists, leaving Demetrios bloody and bruised. If Elazar had not intervened during the worst of the outbursts, Demetrios feared the Roman would have beaten him to death. Beyond the beatings, however, Demetrios faced another torture, a daily battle for survival: near starvation. Marcus withheld food from everyone and everything but himself and his beloved horse.

Demetrios rubbed his bruises, knowing he would be beaten tomorrow and again the day after, and yet, as unbearable as his life was with Marcus, it was at least predictable. If he were sold to a new master, he could face even worse torment: chained in the bowels of a ship, pulling an oar until he died, or hauling stone and rock in bags tethered to his back in a mine, or perhaps following a Roman soldier into battle.

Demetrios wondered if his father missed him as much as he missed his father. Demetrios believed he could be a better son, one his father would love and care for. It was too late now. He just wanted his freedom. At last, Demetrios heard the sounds of Marcus's heavy slumber rumbling through the house. Elazar had gone to sleep as well.

Demetrios glanced at the small corner in the donkey stall that served as his living space, saying a final mental farewell. He had no idea where he would go once he left this place, but he would be free, and with some luck, he might find his father again.

Wrapping himself in his tattered cloak, Demetrios picked up his bag and tiptoed past the animal pens. Marcus's horse whinnied at the sound of his footsteps, and Demetrios froze. He patted the animal on the nose, talking to it softly. "Shh. I have nothing for you to eat."

He entered the connecting corridor to the atrium. Once inside the courtyard, he stood still for several moments, listening. Marcus slept across from the kitchen. To Demetrios, the master's snores sounded like the grunts and snorts of the pigs when they rooted through the muck in their pens.

Alert to any activity that might come from Marcus's bedchamber, Demetrios pushed aside the cloth that screened the storage pantry. He ransacked the shelves, finding a few rounds of dry bread and a cluster of mildewed grapes, enough to keep him alive for a day or two until he could find work. One of the field workers had left behind a water bag, and Demetrios filled it with the brackish water in the impluvium.

Demetrios lifted the heavy door of the entrance gate, easing its weight from the noisy hinges, as he pulled it back far enough to pass through. The muscles in his back strained with the effort, and his crooked leg trembled. When he was outside, he closed the gate in the same way. He took a deep breath then, shaking out the tension in his legs and back, and leaned against the wall. No sound of alarm. He heard nothing but silence.

With no moonlight to guide his path, Demetrios scurried down the hill to the main road, running through the darkness with abandon. At least twice he veered off into the brush, once snagging his cloak in the thorny branches of an acacia tree. Each time, he struggled to retrace his steps. He knew the main road led to Gerasa, but Marcus would take that road as well, so Demetrios decided to cut through the wheat fields into the wilderness. Once Demetrios had eluded the Roman, he could turn back toward Gerasa to search for his father.

But as the first rays of light pierced the horizon, he realized he had not traveled as far as he had hoped. A shepherd carrying a wooden crook called out to him from a distant hill, and from the poor condition of the weed-choked plants around him, Demetrios assumed he was still on Marcus's land. Demetrios could see the road off to his left. The master would come looking for him soon; he needed to hide.

Demetrios turned toward a dry riverbed that meandered around the perimeter of the fields. A trickle of water flowed through the center of the wash, dammed in random places by sandbars and debris. Stands of tall tamarisk lined the far banks, their ferny branches arching high to form tents of shade. Directly behind the green thicket, a sheer stone escarpment loomed over the wash. The rocky wall was too high and too steep for Demetrios to climb, but if he could find shelter under the trees, deep inside their dense curtain, he would be invisible to anyone on the road.

Demetrios skidded down the slope into the riverbed. His bad leg folded underneath him as he reached the bottom, and he pitched forward into the dirt.

He stood, shaking off the pain.

The stand of tamarisk was still a good distance. Grasping a stick for support, he continued on, stepping only on dry ground where his footsteps would not leave an impression. When he reached the trees, he parted their thick, overlapping branches and eased inside the arbor, pulling the limbs closed around him. No breeze stirred; the air was still and the heat stifling. Bees buzzed around the trees' purplish blossoms. The faint, sweet perfume of the flowers made

11

him drowsy. He set down his water bag and dropped to the ground. Tucking his legs close, Demetrios lay back against a mound of dead leaves where he gave in to his need for rest.

He startled awake at the sound of voices, to Marcus shouting, "See the tracks? He's moving south, not east."

Elazar answered, "Yes, Master, I see."

Demetrios sat up. The two men were close, but where could he run? He held his breath, listening, waiting. He was afraid to move. Marcus was clever; the slightest trembling branch, the skitter of tiny rocks could expose him.

Marcus said, "This way. Come on. Pick up the pace."

The voices faded away.

His leg cramped and he stretched out, sighing with relief. He would sleep for a few hours and when nightfall came, set out again on the road. He closed his eyes. Off to his right, a tree limb snapped. A second branch crashed to the ground, and a cloud of birds burst into the sky, screeching. Demetrios sat up with a start. Another limb tumbled down. And another. Entire trees cracked, broke, and fell, as if torn apart by a fierce wind.

Demetrios crawled toward an opening in his shelter. He wanted to look, but he needed to remain hidden. He rose, parted the waving boughs, and peered out.

Marcus! The Roman general sat tall astride his great horse where he charged through the brush, slashing and clearing a path with his sword. With each downward strike, flashes of sunlight sparked from the blade like an avenging flame. Elazar trailed behind him, riding a black-striped donkey.

Spotting Demetrios, Marcus wheeled his mount around and plowed into the thickets, screaming, "Ad victoriam!"

Turning, Demetrios ripped at the branches behind him. Tree limbs slapped his face as he scrambled out of the arbor and floundered toward the rocks.

The dark bay horse, as battle-tested as its master, thundered through the stumpy trees, oblivious to the pokes of thorns and broken branches. It leapt over obstacles as though it had wings. Demetrios ran, pursued by the pounding hoof beats, the shouts of the Roman, and his own terrified panting.

When Demetrios reached the escarpment, he lunged for the nearest handhold, clutching the slippery rock, then lost his grip, falling backward toward Marcus. The horse screamed and reared up, and for a moment, Demetrios could see nothing but the dark underbelly of the beast caked with dirt and sweat. The flying, kicking hooves swirled above his head as he shielded his face with his arms. The horse's front feet hit the ground, and Marcus leaned forward and swooped his sword across Demetrios's elbow.

Demetrios rolled from side to side, terrified of the sword, while dodging the stamping horse. "My arm!"

Marcus pulled his mount close to Demetrios's head. He raised his sword, ready to strike the final blow.

Elazar cried out, "Master, no. Spare him!"

Marcus held his sword aloft, staring down at Demetrios. The scars on the Roman's face looked white against his sunburned skin. His eyes glinted with exhilaration. "Run from me and die," he said so softly Demetrios wasn't sure he had heard him.

Demetrios lay still. The blade hovered above him.

Elazar dismounted the donkey. "No!"

Marcus brought the weapon high above his head, hesitating, his gaze focused on Demetrios. Then he sheathed his sword. "Get up."

Demetrios sighed but did not rise.

With a grunt of impatience, Marcus snatched Demetrios up

by his wounded arm and slung him across the back of his mount. When Demetrios struggled, Marcus slapped him, shoving his face into the horse's mane. "I spared you once. Don't test my patience."

The cut on Demetrios's arm burned; he choked on the taste of dirt and hair, but he remained quiet.

They rode back toward Elazar. Marcus dumped Demetrios at Elazar's feet. He tossed out a coil of rope. "Tie him up. If he wants to run, he can run behind my horse."

Elazar gathered up the rope and looked sadly at Demetrios. "I don't think—"

"Bind his wrists well, or I'll tie you up with him."

"I'm sorry," Elazar whispered as he finished securing Demetrios to the horse.

Demetrios didn't answer. What did it matter if Elazar was sorry? He was still a slave to this wicked man, and now he would be punished.

Marcus dragged Demetrios behind him at a fast clip. Whenever he stumbled or slowed, Marcus jerked the tether, bringing Demetrios upright. Each pull sent a shooting pain down his arm. The rope chafed and burned Demetrios's wrists; a fine stream of blood seeped through the woven knots. The horse kicked up waves of grit, and Demetrios coughed. His tongue felt pasted to the roof of his mouth. Despairing, Demetrios hung his head. Behind Demetrios, Elazar pushed his donkey to keep up with Marcus.

"Perhaps we should give him some water," Elazar called out.

"Not until we're home," Marcus snapped. No one spoke again until they passed through the courtyard gate. Then the master ordered Elazar to take Demetrios to the stables to wait.

Elazar appeared a short time later with a large cup of wine. He untied Demetrios's hands and bathed his wounds in cold water.

14

"The master wants you to drink this."

Demetrios turned his face away. "Why should I? You helped him bring me back."

"Do you think I had any choice?" He offered the cup again. "Please. Drink. It will make your punishment easier."

The wine tasted bitter, as if it had been infused with incense or an herb. It stung his throat when Demetrios swallowed, and after a few more drinks, his head seemed to float away from his body. Each time Demetrios finished the cup, Elazar brought him another. His vision blurred. Demetrios struggled to stay awake. When Elazar gave him the last cup, Demetrios felt as though his ears were plugged with clay. He could barely understand the Jew's words: "He's ready for you."

Demetrios leaned on Elazar for support. As they emerged from the stable, he was assaulted by the heat of a blazing fire. Marcus, resplendent in full uniform, paced the floor. His bronze helmet and cuirass gleamed in the flickering light; the sword strapped to his waist swayed ominously. He was the epitome of the Roman general, ready to conquer new lands.

Marcus glanced at Demetrios, then turned and stoked the fire. Flames shot up, followed by a shower of sparks that seemed to adorn Marcus with a shining crown. The Roman faced Demetrios and drew his blade, raising it high. "Hail to Caesar!"

Caught tight in Elazar's grip, Demetrios fought to free himself. Did Marcus plan to slay him after all?

Even Elazar seemed taken aback. He paused, gazing at the Roman. "Master, we agreed. Not on the face."

"It's my right," Marcus shouted. "He ran away."

Elazar held Demetrios close. "He's young. Not on the face."

"Lay him down." Marcus put away his sword, then stomped toward them. A booted foot swung out and clipped Demetrios

15

behind the knees. Demetrios dropped like a slaughtered ram. The sour wine rose up in his throat, and he thought he would vomit.

Demetrios clawed futilely at empty space while the earth tilted and spun beneath him. Hands grasped his feet and wrists, dragging and pulling him across the ground. He heard the master saying, "Hold him, hold him still." But what did it mean? Where were they taking him? Then a weight fell on top of him. Elazar gripped his arms and pressed them down, grinding his elbows into the dirt. It was hot, so hot. Marcus moved behind him, his heavy steps thumping somewhere near Demetrios's shoulder. Demetrios rolled his head to the side.

Elazar leaned closer. "Look at me." His voice was urgent, commanding.

Demetrios turned toward him. Elazar's dark eyes reflected the firelight. Sweat glazed his face. "What?" Demetrios whispered.

Elazar began to sing words from his strange religion:

"Relieve the distress of my heart, free me from my sufferings;
See my misery and pain, forgive all my sins."

Pain seared Demetrios's shoulder. He smelled cooking meat. Close to his ear, Elazar kept repeating the words, a constant humming, a prayer: "forgive all my sins . . ."

Demetrios felt a searing burn on his arm and screamed.

CHAPTER
THREE

Demetrios lay in a fever for several days. At times, he was aware of Elazar at his bedside, giving him sips of water, bathing his face, praying to his Jewish god. Demetrios wanted to slip away, to leave this world of sadness and grief, but Elazar kept talking to him, telling him he would live. When the fever finally broke, Elazar was massaging aloe oil into Demetrios's seared flesh. Seeing Demetrios open his eyes, Elazar smiled. "The burn is healing cleanly."

Demetrios touched the scar on his arm. He could still feel the heat of the fiery brand against his flesh. "Marcus treated me like an animal, marked me as something less than human." Demetrios looked at Elazar and narrowed his eyes. "And you helped him."

Elazar took a step back. "You broke the law. I did what I had to do. He spared your face. For that, you should be grateful." He leaned over the bed, his fingers stroking Demetrios's brow. Elazar's expression softened. "I tried to protect you. Forgive me for my sins."

Demetrios pushed his hand away. "I just want to be away from this misery."

Despite Demetrios's resentment toward Elazar, the two of them formed an uneasy alliance, for Demetrios had no one else. As the months passed, Demetrios grew into a quiet and sullen slave. He rushed through his chores, leaving them partially finished. When Marcus questioned him, Demetrios acted confused. Demetrios began to steal. He took food from the master's table: small things at first, like a crust of bread or a handful of olives. When Marcus said nothing, Demetrios grew bolder. He stole boiled eggs, bowls of goat's milk, fig cakes, even a jug of wine. Alone in his sleeping quarters in the donkey stall, Demetrios devoured his treasures so quickly that he sometimes threw them up later.

One evening after Marcus had gone to bed, Demetrios snuck into the room with the statues of gods and took the one of Mercury. He knew little about the god, other than he had wings on his heels and wings on his helmet, but he liked the idea of a deity who could fly. He prayed to Mercury, asking to be freed.

Elazar disapproved. "That idol can do nothing for you." He surveyed Demetrios's room, his gaze focused on the scraps of food stashed in the corner. "You should stop that. When the master catches you, he'll give you worse than a branding."

Demetrios moved Mercury close to the head of his bed where he could look at the god before he went to sleep. "I don't care."

Despite Elazar's fears, Marcus paid little attention to either of them. He struck Demetrios less often and spent long hours in the house, drinking until he collapsed on the floor. When he would awaken, he'd roar into the courtyard, confessing, "I'm cursed. This place is cursed." Some days he brought out his sword, swinging it wildly as though he were fighting an invading army. Then he would drop to the ground and bemoan his fate. "I should have died on the battlefield," he'd wail as he covered his face with his hands. Other times, he'd simply lounge on a bench in the courtyard where he'd snore until sunset, wake, and saunter inside grumbling for more wine.

Early one morning when the stifling heat parched their throats like dead leaves, Marcus summoned them both before him. He spoke first to Elazar, "Go to Gerasa and bring my bride and her family back to the villa for the betrothal feast. We need time here to get everything ready, so don't arrive before midday."

Elazar glanced at Demetrios. "Shall I take him?"

Marcus shook his head. "Do you think I'm a fool? He stays here. I have plans for him."

As Demetrios and Elazar walked back to the animal pens, Demetrios asked, "Is it true? The master is getting married?"

"It was settled a couple of months ago." Elazar did not look at Demetrios when he spoke.

Demetrios nodded. "And we're going to have a feast." That meant workers would be coming with carts of fresh vegetables and fruit. If they were inattentive, he might be able to snatch a few things for himself.

As if sensing Demetrios's plans, Elazar gave him a sharp look. "It's not for you. It's for the bridal party. Marcus wants to impress. Her father is a wealthy stonemason. He's hoping the father will increase her dowry."

"What is she like? Have you talked to her?"

"I've only seen her once. She's young." He hesitated. "About your age. Much younger than the master."

Demetrios wondered what kind of young woman would marry a brute like Marcus. "Is she pretty?"

Elazar laughed. "She's a Gentile. I didn't notice." He took Demetrios's arm and handed him a spade. "You need to shovel out the dung. The master wants the pens spotless."

"Why?."

"Do your best." Elazar placed his hand on Demetrios's shoulder. "He will be watching you," he said, looking into Demetrios's eyes, "and I won't be here. Do you understand?"

"Yes." Demetrios's heart ached as he watched Elazar stride out the front gate. Elazar could come and go at the master's will, but he was trapped in this miserable house.

The workers arrived a short time later. Hearing the noise, Demetrios set down his spade and crept through the corridor to the atrium to spy on the preparations. Men hauled in crates of figs, pomegranates, cucumbers, leeks, olives, and lentils. Others carried in solid blocks of cheese and baskets of bread, spices, and eggs. Several people brought in extra tables and couches to expand the dining room for the guests. The cooks had fired the large ovens, and heat poured out from the kitchen.

Marcus stood in the center of the courtyard, barking out commands. "Move those cushions out of the sun," he said. He whirled around, yelling at a man carrying a large platter on his shoulders. "Break that and you'll regret it." Nothing seemed to please him. When the first amphorae of wine were delivered, he sampled every vessel, filling his cup. Then he spat on the ground. "This tastes like piss. Bring me something better."

The farmer said, "This is the best from your vineyard, Master."

The blood rising in his face, Marcus clenched his fists. "Perhaps it would taste better with your body in the ground. I told you I want the best. Get it. Now." At that moment, he caught sight of Demetrios. "What are you doing here?"

"I . . ." A worker strode past Demetrios with a jar of honey, and his mouth watered. With all of the confusion, no one had thought to give him anything to eat this morning.

Marcus frowned and marched toward Demetrios, his hand raised. Before he could strike Demetrios, one of the workers interrupted him. "Master, we're ready for the pig."

"What?"

"The oven is hot. The spices have been ground."

Turning toward Demetrios, Marcus said, "Take a couple of men with you. Get the suckling we've been fattening all week." He grabbed Demetrios's wrist, his fingers digging in deep. "And then finish your work."

Demetrios held the gate while two workers dragged the suckling pig from the pens behind the stables. The poor thing squealed so loudly Demetrios winced. The men cut its throat then drained the blood into a bowl for sauce. They washed the pig, rolled it in coarse salt and ground cumin, and speared it on a bronze spit. As they hefted the seasoned suckling to carry it back to the oven, one of them said to Demetrios, "A pity you have to stay back here."

"I do what I'm told," Demetrios said.

After they left, Demetrios shoveled out the first stall, replenished the mangers with the skimpy layers of fresh fodder, and hauled water from the cistern to fill the troughs. Each time he completed a task, he circled back through the corridor to the atrium. The scent of roasting meat tantalized. Platters of sweet cakes, cheeses, and grapes filled one table. Workers rushed from the kitchen to the dining room and back again, shouting to each other as they passed.

Marcus, ever watchful and impatient, roamed through the crowd, his cup in hand, drinking nonstop. The master's gait had already become unsteady. Marcus's mood could shift from irritable to dangerous and unpredictable when he was drunk. Even the donkeys shied away from the Roman when they smelled the alcohol on his breath. Demetrios returned to the animal pens.

By midday everything was ready—except the stables. One dirty stall remained, but Demetrios was exhausted. He drank a cup of water and then, abandoning his spade, returned to the corridor to watch for the arrival of the bride. He wondered what it would be like to serve both mistress and master. Would she be kind?

Marcus had ordered the workers to stand in regimented lines on either side of the impluvium, where they were to greet the guests. The fierce midday sun beat down, and a couple of boys tottered on their feet. After a final inspection of the tables, the food, and the workers, Marcus whipped open the front gate. Elazar and the guests had not arrived. He glared at one of the cooks, whose face dripped with sweat. "Where are they?"

"Perhaps they were delayed, Master. They'll be here soon," another man ventured.

Marcus yanked him from the line. "Is that what you think? Then run to the main road as fast as you can to watch. Don't come back without them."

The man scurried out the gate down the path. The rest of them waited. When one of the swaying boys dropped to the ground, Demetrios stepped forward to help the young man to his feet. Marcus pivoted and kicked Demetrios viciously in the stomach that he staggered and fell. Several men gasped but no one moved to help Demetrios or the boy. "I told everyone to stand still," the Roman said, his voice cold as he turned away.

The worker did not return with news. Elazar and the bridal party did not come. Marcus paced from the dining room through the vestibulum to the gate and then back across the courtyard to the kitchens where the fires had cooled. Demetrios crouched in the corridor, watching. He knew he should go back to the animal pens, but he wanted to see the bride.

Midday passed, and the shadows began to lengthen. Marcus

paced the atrium like a chained jackal, his gaze centered on the front gates. Everyone else remained in their assigned positions, waiting. One of the workers timidly asked for a cup of water, and Marcus whirled around in a fury. Charging toward the man, Marcus upended the nearest table. Food and crockery went flying. Some of the workers jumped back; others ran toward the gate. "Get out," Marcus screamed as he threw an empty platter after them. "All of you. Go!"

The men fled the house, with Marcus chasing them through the courtyard. When the last one dashed out the door, Marcus slammed the gate shut and stomped through the rubble to his bedchamber where he continued his rampage, breaking oil lamps and throwing furniture. Then it was quiet. A few moments later, Demetrios thought he heard the master snoring.

Demetrios planned to be quick, in and out of the dining room before anyone noticed. He entered the atrium and stepped carefully over the broken pottery toward the remaining tables of food. He scooped up a glob of melted cheese and licked every morsel off his hand, sucking his fingers clean like a hungry babe. He tore off a chunk of bread and stuffed it in his mouth. He reached for the roasted pig, peeled off a long strip of juicy meat: blistered and seasoned skin with large bits of steaming flesh clinging to it. The suckling was still hot from the oven, so hot it burned his tongue as he ripped pieces off and swallowed. Pausing, he glanced at Marcus's bedchamber. The master slept in a drunken stupor; Demetrios resumed his scavenging.

Emptying a basket of fresh figs, Demetrios refilled the basket with the best delicacies he could find: more pieces of the pig, the freshest bread, handfuls of olives and grapes, a cupful of cooked lentils seasoned with parsley and leeks. He flicked the dead flies from a couple of honey cakes and added the sweets to the pile. His basket was overflowing when he finally left the dining room.

Before Demetrios neared the stalls, Marcus appeared. The Roman grabbed Demetrios by the back of the neck, choking him. "Thief. Do you think I don't see?"

Demetrios jerked, struggling to free himself. He could barely breathe. The basket tumbled from his grasp.

Kicking aside the spilled food, Marcus shoved Demetrios into the animal pens with such force they both stumbled. He slammed Demetrios against a wooden post.

Demetrios gripped the upright, slid down, then pulled himself to his feet, his ears ringing. A fresh cut above his eye trickled blood down his cheek. Behind him, he heard Marcus say, "You need to learn a lesson."

There was a sudden, sharp crack, like someone stepping on a lamp or a piece of broken pottery. The air whistled above Demetrios's head, and he turned toward the sound. The first lash caught Demetrios on the shoulder, just above the brand, cutting into his skin with a lick of fire. He shrieked once and was quiet. Demetrios twisted to one side, but the Roman was too quick for him. The second lash hit Demetrios across the upper back, overlapping the first.

Marcus laid the whip well, each stroke curling over the last, ripping new wounds on top of the old, the whip embracing Demetrios with its single, vicious tentacle, stinging and biting as it lacerated his flesh.

How many times did Marcus strike him? Twenty? Thirty? Demetrios lost count. Blood blisters burst into streams. Strips of cloth and raw skin caught in the leather strap; a faint red mist clouded the air. Demetrios refused to allow Marcus to see his suffering, refused to cry out, but with each crackling snap, he writhed and twisted, caught by a horrible sense of anticipation, the knowing of the agony that was to come.

Demetrios's silence incited Marcus into a savage frenzy. Marcus turned from side to side, whirling the lash through the air so quickly it sang. "You want mercy?" the Roman screamed. "Then beg for it."

But Demetrios said nothing. He clung fast to the post, vowing he would not fall, he would not speak, no matter how many times his master flogged him. He would not beg, even if he were whipped to death. His tears dripped down his face, mingling with the blood that flowed from the stripes on his shoulders, but he never made a sound.

Then, miraculously, it stopped. Demetrios sagged to the ground.

Marcus stood above him, gasping for breath. "Don't move. I need . . . water." He crossed over Demetrios's crumpled body and turned toward the trough.

Demetrios raised his head, swiped his arm across his dripping nose. Every small breath was torture. He watched the Roman dip a cup into the water and stride to the first stall.

His back to Demetrios, Marcus sat on a stump talking softly to his adored horse while washing his hands. When the horse neighed, Marcus comforted him. "Shh. He'll be gone soon."

Demetrios knew then: the Roman intended to kill him.

Demetrios crawled out of the stable toward the rear gate. Clutching the wall, he pulled himself up. A piece of stone broke loose, falling into his palm. Someone long ago had carved an inscription into the rock; slowly he traced his fingers over it: Two letters—Demetrios could not read them—twined as one symbol in the way lovers joined their initials. But there was no love here. He turned the stone over, measuring its weight in his hands.

"You still walk?" Marcus said as he lumbered toward Demetrios. He raised the whip.

"No!" Demetrios shouted. He lunged at Marcus, finding strength in his terror.

They hit the ground together, Marcus falling backward into the stable, Demetrios on top of him. Marcus flailed beneath Demetrios's weight, his hands pummeling Demetrios's bloodied back. The Roman dug his fingers into Demetrios's open wounds and ripped away pieces of skin. Demetrios screamed, drew back one hand, and pounded the stone still in his hand into the monster's face. Blood spattered across Demetrios's wrist, every drop stinging his skin with its heat. He heard the Roman's nose crunch beneath the blows. Marcus's grip on Demetrios's back relaxed, his hands dropping away, sliding down Demetrios's ribs like rain-soaked leaves.

Demetrios hit Marcus again. "Stop!" Demetrios cried. "Stop torturing me." He bashed the rock into Marcus's face, over and over, the impact driving through his body. Blood and tissue and stone: all the same.

Finally, breathless, Demetrios stopped. Marcus had not moved for some time. Demetrios dropped the stone and stood, staring at the unrecognizable mass that was once the Roman's face. "Marcus?" he whispered. No response.

Demetrios backed away from the carnage. Clutching his stomach, he doubled over and vomited, then wiped his mouth and staggered toward the body, his limp more pronounced by his weakened state. The Roman lay on the ground, the blood pooling black beneath his head. His body seemed oddly shrunken, diminished, his broad chest shriveled. Despite his pain, Demetrios straightened, pleased that he could stand above Marcus at last. Mercury had answered his prayers. He was free.

Marcus was dead. Demetrios had killed him. But it was justified, wasn't it? He did what he had to do to survive. Demetrios nudged Marcus's leg. "Master? Can you hear me?"

Then Demetrios panicked.

Demetrios knew that slaves who murdered their masters faced terrible punishments: sentenced to labor in the mines or suffered crucifixion. Those sent to the mines often lost their sight due to the absence of light. They toiled naked in deep shafts underground, picking out the ore with iron tools, slowly choking to death from the dust and debris. The average mine slave lasted seven months, and when he collapsed, his body was tossed into an abandoned cavern, where it was left to decay. Death by crucifixion was not as lingering, but no less painful. Suspended by his arms from the crossbeam, the victim was asphyxiated by his own weight dragging him down. Carrion birds picked at the flesh while the crucified slave was still alive.

What would he tell the workers when they returned? What would he tell Elazar? He needed to hide Marcus's body. No one could ever see, no one could know. He could cover it with dirt or rocks, but he would have to dig a hole. But where?

Panting with fear, Demetrios stumbled out of the stable toward the rear gate. His strength rushed from his body in a whoosh of exhaled breath, and he fell. He wept then, the tears falling freely. Where was Elazar? Why hadn't he come home? He needed Elazar; he would know what to do. Unable to lie on his back, Demetrios rolled onto his stomach, buried his face in his arms, and slipped off into a troubled sleep.

Demetrios woke to someone shaking him. Dusk had arrived along with Elazar.

"What have you done?" he cried.

Demetrios shrugged, then wished he hadn't moved, as the scabs across his back tightened and cracked. The remaining shreds of his cloak had stuck to the dried blood. "He beat me."

"He's beaten you before. But you killed him." Elazar tore at his own clothes and hair. "Why, oh why, did you do this? They will crucify us both."

"Not like this. Not with a whip." Demetrios reached toward Elazar, then moaned; the smallest gesture brought on new misery.

Elazar stopped his own lament and stared at Demetrios. He motioned for Demetrios to turn over to his side. "Let me see." Gently, he lifted the tattered cloak from Demetrios's back. "So many stripes."

"Hurts."

"Shh. I will take care of it." Scooping the groaning Demetrios into his arms, Elazar carried him to the trough where he washed Demetrios's wounds and treated them with a soothing balm. Then he wrapped him in a blanket and took him to Marcus's quarters, giving him a cup of drugged wine. "Sleep. Tomorrow you won't remember."

But Demetrios did remember, of course. He remembered every time he touched his scars.

CHAPTER
FOUR

Demetrios woke to the sound of voices at the courtyard gate. Had Elazar summoned the authorities? Demetrios strained to hear the conversation.

"The master was supposed to pay us," a man said.

"I told you," Elazar said. "He's gone." Coins jingled, then Elazar added, "A denarius to each of you for yesterday's wages. Come back tomorrow if you need to talk to the master."

"But—"

"Tomorrow." The gate banged shut.

Elazar entered the room a few moments later carrying a small bowl of goat's milk.

"Who was that?" Demetrios asked.

Pulling a stool close to the sleeping couch, Elazar handed Demetrios the bowl. "Drink this. It will give you strength. Those men were two of the workers from the betrothal feast yesterday. I told them Marcus had to leave for urgent business. I think they believed me. The money helped. But they'll be back tomorrow." He paused. "How do you feel? Can you walk?"

Demetrios shook his head. "I hurt everywhere."

"We cannot stay here. We must leave before nightfall. We have to be gone before the men return. Perhaps you could ride a donkey?"

"Yes, I will try." Sipping at the milk, Demetrios closed his eyes. He didn't want to think about going anywhere. He wanted to sleep. The stripes across Demetrios's back burned every time he took a deep breath; he could barely raise his arms. When Demetrios had knocked the Roman down, Marcus had clawed at Demetrios's open wounds, his fingers ripping apart bloodied flesh even as he died. If Demetrios had not fought back, he would be dead.

Elazar brushed the matted hair back from Demetrios's forehead. "Listen to me. You have to get up. Now. We have work to do."

Demetrios set down the bowl and gazed at Elazar. "What about the master?"

Elazar offered his arm. "I'll show you."

Demetrios leaned against Elazar, his legs shaking as he and Elazar stumbled out of the sleeping chamber to a ridge overlooking the refuse trench. When Elazar wrapped an arm around Demetrios's waist to steady him, the young slave gasped and cried out. "Please. Be careful what you touch. My back, my wounds." He slumped, pulling Elazar toward the ground, but Elazar dragged him to his feet. "I want to go back to bed," Demetrios said.

"First, you must see."

Blinking in the glare of the blinding sunlight, Demetrios shaded his eyes. A sweep of Elazar's arm displayed the darkness below, the piles of trash, and a strange bundle wrapped in a tattered carpet. "He's down there. The carrion birds will find him soon enough." He faced Demetrios, his brow creased. "You murdered him. If anyone learns of this . . ." He swatted an insect crawling on his neck.

"You don't understand. I did what I had to do. He said he was going to kill me."

"I do understand. And you may have provoked him, but it doesn't matter. Now we must flee."

Demetrios stared at the draped body. Marcus had always been fearsome, a brute who stood taller than most men, but he seemed so small now. A sour, putrid odor wafted from the rug. "He's really dead." The sight of Marcus lying broken in the refuse trench gave Demetrios strength. He pushed Elazar away and stood without assistance. "I can walk."

Elazar turned Demetrios toward him. "We'll never speak of this again. Tell no one what happened here. And when we leave this place, we will know nothing of a retired Roman general named Marcus or of his villa near Gerasa. Nothing. Do you hear me? Nothing. We are Elazar and Demetrios, two traders traveling the road."

"And what do we know about trading? I've never lived anywhere but here and with my father."

Elazar sighed. "I know a little. Perhaps enough to start. I've traded for Marcus in Gerasa and Philadelphia."

"But we have nothing to trade."

"Marcus has many fine things for trading. We'll take everything we can carry."

Demetrios considered this for a moment. "Where will we go?"

"We should go south, far beyond the reach and wrath of the Roman authorities, to Nabataea. There'll be no mercy for either of us if we're caught. King Aretas rules Nabataea. He pays tribute to Caesar to maintain the peace but doesn't welcome Roman interference. The authorities won't follow us into Nabataea, and no one will know us there. But we must leave today. Whether you are ready to or not."

"I told you I could walk. I want to go. I want to be free." He paused. "But you're certain we'll be safe there, in Nabataea?"

"Yes. If we're careful, and if the legionaries don't find us before we get there."

They returned to the stalls where Elazar had already begun to pack. "We'll take the four donkeys, the goat, and anything else of value we can sell or trade." Elazar pointed to a tied bundle next to the animals. "I've searched the house, but we should look again."

Demetrios thought for a moment. "When Marcus collected payments from his steward, he always took the coins to his bedchamber. I never saw his hiding place, but there might be money in his private room."

Inside Marcus's sleeping chamber, Demetrios picked up a walking stick propped against the wall. The top of the staff was adorned with a handle carved into the fierce visage of Mars. Demetrios twirled the stick around, studying the scowling god's face. Most of the details had worn away from use, but the distinctive shape of the plumed helmet remained, a reminder that this deity protected the military. Alas, Mars had failed to protect Marcus. Demetrios trailed his fingers over the smooth wood. The staff felt sturdy, solid; it would provide a fine support for his twisted leg. The thought of being able to take whatever of Marcus's treasures he wanted made Demetrios forget the worst of his pain.

Seizing the walking stick, Demetrios paced across the bedchamber, opening the wooden chests and upturning pottery vessels; but the chests had been emptied by Elazar, and no jewels were hidden in the crockery. He circled the sleeping couch a second time, studying the mosaic floor. The design changed near the corner where a dark line cut through the pattern of leafy branches. He stepped on the line, and the floor beneath his feet shifted. He walked across the space again, feeling the stones wobble. "I think

I found something."

He drove the staff into the crack and shattered a section of the floor, exposing a small square hole. Elazar reached inside and grabbed a bulging purse and a handsome ivory-handled dagger bound in a leather sheath.

He handed Demetrios the dagger and then counted out the coins.

"He starves us," Elazar said and gestured to the hole, "but he secretes his wealth under a rock."

Transfixed by the dagger, Demetrios drew it from its casing. The blade had been polished to a brilliant sheen. "A gift from the gods," he said. He turned it over, studying the fine craftsmanship. "Fair payment for our suffering." He stroked the precious stones embedded in the handle and shivered, feeling the presence of the Roman's ghost.

The expression on Elazar's face registered distaste. "Beware of divine gifts. They may carry a price you don't want to pay."

Demetrios managed a grin. Elazar followed many Jewish superstitions that amused Demetrios. He held out the weapon, urging his friend, "Take it, feel the perfect balance in the hand. It's a treasure."

Elazar shook his head and refused. "That thing has tasted too much blood for my comfort."

They hurried to finish loading the donkeys. Elazar grasped a donkey's halter. "Are you ready?"

"Yes. Why don't we take Marcus's horse? It's a strong, lean animal."

"It's too dangerous to travel with a Roman soldier's mount. Someone might ask questions. Let's go."

"Wait." Demetrios rushed back to his sleeping quarters to return with a small carving of Mercury.

Elazar frowned. "Must we take this idol?"

"You have your god. I have mine." Demetrios wrapped Mercury in a cloth and placed him carefully in a bag. "Besides, he answered my prayer. I asked him for my freedom, and now I have it."

"That statue didn't set you free. You killed Marcus."

As they passed through the courtyard gate, Demetrios turned for a final look. The house, which had seemed so grand when he and his father first arrived, now reminded him of a fortress, a place where terrible secrets were locked away. Elazar's comment echoed in his mind: *You killed Marcus.* If a stranger gazed at Demetrios, would he see the blood on his hands? The guilt? If Demetrios hadn't struck Marcus down, how long would it have been before Marcus killed him? Demetrios shuddered; his guilt was outdone only by the thought of what would have happened to him had he not slain Marcus.

"Hurry up," Elazar called. "We want to be far away from here before nightfall."

Demetrios urged his donkey into a trot. The road trailed out before him like a promise for the future. Elazar and he were together on their way to freedom, but Demetrios felt utterly alone.

Demetrios soon discovered the trotting gait of a donkey jarred and rattled his bones; each bouncing step reminded him of forgotten bruises and injuries. He pitched forward and wrapped his arms around his donkey's neck, moaning softly. Elazar, determined they should reach the Jabbok River before they were overtaken by complete darkness, pushed Demetrios to keep moving. "You can rest tonight."

Once they were far away from the villa, Demetrios felt free

to question Elazar. "Where were you when I was left alone with Marcus? If you had come home sooner, none of this would have happened."

"There were problems."

"What do you mean?"

"I did exactly as Marcus ordered. When I knocked on the door of the bride's home, a female slave answered. Inside the house, the bride's father was shouting at his wife, who was weeping. I tried to enter, but the slave blocked my path. She told me the wedding was canceled, that I should take word to my master. Then she slammed the door." He faced Demetrios. "You know too well what Marcus would have done. I couldn't go back without the bride, so I pounded again on the front door. The father opened it. He was so enraged I thought he might strike me. He yelled that I should leave, that his daughter had run away. There would be no betrothal feast, no wedding."

"So you left Gerasa then?"

"No." Elazar's shoulders sagged. "I couldn't go home without her. So I searched for her. I went to the marketplace, talked to the neighbors. No one had seen her. No one knew what had happened. A woman who lived in the house across the street from the stonemason's family told me there had been a terrible argument shortly after dawn, and the father had thrown her out of the house. She said the bride fled into the wilderness. She had vanished. Still, I kept looking. I rode down every street, asking anyone who would speak to me if they knew where she was. I never found her."

Reflecting on Elazar's story, Demetrios hesitated a moment. His brow furrowed and he shot a quick look at the older man.

"You should have come back sooner."

"You blame me?" Elazar said, his voice rising. "I warned you not to steal."

"It's not my fault. Marcus fed his pigs, but he didn't feed me. I was hungry. All of that food spoiling in the heat. I—"

Elazar grabbed the halter on Demetrios's donkey and jerked them both to an abrupt stop. He held up a hand. "Listen. Do you hear that?"

Demetrios listened. Birds twittered in the brush below as they pecked the ground for seed. He glanced at Elazar. "What?"

"We're being followed."

Demetrios stiffened as a gust of wind carried the sound: three, maybe four men talking loudly. There were no hoof beats, so whoever followed was on foot.

"Hurry," Elazar said, keeping his voice low. "Into the trees. Now."

Leading the animals down a slope, Elazar urged them into the undergrowth where they could hide among the thickets of scrub oak, poplar, and tamarisk. "Keep the goat away from the wild oleander, that bush with the white flowers," Elazar whispered. "It's poisonous." He placed his hands on two of the donkey's muzzles to calm them and motioned for Demetrios to do the same.

Demetrios squeezed between his two donkeys and wrapped his arms around their necks while he fought the desire to run. Marcus had hunted him down with a sword. What if these men were armed? The tamarisk he had crouched under had covered him like a cloak; these trees, with their wide, sprawling limbs, provided little protection. The sky hovered in that twilight space between evening and night, and Demetrios held his breath, willing the sun to set. The men were close. He could hear their voices clearly now.

"I still think he was killed by bandits," one of them said. "You saw the villa. Nothing of value left."

Through the trees, Demetrios glimpsed four silhouettes spanning the road. Only one of them carried a torch, its flame casting a flickering light across their grim faces.

"Why would bandits attack a Roman's house? He was a warrior and well armed," a second man said.

"What about his slaves? Elazar and the one with the limp? Where are they?" another one asked. "Do you think one of them killed him?"

The man laughed, and Demetrios raised his head as he recognized one of the cooks from the betrothal feast. Elazar gave Demetrios a warning look, touched a finger to his lips. "That cripple is too weak to do anything," the cook added.

The first man sounded more worried than the others. "Well, I don't want to be accused of murdering a Roman general. We need to find both of those slaves and get them to answer our questions."

The group paused to study the ground. "Can you see any tracks?" the cook asked.

"It's too dark," a companion said. "We'll search for them again tomorrow." They turned back the way they had come.

Afraid to speak, Demetrios clutched his donkeys and gazed up at the sky. Faint stars pierced the twilight, but Elazar did not move. Demetrios waited, wondering if they would sleep here, standing on their feet. The heavens deepened to black, the shapes of the trees disappearing in the night. Elazar touched Demetrios's arm, pointed to a place behind them. "I believe the river is over there. We'll camp along the banks tonight and be gone by dawn."

Although Demetrios and Elazar could not see in the darkness, the animals found the water quickly. "I'm cold," Demetrios grumbled as he tethered the donkeys to a tall poplar. The first day of their journey had broken open his scabs. His fingers were wet after he touched his wounds, but he did feel stronger. His misery had shifted from agonizing pain to a constant throbbing ache.

"Wrap yourself in your cloak and sleep next to the animals. We can't build a fire. It would draw attention." Elazar washed himself and said a prayer. Then he curled up on the ground and closed his eyes.

Demetrios tried to sleep, but he kept seeing the image of Marcus's crushed skull, of the blood that had stained his own clothes. The cloak fit poorly. He snugged the extra length of fabric around his waist to keep the cold night air away. He scraped his fingers against the rough wool as he imagined the crimson beneath his fingernails. A fever came over him, wracking his body with both chills and heat. He groaned. At some point during the night, Elazar covered Demetrios with a carpet, but Demetrios kicked it off, for the rug reminded him too much of the wrapped body in the refuse trench.

In the early morning, Demetrios found it difficult to stand. He grabbed the branches of a tree and pulled himself upright, stretching and massaging his legs as he gripped Marcus's staff and took a few steps.

Elazar watched him but did not offer to help. "We need to cross the Jabbok today."

The donkeys balked at fording the muddy waters of the river. Demetrios offered to lead them through the fast-moving current. "You guide the goat across," he said to Elazar. "I'll bring the spare donkeys with me. If you need help, call out."

On the opposite bank, while the donkeys shook themselves out and Demetrios repacked their belongings, Elazar explained their route. "Philadelphia is south of here, but we won't go into the city. It's too dangerous. There are people there who know me and Marcus." He drew a circle in the mud for Philadelphia and then sketched a line around it. "We'll take a shepherd's trail south. It's less traveled. If we can keep moving at this pace, we should be in Nabataean territory by tomorrow or the next day." He looked at Demetrios. "We cannot rest again until we leave the Roman Empire."

They rode for another full day, stopping only to sleep for a few short hours, then rising to leave again well before dawn. Demetrios felt every jolting bump in the rough terrain and fought back his rising nausea as they trotted along a path that twisted over steep hills to the valleys below. Large herds of sheep had grazed native grasses down to stubble, leaving bare ground in their wake. Elazar pointed at the horizon. "We should be close to Nabataea soon. We'll stop at the next village."

"Why can't we stay on the shepherds' trails?" Demetrios feared the questions people would ask them.

Elazar pointed ahead. "We begin trading now, and we need to learn from the villagers. Soon all of the trees will be gone, and you'll see nothing but sand and rock. They know where to find the next spring, how far it is to the closest oasis, and what dangers lurk."

Late that afternoon, Demetrios and Elazar spotted their first stop as free men. As they approached the ramshackle cluster of mud-brick huts and tents, Elazar brought their donkeys to a halt. "Remember this. We are traders. We know nothing about a Roman general named Marcus, and we've never been to Gerasa or Philadelphia."

"I understand." But what would he say if someone asked him where they came from? He had no knowledge of the world beyond his life at the villa and with his father. He had never traded with anyone before. Surely these people would see through their lies.

"What if they ask us where we have come from?" Demetrios asked as the donkeys strolled closer to the village.

"You tell them you've come from nowhere," Elazar said. "That you have no home but trade and travel."

Feeling vulnerable as they rode into the village, Demetrios kept his head lowered, hunched in the folds of his cloak. He panicked that someone would see his scars.

He and Elazar wound their way down narrow alleyways past a fenced pen where camels lazed near the well in the center of the settlement. A man wearing a long mantle fastened with a girdle leaned against the outside wall of one of the dun-colored houses, watching them. When Elazar and Demetrios stopped to draw water for their animals, he strode toward them.

"You come from the north?" the stranger asked as his eyes searched the travelers' possessions.

"We've traveled a far distance," Elazar said and passed the bucket to Demetrios. "Take care of the donkeys." The stranger invited Elazar to sit on a bench with him outside his home.

While Demetrios watered the animals, Elazar and the stranger sat, gestured with their hands and talked. Demetrios watched them both with narrowed eyes. Elazar was taking a foolish risk speaking to this man. What if he asked questions they couldn't answer?

Demetrios edged closer, wishing Elazar would end this conversation so they could leave. Elazar ignored Demetrios's glare. Instead, he and the villager discussed the weather and the dangers from bandits in the wilderness. The man never asked their names, and Elazar didn't offer them. The villager bragged about his large herds of sheep and goats. Demetrios, terrified that Elazar would expose them, listened intently to every word. When Demetrios heard footsteps, he glanced back. Several children peeped at them from behind walls and open doorways. No one else came forward.

The man said loudly to Elazar, "Your goat looks healthy."

Elazar rose and took the goat from Demetrios. He brought it

back to the shepherd, returning to Demetrios a few moments later carrying a small wooden box. The man led the goat away.

"Why did you talk to him?" Demetrios said as soon as the villager was out of sight. "It is too risky for anyone to know who we are. You told me so yourself."

"And if I had said nothing? He would have wondered more." Elazar cradled the box in his hands. "We're traders now, eager to bargain with strangers. If I had refused to speak to him, he would have been suspicious."

Demetrios was quiet for a moment. Then he asked, "How did you know he wanted the goat?"

Elazar laughed. "I've learned much in my time with the Roman. When you trade with someone, look first at his hands. If his nails are clean, he has others to do his work. He won't flinch at a higher price. Once the negotiations have begun, watch his mouth. He will lick his lips when he thinks the bargain is about to be made." He handed the box to Demetrios. "Frankincense for the goat. It's an auspicious beginning."

Leaving the village, they progressed steadily southward away from their past and deeper into the unknown. The landscape changed, grew more arid and barren. Small stands of tamarisk gave way to broom trees clinging to life, their branches dry and brittle, the tiny white flowers crumbling to dust when Demetrios touched them.

A constant wind kicked sand in their faces, and Demetrios began to wonder when they would ever find a place where they could begin their new life. He had never imagined his freedom to be like this: riding across endless stretches of empty land, rationing food and water, always on the watch for the Roman authorities. It did not feel like freedom at all.

Then one morning when they broke camp, Elazar handed Demetrios an extra round of bread. "Eat. Celebrate," he said. "We are far beyond the border of Decapolis. We are well into Nabataea. Caesar has no real authority here." He smiled before he took a bite. "We're safe now."

Demetrios nodded. "And we're finally free."

CHAPTER
FIVE

The next afternoon they crossed a valley near the Sea of Salt and headed toward Petra, the capital of Nabataea. Elazar claimed it was renowned for its beautiful pink stone buildings and bustling markets. He estimated they had traveled almost a hundred Roman miles. "We are close to the King's Highway now," Elazar said, peppering the horizon with glances. "It is a popular route for spice and silk traders." Then he smiled at Demetrios. "We'll be right at home."

The long trek had exhausted and depleted them; even their donkeys walked with a flagging step. Demetrios's cheeks were chapped and burned from the dry wind and blistering sun. Hunger pangs ripped at his belly, but when he chewed on the remains of their crumbly bread, all he tasted was sand.

Together, they urged the reluctant donkeys into the salty riverbed. The water in the wadi had been tainted with layers of brine, leaving white stains on the animals' legs as they waded through the puddles. Although Demetrios dreaded the company of men, he looked forward to returning to a village where he would dine on fresh bread and vegetables and sleep under the protective cover of a solid roof.

As they rode south along the eastern coast of the Sea of Salt, Demetrios asked, "How much longer until we reach Petra?"

"Hopefully, shortly. I pray every night asking for guidance," Elazar said, his face turned to the sky.

Demetrios wanted to find a permanent home where he could live safely and end this journey.

Elazar paused as they reached the road, and then led the donkeys toward a limestone bluff on the horizon. "The traders say there is an oasis hidden in that mountain. We should camp there for the night."

From this distance, the tall, rocky ridge appeared to be an impenetrable wall. "Why?" Demetrios asked. "It's still early. We could reach a village before sunset."

"A storm is coming. We need shelter before then." Elazar pointed at the sky behind them.

A strange scent filled the air, an odor of burning dirt and debris, stinging Demetrios's nostrils and throat. He glanced back. A cloud of brown floated above the ground, rising and twisting slowly beneath the brilliant blue sky. It appeared no more dangerous than the frequent spinning funnels of wind and sand they had encountered along the way.

Elazar brought his mount alongside Demetrios, riding close. He slapped the backside of Demetrios's donkey and then kicked his own. Both animals leapt forward. "Get all four of them moving," Elazar shouted over the noise of the donkeys' frantic braying. "That storm will tear up everything in its path."

They rode around the base of the foothills and then cut through a narrow opening in the rocks barely wide enough for the animals to pass in pairs side by side. At first, it seemed they had entered a dry canyon, but then the ravine opened to a stunning natural garden. Water burbled from a spring at the top of the rocks. Multiple streams cascaded from clefts in the walls, spilling over moss-covered stones to deep pools below. Date palms, laden with ripe fruit, lined the perimeter of the oasis in neat rows, as if they had been planted in an orchard.

"A marvel," Demetrios said as the donkeys danced with excitement through the lush green grass. "How could such a place exist here?"

Elazar smiled. "Yahweh provides. Some say Moses himself struck these rocks and commanded the water to pour forth." He slid off his mount and motioned for Demetrios to do the same. "Let the donkeys drink their fill at the pools while we set up camp."

"Your Yahweh has not been so kind to us in the past."

Elazar gave Demetrios a disapproving look. "I'm not surprised a pagan would say that. Yahweh's plans are mysterious, beyond the understanding of men. Hand me that rope."

As they pitched their tent, the sky turned, changing from a pale washed blue to a dull brown; the sunlight became filtered and murky. Elazar helped Demetrios tether the donkeys close to the trees, but the animals were skittish, tugging at the ropes. "My people call this a sharav," Elazar said. "The traders have another name, the 'winds of misery.' We will be listening to those winds howl for days."

Shortly before sunset, a large caravan arrived, spreading out around the rocks near the entrance. The group consisted of a single trader with his multiple wives and children, his sons-in-law and grandchildren, a bevy of tents to house them all, and six camels with an equal number of donkeys. The leader of the clan introduced himself as Shumrahu and invited Elazar and

Demetrios to dine with him.

Demetrios wanted to decline. The fear of unwanted questions, the need to keep his past secret, made him recoil from speaking to strangers.

But Elazar insisted. "We will share this small space for several days. It would be wrong to refuse his hospitality. We have nothing to hide. Remember."

They gathered in Shumrahu's tent where the man introduced his family. The names and faces whirled past Demetrios as a blur of quick glances—except for one: Tabitha. His gaze settled on her as her father told her tale. Still unmarried, she was the youngest daughter of Shumrahu's deceased first wife. Tabitha had sun-darkened skin that glowed with a healthy blush. Her brown eyes sparkled with flecks of golden light. She was an unsolved mystery.

"What is your name?" she asked Demetrios.

"They ca-call me Demetrios," he stammered, feeling the fool.

"Demetrios," she repeated as she tapped an elegant finger near the corner of her mouth. When she smiled, her tiny white teeth sparkled like polished ivory. "My mother named me after the gazelle because she said I was fleet of foot."

Shumrahu grasped her arm and pulled her back. "Help the women with the meal."

Tabitha returned and served the bread, balancing a large basket against her round hip. While Elazar and Shumrahu talked and the various wives disciplined their squabbling children, Demetrios watched Tabitha. She moved among the others like an exotic fish gliding through dark water, her body swaying sinuously against an invisible current. Her fine cloak hugged the shape of her torso, accentuating the curves of her body. When she caught him staring, she smoothed her long, black hair. She tilted her head as though she were listening to whispers from the gods, and her gold loop earrings shone like drops of sunshine.

Demetrios extended his opened palm to request a round of bread. She placed it into his hand, and let her fingers linger. "You've ridden a long distance," she said. "Where do you come from?"

Demetrios took a deep breath, wondering what he should tell her. Then someone shouted for more bread, and she stroked his palm once more before pulling away.

Elazar nudged him. "Be careful," he whispered. "She's much too bold."

Demetrios could only hear the sound of his pounding heart. He had never seen a woman so perfect, and he thought she liked him, too. That night, while Elazar slept, Demetrios tossed and turned on his mat, his thoughts filled with images of the beautiful Tabitha.

The sharav took its toll on all of them. Dust and grit settled in their hair, their clothes, and coated their food. The screaming wind sucked the moisture from their bodies, creating a thirst that could not be quenched. Demetrios sat by the entrance of their tent, watching the activity in Shumrahu's camp. When Tabitha was sent to one of the pools to draw water, Demetrios, who craved a cool drink, found excuses to fill his own bucket.

Tabitha seemed pleased to see him. "I will be here every morning."

Demetrios spoke to her about his travels, careful not to speak of Gerasa. Tabitha teased him about his strange accent and stroked his arm when she thought no one was looking, but her father, Shumrahu, was no fool. He called out to her, "Your family waits for their water, Tabitha."

Laughing, she ran back to her father's camp. Demetrios walked

to his own tent, aware of Shumrahu's piercing gaze following his
every step.

On the morning of the third day of the storm, while Demetrios
and Elazar braided rope outside their tent, Shumrahu approached.
Elazar invited him to sit and turned to Demetrios. "Fetch some
fresh water for our guest."

He readily complied, hoping to find Tabitha at the pools, but
she was nowhere to be seen. When he returned, he found Elazar
and Shumrahu engaged in a serious conversation.

Shumrahu smiled at him. "Your uncle tells me you are a hard
worker."

Elazar's subtle nod warned Demetrios not to comment on
their true relationship. Taking a ladle, Demetrios skimmed the
scum of dust from the water's surface. "I do my best." He poured
a cup for Shumrahu.

The caravan driver sipped greedily and then turned to Elazar.
"He's polite to his elders, too, I see." He frowned. "But he has a
limp."

"An old injury," Elazar replied. "It doesn't give him trouble."

Demetrios cringed. Was Elazar thinking of selling him as
a slave to this man? He resisted the urge to run. After all the
risks the two of them had taken, how could Elazar even consider
such a thing? Demetrios had trusted his life to Elazar, but at the
first opportunity, his friend was ready to betray him. Demetrios
clenched the ladle handle, wondering how he could escape.
Where could he go? Out into the brown haze that walled the
sky, lost forever in the desert?

"And he is kind?" Shumrahu asked. "My daughter is a gentle
child. She needs kindness."

Was it possible? They were negotiating a marriage contract. Did Tabitha's father want her to marry him? He started to speak on his own behalf, but Elazar held up a hand to silence him.

"My nephew is kind to all. Animals and people alike. He'll be a good husband. You'll be blessed with many grandchildren."

Shumrahu chuckled. "I have too many now. But that is all well. It's settled then?" He gazed at the horizon, staring at the stately palms that bowed in the wind. "The storm will be gone by morning. A lucky time for a wedding. But we've delayed here too long. After the ceremony, I will kiss my daughter farewell. Our caravan leaves before dark tomorrow. We are going to Petra." He returned the cup to Demetrios. "Be good to my Tabitha."

"I'll keep her safe," Demetrios whispered, stunned.

Elazar stood as the trader prepared to go. "The dowry?"

Fearful that Elazar had offended, Demetrios wanted to say that he cared nothing about a dowry. He cared only for Tabitha; she offered him a life he had never dared to imagine.

For a fleeting moment, Shumrahu's friendly expression darkened. Then he smiled at them both. "She's a jewel unto herself. Worth more than all the coins I have." His hands weighed an imaginary purse. "I offer two fine camels, a donkey, myrrh and frankincense, and a bundle of silk. I think you'll be more than satisfied."

Elazar nodded. "Agreed. We'll begin the ceremony at dawn."

After the trader was out of hearing, Demetrios turned to Elazar, still not believing his good fortune. "Why does her father want her to marry me?"

"Shumrahu is crafty, but the size of the dowry tells me more than his words." He smiled. "He's a desperate man with too many unmarried daughters, and this one, in particular, worries him. His wives dislike her. He sees how she flirts with you, how she finds reasons to meet with you. He wants to avoid trouble." Elazar grasped Demetrios's arm; the fine lines around Elazar's brown eyes deepened into a frown. "Do not touch her until we are far from here. Until they have crossed beyond the hills to the south. Do you understand?"

Demetrios nodded. He imagined himself and Tabitha sharing a comfortable house near the coast where he could farm. He was good with animals. They could have sheep and goats, a few donkeys for local transport. She would bear him many fine children: strong, healthy sons. He would dress her in the finest clothes, cover her fingers with gold rings. When she went to the market, people would stare at her beauty. He would be the envy of every man. "We cannot go to Petra now. What should we do? Will you go back to your people after we're married?" he asked Elazar. Elazar had no surviving family, but perhaps he would prefer to live with fellow Jews.

Elazar set down the rope he had been braiding and stroked his beard, considering the question. "I will stay with you, of course," he said finally. "I have no other choice. Let me think about where to go."

In his fantasy, Demetrios had forgotten about the brand on his shoulder and the scars on his back. "What do I tell her when she sees?" He felt his face flush. "What do I say?"

"Let her see nothing until after the ceremony and after we have left the oasis."

"But she will ask once we're alone."

His voice rising with irritation, Elazar said, "Tell her you fell into a fire at a blacksmith's shop when you were a child." He pulled open the tent flap. "If you value your life, you'll never tell her the truth."

Demetrios walked toward the pools to fill the water bucket, hoping his Tabitha would be waiting for him.

She was there, in the protective care of her aunts. He circled the crowd, but he could not get close to her. Dozens of small children—the grandchildren of Shumrahu—blocked his path as they played games of chase and capture. When the older women were momentarily distracted by a small boy who fell and cut his cheek, Tabitha seized the opportunity to give Demetrios a message. She squeezed behind him, leaning close to murmur in his ear. "Meet me here tonight, when the moon is at its highest point in the heavens." He stared at her as she pranced off with her family, uncertain that she had spoken to him at all. However, when he filled his bucket and drank, he decided that the water had never tasted so sweet. He then returned to the tent to help pack for their departure after the wedding.

In the dark tent, Demetrios lay next to Elazar, listening and waiting for him to fall into a deep sleep. Elazar dictated every moment of his life. Demetrios shifted his weight, moving farther away from Elazar. No one knew what Demetrios had done; no one would be looking for him now. Perhaps it was time he and Elazar separated.

Elazar murmured in his sleep, and Demetrios stared at the shadows above him, restless and impatient. Why did Tabitha want to meet him alone tonight? Did she want to run away with him? The moon had already crossed over the sky before Demetrios decided it was safe to leave his tent. He worried Tabitha had not waited. He found her there, though. She sat cross-legged on the ground, her shoulders draped with a woolen blanket.

"I'm sorry I'm late."

When she heard his voice, she looked up at him. "I knew you would come, my husband."

Demetrios blushed at the familiarity. How could any woman be so beautiful?

She rose and took his hand, leading him away from the camp to a sheltered grove far away from the sight of any tents or prying eyes. After spreading out the blanket, she sat and patted the space next to her. "Come closer. Talk to me."

The moaning of the wind faded away as he dropped to the ground and moved toward her. She traced the planes of his cheek with her fingers. "Who are your people?" she asked.

"My father is dead. Elazar's my uncle. My only family."

She tilted her head back, watching him, her gaze questioning. "My father says your uncle is a Jew. What do Jews ask of their wives?"

Demetrios didn't reply; he knew so little about Elazar's beliefs that he had no answer. She clasped his face, pulling him toward her. "Do not be afraid," she whispered. He froze for a moment. Her lips feathered over his neck, and he trembled. Demetrios leaned forward to kiss her, but he bumped his nose against hers. Laughing, he wrapped his arms around her instead.

Tabitha giggled and nestled in his awkward embrace. Her hair smelled like richly oiled wood, earthy and mysterious. Demetrios breathed in her scent.

A hand clamped down on Demetrios's arm. "Release my daughter," Shumrahu said, as he yanked Demetrios to his feet. "You shame my house!"

"What?" Demetrios stumbled, jerked loose, and Shumrahu lunged at him, snatching at Demetrios's cloak. The fabric ripped at Demetrios's shoulder, a large torn flap falling down to his waist. Furious, Demetrios raised his fist, but Shumrahu was too quick. He grabbed Demetrios's wrist and twisted his arm behind his back.

"Let me go!" Demetrios screamed. He started to struggle but Shumrahu twisted harder. Demetrios groaned.

As Shumrahu's hand grazed Demetrios's bare back, Shumrahu

paused. "What is this I feel? What lies have you and your uncle been telling me?"

"Nothing! Nothing at all!" Demetrios said with clenched teeth.

Shumrahu squeezed Demetrios's wrist, his calloused fingers grinding into Demetrios's bones. "I see what you are!" Shumrahu shouted. "The brand, the marks of the lash. You're an escaped slave or a criminal or both. I should report you to the Roman authorities. The dishonor! You'll never marry my daughter."

Behind them, Tabitha cried out, "Father!"

Shumrahu shoved Demetrios away. "I said go! Do it now before I change my mind." Turning, he reached for Tabitha and dragged her toward his tent. Her head was down, her hair falling about her face.

Demetrios drew his dagger, the same dagger he had taken from Marcus's villa. "Shumrahu," he shouted. "Stop!"

Shumrahu faced Demetrios. At the sight of the weapon, he hugged Tabitha tighter, reached into his girdle, and brought forth a dagger of his own. The blade flashed in the moonlight as he pressed it against his daughter's neck. "If you come near her, I'll slit her throat first and then your own. You'll bring no more dishonor to my house."

Tabitha leaned into her father's cruel embrace, her gaze focused on Demetrios. "Go," she said. "Please go."

"Tabitha . . ." Demetrios said, hesitating.

"You heard her," Shumrahu said, his gaze racing back and forth between Demetrios and Tabitha.

"Go. Take the two camels and go!"

Demetrios sheathed his dagger. Shumrahu lowered his weapon and pulled Tabitha away. Demetrios heard her weeping, but she didn't look back.

Clinging to his tattered cloak, Demetrios ran to find Elazar.

"Elazar!" Demetrios cried as he entered their tent. "Wake up!" Demetrios shook him. Hard. "Get up, get up. Something terrible has happened."

Elazar rolled over, stared up at Demetrios, his eyes blurry from sleep. "What?"

"Shumrahu knows. He caught us together, and he knows. The marriage is canceled. He threatened to report us to the Roman authorities. He took Tabitha."

Elazar sat upright. "What? What have you done?" He clambered to his feet. "Oh, Demetrios, did I not warn you? Load the donkeys. Break camp now, quickly." He pointed to the bundles stacked in the corner. "Get those packs on the animals. Hurry."

"But what about Tabitha?"

"It is done. You've seen to that." He tossed one of the packs to Demetrios. "Move."

In rapid succession, they strapped their belongings to their animals and pulled down the tent. They could hear shouting from Shumrahu's camp, women wailing. Demetrios moved toward Shumrahu's tent, but Elazar stopped him. "There's nothing you can do. We've got to go. He warned you once, he may kill you next."

"And Tabitha?"

"He loves her. She'll live. Hopefully." He pushed Demetrios toward the animals. "Come on."

As they prepared to flee, Demetrios asked, "How will we find our way in the dark?"

Elazar swept his arm toward the night sky. "Shumrahu said he was en route to Petra, so we'll turn north, toward Jericho. Follow that star."

"We cannot go to Jericho. It's in Roman territory."

"They will not know us there. Jericho is ruled by Herod, a Jewish king. He answers to Rome, but if you're more careful,"

Elazar cast a pointed look at Demetrios, "you won't have to worry."

"What about Shumrahu and the authorities?"

"We will have to risk it."

Near the entrance of the oasis, two camels had been tethered together far from the rest of Shumrahu's animals. Demetrios slowed to examine them. "These were part of Tabitha's dowry."

"Leave them."

"No, Shumrahu took Tabitha. These are mine." He untied the camels. "Besides, he said I could take them."

Demetrios stepped on something hard in the sand and paused to pick it up. It gleamed in the night light. A golden hoop earring. One he admired the first time he saw Tabitha. He folded his fingers over it. *Tabitha.* Tonight, they had to flee, but someday, he vowed, he would find her again.

Elazar stopped and turned to face his friend. "Yes, I see. Not a dowry, now, though; it is for his honor. To pay for his shame at breaking the contract. Well, we must still ride as swiftly as the winds of a sharav. Shumrahu could feel different tomorrow."

They traveled at a brisk pace, leaving the desert behind them, moving back into the hills toward Jericho. They approached a village but did not enter. Instead, they continued on toward a cluster of caves near the Sea of Salt.

"Why won't you listen to me?" Elazar asked. "I told you not to say anything."

Demetrios scowled. "I didn't. Shumrahu knew when he saw my scars. The marriage was your idea, not mine! I never wanted to speak to anyone in Shumrahu's camp. You see what happens when we talk to strangers. Nothing but trouble."

"We must find a place to settle down and trade," Elazar said. "Jericho is fine but we should continue north. The further away from Nabataea and where no one will have heard of Marcus's death, the safer we will be. We could go to Galilee."

Demetrios had lost Tabitha. What would become of her? How would he find her? "What is in Galilee?"

"The traders say Herod Antipas is building a new city on the southern coast of the Sea of Galilee, a town he named Tiberias in honor of the Roman emperor. Shumrahu even said that Herod is offering free land to those who will settle there."

"Do you think we could get some free land?"

"Maybe. It is at least a three-day journey north of Jericho. Galilee is the home of my ancestors." As though he were praying, Elazar bowed his head for a moment. "I've been gone too long. I yearn to return to my people, to study the teachings of Yahweh." When he looked at Demetrios, his eyes glowed with joy. "They say there is a synagogue in Tiberias."

"I'm not Jewish. What about us and our trading?" He remembered Tabitha's questions about his family; his chest ached.

"I can't live in Tiberias itself, of course. It would be improper for me, as it's built over a burial ground." He pointed to the purse at Demetrios's waist. "But you, my friend, will build a fine house in the city with our new wealth. Together, with our camels and experience, we'll become the most successful traders in Palestine."

"Successful? We will be wealthy?"

"Possibly. If Yahweh provides."

"Good." Demetrios was unsure about Elazar's grand plans. What about the Roman authorities? What if someone recognized Elazar?

Smiling, Demetrios shook his head. "Let's go."

They chose an empty cave high up on a ridge where they could see the valley below, a good vantage point to see if Shumrahu pursued them. Elazar told Demetrios, "To the Nabataeans, honor means all, and the cancelation of the marriage contract has brought shame upon Shumrahu's house. If Shumrahu does not come before morning, it means he has accepted our taking of the camels as compensation for his shame."

"They are fine animals."

Elazar agreed. "They can carry so much more than a donkey." He crept into the cavern. "Come, let us prepare our beds."

The cave's floor was stained with soot, and a chill wind whistled through cracks near the ceiling. Elazar gathered broken branches of broom trees and stacked a pile of deadwood for their fire. After Demetrios unloaded the packs from the camels and donkeys, he took his blanket to make a bed outside, near the entrance.

"Aren't you going to sleep inside? It's warmer in here."

"I'll keep watch for Shumrahu." He hoped Tabitha would be the one who pursued them, though, not Shumrahu. If she truly loved him, she wouldn't care about his past.

Elazar shrugged. After banking their small fire, he turned his face to the wall and slept.

Demetrios did not sleep. He held Tabitha's earring close to his face, imagining he could still smell her perfume. Sighing, he hooked the wire backing through the fabric on the inside of his cloak and twisted it into a knot. He closed his garment, and it disappeared for no one to see.

The cold night seeped into his bones, bringing new aches to his wounds, but his heart hurt even more. He leaned against the rocks, hearing Shumrahu's words again and again. *An escaped slave or a criminal or both.* His own fingers traced what he could reach: the crisscrossed scars of the whip, the perfect burned imprint of the Roman on his left shoulder. A slave's brand. The monster's claim of ownership. A jackal howled at the crescent moon, and he listened, watching, waiting, wondering what it meant to really be free. No matter how far he ran, he was still held captive by Marcus.

Dawn broke with the morning sun cutting through the thin clouds, streaking the sky with a blinding light. Demetrios removed the dagger he had hidden in his bed. The needle-sharp tip of the double-edged iron blade glinted with flashes of silver and gold, winking at him like a malevolent eye. But the true eyes of the dagger rested in its hilt, a handle formed of a single piece of ivory cut roughly into the shape of a woman. Two perfect lapis lazuli stones had been set into her flat face, beads the color of the deepest waters of the Great Sea. A blue that spoke of fathomless mysteries and wisdom. Gazing into those eyes, Demetrios felt the weapon's power.

The dagger was indeed a treasure.

He turned the handle over, admiring the way the woman's breasts nestled comfortably in the cup of his palm. He stroked the ivory grip with his fingertips, feeling the smooth curve of the woman's shape. Tabitha.

With the knife handle grasped in his hand, he assumed a fighting stance; he twisted the dagger in front of him, jabbed at his invisible opponent's torso. He slashed to the right, to the left. The blade sang through the air. He stopped, his breath coming in quick gasps. In the mere possession of the dagger, he felt a greatness and a power. He lowered the knife, holding it close to his neck. The cold iron numbed his flesh. Then, slowly, he moved the dagger downward, pressed the blade into his shoulder, and sliced.

With the first cut, the knife skimmed over his scar. A slight scratch, then a painful stinging like an animal bite, with teeth cutting through flesh. Demetrios pressed harder, sliding the blade across his skin again and again, careful never to go too deep, never to push to muscle or bone. As the blood streamed over his hand, the dagger became too slippery to manage, and he dropped it. Still calm, he wandered into the cave where he struggled to mix a paste of clay and animal dung with water from his goatskin bag. Tomorrow and for many days to follow, his arm would be almost useless, too sore to move or lift any weight, but at this moment, he felt only a strange exhilaration. When the plaster turned red, he woke Elazar and showed him what he had done. "The slave brand is gone."

Startled, Elazar stared at him, not comprehending. "Who hurt you?" He reached for Demetrios's arm, examining the poultice and the wound. "You did this? Why?"

"Marcus still owned me."

Violence had freed him—twice.

CHAPTER
SIX

Demetrios and Elazar rode north along the Sea of Salt. On the afternoon of the second day, they reached Jericho, a thriving community located near the Jordan River. Elazar explained Jericho was famous for its balsam shrubs; the oil was used as a perfume and in religious ceremonies. "We should purchase some while we're here. We could sell it in Tiberias."

Jericho had been destroyed during a prior revolt and then rebuilt on the ruins. Located in a lush river valley, dozens of palm trees graced the winding and narrow streets. Elazar told Demetrios they should camp along the Wadi Qelt in the shadow of the Herodian palaces where the water was fresh and clear, and the donkeys and camels would have ample grass nearby to graze.

Demetrios gazed up in awe at the massive buildings of Herod's palaces. An impressive pedestrian bridge spanned the wadi, connecting the palace structures on both sides of the wash. A walled portico surrounded the courtyards and reception halls of the northern wing; near the southern wing, an aqueduct fed water to both the sunken gardens and the enormous pool. "It looks

Roman," Demetrios said, thinking of Marcus's much smaller villa. He watched uneasily as a guard paced the perimeter.

"Not Roman but the home of a Jewish king," Elazar said. "Herod's winter palaces. It's too early in the season for him to be here. I doubt we'll see him or any of his family."

Demetrios flinched under the watchful eye of Herod's guards. Demetrios had washed his hands again and again with both water and sand, but he still felt stained by guilt. A close look by one of those trained guards would reveal his true condition: a runaway slave who had murdered his Roman master. At night, when Demetrios slept, he smelled the final fetid exhalations of Marcus's breathing across his face. He glanced again at the palace; a guard had paused in his patrol to peer down at the camps along the wadi. What if that man knew Marcus? Turning his back to the palace, Demetrios crept into the tent he and Elazar had pitched.

That evening, as Elazar and Demetrios huddled close to their fire, talking about the upcoming journey to Tiberias, a small caravan straggled into the camp. The elderly man leading the group had a bleeding head wound and slumped over the back of a donkey while an old woman guided them toward Elazar's and Demetrios's tent. One other donkey, carrying only a few empty, sagging packs, followed with several more women and children trailing behind it. Elazar rose to greet them.

The man slid off his animal, staggered, pressed his hand to his head. "My friends, do you have food to spare?" he asked. "My family and I are hungry." He spoke timidly, seeming fearful to intrude.

"Yes, of course," Elazar answered. "Please, sit." He nodded to Demetrios. "Bring us some wine and bread."

While Demetrios poured cups of wine, the newcomer related his tale. "Our caravan comes from the west, Jerusalem, from the Feast of Booths. There was so much to see, so many people to visit, that we delayed our departure by two days. By the time we left Jerusalem, everyone else had gone. Bandits attacked us on the road. You see the result." He sighed, reached for the cup of wine Demetrios handed him, and drank.

The old woman began to weep. "They took everything," she said. "Our blankets, our food, our money. And they beat my husband, my poor Phinehas." She patted him on the shoulder.

Phinehas added, "We're lucky to be alive."

"Where are you going?" Elazar asked as he broke pieces of bread to share. He motioned for Demetrios to pour more wine.

"To our village. Betharamptha. East of here," Phinehas replied. He studied Elazar for a moment. "Perhaps you would like to join us?"

Elazar shook his head. "I'm sorry, but we travel north. To Tiberias on the Sea of Galilee." He stirred the fire. "How many bandits were there?"

"Three. I fought them, did my best to protect the women and children, but they still managed to steal everything." The men talked for a little while longer about the terrain, the weather, the conditions and challenges of travel, the places to avoid, and the places to find refuge. But before long, it became apparent that the strangers were weary. At a lull in the conversation, Phinehas rose and excused himself. "I'm sorry, but we're all exhausted, and we still have a good distance to go tomorrow." He sighed. "After this, I fear I'll never return to Jerusalem. Brigands control the Jerusalem road. It's too dangerous for anyone to travel."

"Please, make your camp close to our tent," Elazar said. "You'll be safe here."

"We thank you for your kindness," Phinehas answered.

Demetrios crawled into the tent and spread out his sleeping pallet. As he dropped off to sleep, he heard one of the women lamenting their fate to Phinehas. "Please tell us that's not true. Surely we'll visit the Holy City again." Phinehas didn't answer.

Early the next morning, Elazar gave the group rounds of bread and a filled water bag. They departed as bedraggled as they had come. Phinehas waved a final farewell as he climbed the road to the east.

"Do you think we should have accompanied them?" Demetrios asked. "For their safety?"

"Their village isn't far. Bandits won't bother them now."

"Still . . ."

"I know what we should do," Elazar said, turning toward Demetrios. "We should become caravan drivers. We'll be more than simple traders. We can escort the pilgrims to and from Jerusalem."

"You said we were going to Tiberias. Besides, the Jerusalem road is dangerous. You heard Phinehas." Demetrios had the dagger, but he didn't relish the idea of using it to fend off bandits.

"Phinehas was foolish. We are not. He made mistakes. We won't." Elazar's eyes glowed.

"What do you mean?" Demetrios asked.

"There are three major festivals in Jerusalem." Elazar ticked them off on his fingers. "The Feast of the Passover, when we honor my people's exodus from Egypt, the Feast of Weeks, in which we present the first fruits of harvest at the Temple, and the Feast of Booths, to celebrate the fall harvest. Pilgrims travel to Jerusalem for all of them. Not only can we trade there, but we can escort the Jewish pilgrims safely from Tiberias to Jerusalem and back. Bandits attacked Phinehas and his family because he was an old man accompanied by a handful of women and children. His party was too small and lacked protection. But we have four donkeys, two camels, the two of us, and if we gather a large group, we'll be safe. We could hire another caravan driver if we needed to."

Demetrios poked at the ashes of their fire, making sure the coals were cold. "Another driver? Who?" Demetrios disliked the idea of working with strangers; they couldn't be trusted.

"I don't know. We'll find someone in Tiberias." Elazar grinned. "Just think of it. We'll be the largest caravan in Galilee." He tugged at the ropes on their tent. "Come. Tiberias awaits."

Three days later, they entered Tiberias through the southern gate. Off to their left, a Roman-style theater had been cut into the side of the hill. Elazar frowned when he first saw the structure. "Now that is a Roman building," he said. "Let us hope they do not indulge in pagan spectacles."

Demetrios was dazzled by the theater's huge curved limestone walls and rows and rows of seats. He guessed it could hold the entire population of Gerasa. He had never seen a city like Tiberias. More sprawling than any of the small towns they had passed through, Tiberias was also a place where the buildings, the streets and carts, even the donkeys, were clean and new. "Herod Antipas founded Tiberias ten years ago," Elazar said as they led their animals along the paved cardo. Several people turned to watch them as they passed by.

"Why are they staring at us?" Demetrios asked. He felt increasingly conspicuous.

"They're admiring our fine caravan." Elazar nodded at a couple of elderly Jewish men and kept walking. He pointed out other magnificent buildings that dotted the rolling hills overlooking the water. "Over there is a stadium. And I believe that's a mint or some government office. Do you see that hill? It is known as Berniki Hill. That palace on its crest belongs to Herod, too." Elazar's voice dropped to a whisper. "The old fox built his wealth upon political influence and taxes."

"Berniki Hill?" Demetrios asked.

"Herod named the site after his daughter."

Tiberias hummed with frenetic energy. Laborers hauled carts of cut stone along the winding roads; the sound of pounding hammers rang in the air. Everywhere Demetrios and Elazar looked, the construction of glorious mansions and small two-room houses continued unabated. Wealthy women and slaves crowded the shops that lined the street on their right, where they bargained for wine, fruit, clothing, jewelry, baskets, bread, cheese, and household goods. Between the buildings, stone steps led down to the Sea of Galilee; a faint mist clouded the view of the dark-gray mountains across the water.

"Make way, make way," a voice behind them shouted.

Demetrios and Elazar moved to the side to let a slave-borne litter pass, but the litter paused, blocking the road. The curtain parted and a round-faced man, his hair cropped short in the popular Roman style, leaned out. He wore a white woolen tunic bound with a heavy leather belt. "I knew I saw camels." He looked at Elazar. "Are they yours?"

"They are." Elazar touched Demetrios's shoulder. "I am Elazar, and this is my business partner, Demetrios. We're caravan drivers from Nabataea."

A smile split the man's face, crinkling his eyes into tiny slits. "I am Tertius. And have you come to Tiberias to stay, or are you traveling elsewhere?"

"We hope to make our home here," Elazar said.

"Oh, that is fine indeed. Tiberias is fast becoming a city of the world." He gazed at the camels. "Such stately animals. Tell me, is it true they can travel hundreds of miles without water?"

"I don't know. They can go a good distance, though. More than a donkey."

"Indeed." Tertius squinted at Elazar. "You look so familiar. Have we met before? Perhaps somewhere in the Decapolis?"

Demetrios tensed, but Elazar replied smoothly, "I fear I have a common face. Demetrios and I have been trading in Nabataea. This is our first time travelling this far north."

"My mistake then. Well, I would love to talk to you more about your camels, but I'm off to meet a friend. Perhaps another time." He reached to draw the curtain, then hesitated. "Be sure to ask in the wine shop about the wine from Tertius's vineyards. My steward produces the best wine in all of Galilee." He lay back on his cushions and ordered his slaves to proceed.

As soon as Tertius was out of sight, Demetrios lashed out at Elazar. "I knew we should never have come here! There are Romans everywhere. It's only a matter of time before we're caught."

"Nonsense. I've never seen Tertius before, so it's impossible that he recognized me. You worry about nothing." He clapped a hand on Demetrios's shoulder. "Come, let us see more of this fine city."

Demetrios and Elazar continued exploring the marketplace, but they had gone only a short distance before a woman with loose, flowing hair stepped out from the back of one of the shops and beckoned to Demetrios. "Do you want some entertainment?"

Demetrios, attracted by her friendly demeanor, slowed. The way she touched her hair and smiled at him reminded him of Tabitha.

Elazar grabbed Demetrios's arm. "Don't talk to her," Elazar said as he pulled Demetrios away.

"Did you see her eyelids? So blue."

Elazar kept dragging Demetrios along, away from the shop.

"The blue eyelids advertise that she's a prostitute."

Amazed that a harlot could so openly ply her trade in the marketplace, Demetrios glanced back. But the woman had disappeared.

Demetrios and Elazar then strolled down the hill to the shore where fishermen salted their catch and spread the fish out on drying racks. At a vendor's booth, Elazar picked out a fresh fish for their supper. "We'll eat well tonight," he said as he wrapped the tilapia in a damp cloth. "Tomorrow we'll begin the search for our new homes."

That evening, after Elazar had fallen asleep in their tent, Demetrios thought about their first day in Tiberias: so many people, expensive goods he had never imagined, food he had never tasted, and that woman with the painted eyelids. The color made her eyes appear huge, and she had smiled at him as if she knew him. Her mantle had been loose, sliding off one bare shoulder. When she waved at him, her hips swiveled and turned, mimicking a seductive dance. A woman like that could teach him the ways of men and women, and the secrets they shared; he would never again embarrass himself with awkward kisses or clumsy embraces. Demetrios opened his purse, turning over the coins he carried. Was it enough? Tiptoeing out of their tent, he reached the flap, which served as a doorway, took one look at Elazar's sleeping form, and headed out for the marketplace.

Most of the streets in town were quiet, but a light burned in the window of the shop where he had seen the prostitute. A man exited the shop as Demetrios approached, looking furtively up and down the street. When he saw Demetrios standing there, he froze, then turned and hurried away.

Demetrios waited, walking back and forth. The woman stepped out from the building, smiled. "I thought you might come back," she said. "Come in."

Four oil lamps, suspended from chains in the ceiling, cast an eerie glow across the room. The interior of the shop was dank and dirty, and it reeked of other men's sweat and other bodily odors, not at all what Demetrios had expected.

The prostitute stood under the light; her hair was braided and bound in a net. The blue paint on her eyelids had creased into a blurry smear, creating the illusion of a bruise. "I am Shappira. What is your name?"

Demetrios's mouth had gone dry. He swallowed. "Demetrios."

She smiled and held out her open palm. "The fee is one denarius for the night. You won't be disappointed."

Demetrios reached for his purse, removed the coin. Shappira took it from him and dropped it into a box at the back of the room. Turning, she walked toward him and slipped off her mantle. She wore nothing but a sheer tunic underneath. Shappira traced the shape of her curves with her fingers, hesitating, trailing them up her body and then down again. Demetrios's own fingers burned. He wanted to touch, but he was unsure.

Shappira tilted her head, licked her lips, which were cracked and puffy from other men's kisses. Then, slowly, her gaze focused on Demetrios. She reached up, removed the net around her hair, and unwound her braid, one strand at a time. When she had finished, she held out her hands, inviting him closer.

Demetrios stumbled toward her. "Should I take off my cloak?" His voice croaked, and he flushed.

"Of course," Shappira said. "I will help you." As she leaned forward, her tresses, heavily oiled, fell around Demetrios's face. He caught the faint odor of perfume, a fragrance of richly oiled wood. For a brief moment, Demetrios thought of Tabitha. But this was not Tabitha, a woman who was pure. Shappira's perfume had been defiled and soured by the touch of many men. Demetrios coughed.

Ignoring Demetrios's discomfort, Shappira deftly unfastened the pin at his shoulder and slipped his cloak from his body. Then she grasped the hem of his tunic and pulled it over his head. She set both his cloak and tunic on a table next to the bed. Dressed only in his loincloth and sandals, Demetrios stood before her, shivering. She was so bold!

She touched his face, stroked his cheek. "You're young." Shappira kneaded Demetrios's shoulders, pulled him closer. "Relax," she breathed into his ear.

Demetrios closed his eyes. She had a strong grip, sensual and fluid. He sighed, knowing she would teach him everything he wanted to know.

Shappira released him. Demetrios opened his eyes. She had stepped back and was staring at him. Frozen for a moment, she reached up and removed a lamp from a chain and brought it to his shoulders.

"What is that?" She pointed to where Marcus's brand once was. "What happened to your back and arm?" Her friendly demeanor had evaporated.

"I fell into a blacksmith's fire," he said, remembering the lie Elazar had told him to give to Tabitha.

"Are you sure?"

Shappira guided the pale light over his bare twisted leg, frowning. "The fire didn't do this," she said. "What is wrong with you? Are you cursed by the gods?"

"No, no. The fire. I—"

"I don't mind a warrior's battle scars, but these are . . ." She pointed to the marks on his body. "You're hideous, disgusting. And that leg. A punishment or a curse, it doesn't matter. Your ugliness makes me sick." Gagging, she tossed Demetrios his cloak and tunic. "Get out!"

Demetrios clutched the garments close to his chest. "But my money! I paid you!"

"Do you think I want to be tainted by your touch? I don't want your disease." She raised the lamp, tilted it slightly so that hot oil dribbled. "If you don't leave now, I'll give you more scars."

Demetrios struggled into his clothes and staggered into the empty street. The door slammed behind him. Outside the house, two eyes peeked out from a figure crouched under an archway at the end of the street. Not knowing who or what it was that stared at him, Demetrios turned and limped away.

Removing Marcus's brand had made no difference. Demetrios was still cursed by his past. He leaned against a wall and, breathing hard, rubbed his leg. He had been rejected by his father and now twice more. He would never be rejected again.

CHAPTER
SEVEN

Three days later, Elazar guided Demetrios up one of the western hills to a patch of land that commanded a stunning view of the Sea of Galilee. Below, the white sails of boats drifted over the shimmering water. "This is where you will build your fine new house, Demetrios of Tiberias."

"Demetrios of Tiberias. Is that my name now?" The words sounded strange to his ears, as though he had transformed into someone different, someone who had never been sold as a slave or murdered a man. Someone respectable. He thought again about Shappira. If he had been rich, she would never have treated him that way. He vowed to become as successful as his new name implied, a caravan driver of wealth and power.

Elazar nodded. "Yes. In this city, the citizens have no past or history."

Demetrios pointed to the mansion that towered over his building site. Behind the house, vineyards rolled across the land for as far as they could see. "Who lives there? Do you know?"

Elazar hesitated, then said slowly, "Tertius."

"Tertius? The Roman we met on the cardo?" Demetrios backed away. "I don't want to live here. We'll find somewhere else, closer to the shore." He glared at Elazar. "Romans protect their own. They have no compassion for those who have committed a crime against them—especially murder. You told me so yourself."

"Not all Romans are like Marcus. When I spoke to Tertius the other day in the marketplace, he seemed quite congenial, although a bit preoccupied. He's obsessed with his vineyards, talks about them constantly. He told me that his slave, Elisheba, bakes the best bread in all of Tiberias. He offered to send over a basket and a jug of wine once you're settled. A welcome gift to a new neighbor, the caravan driver from Nabataea." He sighed. "You'll find all sorts of people in Tiberias, Demetrios: Ethiopians, Egyptians, Greeks, Romans, Jews. Herod's gift of free land has brought them from the far reaches of the Empire. To be a successful trader, you must learn to speak to them all."

"I don't want to live next to a Roman."

"He won't bother you." Elazar held out his hand. "Come, let me show you the plans for your new home." Pacing out the layout, he said, "The courtyard will face the street and span the entire front. Big enough for benches, a fountain, and a brazier for cooking and heating. Another room back here where you can dine when the weather is bad. A room over there where you will sleep, another room next to it, and in the back, we'll build a storage room. We'll keep the most precious items there, safely locked away."

As he followed Elazar around the site, Demetrios imagined how he would furnish his house with rugs, a sleeping couch, benches and stools, and tables laden with good food and wine. He and his father had never lived anywhere but in a crude one-room hut, no larger than a cave. At Marcus's villa, he slept in the stables with the animals. But he was Demetrios of Tiberias now, and he could afford a place finer than his father had ever dreamed of. Thanks to Marcus. "With so many rooms, you could live with me."

"Gentiles do not share a roof with Jews. Every time I crossed your threshold, I would need to cleanse myself later."

Demetrios sighed, aggravated by Elazar's Jewish superstitious nonsense. "We share a tent."

Elazar smiled. "That's different. Since Herod built Tiberias over a burial ground, I cannot live within the walls of the city. Jewish law forbids contact with human bones."

"Where will you live then?"

"I've found a small one-room house outside of Tiberias with a courtyard in front and stables in the rear. We'll place the donkeys in the stables and keep the camels in the courtyard."

As they walked back to their camp, Elazar announced one more surprise. "Tertius has gambling debts. He's offered to sell you one of his slaves for a fair price, a boy named Rufus."

Demetrios recoiled from his friend, appalled. "A slave? I don't want a slave. I was a slave. Why would I subject someone else to that misery? No. Never. I will never own another human being."

"To be a successful caravan driver, you must appear successful. Besides, you'll need someone to help you in that large house. And Tertius says the boy is obedient, just a couple of years younger than you. We'll train him to assist us with the animals. You have an appointment with Tertius tomorrow morning." He handed a bulging purse to Demetrios. "Here are three thousand sestertii but offer him no more than twenty-five hundred."

"Marcus gave my father two miserable broken-down donkeys for me."

Elazar nodded. "Marcus cheated your father." He folded Demetrios's fingers over the purse. "Keep this hidden until you agree on a price."

"I don't want to do this."

"It's necessary, Demetrios. If you are wealthy and have no slave, people will wonder why."

"Just one slave? That is all?"

"Yes."

Demetrios glanced up at Tertius's massive home on the hillside. His own house would never be as imposing, but people would still see him as successful, and a slave could be helpful, even decent company, perhaps. If he had money, women would no longer reject him. "We'll meet with the Roman tomorrow then."

"Tertius is a Roman, a Gentile like you. The same rules apply about crossing his threshold. If I enter a Gentile's house, I must purify myself afterward. So, you must do this without me, but you've watched me negotiate often enough. Just remember what I do." Elazar gazed at the sea, watching the fishermen on the shore toss their nets into the water. "While you're buying your slave, I plan to visit the synagogue. Bring him back to our tent when you're finished."

Early the next morning, Demetrios stood uncertainly outside the entrance of Tertius's mansion. Grasping his staff, Demetrios rapped on the front door. A female slave opened it and asked his name.

"I am Demetrios of Tiberias," he said, struggling to sound confident. The words felt strange in his mouth, fraudulent. "I've come to speak to your master."

The woman escorted Demetrios into a large courtyard. Unlike Marcus's villa, which had an air of neglect, Tertius's mansion was tidy and cheerful. Bright sunlight warmed the swept stone floor while wooden benches, stacked with cushions, lined the walls. "I'll fetch the master," the woman said as she left the room.

Demetrios perched on the edge of the bench, holding tight to his walking staff for reassurance. When the master, Tertius, entered, Demetrios rose and, out of habit, started to lower his head, then stopped himself.

Tertius smiled at Demetrios graciously and pulled a stool close. "Please, sit." He clapped his hands. "Bring us some wine," he said to a slave, who responded promptly. Turning back to Demetrios, he asked, "So, you and Elazar are caravan drivers? From Nabataea?"

"Yes, Nabataea." Marcus had been a battle-hardened warrior, but Tertius was soft. His fat belly protruded over his girdle and his face was puffy from too much good food and drink. He had the lazy, easygoing demeanor of someone who had lived in comfort most of his life.

"Your camels are wonderful. A distinct advantage in this part of the world."

"We bought them when we were in Nabataea." Demetrios shifted his weight on the bench and a cushion slipped to the floor. Embarrassed, he scooped it up and tucked it behind his back. He straightened, tried to look directly at the Roman. Did Tertius recognize the lies? Was that a frown on the Roman's face or indigestion? Demetrios couldn't tell. "Elazar said you want to sell one of your slaves?" He coughed as the last word caught in his throat like a fishbone.

A female slave brought the cups of wine and Tertius drank deeply before he answered. "Ah, that's very fine, don't you think? From last year's harvest. I have the best vineyards in Galilee." He set down his cup. "It grieves me to sell Rufus. It really does. He's an excellent cook and a compliant slave. Young, about your age, perhaps. You'll treat him well?"

Tertius spoke as though the deal had already been made, but he had never mentioned his price. "I would never hurt a slave,"

Demetrios said, "but I don't know if—"

Tertius cut him off with a wave of his hand. "What am I thinking? You want to see him first." Turning to another slave, he said, "Tell Rufus to come in here."

When Rufus entered, Demetrios was struck by the similarity in their ages. Rufus was not a boy but a young man, old enough for a wife. His hair had been close-cropped in the Roman style, but it had grown out unevenly, with reddish brown curls trailing down his forehead. Slender and tall, he stood before Demetrios and Tertius, trembling, and for a fleeting moment, Demetrios remembered his own terror when he realized his father planned to sell him to Marcus.

Demetrios swallowed; he felt sick. No matter what Elazar thought, Demetrios could not do this. Would not. He'd never own this young man. Preparing to leave, he reached for his staff.

A young woman rushed into the courtyard, trailed by another slave, who yelled, "I tried to stop her, Master."

The young woman dropped to her knees and kissed Tertius's feet. "Please, Master," she said, her hair falling down around her face, "please don't do this. Rufus belongs with us. This is his home." She began to weep.

Tertius clasped her elbows and gently raised her up. "My dear Elisheba, don't cry. It pains me to see you so unhappy." He brushed the tears from her face. "Everything will be fine. You'll see."

Still standing in front of Demetrios, Rufus moaned, an inhuman, animal sound of suffering. Tertius glanced at Rufus and then turned his attention back to Elisheba, murmuring words of comfort, and in that brief exchange, Demetrios realized two things: Elisheba loved Rufus, but Tertius loved her.

"Take her out of here," Tertius ordered, pushing Elisheba toward the other female slave.

Demetrios rose. "I'm sorry. I've made a mistake." He touched Rufus's shoulder. "You can stay with your master."

Tertius gave Demetrios a sharp look. His jaw clenched and all traces of the softness disappeared; he had become the hard-willed Roman, determined to have his way. He shook his head, then smiled at Demetrios, but Demetrios did not find him as charming as before. "Unfortunately, if you don't buy him, I'll have to sell him at the slave market. His cooking skills will fetch a good price. You see, I'm afraid I have a taste for the dice. Alas, I have debts." He shrugged his shoulders, as if to say, What else can I do?

Demetrios cringed. In the slave market, Rufus would be stripped down to his loin cloth and put on display for people to poke and prod at him, talk about him as though he couldn't hear. Rufus appeared to be sensitive. What if a brute like Marcus bought him? What would his fate be then? What was the graver sin? To own a slave and treat him with dignity, or let him be sold to a beast like Marcus? Demetrios pulled out his purse. "Will you accept three thousand sestertii?"

The expression on Tertius's face broadened into a genuine smile. "Of course. That is more than acceptable." He clapped his hands. "I'll send for the scribe Yohanan. He can draw up the documents."

Tertius poured more wine while they waited for the scribe. No one seemed inclined to talk, and the silence weighed heavily upon the room. Demetrios knew he had paid too much, that Elazar would not be pleased, but he was relieved Rufus would be safe.

Yohanan arrived a short time later carrying his pens and a scroll. He was a small, hunched man with arthritic fingers and squinty eyes, but Tertius claimed he knew the law well. "Yohanan will write out the agreement so that it's binding for all parties," Tertius said.

Demetrios had never signed anything before and could only read a few letters and words. He held the pen over the scroll, hesitating. Yohanan gripped Demetrios's hand. "You are Demetrios of Tiberias. That is your name?"

Demetrios nodded.

"Then draw the pen down like this, across and over."

Tertius signed with a flourish, the money was exchanged with a small payment to Yohanan, and Rufus officially became the property of Demetrios.

As they left the mansion together, Rufus asked Demetrios, "Where are we going, Master?"

"To the tent I share with Elazar." Demetrios stopped. He leaned in close to Rufus and whispered, "And never call me Master when we are alone. Never."

"What shall I call you then?"

"I don't know."

"Yes, Master. As you wish."

They continued down the road.

Back at the tent, Elazar insisted that Rufus could help them with the caravan journeys. "We'll teach him to handle the camels," Elazar said.

But Rufus proved to be terrified of the large beasts. When one of the camels snapped at him, he burst into tears. "Please don't make me feed them, Master," he pleaded to Demetrios. "They're vicious."

Demetrios, taking pity on Rufus, assured him his duties would be confined to the house. "Tertius said you are a good cook?"

"Yes, Master, I can prepare you a fine vegetable stew. Or I could steam a fish in garlic and dill."

Demetrios glanced at Elazar, who frowned with disapproval. "We shall have both today." He counted out some coins and gave them to Rufus. "I have heard that Elisheba bakes the best bread in Tiberias. Is that true?"

"Yes, Master. At least, I believe so."

Next to him, Elazar shifted his weight and cleared his throat, but Demetrios ignored his friend. He had seen how much Rufus adored Elisheba, and Demetrios knew too well the pain of loving someone you could not have. Why not give Rufus a small happiness? "Then be sure to buy some of Elisheba's bread. In fact, I think we should have her bread every day."

Rufus, clasping the coins in his fist, glowed. "Yes, Master. Thank you."

Later that evening, while Rufus washed their bowls and cleaned up, Elazar pulled Demetrios aside. "You're the master. Be firm with him. If you don't assert your authority, Rufus will never respect you."

"I won't strike him or whip him," Demetrios said. "I'm not Marcus."

But Demetrios was not sure it was true, for now he owned a slave, something he'd sworn just a day before he would never do.

CHAPTER
EIGHT

A few weeks later, Elazar hired a man named Caleb to help him and Demetrios with the caravans. "Caleb's grandfather," Elazar told Demetrios later as they discussed the new worker, "was married to my grandfather's sister. That means we are distant cousins."

As Elazar talked about his long lost relative, Demetrios felt a twinge of jealousy. Demetrios had always assumed he and Elazar were a family, as close as brothers. "How do you know this is true?" he asked Elazar. "Caleb could be lying to impress you."

"I don't think so. Our ancestors come from the same village."

Unlike Rufus, who avoided the camels, Caleb was fascinated by creatures and eager to learn how to manage them.

"They're stubborn beasts," Caleb said the next morning as the three men strolled across the courtyard, "but very smart. I can see it in their faces, the way they look at us. But I don't know how to make them obey my commands." He handed the cane whip to Demetrios. "Elazar says that you are good with the camels, that you know their tricks and deceptions."

Demetrios balanced the stick in his hand, studying the two

camels, hobbled together at the ankles. One of them watched him warily, as if waiting for the opportunity to bite, but Demetrios knew a precisely timed application of the cane would suppress that desire. "That's true. I've learned much about them during my travels. Come. I'll show you what I know." He removed the ropes around their ankles and stepped quickly back.

"They aren't as clever as you think," Demetrios said. "You have to show them their food, or they won't find it." He pulled Caleb to the side. "Never turn your back on them. A camel can kick backward with his hind legs, striking a blow powerful enough to break your arm or crush your skull." Turning, he snapped the cane stick twice. "Down."

Both camels eased to their knees.

Demetrios signaled for the camels to rise and passed the cane back to Caleb. "You do it. If one of them looks like he's ready to snap at you, crack the stick across his nose. Lightly but firm enough to show him you are the master."

Caleb cracked the cane in the air, shouting, "Down, down." The camels obeyed. Thrilled, he danced around the animals and turned toward Demetrios, grinning. "Did you see that?"

"Look out!" Demetrios cried as he snatched Caleb away from the camels. A camel just missed viciously biting Caleb's elbow. "Do not turn your back."

Sobered, Caleb wiped the animal's spit from his arm. He glared at the camel who had attacked him. "I am the master."

Demetrios smiled and ordered the camels to rise. "Now try again."

At the end of the day, Demetrios told Elazar, "You made a good choice. He handles the animals well."

Elazar watched Caleb as he left the pens for his home. "We should watch him closely. He may be distant family, but one of the shopkeepers in the marketplace told me he caught Caleb trying to steal a handful of olives yesterday. He didn't report him, but he won't let Caleb back in his shop."

"What?" Demetrios said. "Perhaps he was hungry. I know what it's like to be hungry."

"Yes, and look what it cost you." Elazar tugged on his beard, his face thoughtful. "I won't say anything to the authorities about Caleb either. Not yet." He looked at Demetrios. "But if he steals again . . ."

Demetrios shook his head. "You are too quick to judge."

Two weeks later, at Elazar's suggestion, Caleb moved into the house with Elazar to be near the animals. "I can observe him more closely if we share the same roof," Elazar said.

"Of course," Demetrios said. "And he's Jewish, not a Gentile like me."

Elazar smiled, ignoring the rebuke.

In his own house, Demetrios gradually grew accustomed to, but not comfortable with, owning a slave.

Demetrios had continued to urge Rufus not to call him "Master" in private, but after a few awkward attempts at calling him Demetrios, Rufus reverted to "Master." If Rufus suspected that Demetrios had once been a slave himself, he never mentioned it or otherwise gave away his suspicion.

At times, Demetrios longed to confide in Rufus, to tell him about his life with Marcus, and explain why he hated owning a slave, but he remained quiet. Demetrios despaired that while he was no longer an actual slave, he remained enslaved by the secrets of his past.

As the months passed into a new season, Demetrios and Elazar began making short trips throughout Galilee, where they traded Nabataean spices for local goods, such as flax and wine. They traveled the roads along the western shore of the Sea of Galilee, visiting the small fishing villages. In the towns heavily populated with Jews, the locals were reluctant to trade with a Gentile, so Elazar took the lead. "These are my people," he said. "I understand their ways."

"Yes, I see that. Your people dislike dirty Gentiles." Again, Demetrios wondered if it would have been a better decision for the two of them to have separated after fleeing Marcus's villa; but they were dependent on each other now. Demetrios had no choice but to choke down his resentment.

In the summer, Demetrios and Elazar escorted their first group of pilgrims to the Feast of Weeks in Jerusalem. Before they left for the journey, the Jewish farmers in the Galilee region tied reeds around the first fruits of their crops of wheat, barley, grapes, figs, pomegranates, olives, and dates, and placed them in baskets to be presented at the Temple. As Demetrios and Elazar led the caravan south down the road that paralleled the Jordan River, they were joined by more pilgrims bearing offerings for the festival.

Some of the villages on the route greeted the caravan with music and flowers. Elazar had warned Demetrios to be on the watch for bandits, but they encountered no ruffians, only fellow joyous pilgrims. At night when they camped, Demetrios remained apart from the Jews and felt his difference from Elazar even more keenly. While Elazar joined his fellow Jews in celebration and singing, Demetrios preferred to spend time with the animals. That first caravan trip to Jerusalem took four long days.

As word spread in the region about the new caravan managed

by a Jew and a Gentile, Elazar suggested he and Demetrios expand their venture. "We need to buy more donkeys. Our next pilgrimage to Jerusalem will be talked about by everyone between here and Jerusalem." He purchased three more donkeys from a local farmer two days later.

In his home again after their travels, Demetrios made his offerings to Mercury at the altar he had built in his bedchamber, sharing a small portion of their profits with the god. Later, Rufus could take the collection to a Roman temple. Elazar insisted Mercury was nothing but a pagan statue, but Demetrios knew the god had power. Mercury had answered Demetrios's request for freedom from Marcus and blessed him with success as a trader and caravan driver. It seemed only proper that he maintain an altar to the god.

In the fall, Demetrios and Elazar took their camels and new donkeys and escorted a much larger crowd of pilgrims to the Feast of Booths in Jerusalem. The Jews left the caravan camp in Jerusalem to build temporary shelters of branches and palm fronds, where they lived and feasted for eight days. At the end of each day, they offered sacrifices in the Temple to their mysterious god.

Elazar and Caleb joined their fellow Jews in the celebrations, so Demetrios was left alone to tend to the animals. Demetrios watched with longing as Elazar left the camp; Elazar claimed he had no family, but he had a community of people who believed and thought the same as he did. Demetrios had no one.

After they returned to Tiberias from the Feast of Booths, a venture Elazar declared to be immensely successful, Elazar told Demetrios they needed to take a trip to Sepphoris. "Before Herod built Tiberias, Sepphoris was considered the jewel of Galilee. We should go before the winter rains come, so we can replenish our stock for our next trip to Jerusalem. We'll take Caleb with us."

They left Rufus to care for Demetrios's new home and followed the road west to Sepphoris.

If Tiberias was new and unformed, a maiden city still seeking her identity, Sepphoris was a sedate matron, confident of her stature and beauty.

Expansive mansions more massive than any Demetrios had seen in Tiberias dotted the steep hills. The marketplace had an international flair, with visitors and traders from the coast, Galilee, and the eastern deserts. The air was scented with exotic spices and tinctures. Elazar, Demetrios, and Caleb strolled down the colonnaded cardo where the wheels of chariots had worn grooves into the stone-paved roadbed. Shops lined both sides of the street, selling wares the trio could not find easily in Tiberias, including elegant pottery lamps, glass beads and jewelry, and perfumes.

"Look at the ornamentation," Elazar said, holding a lamp up for inspection. "We have nothing like this in Tiberias. This one has a loop to hook a chain." Taking their time, they visited dozens of pottery shops, selecting only the best lamps to purchase.

Caleb marveled at the colorful mosaic floors in some of the shops. "They look like paintings on the ground," he said, toeing the striking patterns beneath his sandals.

"These floors are plain," Demetrios said. "They keep the designs simple because of the heavy foot traffic, but if you were to enter some of the mansions perched on those hills, you would be dazzled. I remember the floor in Marcus's—" He stopped abruptly, his face flushing.

"Who?" Caleb asked.

"Oh, someone . . ." At a loss, Demetrios turned to Elazar and swallowed, too terrified to say more. Elazar's face had flushed red, too.

"Marcus is someone we met when we were trading," Elazar

said quickly. He pushed past them into the next shop. "Our rope is fraying and old. Let us see if this place has what we need."

They continued to shop well into the afternoon, purchasing beads, swaths of fine fabric, blankets, amphorae of olive oil, baskets to carry their goods, with Caleb packing everything carefully onto the backs of the camels and donkeys. They had neared the end of the marketplace when Elazar noticed a perfume shop. "I'd like to find some nardinum. It's highly prized as a fragrance, and if the perfume is of good quality and the price is fair, we can split it into smaller vessels to sell for a fine profit the next time we go to Jerusalem." He turned toward Caleb. "Wait here with the animals."

Once he and Demetrios were inside the booth, Elazar said, "What you told Caleb earlier, about Marcus. You must be more careful. Our futures are bound together. What happens to you happens to me, and I don't intend to end my life nailed to a cross. Think before you speak. I cannot be here every time to save you."

Demetrios clenched his fist, releasing his grip slowly. "It won't happen again." He picked up one of the vials of nardinum and handed it to Elazar. "How do you know if it's good quality?"

"Harvested from only the finest flowers," the shopkeeper said as he stood close by. "Suitable for anointing kings." He dribbled a few drops on Elazar's fingers.

Hearing a noise outside, Demetrios turned around and glanced up. Caleb had wandered away from the animals and was ambling around a display of hair ornaments and jewelry. While Demetrios watched, Caleb picked up an ivory comb, set it down, examined a small brass pin, put that aside, grazed his fingers across several strands of glass beads. Caleb's hand hovered over another hair pin decorated with tiny lapis lazuli stones.

Demetrios tensed. Caleb had lingered too long over the pin. Did he plan to steal it? Unaware of Demetrios's concern, Caleb scooped up the hair pin and tucked it into his sleeve. When he looked up, he seemed surprised to see Demetrios staring at him from the shop, but he didn't return the ornament.

Demetrios touched Elazar's shoulder. "Excuse me a moment. I want to look at that jewelry."

"Fine, but come back soon. I'm almost finished here." Elazar didn't look up; he was too engrossed in examining the shop-keeper's wares.

Demetrios walked outside and stepped behind Caleb. "Put it back," he said softly.

Startled, Caleb whirled to face Demetrios. "What? What are you talking about?"

Demetrios unrolled Caleb's sleeve and retrieved the hair pin. "I saw you take it, and you didn't pay." He dropped it into Caleb's hand. "Put it back."

Caleb's face blanched, but he set the pin on the table. "Will you tell Elazar?"

"I won't say anything if you promise never to steal again. Do you promise that?"

Caleb nodded.

"Good. Then go stay with the animals. We have a lot of valu-able items packed, and we don't want anyone to take them."

When Demetrios entered the shop again, Elazar was asking the shopkeeper if he could sample a few drops from another jar of perfume. Elazar breathed deeply from the vial the shopkeeper offered, then held it out to Demetrios. "What do you think of this one?"

Demetrios leaned close and inhaled. "It smells of the earth. Like rich, oiled wood." For a brief moment, Demetrios reeled, as the memory of a beautiful woman snuggling in his awkward embrace flashed before him: Tabitha. "What did you say this was called? Nardinum?" Demetrios's throat felt dry.

Elazar nodded. "They say it eases the troubled mind." He glanced at Demetrios. "Perhaps you should add a few drops to your wine before you sleep." He turned to the shopkeeper. "We'll take one jar as well as some of your alabaster vials so we can divide it into smaller portions."

As Demetrios reached for his purse, a man strode into the shop. "So the stories are true," the man said, peering closely at both Demetrios and Elazar. "A Jew and a Gentile are partners in the caravan trade." With Elazar still engaged in paying the shopkeeper, the newcomer addressed Demetrios. He had a patrician chin, but his face was fat and round with dark narrow eyes that never stopped blinking. He made Demetrios nervous. "You have no beard, so you must be the young Gentile named Demetrios." The stranger glanced at Caleb, who waited in the street. "I assume he works for you. And those are your camels?"

Elazar turned to answer but Demetrios spoke first. "I am Demetrios of Tiberias, and this is Elazar. You are?"

"Romulus. Of Sepphoris. Like you, I engage in trade and transport pilgrims to Jerusalem. I've lived near Galilee for many years, but I've never heard of you before. Where are you from?"

"We come from—" Demetrios began.

"Nabataea," Elazar interrupted. "We settled in Tiberias recently."

"From Nabataea? How odd." He grinned and picked at a crust of food in his beard. "And what brings you to Tiberias? Such a far distance from the lands of King Aretas."

For a moment, no one said a word. Demetrios shifted his weight, leaning hard on his staff. The stranger's demeanor made him uncomfortable, as though the man knew more than he revealed. Demetrios wondered if Romulus had seen Caleb steal the pin. Would he say anything? "Romulus is an odd name," Demetrios said finally, his voice soft.

Romulus laughed. "I was named after one of the founding twins of Rome. My mother was the secret lover of an important senator." He gestured toward the two camels kneeling patiently on the ground. "Your animals are fully packed, so I guess you're leaving soon. Safe journey. I'm sure our paths will cross again." Waving his hand in dismissal, he turned and disappeared into the crowd.

As soon as Romulus was out of hearing, Elazar spat on the ground. "Pah! Such a story. The son of a Roman senator? More likely, his mother was a prostitute and his father unknown."

As they loaded their final purchases onto the backs of the camels, Caleb asked, "What did that man want? I've been watching him. He was following us through the marketplace."

Elazar stood still for a moment, staring at the space where Romulus had gone. "He covets our camels."

"Do you think so?" Demetrios asked. "He blinked so fast I couldn't look into his eyes."

Elazar chuckled. "Yes, he blinks like a rapacious raven. But understand this: Romulus may appear foolish, but he is no fool. Beneath that ridiculous face is a man too clever to ignore and I suspect too corrupt to trust. Don't ever turn your back to him."

They left Sepphoris that afternoon. Expressing his concern about Romulus following them, Caleb trailed slightly behind Demetrios, Elazar, and the camels to watch the road for the trader.

They kept a vigilant eye for the brash trader.

CHAPTER
NINE

The first winter rains fell soon after their journey to Sepphoris. As the cold winds howled across the Sea of Galilee, and Demetrios settled into his new home with Rufus to wait out the foul weather, the memories of his own life as a slave, beaten and whipped by his Roman master, began to fade. Demetrios calmed, hopeful his secrets had remained intact, the crimes of his past known only to Elazar; and yet, the unease he felt was always ready to surface.

The rumors started to stir. Like the sudden, violent storms that whipped the normally placid Sea of Galilee into a foamy cauldron, the talk of a new miracle worker intruded upon Demetrios's life with a pervasive, demanding force.

Gossip eddied in the marketplace about a Jewish prophet who lived in the wilderness and foretold the coming of a Jewish Messiah. All through the cold winter months, when trade was restricted, Demetrios brooded and waited, watching the sky for portents. And whenever he ventured out, he heard nothing but more stories about this mysterious Jewish healer. But Demetrios knew the tales were false; they had to be exaggerations and lies, for no one could cure illness and disease with words and a gentle touch.

Then one evening, after Demetrios and Elazar had finished cleaning the animal stalls, Elazar announced he and Caleb would be gone for a while. "We're going to the synagogue in Capernaum tomorrow," he said. "To hear the words of this new teacher."

Demetrios set his bucket down so abruptly it tipped over. "To see a miracle?" He laughed. He started to say more but hesitated when he noticed Elazar's disapproving expression. "Surely you don't believe the gossip?"

"It's not idle gossip. If the stories are true, then the prophecies are being fulfilled. My people have been waiting for the Messiah for generations."

Avoiding Elazar's gaze, Demetrios picked up his bucket. He stepped carefully around the sleeping donkeys, reluctant to engage in an argument. Of all the times for Elazar and Caleb to leave, this was the worst. Passover was only a few weeks away. "You can't go now," Demetrios said. "We have pilgrims stopping by every day to inquire about safe passage to Jerusalem. They are your people, not mine. You need to be here to talk to them."

"My faith requires that I go."

"Your faith, your faith! Your religion makes too many demands," Demetrios said, his voice rising. "Don't eat this. Don't touch that. Don't work on the Shabbat. We have a caravan to prepare for. You can't go."

Elazar backed away, his mouth set in a grim line. "You are not my master. I'm going to Capernaum."

"And who will do the work here while you chase after this miracle worker?"

Elazar didn't answer.

Without another word, Demetrios stormed out the courtyard, slamming the gate behind him.

Days passed. When Elazar and Caleb still had not returned, Rufus brought news to Demetrios from the marketplace. "The fishermen hauled in a huge catch last night. In fact, they're still emptying the nets." He laid a tilapia out on the table, a fine specimen with enough white meat for them to feast for days, and began rubbing the skin with coarse salt.

Demetrios's mouth watered as his slave mixed up a paste of garlic, oil, and dill.

"Did you buy garum?" Demetrios asked. The sauce, made from the intestines of small fish, would be good on Elisheba's bread.

"What, Master?" Rufus glanced up from his work. "No garum today. But oh, I almost forgot. There was a man in the market place looking for you. He wanted to know about the Passover caravan."

"He's not coming here, is he?" Elazar always handled such matters, negotiating with the Jewish pilgrims. Demetrios could not imagine one of them entering a Gentile's courtyard.

"No, he's waiting for you near the fishmonger's stall."

"Me? You should not have promised—"

"Forgive me, Master."

"You didn't see Elazar, did you? He could talk to him."

"No, Master." He wiped his hands on a towel and reached for the wine. "Would you like a drink while I prepare the fire?"

Demetrios sipped from the cup. Heat blazed from the brazier while Rufus worked. At his last count, they had almost thirty pilgrims to take to Jerusalem for the festival, but they needed five more to make a good profit. With such a good catch, the marketplace was sure to be busy. He thought about how many strangers would be there, possibly even some from Gerasa. Elazar should meet with the man, but Elazar was not here. He set down his wine. "Bring me my walking staff. I'll speak to him."

Rufus lifted the stick from its place in the corner, passing it to Demetrios. "Are you sure, Master? I could tell him to wait until tomorrow. Perhaps Elazar will be back then."

Hesitating, Demetrios faced his servant. What if Elazar did not return in time? "No, I'll go." He gripped his staff with clenched fists, seeking reassurance from the weight in his hands. "I'll be back for dinner."

An eager farmer approached Demetrios at the bottom of the hill. "Come taste my honey," he said, thrusting a dripping comb under Demetrios's nose. He gestured to the bowls he had spread out. "It's the sweetest in Galilee. Nectar from the heavens. Priced better than anything you'll find in the city."

Demetrios shook him off. "Not today."

Farmers, merchants, townspeople, and peasants crushed together on the narrow road into the city, pushing toward the marketplace. Shepherds whistled at their herds of goats, struggling to keep them away from the booths stacked with winter figs. Herod's auxiliary troops circled through the mob on horseback and foot, their shouts lost in the uproar.

"Move, move! In the name of Caesar and the King, get out of the way!"

The people dropped back to clear a path for more soldiers who marched in tight formation. Their conical helmets bounced up and down in waves as they jogged along the road. One of the horsemen accompanying them broke rank and rode into a group of spectators that had pressed closer for a better look. He swung his sword and warned them to keep back. There were a few muttered epithets, but no one spoke too loudly. A space opened around the soldier, and the crowd could see why they had been forced off the path. The troops dragged behind them a captured slave: a dark-skinned man with the letter F, for fugitivus, seared into his forehead. His hands and feet were bound, and if it were not for the rope that jerked him upright and pulled him along, he would have fallen face down to the ground.

Demetrios brushed his fingers across his own shoulder, feeling the raised, damaged flesh beneath his cloak. If he had not killed Marcus and escaped, his fate could have easily been the same as this poor runaway's.

Someone pitched a stone at the auxiliaries, striking the horse. The animal reared up, and a farmer in front of the soldiers lost control of his cart. The entire procession halted as his crates of doves toppled to the ground.

The terrified birds flung themselves against the wooden slats; clouds of feathers spiraled into the air. The farmer tugged at his donkey's rope, but the creature dug in its heels and refused to move, its hysterical brays adding to the general confusion.

The slave, sensing he had a receptive audience, raised his head. The wound on his brow had festered. His skin glowed with fever and madness. He blinked, scanning the blur of faces in front of him, seeking one he knew would understand. Then he paused and focused his gaze on Demetrios, a faint smile playing around his mouth.

Demetrios shrank back behind a cluster of men.

Of all the Jews, the soldiers, and the travelers in this place, how did he know? How does one slave recognize the other? Although the sun was warm upon Demetrios's back, he shivered.

A man behind Demetrios said, "I heard they found him in the caves near the hot springs. He belonged to Herod's house. Not a good place to hide."

The woman with him asked, "Where are they taking him?"

"With a group of other slaves to the mines. He'll never see daylight again."

Holding fast to the reins of his skittish horse, the furious soldier confronted the crowd. "Who threw that stone?"

When no one answered, he hooked one of the crates with his sword and smashed it to the ground. Several doves flew out, sweeping low over everyone's heads. "Clear this trash from the road."

Some of the men behind Demetrios laughed and jumped to catch the floundering birds; others complained loudly about the delay. A couple of the women near him finally stepped forward to help the beleaguered man drag his remaining crates to the side. The soldiers began to move again, their captive stumbling behind them.

The slave cried out, "Please! Help me!" before he disappeared into the wall of armored bodies.

"Demetrios of Tiberias? Is that you?"

Over the bobbing heads, Demetrios strained to see who was calling him. He cut across the road and scooted around the people still pursuing errant doves.

"Demetrios of Tiberias!" the voice called out to him with authority.

Demetrios wheeled around. They knew. The soldiers were coming for him. He was caught, trapped like a beetle in the clinches of a scorpion's pinchers. Someone had revealed his secret, knew that he, too, was an escaped slave. Marcus's slave. Marcus's murderer.

"Demetrios! Demetrios!"

Demetrios tried to escape through the crowd, but the throng closed about him. He had to get away. Escape. Again. As he ducked and darted through the multitude, Demetrios realized he would be running for the rest of his life. He would forever be a slave.

"Demetrios!"

He pushed against the backs of a group of men. "Let me through." But the crowd would not part for him.

A hand clutched his arm. He froze. Doomed. He was doomed. And he would be sentenced to die in the mines like his fellow slave. The hand that had seized him spun him around now to face his fate.

Romulus.

It was Romulus.

Weak with relief, Demetrios nodded at the trader. He felt faint, felt the ground tilt. He gripped his staff for support.

"You look like you've seen a ghost," Romulus said, guiding Demetrios toward his booth. "Come see my jewelry."

Demetrios's first inclination was to make an excuse to leave, but that was impossible now. Romulus had him cornered.

"And where is Elazar?" Romulus asked. "I thought he would be with you." Without waiting for Demetrios to reply, Romulus draped ropes of beaded necklaces over his forearms, then called to a passing group of local slaves, "See how beautiful? Tell your mistresses. I have the best in all the Empire." The women giggled and moved on. He turned back to Demetrios. "So many people here today."

Demetrios stiffened, remembering Elazar's warnings about Romulus. "What brings you to Tiberias?"

"News of a good catch travels quickly, eh?" Romulus grinned at him, revealing a fence of yellow, broken teeth. "Like you, I seek good trade. I've already talked to several pilgrims who want to go with me to Jerusalem."

Smiling to hide his unease, Demetrios shook his head. Had Romulus come to Tiberias to steal their customers? Elazar would know how to divert him, but he wasn't sure what he should say. "I fear you may be disappointed. The caravan business is poor this year."

Romulus didn't reply. Instead, he snatched up a handful of combs. "Ladies, my hairpieces long to sleep in your tresses." The Roman matrons turned away, but the slave girl who was with them paused to glance at Demetrios, all the while keeping a basket of bread balanced atop her head. "Lovely," he said, still watching the slave. Her black hair swayed sassily over her hips as she ran toward the marketplace.

Demetrios fingered a string of carnelian stones, feeling the fine chips hidden beneath the knots. He set down the necklace. "Her name's Elisheba. She belongs to Tertius." His own slave, Rufus, still adored her. He found frequent reasons to visit Tertius's house so he could speak to her. It saddened Demetrios to see his servant enamored of a woman he could never have, for Tertius loved her as well.

When Demetrios heard Rufus extolling her many charms, he wanted to say, *Stop. Don't think about it. You cannot have her.* But he could never tell Rufus about Tabitha, his forbidden desire, and so he remained silent. Demetrios turned toward Romulus. "It's been a bad season. Elazar and I have barely enough pilgrims to justify a Passover trip."

Romulus squinted, deep wrinkles furrowing his brow. He picked thoughtfully at his beard, studying first Demetrios's face and then the jewelry on the table in front of him. "Oh? Perhaps I should look for customers to the west, eh?" Grinning, he shook his head. "We will see."

Demetrios didn't comment. If he protested too much, Romulus would become suspicious. He glanced at the steady movement of people going toward the marketplace. To get to the fish market, he still had to push past the booths of figs, onions, and olives and cross to a side street near the sheep pens. "I'm sorry. I have to go." He strode down the cardo, the wide road that divided the heart of the city.

"If you're hunting for fish or pilgrims, the best ones have already been taken," Romulus called after him, laughing.

Ignoring the pleas to "look at my wares," Demetrios wandered through the fish market—his heart still pounding and breath still short from when he'd heard his name shouted before realizing it was Romulus—where the fishermen brought baskets of fresh fish up from their boats for sorting. They culled quickly through the catch, tossing out shellfish and anything lacking scales.

While one group gutted the tilapia with a quick swipe of their blades, others laid the cleaned fish out on wooden drying racks for salting. The intestines would be used to make the fish paste so popular with Romans and Gentiles. Crowds gathered around the prepared fish, arguing and dickering with fishmongers.

Demetrios studied the unfamiliar faces, searching for someone who could be a Passover pilgrim. But there were so many Jews in the marketplace today. He wished he had thought to ask Rufus the man's name or even for a description. As he turned to leave, he heard someone call out, "You want Demetrios? The caravan driver? He's over there."

A Jewish man, wearing a traditional striped headdress and a linen mantle cut to fit his narrow shoulders, strode toward Demetrios. The man's eyes widened in surprise as he came closer. "You are . . . ?"

"I'm Demetrios of Tiberias." He smiled at the stranger. The Jew's beard and hair were neatly trimmed and oiled, and his skin was smooth. Clearly he had slaves to do the labor for him.

Taking his time to reply, the Jew examined Demetrios with an air of disdain. "It's just that you're a Gentile. I was expecting . . ." He cleared his throat. "Do you take pilgrims to the Passover festival?"

Demetrios flinched. The Jews had so many rules about what to eat, when to work, and how far they could travel on the Shabbat. Elazar should be here to talk to this man, not him. His smile fading, he nodded. "Yes, I'm a Gentile, but my business partner is Jewish. He'll see that your traditions are protected."

The Jew flicked an invisible speck of dirt from his expensive purse, a bag that bulged with coins. Gold rings glittered on his fingers. "And what is your fee for these services? We have thirteen in our party."

Thirteen! With the thirty pilgrims who had already committed to their caravan that would make forty-three. Plus the pack animals. What an impression they would make as they entered Jerusalem. Everyone would be talking about them. Elazar would be so proud of him if he brought this many travelers into the group. But how much should he charge? Two denarii per day was standard, but the additional people would also mean additional costs. "Five denarii per person per day for the journey. It may sound high, but we have the safest caravan in Palestine. We've never been attacked by bandits. Not once."

The Jew nodded. He glanced at the people milling around them, then stepped forward, leaning close, his voice almost a whisper. A strong scent of cinnamon mixed with olive oil wafted from his hair. "There is something else. One of us requires a donkey—a pure white donkey—to ride into the Holy City. I've been told they're rare. Is that also extra?"

Demetrios tried to recall all of the donkeys they had in the pens. Were any of them white? "No spots at all?"

The Jew shook his head.

"I think that can be arranged," Demetrios said. "The fee for riding a donkey is seven denarii per day."

"So expensive?" The Jew stared at Demetrios, the silence grow-ing between them. "The Rav would not be pleased," he said finally. "But the prophecy requires . . ." His voice trailed off.

Demetrios gripped his staff. Who was the Rav? The keeper of their purse? But this Jew seemed to speak for all thirteen. "A white donkey requires a special diet to keep him pure. I can assure you we're making very little profit."

The Jew still seemed unconvinced.

"We have two camels," Demetrios added. "The only caravan in the region with them. That increases the cost, of course, but we can transport anything you desire." Propping his staff against a wall, Demetrios held up his palms to show he was honest. "You know my name, but I didn't ask yours."

"Stop, thief!"

Three boys barreled into the throng, elbows and purloined figs flying. Startled, Demetrios lunged for his staff and stumbled. The walking stick dropped from his fingers. A stone struck his shoul-der. He turned, reeling, his crippled leg collapsing, and dropped to his knees.

Another stone hit his back.

A stone! No. A rock. The size of his fist. It crushed bone and flesh beneath the blows. And, once again, Demetrios relived the crack of Marcus's lash in the air. A scream pealed through the marketplace. Demetrios fought off his rising panic. No, not his voice. A woman shrieked near the fish vendor's booth, shouting for help. Demetrios repeated the words to himself: I am in the marketplace. Struggling to his feet, he reached out for assistance. Someone pulled on his arms. Or did they push? He tilted back-ward, falling, striking his head against a rock, sinking into an abyss of darkness, knowing nothing he perceived was true.

Chapter

Ten

Demetrios awoke to a blank space in his memory and the smell of fish.

"Good. You're all right. I was worried." A man knelt over him, pressing a damp, sour-smelling cloth to his forehead.

"Who are you? Where is the Jew?" Demetrios's awareness of time was like a tangled fish net: twisted with knots of confusion. He closed his eyes again, trying to fill in the gaps. He had been looking at the fish, and there was a well-dressed Jew. Had they spoken? Yes, the Jew wanted something, something unusual. What was it?

"I'm Matthias," the man said. "You were mumbling many things about a slave and master."

Demetrios's heart seized. He propped himself weakly on an elbow. Had he spoken of Marcus in his fugue? Had he confessed his crimes? What would he do if this stranger knew?

"You mumbled about your slave, Rufus. I know him. He always buys his garum from me. I was hoping to see him today."

"Stinks." Demetrios collapsed again and pulled the rag away

from his face. It hurt to speak. His lips felt thick. What was wrong with his mouth? Opening his eyes, he tried to sit up but fell back. The fish odors made him queasy.

Demetrios leaned into the drowsiness, listening to the drum beating against his skull. He tasted sand—and blood—on his tongue. "I'm thirsty."

Matthias poured a cup of wine and brought it to him. "Take slow sips. You've got some nasty bruises and a few cuts but nothing that won't heal."

"Is he still out there?" He swallowed, grateful for the drink. There had been boys throwing things. Figs? Rocks? What had hit him? "Who threw the stones?"

"What stones?"

"Did he leave?"

Matthias looked at him then, a strange expression in his eyes. He set down the cup. "This man you were speaking to. What do you know about him?"

Demetrios tried to remember. The Jew said his name was . . . but there was no name, nothing he could recall. "Nothing." He had an uneasy feeling, a sense that something bad had happened in the marketplace. Why wouldn't Matthias tell him?

The fishmonger rose. He kept his back to Demetrios. "You didn't fall. You were pushed."

"But he wanted a pure white donkey. I remember now."

"He shoved you to the ground. You didn't fall. I saw him."

Demetrios touched the bump on the back of his head and winced. "The Jew? Why would he push me? We were talking about the Passover caravan."

Matthias turned toward him. "I don't know you, Demetrios, but I like Rufus, and he speaks highly of you. You are . . ." He hesitated a moment. "A Gentile." His voice dropping to a whisper, he leaned close. "His name is Judas. Some call him Judas Iscariot. They say he—" He stopped speaking, stood, and closed the tent flap. "The marketplace has too many ears," he explained as he returned to Demetrios's side. "I'm not one to indulge in idle gossip, but this Judas has been in the marketplace for several days, asking all sorts of questions about the local caravans. How big are they? Are they safe? When will they leave for the Passover festival? Does anyone protect them? People have begun to talk. They suspect he may be a brigand looking for a group that's vulnerable."

Ignoring waves of dizziness that caused the ground to shift underneath him, Demetrios sat up. "Are you sure? Who told you this?"

Matthias shrugged. "Perhaps it's as I said. Gossip. But you should be careful. Did you notice his fine clothes? Not many peasants dress like that."

What Matthias said made no sense. Was Judas targeting his caravan? He glanced at the fishmonger. "Do you think he's a bandit?"

They were interrupted by a voice calling from outside. "Matthias, are you there? I want some garum."

"I'm here," Matthias said, shouting loud enough to be heard. "I'll be out in a moment." He leaned over and grasped Demetrios's hands, pulling him awkwardly to his feet. "That's better. You're standing now. I have to get back to my customers. Do you think you can walk?"

Demetrios swayed and caught his balance. "Do you have my staff? I need my staff."

"Yes, of course. Here you are." He planted the heavy stick in Demetrios's hand and wrapped his fingers around it, steadying him as he leaned slightly to one side. With a firm grip on Demetrios's shoulders, he guided him to the door. "If you go slowly, you'll be fine."

"But I—"

"Almost there." Before Demetrios could say another word, Matthias escorted him out of the booth into the path of the waiting customer.

The man looked up, startled. "You're not Matthias."

"He's—"

"I'm here, Jonas," Matthias said. He turned toward Demetrios and for a brief moment, he seemed uncertain. "Would you like me to send for Rufus?"

Demetrios stared at them both. He was aware that they watched him curiously but with no real concern for his well-being. "No, thank you. I can manage." He stepped into the street and scanned the crowd, wondering just how much time had passed since he had met the Jew. Except for a few stragglers poking through the booths, the marketplace had cleared. Judas was gone.

The gate to Demetrios's courtyard swung wide as he approached, and Rufus rushed out. "There you are, Master! I was worried. I—"

Rufus stopped abruptly. "Caesar's mother! What happened? Were you robbed?" He pulled Demetrios into the courtyard.

Demetrios touched his face. His left cheek throbbed. He staggered, floundered for his staff.

Rufus wrapped an arm around Demetrios's waist and pulled him close. "Here, let me help you."

Relieved to be in familiar surroundings, he fell against his servant. "I think I need to lie down."

When they reached the bedchamber, Rufus eased him down to the sleeping couch and began stripping off his bloodied clothes. He handed Demetrios a fresh tunic. "I'll fetch a basin of water."

Demetrios nodded. Once his servant had departed, he explored his injuries more thoroughly. His upper lip was cut and swollen, but his front teeth were intact. Gently, he probed the other scrapes and bruises with his fingers. Ribbons of dried blood streaked down his arm, and his left elbow was bruised. The back of his head felt like an egg was nesting in his hair. Pain radiated from multiple places on his arms, shoulders, head, back, and even his legs—as if he had been struck over and over by a hard object. Sighing, he lay back down and closed his eyes. He had almost fallen asleep when Rufus reentered.

"Master, I'm sorry, but there are visitors at the gate." Water sloshed onto the floor as he set the basin down.

"Visitors?" The news seemed absurd. No one ever came to his house. "What do they want?"

"They'll wait for you, Master." With a gentle touch—so light that it felt like feathers whispering over Demetrios's skin—Rufus began to clean the wound on Demetrios's shoulder. "There are three men," he said, his voice as soft as his ministrations. "I don't know the name of the third, but the other two are Elazar and Caleb." He rinsed out the rag in his hand; the water in the bowl turned the color of rust.

Demetrios grasped his servant's wrist. "Elazar? He's here? At my home?"

Rufus nodded.

Something must be wrong. Elazar never visited his Gentile home.

He released his grip on Rufus and stood. "No," he said, waving his servant off as he wobbled unsteadily. "I'm fine. I'll dress myself. Tell Elazar I'll be there shortly."

After Rufus left, Demetrios spread his tunic loosely over his shoulders, fastening it with a bronze clasp. He couldn't disguise the split lip, but most of his other injuries were hidden by his clothing. He fingered the clasp. Elazar had been so careful about following the laws of his faith, and now, he walked across burial grounds in Tiberias and visited the house of a Gentile? Demetrios rubbed his hands against the soft fabric of his tunic. His palms were slick with cold sweat.

Rufus must have been mistaken. Only two people, Elazar and Caleb, waited at the entrance, both standing as silent and steady as wooden posts driven into the ground. This morning Caleb brazenly wore a scrap of red silk twisted in his headdress. The cloth bore a remarkable resemblance to a larger piece they had purchased in Sepphoris.

At the sound of Demetrios's footsteps, Elazar turned, his face registering his shock. "What happened to you?"

Demetrios forced a laugh. "A brawl in the marketplace. Someone knocked me down when I got in the way of some thieving youngsters." Stepping into the street, he took Elazar's hands into his own. "I'm honored you've come to my house." His voice held an optimism he didn't feel.

Elazar glanced over Demetrios's shoulder, avoiding his friend's direct gaze. He eased his hands from Demetrios's grip. "I bring news. I will not be there for the caravan this time."

Demetrios stepped back into the security of his own courtyard. An invisible line separated them. "What do you mean? We are always together on the caravans." He turned to Caleb for confirmation.

Caleb looked at Elazar and shook his head. "I'm going with Elazar."

"You can't! If you both leave, who will tend to the animals? I cannot bring them alone."

"I've hired a caretaker," Elazar began. "He'll stay at my house until—"

"Silas," Caleb interrupted. "He's my cousin. He'll do a good job. You'll see."

Demetrios shook his head. "No. No. You can't leave now. Passover is coming. We have work to do." He focused on Elazar. "It was your idea to come to Tiberias, to lead the caravans. We agreed to do it as partners." Elazar refused to look at Demetrios. "How can you do this to me? After all we have been through."

For a few moments, no one spoke.

Then Elazar broke the silence. "We've been to Capernaum." He stroked his beard, examining the boards that formed Demetrios's gate. He faced Demetrios. "Perhaps you've heard of the prophet who came out of the wilderness some three seasons ago? They called him John the Baptist."

"The one beheaded by Herod?"

Elazar nodded. He paused. "The Baptist prophesied a king was coming, a Jewish king who would reunite the tribes of Israel. That promise has been fulfilled. Our Messiah is here. In Capernaum."

"We saw him yesterday," Caleb added.

"I don't care," Demetrios said. "Capernaum. And what does your Messiah have to do with the caravan?"

Elazar smiled. The curve of his lips cracked the desert-etched lines in his skin into a spider web of tiny wrinkles. His expression reflected a strange compassion. Did Elazar pity him?

"We have a higher calling now than to guide caravans." Raising his head, Elazar turned and stared pensively at the eastern horizon, watching the water birds dive into the Sea of Galilee. "So many years we've waited. For generations. We've suffered slavery, exile, oppression. Our prophet Isaiah named him Prince of Peace. But he's also a king, descended from the House of David. Now he's come to set us free."

"You're not a slave, Elazar." Demetrios wanted to add, Not anymore, but they had agreed never to speak of that. No one in Tiberias knew about their former lives.

Elazar looked at Demetrios, the lines of his face deepening with sorrow. He curled his hand into a fist and thumped his chest. "I wear my chains here. For who I am and what I've done."

"What did you do?" Caleb asked.

"Nothing." Elazar snapped out the word so quickly they all jumped. Sighing, he smiled at Caleb. "It's nothing. I'm just an old man with regrets." He folded his calloused fingers around Demetrios's hands. "There's something else."

Demetrios froze in anger. "Yes?"

"The Messiah asks us to set aside the demands of the world so we will be ready for his kingdom. Some of the Galilee fishermen have already abandoned their boats and nets and given all their possessions to him." He leaned close, his grip tightening, squeezing so hard that Demetrios's palms hurt. "My friend, this is what I ask of you. I want to give my share of the caravan to the Messiah. I want to join his disciples."

Demetrios pried Elazar's fingers loose, recoiling, his body stiffening with pain and distrust.

"After we have worked so hard, you would just give it away? How could you do such a foolish thing?"

"After you deliver the caravan to Jerusalem, sell everything, and I'll take my portion." He paused. "That is my gift to my Messiah." His last words seemed to be swept away with a gust of wind.

"No. You can't. We have debts, the money we borrowed to buy goods in Sepphoris, to build this house. You said . . ." He hesitated. "You said once I was like a nephew to you. Do all your promises mean nothing?"

"The Messiah is here. I have no other choice." His voice took on a hopeful tone. "You'll still have enough to start over. Perhaps with a new partner, a younger man than I."

Demetrios shook his head. He would never work with a different partner. No one else could be trusted, and he couldn't do this alone. "No, you can't do this. It will ruin me." He backed away. "No."

"Demetrios, listen to me. You can—"

"Elazar, you ask too much of your friend," a voice said from the shadows.

Startled, Demetrios looked up to see Judas, who walked down the hill toward them, floating out from the shade of the trees like an elegantly attired specter. Had he been spying on them?

Before Demetrios could inquire, Judas spoke. "Forgive me for intruding, but I overheard your conversation." He turned toward Demetrios. "Your Roman neighbor's mansion is lovely, Demetrios. You're fortunate to live in such a fine area." Facing Elazar, he said, "The Rav doesn't ask that you give him your possessions. Only that you renounce your worldly desires."

Elazar turned sharply toward Judas, then looked at Demetrios. "You know each other?" he asked Demetrios.

Judas stepped forward. "You asked my name in the marketplace, but we were interrupted. I am—"

"I know who you are. Why are you here?"

"Judas is with us. We're going to Capernaum together," Elazar said.

"He introduced us to the Messiah," Caleb added.

Demetrios sucked in a breath. "The Rav and the Messiah? They are the same?"

"I don't—" Elazar began.

Judas cut him off. "Some say the Teacher is the Promised One, the Messiah. Yes."

Demetrios's vision blurred, and he leaned against the gate. He wanted to lie down. He blinked, bringing the world back into focus, and looked closely at Judas. Despite the mayhem in the marketplace, the Jew was unscathed. His embroidered cloak was still fresh, his sandals clean. The hammered gold rings on his long fingers reflected sparks of light. If the pilgrims who traveled with Judas were equally prosperous, it would be wise to court his business. But he couldn't forget Matthias's strange warning. Was this man a brigand plotting an attack on the caravan? Had he befriended Elazar only to deceive him? Appalled by his own audacity, Demetrios slid both his mantle and tunic off his shoulder, exposing the bruises and cuts. "Did you push me?"

"Certainly not." Judas shook his head. "The marketplace was crowded. Anyone could have done that. I pulled you to safety."

"Someone struck you?" Elazar asked.

Demetrios stared fixedly at Judas. "Witnesses in the marketplace say differently." Draping his tunic and mantle over his shoulder, he closed the clasp.

He wanted to trust Judas; he wanted the extra thirteen in his caravan; he even wanted to find a white donkey for them. But what if Matthias was right? Elazar's friendship with this man could be placing their caravan—even their lives—in jeopardy. It worried him as well that Elazar was so quick to follow this Rav, this Jew they called the Messiah. Elazar had promised to stay with Demetrios. Now, after everything the two of them had shared, he wanted to go? To follow an itinerant prophet all over Galilee? He turned to Elazar. "And what about this Messiah, this Rav who claims to be anointed? Kings are anointed. How do you think Herod will feel about your teacher calling himself a king?"

"You don't understand," Elazar said. "The Messiah isn't—"

"We've seen miracles," Caleb interrupted. Ignoring Elazar's warning touch, he continued, "Amazing sights you would not believe! He causes the lame to walk and the blind to see."

"Miracles are a fool's wish!" Demetrios spat on the ground.

"I never thought you were a fool, Elazar." A slow rage burned in Demetrios's belly; he felt sick. Elazar and Demetrios were family; Elazar had said so himself. Who was this Messiah, this so-called miracle worker? What lies did he tell to seduce Elazar so easily? Demetrios gripped the gate, wishing he could slam it shut in their faces and make all of it go away.

"No, no, it's true." Caleb fairly danced on his toes with excitement. "There was this old woman with clouded eyes, and he put his hands over her face, spoke a few words, and then she could see. We were there when this happened. Ask Elazar. It was a miracle." Flicking an unruly lock of hair from his eyes, he grinned. "Come with us, Demetrios. He could help you."

"How? What could he do for me?"

Demetrios stared at the young man. Caleb had referenced what was never acknowledged: Demetrios's own infirmities. He stopped leaning against the gate and stood up straight, glaring at Elazar. "Does your miracle worker have a name?"

"Jesus," Elazar said. "From Nazareth."

"Do you believe this Jesus of Nazareth performs miracles?"

"I know he does," Elazar said.

Judas, who was standing behind Elazar and Caleb, tipped his fingers to his own forehead in an ironic salute. Was the gesture an offer of reconciliation, or the smirk of victory? Turning to Elazar, Demetrios said softly, "We share a long history." He stopped. He wanted to say more, to remind Elazar of the secrets that were part of that history, but not in front of Caleb and Judas. Would Elazar ever divulge the murder to anyone else? Could he be trusted? "Please, Elazar, for the sake of our friendship, I ask—"

"What you say is true," Elazar agreed. "Our lives have been yoked together out of necessity, but now we must separate. This path I take? You cannot follow. You, Demetrios of Tiberias, and

I, Elazar, son of Jeremiah, are of two different nations. I belong to the family of Abraham, and you are . . ." Leaving the statement unfinished, he looked away.

"An unclean Gentile," Demetrios snapped, "who worships idols and prays to pagan deities?" He stomped his foot. "Say it then. Dirty Gentile! Is that what you think?"

Elazar held up his hands in rebuff, his brown eyes darkening with anger. "Do not do this, Demetrios. You don't want to do this."

Caleb interjected, "I don't think—"

"You are no better than I am, Elazar. We have the same blood under our fingernails. Don't forget that," Demetrios shouted. "Don't forget the Roman."

As Elazar gasped and stepped back, Judas grasped Elazar's arm. "Come. Jesus is waiting."

Elazar hesitated, gazing deep into Demetrios's eyes. "Your sorrow makes you speak rashly." Lowering his head, he added, "Forgive me." He turned to go.

Caleb glanced at Demetrios, shrugged, and then followed his companions.

Too stunned to react, Demetrios watched as the three made their way back to the heart of the city. He longed to call out to Elazar, to ask him to reconsider, but remained quiet. As they crested the rise of the next hill, the road narrowed, causing them to meld into a single file, their separate shadows converging into a solitary black streak across the pale, gray sand. To Demetrios they seemed no longer three separate individuals but one being, with a unique purpose and destiny all its own.

Gone! He ground his heel against a rock and turned his back to them and banged the gate shut.

Let them go!

CHAPTER
ELEVEN

The following morning, Demetrios dressed for a journey to Capernaum, hoping to find Elazar and convince him to return to Tiberias where he belonged. He must change his mind about this madness with this Messiah. It would only lead to trouble for Elazar and Caleb, plus it would ruin him.

As Demetrios draped his cloak carefully over his bruised shoulders, he thought about Caleb's claim this Jesus was a miracle worker. Did Jesus cast some sort of spell over both Elazar and Caleb? Did he promise them riches for their loyalty? More importantly, what had Elazar said to Jesus about his and Demetrios's past? Demetrios needed to bring Elazar home before all was lost. He and Elazar were linked by their history, by secrets that could destroy them if revealed. Such bonds were not meant to be broken, not this way.

The first thunderclap shook the house as Demetrios reached for his staff. Moments later, a hard rain thrummed the rooftop and pelted the courtyard gate.

Fuming, Demetrios peered out his window at black clouds that weighed down the sky. How long would he have to wait for the storm to clear? What if Elazar left Capernaum before Demetrios arrived? Demetrios stomped across the floor. Even the weather conspired against him.

The wind howled and tore at the roof of Demetrios's home for two more days. Rufus set out bowls and basins to catch the drips pattering from the ceiling, but with each clatter of the outside gate, a new puddle seemed to form on the floor at his feet. Demetrios paced, unable to control his impatience.

With every passing day, the possibility of bringing Elazar back faded. Trapped inside the walls of his home, Demetrios tried to imagine what Jesus was like. Most of the Jews he had known were reluctant to call attention to themselves, for fear that Rome would view them as potential insurrectionists.

But, according to the rumors, Jesus had been attracting large crowds. Did Jesus hope to foster a rebellion? Were his magic healings simply a means to court followers? Elazar could be arrested. Who knew what would happen?

Demetrios sipped at the cup of wine Rufus had brought him and sighed. If nothing else, he should warn Elazar of the risk. He pulled back the bedchamber curtain, agitated by the constant rain. How much longer would he have to wait?

Just before dawn on the fourth day, he awoke to silence. Rufus tapped lightly on the door. He balanced a tray of food in his hands. "Elisheba is here, Master. I hope you don't mind."

"Elisheba?" First, no one ever came to see him, and now it seemed he had a steady stream of visitors, including a slave from another man's house. "Why?"

"The wind broke the tiles on Tertius's mansion, and after the workman fixed his roof, he was kind enough to send him here to put down new thatch and reroll the plaster over your bedchamber. Elisheba came with the workman." He held out a cloth-wrapped bundle. "She brought several loaves of her fresh bread."

Demetrios set the tray aside. "Wrap up some of the bread with a block of cheese. I'll take it with me to Capernaum."

"You're leaving today?"

Demetrios nodded. "When the workman is finished, you can walk Elisheba home." He turned away when he saw Rufus blush. He shouldn't encourage their courtship. Nothing good could come of it.

After dressing, he made his oblations to Mercury, the guardian of merchants and travelers, adding a special entreaty for the deity to speak favor to Elazar's god, Yahweh. The terra-cotta figure on the tiny altar maintained a fixed gaze to the heavens.

Taking up his staff, Demetrios sank down on his sleeping couch, thinking about his quest to bring Elazar home. Capernaum: Other than the Messiah, what promise did Elazar find there? The place was a dirty, sleepy fishing community where the small black basalt houses were crammed so close together they made the streets feel stark and gray. The synagogue was equally plain. Holy buildings should be imposing, like the Jewish Temple in Jerusalem or the Nabataean temple in Petra. Demetrios never understood why Elazar made so many visits to the synagogue in Tiberias. What wisdom did he find there? What more wisdom did he hope to find in Capernaum? However, if Elazar was still in Capernaum, he would not be far from the synagogue there, for Jewish healers often practiced their arts in such buildings.

When Demetrios stepped out into the courtyard, Elisheba was still there, laughing at something Rufus had said. Demetrios cleared his throat.

Elisheba raised her hand to her mouth, and they both fell silent. Rufus turned to face Demetrios. "Yes, Master?"

Uncomfortable with the happiness he saw on his servant's face, Demetrios ducked his head. "Nothing. I should be back later this afternoon." He heard their continued banter as he pushed the gate closed behind him.

In Capernaum, Demetrios climbed the hill to the synagogue and lingered outside the heavy wooden doors, listening to the murmur of the voices from within. A Gentile was not welcome to enter, and he had no idea how long he would have to wait until he could speak to someone. The Jewish god mystified him. Elazar told him Jews were not allowed to create any depictions of Yahweh's form, lest they worship graven images, but how could a person worship a god he couldn't see? A proper god needed a fine house, statues and images to remind his servants of his power, and regular obeisance.

Demetrios searched for a place to sit.

Two men—Pharisees by their dress—emerged from a side door. They wore formal mantles with blue fringe trailing from the hems, fringe so long it brushed the ground. Leather amulets were tied to the men's foreheads and left hands. Phylacteries, Elazar had said they were called. The Jews used them as prayer boxes. It must be their Shabbat day. What else had Elazar said about the prayer boxes? The larger the phylactery, the more pious the Pharisee. It was not a compliment. The two Pharisees stopped in surprise when they saw their visitor. "Gentile, what do you want?"

If Elazar was not here in the synagogue, Demetrios reasoned he must be with Jesus. He gripped his staff and stood up straight. "I am looking for—"

The short Pharisee with a rounded belly cut him off. "Keep your idols away from our house." He pointed to the staff Demetrios carried, his walking stick adorned with the carved head of Mars.

"Put it down over there." He waited until Demetrios had propped the staff against a tree across the street. Then he said, "Who is it you seek?"

"Two men," Demetrios answered. "One is named Elazar, and the other calls himself Jesus of Nazareth."

"Blasphemer!" the taller Pharisee exclaimed. His beard twitched as his lips turned up in a sneer. "I know nothing about your friend, but you'll find your false prophet speaking to his followers in a wadi to the west. The crowds have beaten the grass flat. The trail is easy to see." He peered down his nose at Demetrios, his mouth puckered in disgust. "Go listen to the words of the heretic. You don't belong here, idol-worshipper." Turning their backs to Demetrios, they entered the synagogue.

The trail they mentioned wound through fields choked with darnel weed. Narrower paths branched off to the left and right, twisting back over themselves and then to the main road. On every track the brush had been trampled down as if a vast army had marched across the land. All of the paths finally converged and ended abruptly at the top of a cliff overlooking a sweeping dry riverbed.

Demetrios stopped there, astonished by the tableau he saw below. People of every class, every age, every nationality swarmed the wadi. Samaritans shared bread with Jews, ignoring the long-standing distrust between the two groups; wealthy merchants sat on woolen rugs side by side with their slaves; and tax collectors, despised by everyone, joked with peasants.

Greeted by tendrils of gray smoke, Demetrios worked his way down the hillside into the valley.

The spicy fragrance of simmering herbs and vegetables floated on the breeze. From above, he had not noticed the women, but now he saw young mothers nursing their babes while older women prepared the midday meal. The children who were big enough to walk didn't walk but ran in and out of the various camps, darting between the adults and the small fires. A couple of crones, with toothless caved-in mouths, pointed and laughed when Demetrios nearly tripped as a toddler crashed into his legs. The child sat down hard but didn't cry out.

An old woman tending a fire looked up. She was so frail her chin quivered when she spoke, but her words carried, "Martha, get your sister. Don't let her wander off." She paused, staring at Demetrios. "Yes?"

The ancient probably watched everything that happened in this wadi. "Jesus of Nazareth. The one they call the Messiah. Is he here?" Demetrios asked, his eyes darting here and there for a glimpse of Elazar or even Caleb.

She pointed to her left. "With that circle of Jews. The one in the center." She returned to stirring her pot.

The Jews had formed a wall of bodies that was nearly impenetrable. Demetrios walked around them several times, craning to see over their heads. "I need to get through." No one noticed him. He nudged a burly back with his staff. Several of the Jews turned around.

Assuming an air of authority, he waved his staff at them. "Is that Jesus? I need to talk to him."

"Wait your turn, Gentile," one of the men said. "We were here first."

When a man in front of him knelt to tighten the strap on his sandal, Demetrios seized his opportunity. Over loud objections, Demetrios pushed past them. Jostled from all sides, he found himself standing directly in front of a small group of Jewish men who talked all at the same time, barely listening to the answer to one question before someone posed another. But which of them was

Jesus, Elazar's Messiah? The husky man in the fish-blood-stained cloak whose abrasive laughter drowned out the conversation? The tall slender one with calloused palms and a sunburned face? Most of the men appeared to be listening to the latter.

Herod had spies everywhere, and such a raucous group was certain to draw negative attention. As Demetrios pulled his cloak up to shield his face, a familiar form stepped forward and pumped his fist into the air. "Hail to the Messiah," he cried, "the new King of the Jews." Judas! Demetrios tried to step back but was blocked by the crowd.

Immediately, several people picked up the chant: "Hail to our King!" Others waved their fists. "Hail to the King of the Jews!"

Someone behind Demetrios shouted, "He's not our king. Herod is king of the Jews! He speaks for us."

They began pushing each other. A man pointed at the Herod defender. "Heretic! He blasphemes." Jesus's supporters grabbed the speaker and punched him in the mouth.

One of the brawlers slammed into Demetrios's shoulder; Demetrios nearly collapsed. Blindly, he spun around, pressing against the surging bodies. He had to escape, to get out before it was too late.

A hand tugged on his wrist. "Demetrios, over here."

"Elazar!" he cried, catching his breath as they tumbled free. "I'm so glad I found you."

Elazar guided him away from the commotion. "Why are you here?" he said, confused.

While the Jews continued to yell and argue behind them, Demetrios stared at his friend. Elazar's face was crusted with dirt, and he looked tired. Grasping his staff, Demetrios stood up straight. "I should ask you that question. Did you hear what they were saying? They called him a king. Do you know what that means? Insurrection, rebellion. They want to start a war." He was shouting now, desperate to make Elazar listen to him.

People turned toward them, gawking as if they were a pair of squabbling birds. "Your Messiah will bring down the Roman boot. And when you get caught—for you will be caught—you'll be crucified." He shook his head. "I care about you. I don't—"

"Demetrios . . ." Elazar touched his fingers to Demetrios's lips, warning him to be quiet. Embracing his friend, he pressed his mouth against Demetrios's ear. "Let us go where we can talk in private."

He led Demetrios north, to a trail that twined up the opposite side of the wadi. "We will be alone at the top. Do you think you can manage the climb?" Demetrios studied the path. Most of it was sloping, but someone had cut rough steps into the rocks near the ridge. He nodded. "I have my staff."

They ascended in silence, the sounds of the crowd falling away behind them. Despite his age, Elazar still walked with a strong step and straight back.

Near the top of the stairs, Elazar paused to assist Demetrios up the final steep steps. Then he crossed the ridge to stand and gaze at the gathering below. "Isn't it magnificent?"

Demetrios joined him but didn't comment.

Jesus's followers sat cross-legged in a circle on the ground off to the right, while the slender man, the one Demetrios assumed to be the Messiah, walked among them, touching the shoulders of one man, placing his hands on the head of another. Judas followed closely behind, mimicking the Messiah's gestures of compassion.

Several families were packing up to leave. The men took down the tents while the women collected their children. Their shrill voices quavered in the gusting wind, "Eli! Jonah! Rebeccah! Over here. Your father's waiting." The children screamed with laughter as the swirling breeze snatched the black-striped tent flaps from their hands.

Others had decided to remain in the wadi. Some traveling merchants had laid out their heavy carpets side by side, creating a floor where they could play dice. They crouched on wooden stools, their heads bare to the sun, shouting out their wagers, showing no interest in Jesus at all. Slaves with large jugs of wine balanced on their shoulders moved easily in and out of the noisy group, ready to pour a cup.

On the far side of the wadi, a small group of peasants huddled in the shade with their backs to the game. Unlike the merchants, who wore ankle-length robes of fine linen embroidered with threads of scarlet and blue, the peasants were dressed in plain woolen cloaks that fell just below their knees. Their hair was long and matted, their beards uncombed. The shepherds among them carried the crooked staff that marked their trade, and all of them watched Jesus intently, leaning forward to capture every single word. Whether from fear or doubt, they made no attempt to join the circle of followers. Demetrios often felt like those peasants must feel: an outsider. But the difference was those shepherds had wives and families. Demetrios had no one.

"Why do they come here?" Demetrios asked.

Elazar turned toward him. "The Messiah helps those in need." He offered no more explanation. "Why did you come, Demetrios?"

"To take you back to Tiberias." His hip hurt from the climb; he shifted his weight. "Herod tolerates no dissent. He beheaded the Baptist for insulting him. What do you think he'll do to Jesus? To his disciples? Are you one of them now?"

Elazar started to argue, but Demetrios grasped Elazar's arm and pulled him around to face him. "You've made a terrible mistake. Come home with me. Where you belong."

Doubt flashed in Elazar's eyes.

His expression hardened.

He shook his head and stepped to the side, pulled himself free of Demetrios's grip, his gaze again focused on the wadi below. "No, you're wrong. The prophecies foretold of a Messiah, a son of David. Jesus fulfills all that is written."

"Where is Caleb?"

"He's no different than the others who expected miracles. He left."

"Where did he go?"

Elazar shrugged. "Caleb is like the sails of a boat in a storm. He changes direction with each shift of the wind. You may see him again in Tiberias. Or elsewhere. I have no idea where he is."

"Perhaps Caleb saw the truth. He knew Jesus and his followers were trouble. He left for a reason. You should leave, too."

"I can't do that."

Demetrios started to speak but stopped. What could he possibly say to Elazar that would change his mind? He squeezed his hands into tight fists. When he unfolded them, the whiteness of his palms ebbed pink. "You're my friend, you cared about me."

"Your father was a cruel man, Demetrios. I'm sorry for that."

"Cruel? Is that your word for it?" He felt his face flush as he glared at Elazar. "Before the Roman, my father beat me almost every night of my life, leaving me with this." He tapped his twisted leg. "When I was no longer of use to him, he sold me off like an animal so he could pay his gambling debts. Do you call a man like that a father?" Awkwardly, he touched Elazar's shoulder. "I know we come from different nations, but I think—"

Elazar removed Demetrios's hand. "You're not a child anymore. You don't need me." The wind tugged at Elazar's hair, and he brushed a strand out of his eyes. A slow smile crept across his weathered features. "You need a wife."

"A wife? Tabitha—"

"Tabitha was a mistake. You made a mistake. But it doesn't have to be that way now. The past is the past." He paused. "Your new wife would never know you were once a slave. You've taken care of that."

"You think my scars don't matter? And what about this?" He jerked the hem of his cloak up to his hip, exposing his left thigh. The leg above the knee twisted inward at an awkward angle; ugly indentations in the rippled flesh marked previously broken bones—the gift from his father, now healed. "Do you know what the prostitute in the marketplace said about me?"

Elazar stepped back, frowning at Demetrios. "You go to the slums of Tiberias? Mix with those thieves and prostitutes and who knows what else lives down there?"

"Don't look at me like that. Where else would I go?"

"Not there."

"Shappira? The one who plies her trade along the shore? Well, she refused me altogether. Said my body gave her nightmares. Told me I couldn't pay her enough to make her touch me." The memory of her mocking smile brought the taste of ashes to his mouth. He didn't mention her other remark, that the gods must have cursed him for what he had done. What woman would marry a man like him, deformed and a man who had committed murder?

After a brief silence, he turned back to Elazar.

"The prostitutes reject me."

Elazar said softly, "You seek love in the wrong places." He straightened the cloak over Demetrios's leg. "Look for a Gentile who tends to her house and keeps her body pure."

"No, I don't think I can find a wife."

One of the gamblers was collecting the winnings from the

game. When his basket was filled, he carried it over to Jesus and knelt before him. Jesus blessed the man while Judas took the coins and counted them. Why were they paying tribute to the Messiah? Did they expect him to grant favors, to perform miracles for money?

Jesus looked like a charlatan to Demetrios, a cheat who deceived the foolish and the desperate. Demetrios massaged his leg, squeezing the soreness from his muscles. It was a mistake to climb up that stairway. He could walk miles on a good road but steep hills always caused distress. He sighed. Tonight he would need to soak his legs in salt water.

"I told him everything," Elazar said, breaking into the silence.

Demetrios straightened. "What? Who?"

"Jesus. I told him what we did, what you did. I confessed our crimes."

"You confessed?" Disbelieving, he stared at Elazar. "You told him? Everything?" Then the full implications of Elazar's revelation hit him. "No," Demetrios said. "No."

He raised his staff and lunged toward Elazar.

But Elazar grabbed the stick and yanked Demetrios off-balance. The two wrestled for the staff. Demetrios wrenched it back as Elazar held on. The wood slipped between their sweaty fingers, but neither would give up the struggle. They fought their battle in silence, punctuated only by the heavy rasp of their breathing.

Finally, Elazar shoved Demetrios away from him.

"You would strike me?" Elazar cried, his chest heaving as he danced out of reach. "I protected you, I took care of you, and this is what it comes to?" His face purpled with rage.

Demetrios staggered, grasped his staff, slammed it into the dirt, trembling with fury like a palsied old man. "Do you think he'll keep this secret? How long before Jesus turns us over to the magistrate? What then?" Heat rushed to Demetrios's cheeks; he felt ill, feverish. Elazar was his friend, his only friend. How could a trusted friend do this? Swaying, Demetrios backed away.

"We made a vow. No one was to know. A vow." Tears burned his eyes. "No one." This Jesus. This Jesus was a demon, an evil spirit with the power to persuade Elazar to confess the one sin he should never have confessed. This Jesus. Elazar had doomed them both.

The sky, bleached white by the afternoon sun, shimmered. Barren rocks glittered like jewels in the brilliant light. Elazar had become a disappearing shadow. Their friendship was gone forever, poisoned by a broken promise.

"You betrayed me," Demetrios snapped.

Then he lurched across the granite ledge, searching for the path, the stairway a black hole under his feet.

Several times he lost his footing on the steps as he stumbled and slid over the rocks. Stones showered around his feet as Elazar scrambled to keep up. "Demetrios, wait. I'm sorry. Let me help you."

Demetrios didn't reply.

Instead, he picked up his pace.

CHAPTER
TWELVE

In the wadi, Demetrios stood still, trying to absorb what had happened. Elazar came up behind him, but Demetrios didn't turn around. He didn't want to see his friend's—his betrayer's—face. Not now, not ever again.

Elazar touched Demetrios's elbow, and Demetrios jerked away. "Marcus was a monster," Demetrios said, his voice barely above a whisper. He gazed at the staff in his hands, as he spun the point of the stick slowly in the dirt. "When he finished with me, he would have turned his wrath on you. I saved you. I saved both of us. If it weren't for me, you would still be a slave." He took a deep breath. "And this is how you repay me. With betrayal."

Elazar stepped in front of him, gazing at Demetrios as though he wanted to remember his face.

"Get away from me," Demetrios shouted. He raised his staff again, threatening to bring it down, but froze. The bitter words had slipped from his lips before he could stop them. The two of them had worked so hard, planned a good life, and Elazar had tossed it all away for the promises of a charlatan. Demetrios wanted to weep.

Elazar hesitated a moment longer, then said, "Good-bye, my friend."

He turned and walked away, never looking back, as he continued up the wadi to speak to his new friend, one of the Jews who had been sitting near Jesus.

Demetrios watched Elazar and the other man until they were out of sight.

"Make way! Make way!"

Demetrios jumped. He had forgotten about the gambling merchants. They were all leaving now, their voices loud with alcohol and ennui. The air swirled with dust as their slaves shook out the carpets and rolled them up. After hefting the rugs onto their shoulders, two of the slaves pushed past Demetrios and staggered toward the path to Capernaum. "Up, up. Easy. Keep it level." Four more slaves, their bare chests glistening with sweat, lifted a litter.

One of the merchants in the litter patted his sunburned scalp with a damp cloth while his companion lay back in a pile of pillows shouting out orders. "You, be careful there. Hold your side up higher or I'll fall out." He flicked a slave on the back with a short strap and then snatched his curtain shut. The slaves groaned as they jockeyed their burden along the wadi. When they reached the trail that led to the top, the lead man on the left called out a cadence, directing the four into a march up the hillside.

A couple of peasants elbowed past. "A wasted day," the first man said. "I should've cleared the weeds from my fields."

His companion grunted in agreement. "Just fancy words and empty promises. The real Messiah would bring down fire from the heavens to purge the earth of Rome." He paused and cast a knowing look at Demetrios. "And all her pagan servants." The two followed behind the merchants, grumbling about "false prophets."

Demetrios started after them, prepared to tell them he had as much right as they did to be here, but he held back. Those Jewish peasants knew nothing about what he had suffered, how hard he had worked. But still, their words about Jesus made him pause. Perhaps this Jesus of Nazareth wasn't a healer after all, and the peasant was right.

Jesus's talk had ended for the day. All the tents had been packed and carted off, the cooking fires extinguished. Gathering up their implements, farmers and shepherds departed for their homes. Of the devoted circle of Jews that had surrounded Jesus, only a handful remained, and these men, too, began to leave in groups of two and three, calling out farewell as they walked back toward Capernaum.

Judas, the last to go, kissed Jesus on both cheeks, then left in the same direction as Elazar. Except for a few stragglers ascending the cliffside path, Demetrios and Jesus were alone.

The wind soughed through the small branch canyons like the mournful cry of a gull. The shadows lengthened across the valley floor. He knew he should leave with the others, for it was dangerous to travel a dark road, but Demetrios stayed—watching, waiting.

Would Jesus report him and Elazar to the Roman authorities? If Jesus did not speak to him soon, then Demetrios would ask. He approached the Messiah.

Jesus held out his hands, palms upturned in greeting. "What do you need?"

"I want—"

"Teacher," a man shouted. Demetrios stopped. Jesus had not been speaking to him.

"Rav," another man called. "Come over here."

Demetrios turned, straining to see the newcomers. The first cry had originated in the rocks above, the second from somewhere to his left.

A woman's wail cut through the air, shrill and piercing. "Master, oh Master, help us. My baby's ill."

They were upon him now.

The beggars, the outcasts, the shunned, the unclean, the possessed, and even the dying rushed in from their hiding places; they crawled out from behind large boulders and stands of tamarisk and brush; they stumbled over rocks in the wadi, falling on their knees. They closed around Demetrios and Jesus, pushing and shoving, the stink of their diseases falling upon Demetrios like a noxious rain. Arms wrapped in bloody bandages reached out to touch him. No, they sought to touch Jesus, but they still brushed against Demetrios. Tears streamed down cheeks pocked with sores, faces so disfigured Demetrios feared to breathe the air he shared with them. Several of the people, inhabited by evil spirits, rolled on the ground, stuffing handfuls of dirt into their blackened mouths. Demetrios backed away, but too late. He could not escape the madness.

The crowd grabbed and tugged at Jesus's clothes, some of the weaker members dropping like dead leaves at his feet. Moving patiently among them, Jesus stroked dirty heads teeming with lice. His lips kissed oozing wounds and whispered words that seemed to offer comfort. Unlike the earlier followers who had expressed their doubts, these people adored him, and Demetrios was afraid. No man should have this power!

If so many people revered Jesus, what would the authorities think? Would they listen to him, do his bidding out of fear? Demetrios was determined that no one would return him to a life of slavery. Not Elazar. Not Jesus. Not even Rome. Demetrios didn't know yet what he would do, but Elazar needed to be silenced and Jesus stopped.

A woman fell to the ground in front of Jesus, her black hair fanning out over her back. "Master, master, heal my husband. He can't walk. I'll take you to him."

Another beggar, wearing only a loincloth, tugged on Jesus's robe, trying to lead him away from the mob. "We're hungry. My children have nothing to eat."

A rough hand clamped onto Demetrios's arm, pitching him off-balance. "Give me money." A fat, red-faced man with rheumy eyes held him fast, flecks of white foam spraying from his cracked lips as he snarled out his demand. "Coins, denarii, money!"

"Let go of me."

Laughing, the horrible creature twined his fingers into the folds of Demetrios's cloak and pulled him closer. "I saw your purse. Give it to me."

"No!"

Demetrios braced his staff against the man's chest and shoved, sending them both reeling. The stranger toppled into the stamping horde. Demetrios lurched backward, stumbling over a small figure crouched behind him. His fury rising, he whirled around, ready to strike. "Get away from me."

He had been tripped not by a person but by a bundle of clothing stacked slightly higher than his knees. He stared at the mound of fabric on the ground. The garment was made of fine wool, dyed the deep rich blue of the rare indigo plant, like sea water bubbling in a dry wadi. Silver silk threads woven throughout gave the fabric a glossy sheen. This was a piece much too valuable to belong to one of these beggars. He reached for it.

The bundle moved.

"Don't touch me." A woman's voice spoke with surprising force from beneath the heap.

"What?" His hand remained suspended above her.

"Don't." A head emerged from the drape, covered in a layered tunic that masked everything but a small opening for her eyes.

But oh, those eyes—the color of loamy, fertile earth high-lighted with flecks of golden light, deep brown eyes with lashes as thick as the fringe on a Pharisee's shawl.

She rose, and the cloak assumed a human shape.

A double belt embroidered with red and white squares circled her waist; a veil of the same fine wool covered her head. Despite these attributes of wealth, the newly sewn patches in her clothes revealed a recent descent into poverty. A crust of mud caked the shoulder of her cloak. She peered at Demetrios through fluttering lashes. "You mustn't. It's too dangerous."

Demetrios trembled. She had such a gentle, kind voice. Unlike the prostitutes, this woman would never shame him, never mock him. He reached out to wipe the dirt from her garment.

"No," she snatched her cloak up as though he had slapped her, "you can't."

He caught a whiff of her perfume, a scent powerfully sweet with a hint of musk, earthy and rich. When a wisp of hair escaped from the curve of her veil, he fought the temptation to tuck it back into its proper place. Who was she? Why was she here? Most women who veiled their hair were married Romans or Gentiles, but where was her husband? Why would he leave her alone in this place? "I won't hurt you." This time he didn't hesitate and reached out for her.

With a terrified cry, she turned and fled.

"Wait!"

She raced against the ebbing flow of people, ducking and dodging, never once making physical contact with anyone, until she disappeared at a bend in the wadi.

Demetrios could never run that fast and clearly she didn't want to be found. Turning, he searched for Jesus among the confusion.

The Messiah hastened down the sandy wadi toward his disciples, his quick steps flying over the ground. Behind him, the multitude followed like a trailing wind, still beseeching him for aid.

CHAPTER
THIRTEEN

The fear of what Jesus might do preyed upon Demetrios. During the day, when he worked alone with the animals at Elazar's house, Demetrios kept watch for the arrival of the magistrate. At night he drank wine to help him sleep. He stopped visiting the marketplace and sent Rufus instead, who brought word of more pilgrims seeking safe passage to the Passover festival. If it weren't for the caravan, Demetrios would have already fled Tiberias. But where would he go? Whom could he trust?

Despite his fears about Jesus, Demetrios could not stop thinking about the strange woman at Capernaum. She was so graceful; her voice so kind.

One night, he dreamt of her.

He imagined her entering his bedchamber on the intoxicating trail of her perfume, an aroma both sweet and pungent. She wore nardinum, the same expensive scent Demetrios and Elazar had purchased in Sepphoris. Her veil obscured her features, but

Demetrios knew she would be beautiful when he gazed upon her. Her cloak rustled like a whispering breeze in the darkness. The embroidered woolen tunic had been transformed into a filmy, almost diaphanous robe. Although he couldn't see her face, he could see the shadow of her slender naked body. He pictured her kneeling by his bed, her breath caressing his cheek. Her hands arched over his face, but she didn't touch him. The air glowed. "Demetrios . . ." Her voice flowed like a cool river; still, his flesh burned. She smiled and leaned close enough to kiss. But did not.

Like an evanescent vision, her shape waxed and waned in the moonless night. Her hair, the color of kohl, was bound up in a magnificent shining coil. Her gold-flecked eyes reflected the sun, even in the darkness. He sensed this woman would never reject him.

When he reached for her, his fingers fluttered through empty space. Demetrios called out to her: "Please . . ."

A man's hand clamped over his mouth, and Demetrios knew he was no longer dreaming. Demetrios opened his eyes, staring at the shadow near his face, listening to the ragged breaths of the other person who stood over him.

"Be quiet. I don't want to hurt you, Demetrios."

Demetrios was quiet.

"Much better." The man removed his hands, sat back on the bed.

"Caleb," Demetrios said.

Caleb laughed. "Sit up slowly, please, and don't light the lamp. I prefer the dark."

"How did you get in here?"

"The storeroom at the back of your house does provide easy access."

"It's locked. Rufus sleeps at the door."

The soft clink of metal pinging against stone cut through the quiet night as Caleb tapped an object on the wall. "Not if you have a key. Rufus is a poor guard. An earthquake could toss him out of bed, and he would still be snoring like a goat. Unlike you"— he paused—"so much flailing and mumbling. You kept calling to someone. Did you know I was here?"

Demetrios sat upright. Pieces of his dream, like strands of shredded rope, tugged at him. Her perfume lingered in the bed-chamber. "What do you want? Did you come to rob me?"

Again Caleb laughed. "I came to warn you, Demetrios. You could be in danger. Romulus knows Elazar and I have left. He covets your camels."

Demetrios managed a dry chuckle. "He's coveted our camels since the first day he saw them." Romulus seemed like a minor worry. "What about Jesus of Nazareth? Did he say anything about me? Have you talked to Elazar?"

Caleb didn't reply. He rose and shuffled across the stone floor, his footsteps now uncertain. "A few days ago, when we came to your house, Elazar said he had regrets. What did he mean?"

"Nothing. I don't know. It's nothing."

Demetrios strained to follow Caleb's movement in the darkness. He thought the young man had stopped pacing somewhere near the storeroom, but when Caleb spoke, the sound came from in front of the window. "I saw you in the wadi," Caleb said. "I haven't talked to Elazar. Is he coming back?"

Demetrios was silent. He had received no word from Elazar since their last meeting. Elazar's betrayal still cut through him, and his friend's absence troubled Demetrios. What if this Jesus repeated Elazar's story to the authorities?

A light breeze ruffled the curtain. Caleb's body formed a

dim shape against the open window. Demetrios looked at Caleb. "Elazar won't be returning to Tiberias." He peered again at the shadowy form, wondering how much of what Caleb said was true, how many of his words were lies to cover his attempted theft. "How could you be in the wadi? Elazar told me you left."

"No, I was there, hiding in the rocks, watching. I'm always watching." Caleb turned and took a step toward the bed, stopped. "I listen, too." He didn't elaborate. "Where did you get that scar on your shoulder? I saw it when I put my hand on you."

How much did Caleb know? How much could he guess? Nervously, Demetrios tugged at his tunic. "An accident. From long ago."

"It looks like a burn. Or a knife wound. Or both?"

"Why do you ask me these questions? Why are you here?" Demetrios struggled to suppress his rising anxiety. A secret, once told, spreads like an uncontrolled fire. If Caleb knew, how long before Rome came banging at his door?

"I told you. To warn you. Without Elazar or me, your caravan is more vulnerable to attack. If it's not Romulus, it could be bandits. The brigands tend to leave their fellow Jews alone, but now you have no Jews working for you."

Leaning back against the wall, Demetrios relaxed. Caleb knew nothing. "And does Jesus have anything to do with this? Matthias, the fishmonger, said Judas could be a brigand."

Caleb resumed his restless stroll around the perimeter of the bedchamber. "You were there for only a short time. You saw so little of Jesus." A sigh. "I wish I could explain it to you. I wish I could believe fully. Jesus does wondrous things, but what he says confuses me." He was quiet for a minute. "And he consorts with tax collectors, beggars, ruffians, prostitutes, even bandits. He excludes almost no one."

Caleb glanced at Demetrios and walked to the bed. The reed mattress sagged as he sat down. "Perhaps this is a test," he spoke in the darkness. "If Jesus is the true Messiah, then the kingdom of Israel will be restored, and there's nothing you or I or anyone can do about it. Just be careful, though. Not everyone wishes you well."

"Why did you come here, Caleb? To steal my food?"

Caleb laughed softly, but there was no amusement in his tone. "You've always been kind to me, Demetrios. I'm not hungry, not yet, but I do need work. I know you need experienced caravan drivers." He leaned close, his hands resting on the bed near Demetrios's elbows. "What do you say? Will you hire me to drive the caravan?"

Demetrios drew back, pondering whether he could trust Caleb or not. Demetrios could not move the caravan alone, but was Caleb the best choice? "Let me think about it. Meet me at the animal stalls the day after tomorrow. We'll talk then."

"Good enough. I'll see you in two days then." He reached for Demetrios's hand. "Here." He folded Demetrios's fingers tightly around a small bottle. "I believe this belongs to you."

"I didn't say I'd—" He stopped, startled by loud voices coming from the street. Someone pounded on the gate to the courtyard.

Caleb touched his arm. "What is it?"

"Shh!" Rising, Demetrios rushed to the entrance of his bedchamber and placed his ear against the door. Rufus was running across the courtyard toward the entrance. The gate crashed open, and a woman, her voice high-pitched with excitement, greeted his servant.

"Is someone coming?" Caleb asked.

"Be quiet. They'll hear you."

On a rooftop nearby, a nervous rooster crowed wildly.

Caleb hurried to the window, sweeping aside the coverings. A pale gray light warmed the sky. "The hour is late. I have to go." The shouting in the street increased. It sounded like a small crowd had formed. Turning, Caleb ran through the storeroom, closing the door behind him.

Demetrios waited until he knew Caleb was gone. Then, returning to his bed, he sat and studied the gift Caleb had placed in his hand. He rolled the tiny bottle across his palm. He recognized it from his storeroom: an oval-shaped container, carved from a single piece of alabaster. Carefully, he snapped the clay seal, dribbling the perfumed oil through his fingers. He brought his hand to his face, inhaling deeply. Nardinum, the scent of the lady in his dream.

CHAPTER
FOURTEEN

Moments after Caleb left, the courtyard gate banged shut, and Rufus burst into the bedchamber. "Master, you'll never guess what has happened."

Still holding the perfume, Demetrios looked up. Caleb's nocturnal visit seemed to be an extension of his strange dream, but Rufus's abrupt arrival reminded him of the activity outside his house. He tucked the vial under a cushion. "Who was at the gate? What is it?"

"Oh, that was Elisheba. She had the most amazing news." Rufus pulled back the curtains, letting in the light. When he turned to Demetrios, his face was shining. "A dead man has been brought back to life. Somebody called Lazarus, she said."

"That's crazy. Who did this?" Even as he asked the question, he knew the answer.

"Jesus of Nazareth." Rufus reached for a broom and began sweeping rapidly across the dirt floor, his words spilling out as he worked. "Everyone is talking about it. They say he's the 'anointed one,' the Messiah, chosen to be King of the Jews."

The idea of bringing a dead man to life was incomprehensible, but Demetrios could not forget how the beggars and the dying followed Jesus and fell at his feet, pleading for help. They believed Jesus could work miracles. Demetrios had sensed the man's influence in the wadi, the way people listened to him, transfixed. Was it even possible he resurrected this Lazarus? If so, what else would Jesus do? The ramifications terrified him.

Rufus remained unaware of Demetrios's long silence. He continued to tidy the bedchamber, prattling on about the news from the marketplace, mixing everyday gossip with the exciting story of a dead man brought back to life. "And then Elisheba said—"

"Stop." Demetrios held up his hand. Nardinum flooded his senses, and he coughed. "Stop talking about the marketplace. Tell me again. From the beginning. What do you know about this Jesus of Nazareth? What did you hear?"

Rufus turned toward him, his face clouded with confusion. "I've told you all I know." He sniffed at the air. "What's that smell? Did something spill?"

"It's nothing." He wiped his fingers on his tunic. "A broken vial of perfume. Now, tell me the story about the dead man."

"Yes, Master." He picked up Demetrios's sandals. "Would you like me to help you dress while I tell you again?"

Demetrios nodded.

"Elisheba knocked on the gate early this morning. She had sold some of her bread in the marketplace—Tertius makes good money from her baking—and she said everyone was talking about it there. Some merchants brought the news." He tied the strap around Demetrios's right ankle. "They said Lazarus was in the tomb four days. Long after the time the Jews believe the spirit remains with the body." His hands poised over Demetrios's other foot, he looked up. "Think of it! Ooh, can you imagine the smell?"

Rufus shook his head and shuddered. "But he told them to move the stone away. Then he commanded Lazarus to get up and walk. And he did. Just like that. Right out of the tomb. Like a living skeleton with all the bindings still attached."

"Who? Who commanded him to get up and walk?"

"You know"—he crouched down again to tie the other sandal, his fingers working the laces through the holes in the leather—"Jesus of Nazareth. Except some of the Jews are calling him the Christos now. Others call him Messiah. But it's all the same, isn't it?"

Sunshine streamed through the open window. Did Caleb wait on the other side, listening? "Was he really alive? It wasn't some illusion? A trick?" He grasped his servant's arm, dragging him toward the bed. "Where is Jesus now?" he demanded.

Staggering, Rufus fumbled to stand upright, but Demetrios still had a firm grip on him. "I don't know. Elisheba said the merchants came up from Jericho. But they told her Jesus performed the deed in Bethany. Then he went to Jericho. To rest. It must be hard work bringing the dead back to life." He took a deep breath. "Will you let me go now? Please?"

Demetrios released him. Rising, he began to pace the room. "So, he's left Capernaum." To reach the valley near the Sea of Salt, Jesus and his followers must have departed the day after Demetrios had seen them. He turned toward his servant. "He's still in Jericho?"

Rufus nodded. "I believe so." He stood quietly, watching Demetrios with a strange expression. "They—they told Elisheba raising the dead man was a sign. Jesus was the true king of the Jews. They said he would soon claim his rightful kingdom."

"A king? No, that cannot happen." Lights flashed in front of his face; a terrible vision of the dead and bloodied Marcus appeared before him. Demetrios reached blindly for his walking staff, the wall, anything. Still, he felt unbalanced, teetering.

Rufus caught his hands. "Master!"

Demetrios tore loose, backing away. He ran his fingers across his scalp, nails digging into his skin. A horrible crawling sensation wormed beneath his flesh. He felt as though his brain was going to burst, like Zeus giving birth to Athena. This was no divine genesis, though, but a realization of a disaster. Bringing the dead to life. Was this the punishment Jesus planned for Demetrios? To resurrect the dead? To give life to the Roman? Bring him back for revenge? "Where is this kingdom?" His voice choked when he spoke.

Rufus shook his head. "I don't know." Cautiously, his eyes still focused on Demetrios, he rubbed his left arm. "I think they were talking about a kingdom in the Holy City, but I'm not sure."

Understanding dawned. "Yes, of course. He will go to Jerusalem for Passover." Roman legionaries were stationed in Jerusalem to control the crowds. Pontius Pilate, the prefect of Judea, would be there to represent the interests of Rome, including the sentencing of criminals. If Jesus planned to turn Demetrios over to the authorities, it would be in Jerusalem, surely.

If Jesus intended to return Marcus to life, that, too, would occur in Jerusalem where his followers could proclaim his power. Demetrios stared at Rufus. "But Jesus is still in Jericho? For how long?"

Cowering from Demetrios, Rufus shrugged. "The merchants were leaving for Jericho today to see him. They thought he would be there for a few more days or a week at least."

"I have to find him." A drumbeat pounded in Demetrios's ears. Closing his eyes, he buried his face in his hands. He had to think clearly. He had to find Elazar. No, Elazar was gone. He had to find . . . He felt a light touch on his elbow.

"Master, are you ill? You're so pale."

Demetrios turned. The itching and throbbing ceased. "I'm fine." He walked Rufus to the storeroom. "I have work for you. Take inventory. Open all the chests. Check everything. Make sure nothing is missing. Count it all, and when you're finished, change the lock on the outside door."

As Rufus lugged the first heavy wooden chest across the floor, Demetrios backed away. He kept talking as he prepared to leave. "Don't forget to check my box of spices. Someone could've stolen something from there." Taking his cloak from the hook, he wrapped it around his shoulders.

Rufus stepped into the bedchamber. "There's a bottle of perfume missing. Is that what broke?" He paused, startled by the sight of Demetrios dressing to go out. "Master?"

Demetrios fumbled with the clasp on his cloak. The pin was bent and didn't close well, but he forced it in place. Then, taking up his staff, he turned to his servant. "Keep checking the storeroom. I'll be back soon." He dashed through the courtyard into the street.

Tertius's mansion reigned supreme at the road's end—a magnificent two-story structure built around a paved courtyard, commanding a splendid view of the city. Although Demetrios's Roman neighbor had departed for the coast a few days ago, the activity of his household continued without cease. Slaves, bearing goods to and from the marketplace, crossed regularly into the house through a pedestrian door in the side wall.

Demetrios did not see Elisheba as he raced past her, mumbling disjointed sentences and fragments of broken thoughts. As he hobbled up the hill, passersby stared at him curiously. Demetrios glared back, challenging them to confront him. He stopped speaking out loud, but his lips continued to quiver as the words swirled through his brain: *Elazar, why did you break your promise? You betrayed me. Do you know what you've done?*

Demetrios wondered if the authorities would be waiting for him in Jerusalem. But he could not cancel the Passover journey. If he did, he'd starve the coming winter. *I won't be crucified. Never,* he thought. Marcus is food for the vultures. He cannot return. Can he? For a fleeting moment, Demetrios imagined Marcus emerging from the trench where they had left him, his body a framework of bone and rag, a fringe of dark hair trailing from his skull, eyes in hollowed sockets following his every move. The whip, rotting but still strong, cracked through the air. All because of this Jesus.

"Demetrios!"

At the sound of his name, Demetrios spun.

Elazar stood near the bottom of the hill, hesitant to approach Demetrios.

"Elazar!" Demetrios was so relieved to see his old friend, he rushed forward to greet him, his anger forgotten. "You've come home."

Elazar clasped Demetrios's hands and stepped back. "I'm glad you've forgiven me. I knew you would understand." He smiled.

"I've heard the story, but it doesn't matter. Forget about Jesus. We have work to do. Our caravan is going to be one of the largest Jerusalem has ever seen, and you and I will take it there. Together."

"No." Elazar's tone was guarded, as though he expected another argument. "You've heard the news? About Jesus bringing a man back to life? I came to insist that you sell everything in Jerusalem. All of the merchandise, the donkeys, even the camels. We can divide the money, and you'll have enough to start your own business. I want to give my share to Jesus."

Demetrios reeled, tottered sideways, then caught his balance. First, Elazar broke his vow, and now he wanted to rob Demetrios of his wealth? Jesus had destroyed everything. "You would have me do all of the work and then take half of all that I possess?" Demetrios said, his voice rising. "I won't do it. I won't." He hesitated, wondering if he should cross this line, but Elazar had left him with no other choice. "If Jesus reports your story to the authorities, I'll say he lied. I'll tell them you killed Marcus. You bashed in his skull for his money and forced me to go with you to keep your secret."

Elazar studied Demetrios for a moment, shaking his head. "You know that's not true. And Jesus won't tell anyone. Your secret is safe." A sudden gust whipped Elazar's hair across his face, and he pushed it aside. He smiled but his eyes were troubled. "Meet me during Passover in Jerusalem. In the Upper Agora. We'll talk after you've had some time to consider my request."

"I don't think so." Demetrios gripped his staff. Leaning forward, he glared at Elazar.

Startled, Elazar raised his hand above his face as if to ward off a blow. "No, don't."

Demetrios squeezed the carved handle, caressing the top of Mars's head. "Don't worry. I'm not going to hit you." He turned away and started up the hill. "Good-bye, Elazar. You traitor."

Behind him, Elazar called, "Jerusalem, Demetrios. I'll meet you there." But Demetrios ignored him and kept on walking.

Following a course that cut to the left of Tertius's vineyards, Demetrios climbed to a promontory of rock overlooking the Sea of Galilee. Boulders, some as large as houses, lined the trail. Many of them bore the marks of previous visitors: the carved inscriptions of lovers and travelers. Today, Demetrios had the hilltop to himself. He perched on a flat shelf of stone.

Below, a cold wind stirred a white chop over the sea's surface. Shivering, Demetrios pulled his cloak closer. He felt the cool smoothness of the metal earring against his chest and remembered his brief encounter and chance at love at the oasis. His sorrow had followed him up the hill like a lion stalking its prey. When he and Elazar had first settled in Tiberias, Demetrios thought his life was born anew. He had left his past behind. People considered him a successful caravan driver and trader. No one suspected he had once been a slave. But love was lost to him now, and Elazar had destroyed everything they built together.

The chill weather sunk deep into his body; his leg ached. Down on the shore, the fishermen had all beached their boats, covering the interior shells with heavy tarps to keep out the rain. Two men dragged a full net of fish over to baskets for sorting. A flock of hungry sea birds gathered in the limbs of a gnarled tree that jutted out from the hillside.

Dry leaves and debris swirled around Demetrios's legs, pummeling his bare skin with stinging little slaps. Huddled in the warmth of his cloak, rocking gently against the force of the wind, Demetrios traced the ridge of scarred flesh that curled from his back over his left shoulder.

His fingers massaging the distorted imprint of the brand on his arm, he closed his eyes, recalling the heat of the fire, Elazar's prayer, "Forgive my sins . . ." Who forgives? Would he be forgiven?

A shrill screech near his ear startled him, and he opened his eyes to see the shorebirds circling. Demetrios looked down at the sea. The fishermen had finished cleaning and salting their catch, throwing the spoiled entrails to the birds. He wished he could be like those birds, able to fly away from the fear that consumed him.

Still watching the fishermen below, he picked at the boulder next to him, prying loose a chunk of rock marked with the initials of two lovers. The letters had been intertwined, crossed over one another as a single design, the lovers' promise to be together always. Did their promise hold? So many vows were broken. The Roman had had a similar stone in his own courtyard.

Demetrios turned the broken rock over, feeling the weight against his palm. Not as heavy as the stone that laid his old master low, but the power lay in the way it was wielded, not in its size. Two crows whirled above the fishermen, their raucous cries floating on the air like a desolate siren song. When they spotted the shorebirds dining on the fish, they swooped down and sent the small flock scattering in all directions. Demetrios stood, threw the rock, and shouted to the crows, "Go! Get out of here!"

The two birds took off.

Fat gray clouds had rolled in from the north, their movement casting silhouettes across the surface waters of the sea. The storm had arrived.

Justice. The gods required it. Jesus had two choices: he could have Demetrios arrested, or he could bring the Roman back to life to exact a greater revenge. No one should resurrect the evils of the past, not even a prophet with magical powers.

He dusted off his hands. Without Jesus, Elazar would come home. Secrets could remain secret. He would be a free man. He had to halt this marching return to slavery and death. He didn't know how he would stop Jesus, but he would find a way.

CHAPTER
FIFTEEN

In the days that followed, Caleb did not return, and Demetrios could not sleep. He believed his pledge to the gods should have terminated his ill thoughts; he would give the gods the justice they demanded. Instead, the thoughts intensified like a raging fever. Even in his sleep, they pursued him as dreams. Nightmares.

His night visions of terror included Jesus, Judas, Elazar, a ghost of the Roman, his father, Tabitha, and her, the veiled woman at Capernaum. She chanted his name like a prayer. *Demetrios, Demetrios, Demetrios. Come to me, Demetrios.* She spoke with a tenderness he had never known. But she opened a door to the ones who cried out for Demetrios to be crucified—to Roman soldiers who came to arrest him; to Marcus who returned for revenge; to the horrors of his past and to the threats to his future.

Despite this, he hungered for her. She was an addiction, a poison by association.

Awakened by his own screams, he lay in his bed, shaking, drenched in the stink of his fear, uncertain of what was real and what was imagined. He wondered how his servant could sleep through the noise, but one night, hours before dawn, Rufus—who stayed in the storeroom nearby—knocked on his bedchamber door. He brought a cup of warmed wine seasoned with incense. "Master, you have bad dreams. You are troubled?"

"Yes." Demetrios sipped at the drink, soothed by its spicy taste.

Rufus brought his lamp closer to the bed. "I want to show you something." He handed Demetrios a piece of cloth.

The linen had been folded and opened many times, handled so often that the writing on it was faint; the first line depicted the moon in all her phases and drawings of stars. Demetrios fingered the fabric, wondering what magic the words in the second line contained, for he couldn't read them. He looked up at Rufus. "What does it say? Do you know?"

Rufus raised his head and recited from memory, "You holy characters and all praiseworthy letters, kindle and burn the heart of Elisheba, slave of Tertius, in longing for the heart of Rufus, slave of Demetrios of Tiberias."

Demetrios returned the cloth to Rufus. "Where did you get this?"

"I bought it from Shappira, the prostitute who works the marketplace, but she didn't make it for me."

"Who did?"

"An enchantress. People go to her for help with their illnesses. If a barren woman wants a baby, she can make it happen. She sells potions and balms. She can put a curse on your enemies or give you a love spell. They call her the Sorceress of Galilee." He traced a finger over the words on the linen. "I told Shappira what I needed, and she gave it to the sorceress, who created the magic spell."

"Does this sorceress have a name?"

Rufus leaned close and whispered in Demetrios's ear. "The other slaves claim it's bad luck to say her name aloud," he said as he pulled back.

"I don't believe in luck." Demetrios poured himself another cup of wine. There must have been another message embedded in the dreams, something he couldn't see. The gods wanted more than he had offered. Or perhaps they were trying to warn him? An enchantress held magical powers, but a prophet who could bring dead people to life also had magic. He wondered if the Sorceress of Galilee was stronger than the Prophet of Galilee, Jesus. Rufus said she created spells. Could she fashion a spell to make people forget? A spell for protection? "How do I find her?"

"She has a boy who lives near the slums outside of town. He'll take you to her." His fingers played with the lip of the wine jug. He hesitated and then asked, "Would you like me to go with you?"

Demetrios considered the possibility. The slums—home to harlots, brigands, and beggars—consisted of a motley collection of a dozen or more small block houses, all of them in ill repair or tumbling down. Garbage and human waste spilled out into a narrow channel that paralleled the street; the scent of misery hung in the air. It would be safer to visit the slums with a companion, but Demetrios had no desire to reveal his secrets to Rufus. "I'll go alone."

Shappira, the one with the blue-painted eyelids, watched him as he entered the settlement. She leaned against her doorframe, her long hair trailing over her bare shoulders, the top of one breast exposed. "See something you like, ugly thing? You don't have enough money." Her jeering laughter followed him down the street. Heads poked out of doorways, and several people clustered around him, begging for coins. When Demetrios shook his staff at them, they scattered.

According to Rufus, the boy lived in the last hovel closest

to the water. He stopped in front of the tiny shelter, picked up a small stone, and tapped on the outside wall.

A hand with fingers curled like a claw drew back the tarp covering the entrance. A small figure stepped out into the sunshine.

The creature's physical appearance left Demetrios speechless. He couldn't bear to look too closely at its face. The boy had normal features from the forehead to his eyes, but something monstrous had happened to the lower half. Below the eyes, his nose was flattened and squashed as though someone had stepped on it. He had no discernible nostrils. Just two tiny holes crusted with phlegm. His upper lip had been split in two, curling up on both sides, exposing dark-pink, toothless gums. His tongue, a useless flap of flesh, wobbled at the back of his throat.

This poor thing couldn't help Demetrios. He couldn't even talk. The boy's hand touched his arm.

Demetrios shook his head, pulled away from the boy's grip. With a face like that, he was surely stupid. Demetrios sighed. "My servant, Rufus, told me to talk to you." He was surprised when the boy nodded. "Do you understand me?"

The boy nodded again.

Demetrios focused his gaze above the boy's nose. He enunciated each word carefully. "I am looking for—"

The boy stopped him, grabbing his wrist and pulling him forward. Releasing Demetrios, he sculpted the shape of a female form in the air.

They were engaged in a strange, childish game, but he found himself struggling to communicate. "Yes, a woman. She's called—"

The boy stopped him, garbling. Each time he made a sound, a thin stream of saliva trailed down the chapped red chin. Yes. No words. Just an affirmative movement. The boy pretended to stare into the distance. He tapped his forehead and nodded again. In

151

his excitement, he gurgled; spittle bubbled out of the hole in his face. He rubbed it away.

Demetrios thought he understood. "You know her. You know where to find her?"

The boy nodded vigorously, gesturing toward the hills to the west. Then he held out his hand and tapped his palm.

"How much?"

Using his big toe, the boy traced two stripes in the sand.

Demetrios counted out two denarii. "Take me to her. Take me to the Sorceress of Galilee." Demetrios looked the boy full in the face and spoke the name Shappira and others were afraid to say. "Endorah."

They walked beneath an endless, bleached sky. Ribbons of light danced on the horizon, teasing Demetrios with the promise of water. The price of so many sleepless nights exacted its toll, and he drifted into a semisomnolent state, stumbling over rocks that leaped out to trip him. When he turned, the roots of old trees snared his feet. He shook his head, struggling to stay awake.

The boy continued to lead him on a circuitous route that criss-crossed the original path, twisting among dead-brown hills and dry washes. Demetrios felt the firmament, a weight as heavy as one of Herod's Temple stones, pressing down upon him, challenging, *Seek the Sorceress of Galilee at your peril. Secrets cannot be told if Jesus cannot speak.* Demetrios glanced at the boy again and again, wondering what had happened to this deformed creature, wondering if he gazed at his own future.

When they crossed the same riverbed a third time, Demetrios grabbed the boy's arm, bringing them both to a stop. "We've been wandering for hours. How much farther?"

The boy unfurled two scrawny fingers.

"Two hours? Two miles?" Did he want two more denarii? The boy didn't answer. They continued on.

They followed a bend in the wash to a natural spring bubbling up from the earth. A strange odor permeated the air. Rotten, like the smell of eggs left too long in the heat. Seafoam bubbles surged from the pool's dark-green depths, clustering around the white stones that bounded the rim. Demetrios coughed. The boy pointed to the pool, then to his mouth. He shook his head.

"I know you can't drink a hot spring. We must be—" He stopped abruptly. "We've turned back toward Tiberias. We're near the outskirts of town, aren't we?"

The boy's eyes glazed with fear. His babbling intensified as he pulled Demetrios around the perimeter of the basin deep into the cliff's shadows behind them. The gloom swallowed them both. Demetrios shivered. Releasing Demetrios, the boy raised his hand, waving farewell. He took one step back and . . . disappeared into the darkness.

Demetrios muttered a curse. A steady thumping, soft and muted, rumbled from inside the cliff wall. Demetrios struck his staff against the rock. "Where are you?" Again, the tapping resounded. "Keep pounding. I'm coming." Moving toward the sound, he cried out when his feet dropped from beneath him, his hips bouncing off a steep incline as he fell into a hole. Demetrios reached desperately for a handhold, but the walls were slick, smooth, his fingers scratching helplessly at the rock. His weak leg collapsed as he fought to gain his balance, and he hit the bottom of the chasm with a hard thump. Demetrios lay there for a moment, fighting to catch his breath. Then he pushed to his feet; sharp pains shot down his back and legs, but he ignored them.

Where was he?

Sheer rock formations towered around him, enclosing him in a chasm just wide enough to stand. He reached above his head, searching for the ceiling of the cave or a means of escape. A sliver of sky, no wider than a fingertip, pierced the blackness. The rough stone closest to his face was striated with irregular grooves shaped like the exterior curves of the oyster shells he had seen traded in the marketplace. The lines flowed in a horizontal pattern, following the path of the chasm.

He had tumbled into a deep wadi canyon, sculpted by wind and water. In the arid months, birds and rodents nested in such hollows; when it rained, flash flood waters drowned everything trapped between the walls. Demetrios kicked up a cloud of dust, grateful for dry ground. "Boy." His shouts evaporated, absorbed by the porous stone. No one could hear him; no one could find him. "Boy!" A sense of panic infused the word.

Fingers closed around his wrist. He yanked his hand away, but the fingers only gripped him more firmly. "Stop! Who are you?" Demetrios demanded. Flecks of spittle showered Demetrios's head as his captor tried to speak. *The boy!* Demetrios relaxed—a little. He wondered if the enchantress could assume the form of a defective child.

Still spitting with excitement, the boy placed Demetrios's hand on his own hip, patting it twice, indicating that Demetrios should keep it there. Then he pushed deeper into the canyon, Demetrios lurching behind.

Whistling through tiny fissures in the walls, the wind made a mournful cry, like the wail of a dying animal. A spirit trapped by the sorceress? Demetrios never had the chance to ask, for when the boy heard it, he ran, dragging Demetrios behind him. The keening faded as they ascended the trail. They emerged from the passage into a hidden oasis.

Steep hills surrounded the green valley on three sides, the wadi canyon creating a fourth wall. The setting was a fortress. No one could enter without detection. He saw no evidence of a house or building, but someone worked here. A full stream gushed from a split in the rocks above them, spilling down the hillside through a partially covered man-made aqueduct. At each drop of elevation, gates controlled the flow of water into the fields below.

The farmer had cultivated two fields: one of barley and one of grass, separated by a dense hedge of buckthorn. A family of goats grazed on the grass. The nanny kept her two kids close, while the billy moved up the hill. "Is this Endorah's place?"

The boy pointed to the hill closest to the fields. Crude, stone steps had been carved into the rock, but Demetrios saw nothing at the top. No house, no enchantress waiting. A spinning breeze twisted over and up the steps, stirring a dusty goat-hide tarp that rested against a crevice in the hillside. The door flapped a couple of times in the breeze and then dropped shut. He looked at the boy for confirmation. "Up there?"

The boy nodded.

"Take me to her," Demetrios said.

He shook his head.

Demetrios headed toward the stairs. As he walked past the goats, the kids bleated and butted against their mother, demanding a teat. The nanny nudged her crew toward Demetrios and nuzzled close. They were fat, sassy animals, well cared for. The kids, beyond the age of weaning, shared similar markings: solid black bodies with white forelegs, white patches on the forehead, and a white tail. No, not similar, but identical. Exactly the same age, exactly the same in appearance. Twins. Most people considered twins to be good luck, but Demetrios had never liked twins. His father's lies about Demetrios being a surviving twin had caused

155

Demetrios great suffering. To Demetrios, twins were an ill omen. He paused on the steps. "Boy, are you coming?"

His back to Demetrios, the boy remained sitting on the ground, picking at his rags. Demetrios glanced at the goats, shrugged. The gods demanded their answers. He continued up the stairs. At the top of the stairs, he studied the hide door for a prolonged moment, then drew the tarp aside and entered Endorah's lair.

A small fire smoldered in a depression in the cave's floor, sending up lazy curls of fragrant smoke that transformed from gray to blue as they reached the domed ceiling. Fascinated, Demetrios twined his fingers through the hazy plumes. He sneezed. The fire sparked, and he jumped back, grazing an oil lamp suspended from a chain in the ceiling. The lamp flared and burned out. "Endorah? Anyone?"

Demetrios listened for an answer. He heard nothing but the sound of the goats outside and the fire's intermittent sputter. Taking a lamp from one of the chains, he touched the wick to a coal, bringing more light into the room.

Endorah had furnished the cave like a comfortable home with cushions, tables, and blankets, but there were other items, talismans and charms, that indicated her trade: several sealed jars with mysterious inscriptions, baskets of feathers and fur, and a mounted black carrion bird with a dead mouse hooked in its talons. A net strung across the ceiling harbored dried plants and herbs, a few of which Demetrios recognized—like the mandrake with its long jagged leaves—but others he had never seen before.

The table closest to him displayed neat rows of small bones. He grazed his fingers over the smallest specimens: leg bones from rabbits and birds. On the corner of the table, hidden behind a vessel of colored stones, he discovered a human finger, with the flesh and nail still attached. He picked it up.

156

"Welcome."

Dropping the finger, Demetrios pivoted to face the sorceress.

She was tall. Much taller than he'd expected her, or any woman, to be. She had smooth golden skin and a long, elegant nose that tilted up on the end. Her shapely body, full and inviting under the thin fabric of her tunic, moved with every breath.

Stunned by her overpowering sexuality, Demetrios stepped back.

When she removed her scarf, tangled loops of gray hair fanned out over her shoulders. She parted her fleshy lips into a smile, exposing dark-brown teeth.

Demetrios shivered.

She motioned for him to come closer. "What is your desire?"

CHAPTER
SIXTEEN

Demetrios fumbled for an answer. "Are you—?"

She cut him off with a hoarse laugh, breaking into a hacking cough. "Endorah." She cleared her throat. "The one you seek." Pulling a small table up close to the fire, she knelt behind it. "Sit. Place the lamp near your face. Endorah prefers to see her visitors in the light."

Holding the lamp close, he remained standing.

Endorah leaned toward him, peering with narrowed eyes. "You work with donkeys and camels."

Demetrios nodded. "I drive a caravan."

"From a city south of here. You are the caravan driver from Tiberias."

He jerked back, the lamp in his hand spilling drops of hot oil. "How do you—?"

"The boy told me."

"But the boy never . . ." He turned toward the tarp door. The boy hadn't entered the cave.

"The boy talks to me." Her tone left no room for argument.

She fixed her unblinking gaze upon him.

Demetrios wanted to leave, but he needed his answer. He thought of the fate of the farmer's doves the morning he met Judas, how they were crushed under the rush of the crowd, nothing left but bits of feather and bone. In this cave, alone with Endorah, he felt as trapped as those doves. Holding the lamp steady, he backed away.

Turning her attention from Demetrios, the sorceress rummaged through a pile of blankets on the floor. "Here." She tossed him a rolled reed mat. "Sit down. I won't ask you again."

Demetrios caught the mat by the corner. Perfumed dust rained over his hands; the lamp's flame flared and died. If she could control light from afar, she had powers he hadn't even imagined. He sat.

"Much better." She spread a cloth over the table. "You've come to me for help. I can do that, but you must heed my words closely." She took the lamp from his unsure hand and expertly trimmed the wick with her teeth. Mumbling a strange chant, Endorah searched the jars stored under a table behind her. She turned over a jug, set it upright. "I have some more oil here."

Demetrios leaned forward to see her more clearly. Her lithe body and unlined face suggested she had seen fewer than twenty summers, but the gray hair and decaying teeth confused him. Had she cast a spell to make her elderly body seem young? When she tossed her head, the ropes of her matted gray hair slithered across her shoulders like serpents sliding through the grass.

"Your lamp is ready." She smiled briefly, then smacked her lips. The lustful hunger in her eyes made him squirm.

"I want—"

Endorah stopped him with the halting gesture of her hand. "Endorah knows what you want, but that's not what you need. You have a shadow over you, a darkness not easily revealed." She paused. "You need me to read a liver."

"A liver! I can't afford that." He shook his head. She was a haruspex, one who divined the future from animal entrails. It was said that Caesar himself consulted a haruspex before he entered battle. The organs revealed the enemy's weaknesses. The sorceress had already guessed Demetrios was a caravan driver. What knowledge would she divine from a liver? He pushed back from the table.

"Endorah knows what—"

A commotion outside the cave stopped her.

The boy, who must have been standing near the entrance, screamed. First one goat, then a chorus, bleated in terror. The boy screamed again.

Demetrios froze.

"Your goats!" Demetrios raised his voice to be heard over the uproar outside.

"I could give you a fine liver reading." Although she shouted, her calm expression never wavered. She knelt by the fire, stirring the coals. "I'm the best you will find outside of Rome."

The distressed cries of the goats intensified, as did the boy's screaming. Demetrios turned to Endorah. "The boy and your goats. They're in trouble." He clambered to his feet.

"Sit down."

A single, ear-splitting shriek ended the discussion. Then . . . silence. A heartbeat later, one goat bleated plaintively, like a sobbing child.

"It's done." Endorah motioned to the table. "We must begin."

Demetrios stepped back as the tarp parted and the boy entered, bearing a large basin filled with a bloody mass.

"Our liver." She smiled broadly. "Put it on the table here in front of me, close to the fire where we can keep it warm. The blood needs to flow freely for as long as possible."

Streaks of blood smeared the boy's cheeks; the rags on his body dripped with gore. He waggled his useless stump of a tongue at Demetrios. A trickle of pink-stained spit dribbled down his chin.

Demetrios turned to look at the basin on the table. The liver breathed a light steam. Demetrios had seen animals slaughtered for sacrifice, but this butchery made his stomach churn. Wiping the beads of sweat from his brow, he sank to the reed mat.

Endorah leaned over the bowl, examining the contents. "Excellent." Looking at Demetrios, she touched a bloody finger to her lips and grinned. "You won't be disappointed."

She turned back to the liver. "You've done well, Boy. Indeed." Her fingers flowed over the organ's surface. "Splendid lines. Good form and shape. This liver will tell me much."

Rising, she clapped her hands. "Now, Boy, bring me water so that I may wash properly."

After the boy had departed, she took a stick and drew a line in the dirt as she walked slowly around Demetrios. "I adjure you by him who divided the staff in the sea, bring down the veil between good and evil. Separate and consecrate this sacred place and protect it from the eye of the cataract, the eye of the evil spell, the eye of venomous speech, the eye of the dark house, and the eye of open space." Her words were a mix of Aramaic and Greek, as though a single language could not contain the power of her magic.

She paused in front of Demetrios and tossed a fine powder into the glowing coals. Bright-colored flames shot to the ceiling of the cave; Demetrios shielded his face while the sorceress cupped her palms toward the fire. She muttered an incantation in Aramaic. "Adjured are you, spirit. Honor our claim."

The boy returned with the jug of water and a handful of fresh mint leaves. Taking the mint, she placed it in the bottom of an earthenware bowl. She turned to the boy. "Pour in the water." When the bowl was full, she lifted the basin with the liver and directed the boy to carry the mint-scented water. "Follow me closely, Boy, and do exactly as I tell you."

Together, the two of them walked single file in the circle around Demetrios, the fire, and the table. As she passed by the simple altar she had created on the table, Endorah hefted her basin high. "Seal and protect this space from evil tormentors, from evil eye, from demons and spirits and all shadow-spirits, whether they be male or female. Consecrate this place."

Behind her, the boy lifted his bowl, gurgling an unintelligible response. His eyes rolling back in their sockets, he sprayed a fine stream of saliva from his unformed lips. Demetrios cringed. The sorceress remained composed, but the boy seemed completely deranged.

They paced the circle two times, each time pausing for Endorah to stand at the altar, raise her basin, and repeat her incantation. "Seal and protect this space from evil tormentors, from evil eye, from demons and spirits and all shadow-spirits, whether they be male or female. Consecrate this place."

She then made a third pass where she stopped behind Demetrios. Taking a piece of broken pottery, she spit on it and pressed it against Demetrios's scalp. Her lanky hair fell around his shoulders as she leaned forward; her breath burned his neck. "With this good and tested amulet," she whispered, "protect this man against spirits and shadow-spirits." His lungs filled with her scent of decay and mold, the odor of places secretive, dark, and foreign. She was a creature born from a deep chamber in the earth.

For the final pass around the circle, she reversed direction and repeated her spell backward. "Female or male be they whether, spirits-shadow all and spirits and demons from, eye evil from, tormentors evil from space this protect and seal. Consecrate this place." As she concluded her prayer, she stopped at the table and set the basin down. The boy did the same with his bowl. "It is finished." She dipped her hands into the mint water and flicked them dry. "Heed the purification of the gods."

Demetrios blinked as drops fell upon his face. Mint, the herb of healing and comfort.

Endorah closed her eyes and lowered her head then, silent. Demetrios glanced at the boy, who had also bowed his head. Demetrios wondered if he should close his eyes as well. He waited but no instruction came forth. Lowering his chin, he studied the mat under his feet. The reeds were tightly woven by a hand that had done such work often. The sorceress panted, as if she had been running.

She jerked her head up, gazing at something Demetrios couldn't see, and raised her arms high. "I adjure you, good spirit." Then she dropped to her knees and plunged her hands into the liver. Smiling, she faced Demetrios.

"We'll begin in the eastern zone. The region of those who care about us, the friendly portion." Her long, strong fingers worked around the edges of the pulpy mass, kneading and massaging. A thin film of coagulated blood had formed over the organ, but as the enchantress squeezed the liver, fresh red ichor surged out, oozing over her hands. "Oh, this is bad. Very bad."

"What? What do you see?" Despite his distaste, he watched with a sickening fascination as Endorah's fingers manipulated the slippery flesh.

She didn't answer. She moved her hands rapidly over the surface of the liver, then paused, her brow furrowed. "I thought the boy had chosen a liver with a fine form, but I fear I was mistaken." She lowered her voice to a whisper. "Do you see this growth? This monstrosity?"

Demetrios looked. That lump on the liver's edge? A natural variation or a true deformity? He pointed to the place her finger marked. "You think that's an ill omen?"

Endorah nodded. She pressed her lips into a thin, grim line, as if reluctant to bear bad news. She coughed and said, "Despite my efforts, I fear a shadow-spirit pursues you. A darkness with evil desires." She rubbed her thumb slowly around the liver's perimeter, touching the lower left side. "This section is the hostile lobe, the home of the most fearful regions, the place where those reside who wish you the most harm." She waved her hand to the left. "Note how this growth in the hostile lobe invades the friendly regions."

To his horror, Demetrios realized the bump extended to both sides of the liver. "But what does it mean?"

"Someone close to you will die."

His head snapped back. "Die? Is it Elazar?" He hesitated, thinking about the potential loss of his friend, but was Elazar still his friend? "I cannot forgive him. Not for what he's done."

"Have you committed no wrongs? Take care your anger does not bring more evil down upon your head." Endorah tapped the deformity on the liver, then looked up at him, her gaze curious. "Who's Elazar?"

Demetrios didn't answer. Who was destined to die? Elazar? Rufus? Caleb? What about the dreams? Perhaps the sorceress had made a mistake. Perhaps he was the one chosen to die. "Tell me the name. Who is it?"

Endorah shook her head. "The liver doesn't offer names. Only portents." She dipped her fingers briefly into the water and wiped the dried blood from the interior portion of the liver. "Do you see this discoloration?" Her long nails traced the tangle of blood vessels in the graying flesh.

Demetrios didn't see anything significant. It all seemed the same to him. Afraid to contradict her, he gave her the answer she expected. "Yes."

She pointed to a tiny indentation. "There are vipers in your house."

"What? What do you mean?"

"Betrayal. If you have not been betrayed, you will be." She sat back, watching him.

Betrayed? Yes. Elazar. She knew. Or had Jesus already gone to the authorities? He pushed back the fear. "No one lives with me but my servant. He's loyal. He'd never turn against me."

Endorah pursed her lips, thinking. "Your house extends beyond the walls of your courtyard," she said.

Demetrios nodded. "There is someone. A Jewish man. Some claim he's a magician. Jesus—"

"Do not say his name here!" Her hand shook as she stabbed her dirty finger in Demetrios's face. "That hypocrite, that fraud. He speaks against evil spirits, but he knows nothing of my world. I commune with powers he cannot understand. He even frightened away Shappira's customers. In their weakness, they listen to him." She pushed away from the table, started to rise, then settled again on her knees. Her face had turned dark purple, as though she couldn't breathe. Endorah's expression transformed into a mask, her blank eyes looking inward.

Demetrios waited. He wondered if the session was over, if he should leave.

Endorah blinked and looked at Demetrios. When she spoke, Demetrios felt a chill fill the chamber. "The traders have a saying. Do you know it?" Before Demetrios could answer, she said, "When a viper enters your tent, you cut off the head, not the tail." She grasped Demetrios's hand, turning it palm up. Her ragged fingernails traced the lines in Demetrios's skin. "Those who are innocent have nothing to fear. Your hand shows me—"

Demetrios strained to pull loose from her grip, but she refused to release him.

Endorah leaned close, her sour breath warming his face. "Do you see? It must be done quickly, quietly."

"What do you want me to do?"

She smiled. "You have the tool you need, don't you?"

"What tool?"

"You know what you must do. Kill him. Kill Jesus of Nazareth."

Demetrios freed his hand from hers this time. Avoiding her gaze, he swallowed. The Roman Marcus had deserved his fate, but Jesus? Could he murder another man? He glanced at Endorah. She knew about the dagger. What else did she know? "The gods—"

"The gods have selected you. Do not deny them." She paused, watching him closely. "Your journey will give you the answers."

"I should go to Jericho?"

"You choose what you choose, but choose wisely or you will have regrets." She shrugged. "It's not for Endorah to decide." Turning back to the liver, she palpated the organ a final time. It had taken on a dried, shriveled appearance, the edges curling up like the tail of a scorpion. Endorah examined the liver once more and flipped it over. She draped her hands above the altar, her wrists arced. "The spirits are gone from this place."

The boy, who had exited the cave earlier, entered, pushing aside the goatskin door. He stood by her side. As the tarp flapped behind him, bright sunlight flashed into the dim recesses of the cavern. Reminded of the world outside and the troubles that awaited him, Demetrios turned away. He could not stop thinking about Endorah's proclamation. Was she more powerful than Jesus?

What if Demetrios failed the gods? What would happen to him then?

The sorceress handed the boy the basin with the liver. "Dispose of this properly. I'll call for you when I need you."

After the boy had gone, she cleared the cloth from the altar. Demetrios moved to stand, but Endorah indicated he should remain seated. Stepping in front of him, she snatched up the hem of her tunic and began drying her face and hands.

His gaze traveled upward, over her skinny ankles, past her bony knees, beyond her strong, muscled thighs. She wore nothing underneath, not even a simple scrap of fabric for a loincloth.

"Do you see something you like?"

Demetrios shook his head. His tongue felt stuck to the roof of his mouth. "No."

"Are you certain? You won't regret it."

"No." This time he was more forceful with his answer.

Endorah dropped her tunic. "A pity. We could've had fun." She grinned her brown, broken-tooth smile. "Who do you think taught Shappira her skills?" She shrugged when he didn't reply. "No matter. Endorah knows you've come to see her for other needs."

Demetrios sighed. "Yes, I cannot sleep."

"Close your eyes."

He hesitated, but when she repeated the order, he reluctantly closed his eyes. Demetrios heard her walking, her footsteps coming close. She sat down in front of him and placed her hands on his shoulders. Her fingers dug deep into the flesh between his bones. "Your dreams are troubled."

He tensed at her touch and remained rigid. He knew he shouldn't trust her, but she kept murmuring her magic words. Demetrios was determined not to listen.

Endorah stroked his cheek, her touch as gentle as a mother's caress. Her lips brushed his ear, whispering, "Tell me about your dreams. The liver speaks of the future. Your dreams speak of your past. Tell me. What is chasing you?"

He struggled to rise, but she pushed him down. "I must leave," he said. She knew what he and Elazar had done.

"I see . . ." she began and stopped.

He wanted to tell her what he saw. "I can't."

Releasing him, she took a breath. "Endorah can help you." She slapped his cheek lightly, startling him to open his eyes. Then she stuck her open palm in his face. "But first, payment."

The abrupt shift startled him. He stared at her. "How much?" He kept his hands at his sides. He wouldn't reach for his purse until he felt he had agreed to a fair price.

"For my excellent divination of the liver and the potion I will give you? Three silver shekels will do."

Horrified at the expense, he clenched his fists. It was all that was in his purse. "That's too much. I don't have it."

She tossed her head, her hair flying around her face. Her voice elevated to a shriek. "You lie! You lie to Endorah! Three shekels. It's hidden in that secret pouch in your purse." Her fingers shaking with her fury, she held out her hand. "Give them to me."

How did she know? Had she fondled his purse when he wasn't aware? Still, it seemed too much for a liver reading he'd never requested. Terrified of what her wrath would bring down upon him, Demetrios offered a compromise. "Will you accept two?"

She stared at him for a moment, unblinking. He squirmed under the force of her gaze, wondering what disasters she could bring down upon him. Then the sorceress pinched her mouth into an angry grimace and nodded.

Turning his back to her, Demetrios reached deep into his

purse and brought out the two coins. Endorah scooped up the money, tucking it into the folds of her tunic. Once she had been paid, the tension between them eased. She smiled. "Now Endorah will help you."

She took a lamp down from one of the hooks in the ceiling and perused the shelves of clay jars, all lined up in neat rows, like soldiers preparing to march. The wavering lamplight flowed over the artifacts, the pieces of bone, the mysterious secrets of her trade. "We'll begin with this." After hooking the lamp into its chain, she turned and set a small clay pot on the table. "Now I need my grinding stone."

Endorah measured out a handful of tiny, black seeds into the hollow of her stone, crushing them until they produced a clear oil. She took down two plants from her collection in the net on the ceiling. The first plant had a thick stem with fat, green seedpods attached. Breaking off the seedpods, she tossed the stem aside and cut the pods into equal pieces. A white juice seeped from the pods as she ground them with the oil in her stone. When the liquid was fully blended, she poured it onto a leather square and held it over the fire. As the mixture warmed, it dried to a fine, brown powder.

Demetrios fanned his face. "That smells."

Endorah looked up from her work. "Shh." She reached for the second plant, still fresh with supple green leaves and pink flowers. She shredded the leaves and flowers into a separate bowl, stirring them with the brown powder until they were completely coated. Then she scraped the entire contents onto a scrap of goatskin hide where she folded it up into a pouch that she tied with a red cord. She handed it to Demetrios. "Your potion."

"I didn't—"

She waved him off. "We're not finished." Reaching under the table, she produced a small earthenware cup. "You'll need this."

She tapped the rim with a blackened fingernail. "See the line I've marked near the top? Put all of the powder in the bottom of the cup. Then fill it with boiling water up to the mark." She paused. "Now listen carefully. The potion must steep until the water turns the green of first figs. This is very important."

"What about my dreams?" He wanted his dreams to end; he had already made his bargain for justice.

"Your dreams are not to be denied. They hold a truth you cannot see in your waking hours. There is more for you to know." Before he could protest, she held up her hand. "You will sleep, and you will dream, but you'll sleep through your dreams." She cocked her head and gazed at him for a long moment with a calculating eye. "Perhaps the sleep will give you the strength to do what the gods ask."

"And what if I can't do what they ask?" Wishing then he had said nothing, Demetrios refused to look at her.

Endorah ignored him. "The potion is too strong to be drunk like water. It must be measured out in drops. For that, I think you'll need a feather." She rose. "Wait here."

She strode toward the entrance of the cave. When she returned, she carried a basket of feathers. As she picked through them, she mumbled under her breath. "Broken, dirty, too small. I need something that will . . ." She dumped the basket's contents onto the table. "Yes! A stork feather." Endorah held it up for Demetrios to admire: a long, clean wing feather, black and white, with an intact shaft.

Kneeling at the table again, she showed him what to do. "Use this to measure. Immerse the shaft in the potion." She mimed dipping the quill into the cup. "When it fills, seal it." She covered the tip with her finger. "Like this." Setting the feather aside, Endorah leaned close to him and grasped his arm. "Now heed what I tell you." Her voice dropped to a whisper. "When you take your cup of wine tonight at bedtime, spill two drops of this potion into the wine. Not one drop, not three drops. One drop will cause you to have waking dreams that will send you into madness. Three drops will put you into sleep that resembles death but is not death. Two drops. Do you understand?"

Demetrios swallowed and cleared his throat. "What happens if I use four drops?"

Endorah laughed so hard her breath came in short gasps. Tears spurted from her eyes. "Then they'll be placing Charon's obol in your mouth, the payment for your passage into the world of the dead." She stood. "The boy will take you back to Tiberias now."

Demetrios turned to see the boy waiting behind him. Intent on listening to the sorceress's instructions, he hadn't noticed the tarp swing open.

She nodded to the boy. "Use the direct route."

Endorah turned to Demetrios. "The boy will have you at the gate of your courtyard before nightfall." Grinning at him, she winked. "We're much closer to Tiberias than you might think."

As they pushed open the door, she called out to him. "After you use the potion, the plants may talk to you. Be sure to listen."

"The plants?" He had a horrible fleeting image of Tertius's grapevines curling around his neck. "Why?"

"They might have something important to say." With that, she turned and disappeared into the darkness beyond the lamps.

The tantalizing odor of roasting meat greeted him when he stepped outside. Animal organs, speared on a crooked stick, cooked over an open fire. Demetrios's stomach rumbled.

The boy preceded him down the rough-hewn steps. As they reached the fields, Demetrios glanced at the goats. The nanny grazed quietly on the grass with one of her kids close by. The other kid, the twin, lay stretched out in the grass. Flies buzzed over its open mouth, the ground bloody beneath the slit in its neatly eviscerated belly. The little goat rested in quiet repose, its sightless eyes staring at the empty promise of a slowly setting sun.

CHAPTER
SEVENTEEN

Rufus was waiting by the gate when Demetrios arrived home. The lamps had already been lit, and torches rimmed the courtyard. "Oh, Master, you're back!" Rufus rushed forward to pull Demetrios inside the walls. "You shouldn't be on those roads after dark. It's too dangerous."

Slaves were supposed to fuss over their owners, but Rufus's manner made Demetrios squirm. Demetrios had never been so subservient to Marcus. "You worry too much, Rufus," Demetrios said, "I'm fine."

As Rufus hurried to prop some cushions behind his back, Demetrios collapsed onto a wooden bench and stretched out his legs. He massaged the cramping muscles in his thigh. A chalky grime coated his feet and ankles; somewhere during the course of his journey he had also broken the lace on his right sandal.

"Your bath is ready for you, Master. I kept the water hot."

Demetrios didn't answer. He pulled out the goatskin packet and the cup. He set the packet down but cradled the cup in his hands, turning it over to examine it more closely. Ancient words, faint and illegible, scrolled around its base. Was it a spell of some sort? Had Endorah tricked him? Perhaps he should find another cup, one of his own.

"Did the sorceress give that to you? What is she like?"

The sound of his servant's voice so close to his ear startled Demetrios. "She's strange. Old but not old." Demetrios was about to say she knew his secrets, but he stopped himself. He had told his servant enough. He set the vessel down and faced Rufus. "My bath is ready? Then let us begin." Rising from the bench, he reached for the clasp at his shoulder. "Take my cloak, please."

Rufus moved quickly to catch the cloak before it hit the ground. "It's so dirty." He shook out the garment, snapping it in the air. A clinking sound came from the floor, and the gold loop earring rolled to the feet of Demetrios. Fine grit filled the air, floating in the light of the lamps. Demetrios bent down, picked up the token of love lost, and handed it to Rufus.

"Attached this to the cloak when you have finished cleaning it."

"Yes, Master."

Demetrios's cloak had been spattered with rust-colored matter, creating a pattern that curled down one side and around the bottom. Was it dung? Blood? Soot? A piece of the goat's liver? His time in the sorceress's cave seemed almost like a dream.

"I'll have to beat the stains out on the rocks and dry it in the sun."

"Just do your best, Rufus."

Demetrios slipped out of his tunic, letting it drop. Wearing nothing but his loincloth, he walked to the brazier where he warmed his hands for a few moments. "I'm ready now." Turning from the heat of the fire, he stepped onto the smooth stones Rufus had spread upon the ground.

Rufus removed Demetrios's loincloth with a light, deft touch.

His fingers worked at the knots around Demetrios's waist without once touching his skin. "Do you want me to set your purse on the bench?"

Demetrios nodded. The single remaining shekel thumped against his chest as Rufus eased the strap over his head. Fully naked and exposed before his servant, Demetrios cringed at the ugliness of his own body. The soft glow of the coals accentuated the unnatural shape of his twisted thigh bone. Although he couldn't see them, he could feel the latticework of scars on his back prickling across his skin, reminding him of a pain he thought he had long ago left behind. Those marks had healed over, but the wounds beneath the skin still pained him.

A faint breeze waffled the trees, sending out a flare of sparks from the brazier. Demetrios shivered. The night air had taken on a sudden chill. "The water, Rufus."

His servant reached for the first jug.

The heated water splashed over Demetrios's head and shoulders, draining cleanly down his back into the mat of stones under his feet. Rufus washed his back. Demetrios turned so Rufus could wash the other side. "Again, please."

After the second shower, Rufus mixed a balm of coarse salt, olive oil, and sage, spreading it in a thick layer over a strip of sheepskin. He massaged the mixture into Demetrios's shoulders, working his way down his master's back, careful not to press too deeply into the mottled, damaged flesh. The tangy fragrance of the sage soothed, cleansing Demetrios of the taint of Endorah's cave.

Demetrios closed his eyes, thinking again of the horror of the slaughtered goat, the boy's inhuman shrieks. Did Endorah see more in the liver than she revealed? Endorah said the gods had selected Demetrios to murder Jesus, but could he do it? Killing Marcus was justified; Demetrios had had no choice. What if he failed to murder Jesus? How would the gods punish him?

Rufus tapped Demetrios's shoulder, and Demetrios turned toward him, his gaze questioning. Neither spoke, but Demetrios understood. He raised his arms so Rufus could layer the mixture over Demetrios's elbows and wrists.

Still absorbed in his plans, Demetrios gazed into the night, sighing as Rufus stroked each arm. The deed must be done in Jericho, before Jesus could reach the safety of Jerusalem, where Roman legionaries patrolled the streets during Passover. He could leave the caravan for a short while in Jericho, but how could he get close to Jesus? The Messiah surrounded himself with adoring followers and beggars. Beggars. Demetrios smiled. Jesus had embraced the beggars at the wadi outside Capernaum. Perhaps he would embrace another beggar in Jericho, a beggar named Demetrios who planned to stab a dagger into Jesus's heart.

Rufus began rubbing the concoction over his chest and belly. He paused for a moment. He applied another coating of the salt-oil-sage balm, smoothing it over Demetrios's deformed leg. Demetrios held his breath, waiting for his leg to give way or the first sign of revulsion. It never came. His slave treated the misshapen limb with the same tenderness he gave to the rest of his master's body.

But where to hide the dagger? No one could see it, no one could know about it, even after he murdered Jesus. He could strap it to his arm, perhaps, or around his waist, secure beneath his beggar's rags. Then he would cry out to Jesus as he passed, plead with him for help, and when the Messiah approached . . .

Rufus applied the last of the balm to Demetrios's body and stepped back, clapping the mixture from his hands. Demetrios stood quietly, allowing the salt to dry on his skin. It was time for the next phase. "Bring the cool water, Rufus. I need to rinse." His servant continued his work without saying a word. This, too, was part of their ritual. As long as Demetrios remained vulnerable and naked before his slave, Rufus remained mute, his silence a tacit acknowledgment of their proper roles.

The shock of cold water on his bare skin made Demetrios jump; he moved closer to the fire. After a second cool rinse, Rufus tipped a small vial of oil onto his finger, smearing the drops onto the curved blade of a bone strigil. He slid the instrument over Demetrios's skin with quick, clean strokes, removing the grime and unguent from his master's body. He repeated the process several times, finishing with a final warm rinse. Then, taking a clean cloth, he rubbed Demetrios dry. After he had tied a new loincloth around Demetrios's waist, he handed him a fresh tunic.

Demetrios smoothed out the folds. "You may speak now, Rufus."

Rufus turned from packing his bathing tools. He picked up the small vial of oil. "I have a little left. Would you like me to massage your feet?"

Demetrios shook his head. "No . . ." But then he sat on the bench and stretched out one bare foot, and flexed his toes. "Wait . . ." He had stepped on a sharp thorn during his journey to Endorah. "Yes, perhaps. But don't use too much."

"Do you still need help with the Passover caravan, Master?" Rufus's fingers kneaded the oil into the ball of Demetrios's foot.

Demetrios didn't reply. Did he have the assistance he needed? He was supposed to meet Caleb tomorrow at Elazar's house, but after Caleb's nighttime intrusion into his bedchamber, Demetrios doubted he could trust him. Demetrios had no desire to turn Caleb over to the authorities, for he sensed Caleb's thefts were driven by a need greater than pure greed, a hunger for something deeper than wealth. Caleb was good with the animals, and he could manage a recalcitrant donkey but there was still that nagging question: How did Caleb get the key to the storeroom? Demetrios frowned. Did Rufus give it to him? "I'll need your help this time. You'll have to lock up the house and come with me to Jerusalem."

Rufus held the vial in his hand aloft, his face uncertain. "How long does it take to get to Jerusalem, Master?"

Shifting his weight, Demetrios pointed to his feet. "You haven't touched my left foot." The thorn had pierced the heel of his left foot, and it still ached. "The journey to Jerusalem lasts about four days, but we'll take at least six. I want to trade in Jericho."

"I'm sorry, Master, but I can't go."

"What? Why?"

In his confusion, Rufus stoppered the vial of oil and stood. "When I first came to Tiberias, Tertius spoke to a soothsayer who told him I can never travel more than a day's journey from the shadow of Tertius's mansion."

"What are you talking about?"

"If I go farther than a day's journey, I'll die. That's what the soothsayer said. Tertius warned me."

"Tertius told you that so you wouldn't run away. How can you believe such nonsense?" He paused, aware of his own hypocrisy. But Endorah was much more powerful than a common fortune-teller in the marketplace. She spoke to the gods. Didn't she? "Tertius uses that story on all of his slaves."

Rufus shook his head. "Not Tertius. The soothsayer said it. I heard it myself." His face brightened. "Besides, Master, I've found someone to help you. A Jewish boy named Isaac." He knelt again and grasped Demetrios's left foot. "Isaac is young but strong enough to drag the boats onto the shore after a night's fishing. He mends the nets for his uncle, but the man has two sons of his own to feed."

"Why does he want to work for me, a Gentile?"

Rufus gazed directly at Demetrios, his expression hopeful. "Most of Isaac's family died last summer of the fever and chills. Only his mother and baby sister remain. They'll all starve if he can't find good work." Taking a clean rag, he rubbed each foot dry of excess oil. "And you're a good person, Master. I know that."

"I see." The burden of his new responsibility weighed down upon Demetrios. "He can speak for me with his fellow Jews." He stood and looked at his feet. "Tell him to meet me at the animal stalls tomorrow. I'll talk to him then." He could test both Isaac and Caleb at the same time.

Rufus could barely contain his own delight. "Did I do well, Master? Are you pleased?" As he gathered up the oil and rags, he added, "So, you see with Isaac to help you with the caravan, there's no need for me to go to Jerusalem."

Demetrios jerked his head up, impressed. Rufus had solved the problem quite cleverly. Demetrios thought again about the sorceress's warning of vipers in his house. Demetrios trusted Rufus, but could he trust anyone else? Caleb, who broke into his storeroom? Elazar, who had already betrayed him once? He picked up Endorah's cup. "Bring me the guest's cup this size and fill it with wine. I need a basin of boiling water for the potion. You can serve me in my bedchamber."

Perhaps he would find the answer in his dreams.

Rufus had gone to bed; the water boiled on the brazier in Demetrios's chamber. The wine had been poured into the guest's cup, the powder deposited into the sorceress's vessel. Demetrios held his hands over the steaming basin, hot droplets condensing on his palms, hesitating. Endorah's magic powder awaited the

179

embrace of the bubbling water.

He looked at the cup with the mysterious powder but didn't pick it up. If he dreamed, would he see the woman from Capernaum again? He didn't want to let her go. Did those crushed flowers and seeds contain magic? Or poison? He lifted the basin of boiling water.

As he poured the scalding stream into the cup, the room filled with a fog of conflicting fragrances. First, a sweetness bloomed in the air, like the scent of honeysuckle that flowered on the hills in early spring. That sweetness faded quickly, overpowered by a more repugnant aroma, strange and dark, recalling secret canyons and caves populated with menace. Demetrios brought the cup close to his mouth.

Burning! How it did burn!

He tipped the drink in his hand, splashing hot drops over his fingers. The flesh on his knuckles tingled; a more fierce pain, however, centered in his throat. His eyes blurred with tears, he coughed, choking. The bite of a hot spice stung the back of his tongue. Finding it difficult to swallow, he studied the potion.

Small fragments of leaf and flower floated on the water's surface, while the water itself remained a dirty yellow. Demetrios swirled the mixture with a stick, watching as the brew transformed from yellow to brown to a dull green that resembled the slime on the marshy waters near the southern tip of the Sea of Galilee. Demetrios stirred the potion again. The color deepened into a lush, dark hue—the verdant tint of early figs. He picked up the feather Endorah had given him, ready to measure the dose.

Her instructions to only use two drops buzzed in his ears. He dipped the feather, fascinated by the flow up the shaft.

When the potion filled the quill to approximately the length of his first knuckle, he tilted the feather slightly and lifted it from the brew. Pressing his finger firmly against the tip of the shaft, he brought it to the wine. Slowly, he rolled his fingertip to one side, releasing a single drop. Cover the shaft and then release once more. Another drop fell into the cup. As he set the feather aside, Demetrios saw a single bead of green moisture clinging to his fingertip. Had his carelessness allowed another drop to fall into the wine?

He glanced at the cup, hoping to see traces of the potion floating on the surface, but Endorah's concoction had dissolved completely. He picked up the drink and sniffed. It smelled simply of wine: dark and sweet. Two drops? Or three? He brought the cup to his lips and drank.

"Boy," Demetrios shouted. "Where are we?"

Demetrios took one step and fell, sliding on his back, clods of earth raining onto his head as he plummeted down a deep well. At the bottom of the cavern, his heart stopped. Then it beat, thumping so slowly he could count each measured pulse. When he breathed, stale air, weighted with decay, assaulted his lungs. A huge black bird descended upon him, picking the flesh from his face. Demetrios raised his arms to ward off the creature, but it kept poking, jabbing. Then Endorah appeared and waved it away, shouting, "Be gone, my slave!" When Demetrios tried to rise, she pushed him back, and his head bounced against a cold stone. Endorah placed two pottery shards over his eyes. Even in the darkness, Demetrios could see the wicked spells scrawled across their surface: words in a language he did not recognize but their very essence exuded evil. "I adjure you, black spirits," Endorah said, and around her, the demons danced, slithering vipers with jagged teeth that snapped at Demetrios's throat. The demons sang, "You were chosen. But Jesus still lives. You must be punished."

Demetrios screamed but no sound came forth. His lips had been split, his tongue clipped to a waggling flap. Stone walls rose up on either side of Demetrios. Mute and helpless, he had been sealed in a tomb. Demetrios's heart pounded like rolling thunder, and he pushed against the rock, chewed at the air, spittle flying from his mouth. He had been transformed into Endorah's Boy.

Demetrios awoke in the night with his blanket in his mouth, the taste of wet wool on his tongue. He pulled the fabric free and rolled toward the cup on the table next to his bed. He was still alive. He had deposited two drops, not three, but the dream was a warning from the gods: He could not fail.

CHAPTER
EIGHTEEN

Demetrios dozed through the rest of the night, fitful and restless, and when he woke again at first light, his head throbbed. His vision was clouded, as though a thin veil covered his eyes. He blinked and picked at the woolen threads still caught between his teeth. Endorah had advised him to listen to his dreams. This dream, the one formed by the spell of the potion, told him the gods were merciless.

Jesus must die.

Stumbling to his feet, Demetrios reached blindly for his staff. "Rufus," he shouted. "Bring me water."

Rufus bustled in with Demetrios's cloak and a basin of clean water. "Did you want to wash, Master?"

"No, I want to drink." Taking the basin from his slave, he raised it to his mouth and guzzled, slurping the water like a thirsty animal. Demetrios drank steadily until he had to take a breath. Gradually, his sight cleared, but the dull headache remained. He lowered his head so Rufus could drape his cloak. "Watch the house," Demetrios said as he fastened the clasp at his shoulder.

"I'm going to Elazar's to meet this Jewish friend of yours. Isaac. Is that his name?"

"Yes, Master." Rufus steadied Demetrios when he tilted off-balance. "Are you sure you're well enough?"

The nagging pain at the back of his skull made Demetrios irritable. "I'm fine. Stop asking me that." Without looking at Rufus, he gripped his staff. "I'll be back soon. If Isaac is not worthy, you should assume you'll be accompanying me to Jerusalem."

Rufus frowned but didn't argue.

The sight of Isaac waiting alone for him outside Elazar's house made Demetrios pause. Elazar should be here, not this stranger. Demetrios's chest hurt; a hole had replaced the space Elazar once occupied. Would he ever see Elazar again? Was it even possible for them to rebuild their friendship? And where was Caleb?

He approached Isaac slowly, taking time to form his impressions before he spoke to him. The young man had the build for a caravan driver with well-developed muscles across his shoulders and back. A square-shaped jaw indicated discretion. He wore his hair long, in wavy ringlets, and the beginnings of a first beard dotted his chin. His wide-set eyes glittered with keen intelligence. He was close to Demetrios's own age. Straightening his shoulders, Demetrios wondered how well Isaac would accept his authority. "You are Isaac?"

"I am." Isaac cleared his throat. "Rufus said I should speak to you. You need a caravan driver?"

Demetrios nodded. "You look strong. What other work have you done?"

"I've helped my uncle repair his fishing nets and sails." He turned out his palms for inspection. They were crisscrossed with healing cuts and old scars. "But I fear the awl and needle are hard taskmasters. I prefer working with animals."

His answer pleased Demetrios, as Demetrios, too, found it easier to understand animals than people. He directed Isaac toward the gate that barred entry to Elazar's courtyard. "Come then, let us see how well you handle a donkey or a camel."

Inside, a large water trough divided the courtyard into two sections. The front was reserved for guests and customers, while their camels were tethered in the rear. A row of stalls, used to house the donkeys, lined the back wall behind the house.

As Demetrios stepped into the courtyard, he was struck by the quiet. Where was Elazar's cousin, Silas? Elazar had hired Silas to watch the animals. Silas should have come forward to greet them, but he was nowhere to be seen. Except for a lone donkey drinking from the limestone trough, the place appeared to be deserted. He paused for a moment, then gestured for Isaac to follow him. "This way." The donkey glanced at them curiously as they walked past.

They found Silas snoozing at the back of the courtyard under the thick branches of a stand of junipers. To shield his eyes from the sun, he had drawn his headdress low over his brow. Sometime during his sleep, the headdress had slipped down over one ear, twisting his hair into wild, curly tufts. He lay on his side, his head resting on his arm, while he snored loudly.

"Wake up, you lazy beggar." Demetrios poked the man once in the ribs with his staff. "We're here to examine our animals."

The caretaker stumbled to his feet.

"Ah, Demetrios," a voice behind them said. "Don't be so cruel. It's hot today."

Demetrios whirled around. "Romulus." With dismay, Demetrios realized he had neglected to close the gate.

185

"It seems we meet often." Romulus grimaced with what passed as a smile, his tongue licking his ugly teeth. As he raked his long, thin fingers through his dirty beard, he studied Demetrios.

"Why are you here?" Demetrios asked.

Romulus scratched his chest, flecking bits of dried food from his cloak. "I have business with Silas. Perhaps the better question is, why are you here, Demetrios? I thought you were no longer interested in caravans."

"This is Elazar's house. Of course I'd be here. And you're mistaken. My caravan is still scheduled to leave for Jerusalem."

"Oh?" He peered around Demetrios as though he expected to see someone standing there. "Has Elazar returned to Tiberias? I heard he was following some miracle-worker around Capernaum."

"Elazar's not important. I'm leading the caravan myself this year. A very large one. And this is Isaac." Demetrios pulled the boy forward. "My new apprentice."

Romulus's rapacious gaze pivoted to Isaac. He laughed. "Pretty small, for such a hard job." He shook his head. "But I'm sure you know best, Demetrios. Indeed, I have a new assistant of my own. I sent him to Caesarea this morning with one of my drivers to pick up some spices. Perhaps you know him. Caleb? He says he used to work with Elazar."

"I know him." Caleb's disloyalty stung. He hoped his feelings didn't show on his face, but he also feared Caleb had made a poor choice. Romulus had a reputation for cruelty, with little tolerance for incompetence, and was quick to punish any infractions. How would Caleb fare under such treatment? "Caleb is a good worker. Honest and loyal. You won't be disappointed."

Romulus was nonplussed. "Is that so?" He nodded thoughtfully. "Well, I'll have to watch him closely. And Silas, perhaps we can speak later." He turned to Isaac and tapped him lightly on the chest. "Such a small one to drive a caravan. Well, then, Demetrios, I guess we'll meet again in Jerusalem. Good luck. You'll need it." Laughing to himself, he strode out the gate to the main road.

Demetrios confronted Silas. "Business? What business do you have with Romulus?"

"Romulus?" The caretaker flushed. He had adjusted his headdress so it no longer drooped over his eyes. "Well, I—It's just that Romulus said you weren't taking a caravan to Jerusalem this year, and with Elazar's departure, you were in need of money. He offered to buy the camels."

"My camels? You agreed to sell the animals that belong to me and Elazar? And what is your reward?"

"Romulus said I should keep a few shekels for my trouble and tell you the rest was the full price." He ducked his head, cringing under Demetrios's glare.

Stunned, Demetrios didn't react immediately. Then he raised his staff, ready to strike the caretaker. "Idiot! I should—"

Isaac grabbed his arm. "Demetrios, if Elazar isn't returning soon, perhaps I should stay here with Silas."

"What?" Demetrios lowered his staff.

"Silas could teach me everything I need to know about the care of the animals. And the work would be finished more quickly if I were here all the time."

"Teach you?" Silas asked.

Demetrios nodded, suddenly understanding Isaac's intentions. Silas could pull no tricks while Isaac watched him. "Yes, that's a splendid idea. Silas, feed and water the donkeys. I want to show Isaac the camels."

They passed the trough and crossed to the back of the courtyard where the animals were kept. The two camels were tethered to each other with a strong rope around their ankles. One

187

could not move without dragging his companion with him. They chewed their cuds quietly, but Demetrios knew that could change in an instant.

Isaac stood back, watching the camels. After a few moments, he said, "They seem docile, but I sense they have a temper."

Pleased Isaac was so observant, Demetrios smiled. "You're right. They do." He grasped the cane stick he and Elazar used to control the beasts. "Let's get to work."

Demetrios showed Isaac how to make the camels kneel, how to mount a balanced load on their backs, and what to do if they fought one another. Then they discussed the journey to Jerusalem and when the pilgrims would arrive. Demetrios found he was impressed with Isaac's quick understanding; Rufus had chosen a good man.

The sun slipped behind the western hills as they finished; black fingers of shadow darkened the grounds. Silas went into the house to prepare the evening meal for himself and Isaac. Outside the courtyard, at the crossroad to town, Demetrios bid Isaac farewell and turned toward his home. Demetrios stopped and called out for Isaac to wait. "I need to pay you." He reached into his purse and dropped two denarii into Isaac's palm. "You worked hard today."

Isaac handed him back one coin. "This is too much."

Demetrios refused to take it. "No." He folded the young man's fingers over both coins. "The first denarius is for you and your family. The second is for your clever thinking. Silas will cause no more trouble as long as you remain here. Be sure to eat well tonight. You'll need your strength in the morning. After dinner, go tell your mother that you are moving into Elazar's house and return right away."

A shy smile of pleasure warmed Isaac's face. "Thank you." He clasped the coins as though he were the richest man alive. "You won't be sorry. I'll be here waiting." Jingling the two denarii in his hand, he trotted into the house for dinner.

On the evening of Demetrios's and Isaac's third day of labor together, Demetrios was surprised to see Caleb pacing the street in front of his gate when he returned home. "I need to speak with you," Caleb called out.

Demetrios was exhausted and hungry; Rufus would have his dinner waiting for him inside. His first inclination was to ignore his visitor. Caleb had broken into his storeroom, begged him for work, and then abandoned him. But the young man's agitated state—he bounced as though he wore a hair shirt studded with thorns—made him reconsider. Something had happened. "I thought you were in Caesarea."

Caleb stilled. "You know about Romulus?" His voice was cautious, uncertain.

"He said he hired you to drive one of his caravans."

"Oh, Demetrios, I'd never do that to you. I could never betray you that way. You're better to me than Romulus could ever be. When he came to me, I told him so. I told him—"

"Enough of your deceptions. What do you want?"

Caleb sagged against the courtyard wall. "I want to come back to work for you."

"Why? You've already agreed to work for Romulus."

"I made a terrible mistake. Terrible." His words sounded fevered; a madness glazed his eyes. He paused. "Are we alone?"

Demetrios sighed with impatience. The aroma of steaming garlic and onions wafted from his house. "My neighbors are eating their dinner. Something I would like to do."

"Romulus is an evil man. It was just a trinket. Not even valuable. I wasn't going to keep it. I was going to put it back. Really. But Romulus, he saw me, and he—Look, Demetrios! Look what he did to me!" He leaned forward, waiting silently for Demetrios to come closer.

An ugly bruise swelled under Caleb's right eye, dried blood crusted around his nostrils, and when he opened his mouth, a hole gaped where a front tooth was missing. Demetrios stepped back. "Romulus did this to you? You must report him to the magistrate."

"Romulus never touched me. He's too clever for that. He sent three of his thugs. They caught me on the road on the way back from Caesarea, and look, look what else they did." Caleb pulled the robe off his shoulders, exposing a row of bruises that flared across his chest and along his ribs. "Afterward, Romulus found me where they had left me to die. He told me I should be grateful he didn't have me arrested." Caleb adjusted his clothes, stood straight. "Please, Demetrios, I want to work for you."

Gently, Demetrios patted Caleb's shoulder. He felt sick, remembering only too clearly the bite of the Roman's whip on his own flesh. "What did you steal, Caleb?"

"I don't steal things." He rubbed his nose and sniffed. "It was a bracelet, made of tinted black glass with a bronze clasp." He looked up at Demetrios, blinking back his misery. "Romulus had six of them. I didn't think he would miss one. I planned to put it back."

"He had you beaten after you returned it?"

"No-o-o . . ." Punctuated by his hesitation, the word trailed off. "There was this family. A father, his two sons, and a daughter. The mother was dead from a wasting disease. Anyway, they came to Romulus asking for passage to the Passover festival. They wanted a donkey for the daughter to ride. But Romulus turned them away.

He said he had no free donkeys to spare for lazy children. When I saw the girl, I knew she could never walk the distance to the Holy City. She said she was of marriageable age, but she was as small as a child. Her skin so pale you could see the sunlight through it." He closed his eyes. "I think she was dying, too."

"What are you talking about?"

"I gave the bracelet to the girl."

"So, Romulus has dismissed you?"

Caleb shook his head. "He told me that I owed him a debt now. I'm to work for him until he agrees it's paid. Will you take me back?"

Demetrios didn't comment. He pitied Caleb, but the young man had created a complicated situation. "Oh, Caleb, how could you be so foolish?" Demetrios sighed. "I can't take you back without paying your debt, and I can't be the one who pays it. Romulus is no friend of mine. If he suspects I'm involved, he'll set the price even higher. You know that. I don't think I can help you." Seeing Caleb's hurt expression, he tried to sound more positive. "Take heart. Romulus has spared you. Clearly, he needs you for his caravans. He won't have you beaten again, unless you give him reason. Work for him until your debt is paid."

"I see." Caleb tucked his hands into the sleeves of his cloak. "Several nights ago, I came to your chamber as a friend to warn you about him. And now, when I ask for your help, you turn me away. So be it. I won't trouble you again." He turned to leave.

Demetrios grasped his arm. "Caleb, wait."

Caleb glared at Demetrios but didn't pull away. "Yes?"

"I can't take you back now, but there's something you can do." He paused, seeking the right words.

"What would you have me do? Suffer another beating?"

Demetrios shook his head. "He won't do that again. Not so

close to Passover. Go with Romulus's caravan to Jerusalem. Become his best driver, one he trusts completely. Once we're all in the Holy City, I'll talk to Romulus, negotiate your freedom. If trade is good, he'll be more receptive to releasing you."

"And if he won't?"

"He will if he makes a good profit at the Passover festival. It will be your job to see that he does."

"It may be too late for me by the time we arrive in Jerusalem."

"No, it won't, Caleb." He reached into his purse and removed his one remaining denarius. "Take this to the marketplace and buy some oil of aloe. It will heal your wounds."

Caleb hesitated, then took the coin. "Good-bye. You were a good friend." As Caleb departed, a blanket of thunderclouds covered the sun, and he vanished into the gloaming light.

Demetrios shivered as if he had just seen a ghost.

CHAPTER
NINETEEN

The time for the caravan's departure was rapidly approaching when Demetrios decided to visit the scribe Yohanan in Tiberias. The task the gods had assigned Demetrios was fraught with danger: he could be caught and executed; he could be attacked by Jesus's followers. He had a responsibility to provide for those he loved if something happened to him. Elazar first; even though Demetrios had doubts about their friendship, he recognized his debt to Elazar. Rufus second, for he had taken good care of Demetrios. As a slave, Rufus was vulnerable with no master. And finally, Isaac, who depended on Demetrios for his livelihood.

When Demetrios entered the scribe's small room situated off an alleyway near the marketplace, Yohanan squinted at him, peering through the gloomy light. Once he recognized Demetrios, he greeted him cordially. "Good morning. I thought you had left already for the Passover festival."

"We're still waiting for the last of the pilgrims to arrive before we go." Demetrios perched on a stool across from Yohanan's table. "I want to draw up a document for my heirs in the event I die suddenly or unexpectedly."

"Indeed." Yohanan showed no surprise at this unusual request, but it was a scribe's role to be discreet.

Demetrios dictated his thoughts slowly while Yohanan scratched out the words onto the scroll. A fly buzzed in the corner, hurling itself against the curtain but unable to find an escape. "I declare Elazar to be my sole heir," Demetrios said. "Upon my death, he shall receive my house, all of my personal belongings, the animals and the merchandise in our caravan."

Yohanan, his head down, continued marking the scroll.

"My slave Rufus shall be freed immediately and given twenty shekels."

Yohanan raised his head. The scratching stopped. "The customary time for emancipation of a slave is seven years. You wish to shorten it?"

"Yes."

"Indeed." Yohonan returned to the scroll. "Please continue."

The noise of the fly annoyed Demetrios. He struggled to organize his thoughts. "My assistant Isaac will receive Elazar's house and two donkeys, so he can start his own caravan business if he so wishes."

The scratching stopped again. Yohanan raised his head, his eyes questioning. "Isaac? The fisherman's nephew? The one who repairs sails and nets? He works for you now? And Elazar's house? Do you have that authority?"

"Elazar is no longer my business partner. He has left Tiberias. He gave his house and his share of the caravan to me. Isaac is the sole supporter of his family. I want him to have this."

"Well . . ."

"I have one more bequest to make." Demetrios hesitated, then said quickly, "I want to leave one hundred denarii to Mercury as my praise and gratitude for his gifts."

This time Yohonan pushed back from the table. "I don't go to pagan temples. And I don't think Elazar or Isaac would, either."

"Rufus can take it to Mercury then," Demetrios snapped.

Yohanan nodded. "Of course. Send a Gentile slave to a Gentile pagan temple."

Demetrios could see Yohanan was not pleased with Demetrios's final gift, but these were Demetrios's decisions, not the scribe's. "That is everything," he said.

Yohanan had resumed writing, his head bowed low over the scroll. "A moment while I finish."

When the document was complete, Yohanan asked Demetrios to make his mark. Demetrios no longer needed Yohanan's assistance, for he remembered how he had written his name when he purchased Rufus. Afterward, the scribe rolled the scroll tight, secured it with a leather cord, and sealed it, indicating Demetrios should impress his ring into the seal. Demetrios handed him the fee and paused. He gave Yohanan a second denarius. "I trust you will tell no one about this."

Yohanan dropped the extra coin into his purse. "A scribe maintains all confidences."

That same evening, Demetrios paced his bedchamber, thinking of the choices he had made that would change his fate. The hour was late, the house cocooned in silence. Demetrios studied the three items he had arranged on the table: the dagger, the scroll of his final wishes, and the last of Endorah's potion. He picked up the dagger first, turning it over fondly in his hand. When he looked into those blue beaded eyes, colder than any stone, he felt the power of the blade transferred to his grip. He slipped the weapon in and out of its sheath, listening to its hiss. *Shh, shh, shh.*

Setting down the dagger, he grasped the scroll. Only two people had the authority to open the document: Demetrios and Elazar. If all went well, the seal would never be broken. Demetrios would burn the scroll when he returned from Jerusalem. If he failed . . . He shook his head. The gods had made their promise and sent their warning. He wouldn't fail.

He placed the scroll next to the dagger, thinking about Isaac. He had promise. The young man could drive his own caravan someday. He possessed the skills as well as the charm to court the pilgrims. Isaac knew how to speak to his fellow Jews, how to make them comfortable. The pilgrims trusted him, and even Silas, properly humbled, followed Isaac's direction. Together, Demetrios, Isaac, and Silas had organized the groups and planned the loads for each camel, each donkey. Demetrios wondered about Caleb and Romulus. Would Caleb follow Demetrios's advice?

Demetrios glanced at the liquid in the cup. No longer the color of early figs, the dregs of the sorceress's potion had steeped into the moldy hue of rotting wood. Did this make it stronger? Demetrios poured himself a cup of wine. Dipping the feather into the potion, he measured it out, counting the drops as they slid off the tip of the shaft: one, two. Demetrios picked up the wine, stirring it with his finger. He didn't drink. Not yet.

Demetrios brought the cup of wine to his mouth. The mixture burned when he inhaled its aroma. Tiny flames licked his throat. He lay back against his couch, listening to the sounds of the night, and closed his eyes.

Footsteps. Someone had entered the room.

The curtain in front of the window swayed. "Rufus, is that you?" His servant would be at the door, not the window. Demetrios reached for the dagger on the table, easing it from the sheath. "Who's there?"

A man stepped away from the window.

The door to Demetrios's bedchamber was closed, the window too small for anyone to enter. He had locked the door to the storeroom himself. "Caleb?" Demetrios rose, hiding the dagger in the folds of his tunic. "Show yourself. Speak."

Jesus turned to face him, his eyes bright in the darkness.

Demetrios stood still. "What do you want?"

Jesus smiled but didn't speak. He remained by the window.

"Say something. Why are you here?" The stone floor chilled Demetrios's bare feet as he tiptoed closer.

Jesus extended his hand in greeting but said nothing.

Demetrios lunged toward him, slashing the knife across Jesus's throat. Jesus's hands flew up to touch his neck. A thin red line seeped through his fingers. He couldn't speak now.

Demetrios thrust the blade into Jesus's torso, watching as a single dot at the point of entry spread across Jesus's robes like a blossoming flower. The man stumbled and tilted forward but did not fall. Still holding fast to the hilt of the dagger, Demetrios flexed his wrist upward and outward in a vicious arc. He pulled the knife out just as Jesus dropped to his knees.

Demetrios stared at the dagger in disbelief. The blade was clean!

Taking a step back, Demetrios staggered. His vision faded; he swept his hand across the blankness in front of his face. Who was this man? A shooting pain swelled from his belly across his chest. He grabbed at the window coverings and collapsed.

Demetrios awoke to the washed gray light of dawn. He pulled himself to his feet, gazing at the window, stunned to discover he had sliced his curtain to shreds. He looked for Jesus. Gone. The dagger lay on the floor where he had dropped it. The cup of doctored wine remained where he had left it, on the table beside his bed, untouched.

CHAPTER
TWENTY

Embarrassed by his behavior during the night, Demetrios hid the ripped window coverings under his reed mattress. When Rufus inquired about the missing curtain in the morning, Demetrios told him, "I prefer to wake by the light of sunrise." Demetrios then poured the dregs of Endorah's potion into the dirt.

Only one day remained to pack before the caravan's departure, but that single day was too long. At Elazar's house, the sun dragged across the sky while Demetrios, Isaac, and Silas worked to load their goods. Then Demetrios returned home to gather his personal belongings.

Demetrios planned to rest, but he paced instead, counting his footsteps from one wall to another, gauging the distance in his mind to Jericho. How many thousand steps would Demetrios need to take before his quest was complete? He would not sleep at all tonight; when the moon reached its full height, he would need to meet the caravan gathering at Elazar's house.

It was still dark when Demetrios called to Rufus to tell him it was time to leave. The two of them locked up the house and walked together to Elazar's house to meet Isaac and Silas. As they approached, plumes of gray smoke twisted into the night sky, creating a faint haze that blotted out the starlight. Beneath the pall that lay suspended in the air like a floating veil, more than a dozen small fires lit the camps of pilgrims gathered for the journey to Jerusalem. They came from villages scattered all around Galilee, from the western settlements of Cana and Rumah, and from the communities along the shores of the Sea of Galilee: Tericheae, Gennesaret, and even a few from Capernaum. Another family from Scythopolis planned to join them as they traveled south from Tiberias. Even without Elazar's assistance, Demetrios had managed to create a grand caravan, a parade of people and beasts that would be the talk of the Passover festival.

Now Demetrios led the way around the campfires stretched out along the roadside. "Raise the torch higher, Rufus." He loved this time before the caravan's departure. These final hours of preparation hummed with restless energy.

He felt the anticipation in the excited conversation of the women and children, in the donkeys' nervous braying. Laughing, joking with one another, the men strode from the camps along the road to the courtyard, loading up the last of their belongings. Isaac barked out orders: "Bring me that rope! Is there room for one more basket?" Even the camels seemed more alert as they knelt on the ground with heads held erect, necks pivoting to watch the activity.

The torchlight that illuminated his path faded away. Demetrios turned to find his servant lagging. "Rufus! Hurry up." Pushing the courtyard gate open to its full width, he tapped his foot while he waited.

Rufus ran to catch up; sparks flew from his torch as he jogged and darted through the crowd. When he reached the gate, he faced

Demetrios. "What if I traveled with the caravan for only the first day? I could help you get everyone on their way and then come back here and take care of the house while you're gone."

"Why would you do that? The house is locked up. Tertius's slaves will keep watch."

"But the soothsayer's warning—"

"The soothsayer. The soothsayer," Demetrios waved away Rufus's worries with his hand. "I've told you a dozen times, that's a story Tertius uses to keep his slaves from running away." He stopped, wondering if Rufus would protest again. They had been arguing about this for days. With such a large caravan to manage, Demetrios had decided he needed Rufus's help on the journey. "The answer is no. You're going with me to Jerusalem."

Rufus's eyes glistened. Were they tears from the smoke or from his disappointment? Demetrios couldn't tell.

Rufus shook his head. "But, Master—"

"Stop that!" a man suddenly shouted from behind them. "This is our place!"

"You gallows-bird!" another man's voice cried. "How dare you dump our things on the ground?"

Demetrios strained to see the source of the argument. Like jackals circling a carcass, the crowd of men and boys drifted toward the commotion inside the courtyard. The mood had shifted quickly from happy to menacing, the threat of violence rising with the smoke.

"Come on, Rufus." Demetrios elbowed through the milling throng, searching among the shadowy shapes for Isaac. Where was his assistant?

"What do you plan to do about it?" the first man asked.

Demetrios pushed around the wall of bodies that had formed. "Let me through." No one seemed to hear him. Several tall boys stepped in front of him and stood still, fascinated by the unfolding altercation. "Move!" Without waiting for the young men to comply, Demetrios shoved them aside.

"Watch your step, Gentile," a man muttered. He started to add something more, but Demetrios silenced him with a glare.

Demetrios raised his voice. "This is my caravan." The Jews on either side closed in, pushing him toward the two arguing men, their dislike of him all but palpable. He swallowed and straightened up to his full height. He had to stop this before he lost control of the caravan, but he couldn't do it alone. Where was Isaac? And what had happened to Rufus?

"You insolent cur!" the second man yelled. "You think you're better than the rest of us, Enoch? Why should your daughter ride when we have to walk? I paid for a donkey to carry my belongings. Now you say there's no room?"

Enoch spat onto the ground. "You can carry your own trash, Daniel."

Rufus appeared at Demetrios's side. "I found Isaac," he said, pulling the young man forward.

Isaac rushed to separate the two men. "No fighting here." He inserted himself between them. "No need for this. We've plenty of space for everyone." He knelt to pick up Daniel's pack. "Come. I'll find you a place elsewhere."

But Enoch stepped on Daniel's bag. "This is a matter for men, not boys." He elbowed Isaac out of his way. "My daughter rides." Defiant, he raised his fists, glaring at Daniel. "You want this donkey? Take it from me."

A girl's voice broke the tension. "Father—"

Enoch dropped all bravado to fuss over his daughter. He hurried to the donkey where she sat. "Do you feel ill, my Rebecca? Rest your head on Abba's shoulder." Stroking her face while she leaned against him, he shouted out to the men in the crowd, "Bring water. My daughter is thirsty."

Her shoulders and back rigid with the effort, Rebecca sat upright. She smiled, a vain attempt to dismiss his concern. "I'm fine. If the caravan needs this donkey, then I'll walk." Balancing carefully, she reached up to adjust the scarf on her hair as she prepared to slide off the donkey.

The flame on Rufus's torch flared; in that moment, Demetrios caught the flash of something metallic on the girl's arm. He grasped her wrist and slid back her sleeve, forcing her to sit. He could feel every tiny bone beneath her skin. "Where did you get this?" His right hand gripped her arm, while his left fingered the bracelet of tinted black glass and bronze that circled her wrist.

"Don't touch my daughter, you pagan!" Enoch yelled.

The girl stared at him. She didn't speak.

Enoch shook his head. "We didn't steal it."

"I know that." When Demetrios realized she was trembling, he released her, but he kept his eyes focused on her face. "Where did you get the bracelet?"

"A man gave it to me."

"What was the man's name? Do you remember?"

She tilted her head, a wisp of a smile lighting her features. "Caleb. He was very kind."

Demetrios addressed the crowd. "The girl rides." He turned to Rebecca. "Let me see your arm again."

Grasping her sleeve, she extended her hand. Demetrios examined the bracelet, judging its quality under the torchlight. He couldn't see the details but he recognized fine workmanship. He traced over the delicate etching on the bronze clasp, stroked the smooth polish of the glass beads. Caleb had taken a great risk to give this to the girl. An expensive treasure for Romulus to lose. "Your friend Caleb must be very kind to give you this." He smoothed the cloth over her wrist, hiding the bracelet in the folds. "Guard it carefully."

Daniel had retreated from the argument, but Demetrios could tell he still seethed. He pointed to Daniel's spilled bag. "Gather your things. My assistant will find you another animal."

Rufus touched his arm. "This man wishes to speak with you, Master." He indicated a tall Jew standing next to him.

Demetrios had noticed him earlier. The man stayed apart from the rest of the pilgrims, watching over them with a protective eye. Their unofficial leader? Demetrios grimaced. He didn't need someone else who wanted to control the caravan. "Yes? What do you want?"

The stranger stepped forward; the others cleared a path for him to pass. "I'm Menachem of Cana." He waved an arm, taking in the two men who stood near the donkey in question. "Enoch and Daniel are my people, from the same village. Perhaps I can be of assistance?"

Demetrios wanted to ask Menachem why he hadn't offered to help sooner, but he kept his thoughts to himself. "We have a long journey ahead. Inform your people I won't tolerate any fighting."

"I see. And you are?"

"Demetrios of Tiberias. This is my caravan." The second time he had been forced to say that tonight.

"A Gentile leads us to the Passover festival?" He shook his head. "I wasn't aware." He pointed to Isaac. "I gave my money to him." Without waiting for Demetrios to reply, he walked over to the two men. "Daniel," he said as he placed a hand on the man's shoulder, "you know that Enoch's daughter has not been well. If he's paid for her to ride a donkey, then she will ride. Pick up your bags. You can share space with me."

Enoch lowered his eyes. "Thank you."

Daniel hesitated for only a moment. Then, muttering under his breath, he scooped up his scattered belongings and began to stuff them back into his pack.

Menachem snapped his fingers. "Enough complaining, Daniel. It's a fair decision." He turned to Demetrios. "I'll take care of any problems with my people in the future."

Demetrios frowned. The man's arrogance grated. "Get them moving, then. We need to be ready to depart before daybreak."

Nodding, Menachem led his companion back to one of the camps.

Then Demetrios went to work. In the confusion, the two camels had risen to their feet and were now ambling around the courtyard. He grabbed a cane. "Isaac, get these animals down. We need to finish loading."

"Right." Isaac slapped his stick across the back of the first camel. "Down! Down!" The camels dropped to their knees, ready to accept their burdens. The final packing began.

Demetrios made a last pass around the serpentine line: Camels in front, donkeys bringing up the rear. Except for Rebecca, who rode a black-striped donkey, the pilgrims walked behind the donkeys. Leaving the courtyard, he gazed at the campground. Impossible to tell in the smoke, but he thought the people were ready to go. He gave the order, "Put out the fires." Others echoed his cry, bringing mothers, fathers, sons, and daughters to their feet.

The men and older boys formed a double line leading from the nearby shore of the Sea of Galilee to the center of the camp. Demetrios motioned for Silas to meet him at the fire nearest the courtyard gate. "We'll begin here."

The first row passed two filled water buckets hand over hand to Demetrios, who poured each of them on the flames. As soon as the buckets were emptied, he sent them back down the second line to be replenished.

Silas came running with his stout stick. He stirred the wet ashes carefully, probing for glowing embers. Once he confirmed that the fire had been fully extinguished, he immersed his hands in the cinders. Too much heat beneath his palms would indicate another dousing. As he rose from the campfire, he declared, "This fire is cold." He wiped his face, leaving a black stripe across his brow. "Where next?"

"Over here." Demetrios directed him to a campfire where a family of four waited.

They moved through the campground as a team, quenching the flames and clearing the space. Once Silas had voiced his approval, the pilgrims picked up the last of their bags and walked to the side of the road, where they waited. The caretaker's face darkened with soot and grime as he worked; when he grinned, his white teeth looked like floating stars on a black and shifting sea. Finally, ordering a pause in the effort, Silas commandeered a bucket and dumped it over his head. Then they began again.

As the fires died, smoke and dust—kicked up by the constant activity of people and animals—pooled in a noxious cloud waist-high above the ground. The night was cool, but there was no breeze to clear the air. Unable to see their family and friends, the pilgrims called out to each other in the darkness.

Demetrios, now hoarse from shouting over the noise, pulled his cloak close about his face and plunged deep into the suffocating fog of smoke, dust, and debris, searching for the glow of the next fire. The pilgrims coughed and covered their faces with scarves, but no one complained. They recognized fire as both friend and enemy. A well-tended fire provided comfort and safety; a neglected fire could become a raging inferno in minutes.

As Demetrios finished pouring water over a small, abandoned flame that flickered under a mound of dirt, Silas said, "I believe that's the last one."

"What?" Demetrios turned to see Silas drenching himself.

Black rivulets dripped from Silas's hair. He smiled, shaking his head to keep the water from running into his mouth. "That's the last campfire. We're finished."

"Then it's time. Where is Isaac?"

Silas glanced to his left. "Over there. By the entrance." He handed Demetrios a damp rag. "Here. Wipe your face. You look like you've been sleeping in a brazier."

Demetrios made a futile swipe over his face and hands, but he still felt as grimy as a leprous beggar. He sighed. No time to wash again until tomorrow afternoon when they reached the intersection of the Yarmouk and Jericho rivers. He tossed the soiled cloth back to Silas. "Come, let's find Isaac and give the signal."

They found him waiting just outside the gate. Rufus, who stood nearby, stepped forward. "Master, have you reconsidered?"

"What?" He shook his head. "Rufus, you're going with us."

Isaac ended the discussion by pronouncing, "The animals are ready."

Demetrios nodded. His caravan: a total of ten donkeys, two camels, and more than twice as many people. He would make a fine profit this season without Elazar. But first, they would make an important stop in Jericho.

He spoke to Isaac, "The camels will set the pace at the head of the line. Next, send out the donkeys. The men, women, and children can follow them. Isaac, I want you to lead." He turned to Rufus. "You'll bring up the rear. And I'll be right behind you." He strode to the gate. "Now."

Isaac snapped his cane in the air. "Up, up! Let's go. Up!"

With much groaning and grunting, the great camels rose, towering imperiously above Isaac's head. With a second snap of the cane, the camels strode through the gate. When they stepped into the haze outside the courtyard, the beasts slowed for a moment, their thick-lashed eyes narrowing to slits as they watched the world through a third membrane that protected their eyes from debris. No longer fazed by the smoke, they picked up the pace, tramping down the road.

The first donkey that approached the gate carried Rebecca. She leaned against the bundles on the animal's back, her eyes closed, her head nodding in time to the donkey's gait. Her father walked at her side with his hand on her leg to steady her. His gaze never left her face. When Rebecca's donkey caught the first whiff of smoke from the campgrounds, it balked. Demetrios had to blindfold it temporarily so it wouldn't create a panic among the others.

After the last donkey exited the courtyard, the pilgrims followed the line, forming a ragged group that reached across the road. Local Jews watched from both sides, calling out their blessings as the caravan passed. A few merchants had also put up booths, hoping to make a last-minute trade, and beggars, hiding in the brush, had set out their bowls for the pilgrims, knowing that some of them believed it was good luck to give to the poor before a long journey. Two women in the caravan dropped back to examine the merchants' wares.

Elisheba darted out of the crowd of spectators, bearing a basket of her fresh baked bread. "Rufus," she called.

Rufus ran toward her.

Demetrios whirled around. "Rufus!"

His servant stopped, snapped his head up—his face was

streaked with tears. "Master?"

Demetrios pointed to the dawdling women. "Say good-bye to Elisheba and then get them moving. Quickly. We can't have stragglers on this trip."

Rufus took the bread from Elisheba, squeezed her hand, and said, "I'll be back soon." Then, without another word, he released her and dashed over to the beggars' bowls, where he ripped off a piece of bread to give to them. Elisheba waved to Rufus once more and slipped back into the throng of people lining the road.

Rufus froze, staring at the place where Elisheba had been standing, until Demetrios shouted to him, "Get those women back into the caravan."

"Yes, Master." Rufus scurried toward the women and escorted them back. He glanced at Demetrios, then joined the end of the line. The caravan continued to move down the road toward Jericho.

Demetrios watched until Rufus's shoulders bobbed just above the horizon. A young boy began to sing, his voice as brilliant as a high-pitched flute. "The sun cannot strike you down by day, nor moon at night . . ." Other voices joined him, singing, "I lift my eyes to the mountains . . ." A traveling song that spoke of hope and protection, but the words had nothing to do with Demetrios. They belonged to the Jewish pilgrims. Demetrios patted the knife secretly strapped to his forearm. He had placed his hope elsewhere.

He turned to Silas, who waited beside him.

The caretaker gestured toward the courtyard. "Is it time to lock up Elazar's house?"

"Yes. Everything of value goes with us. Join me as soon as you've finished." Taking up his staff, he walked toward the road. The courtyard gate slammed shut behind him.

CHAPTER
TWENTY-ONE

The caravan reached the outskirts of Jericho on the morning of the fourth day.

Demetrios ordered them to make camp along the Wadi Qelt, just west of the complex of Herodian palaces. They would stay there for two days, just two days for Demetrios to find Jesus, silence him, and return to the caravan, all without drawing attention or raising an alarm.

New caravans had been arriving all afternoon. They spread out across the wide, fertile plain, dotting the landscape with brightly colored flags and goat-hide tents. Every camp had its own contingent of donkeys, and a couple of the caravans had already set up their booths for active trading to barter with the locals for the balsam and perfumes of Jericho, which were highly prized. The settlement had a feeling of permanence to it, but in a few short weeks it would disappear as quickly as it had formed. Romulus's striped flags weren't to be seen, but he would be here soon—if not tonight, then tomorrow evening. Would Caleb be with him?

Demetrios wandered restlessly among the travelers. His skin

itched with a nervous tension; his palms reddened in the sunlight, as if they had been burned by a flame. Holding his hands
out in front of his body, Demetrios watched his fingers tremble
like a withered branch quaking in the wind. He looked around
quickly to see if anyone else had noticed and then tucked his
hands back into the folds of his cloak. This morning, as they set
up their camp, other travelers had stopped by to gossip and share
news. Many of them talked about the strange prophet preaching
and healing people at the river. Demetrios knew then that he had
guessed correctly: Jesus was here.

The Passover festival began in one week in Jerusalem. If he
allowed Jesus to escape to the Holy City, it would be too late. The
Roman presence there would be too strong, and it would be too
easy for Jesus to disappear among so many Jews. Lost in thought,
Demetrios strode past his own caravan across the boundaries of
another camp where he bumped against a stranger.

The man turned and stared at Demetrios, making Demetrios
flinch. He wondered if the man had felt the dagger strapped to
Demetrios's arm. "Sorry," Demetrios muttered, lowering his head.

The stranger shrugged, turned away.

Demetrios straightened and moved rapidly toward his own
camp. Isaac waved to him as Demetrios approached. "You're back.
I've almost finished here." He fed a rope through the last donkey's
halter and tied it to a stake in the ground.

"I like the way you've placed the bells on their necks." Demetrios
wrapped the excess cord around a stone weight. With the tether and
the weight, the donkeys had enough slack to graze but could not
stray. "The ringing will alert us if someone tries to steal our animals
during the night." He smiled. "You've learned well."

After testing the rope once more, Isaac swiped his face with a
rag. "It's so much hotter here than in Galilee."

Demetrios handed his goatskin bag to Issac. "I believe it's because we're so close to the Sea of Salt. Something about the water draws the heat."

Issac raised the bag and gulped away his thirst.

"Where is Silas? I thought he was going to help you feed the animals later."

The young man laughed. "He's in his usual place, sleeping in the shade."

"He should be here. And Rufus? Is he in my tent?"

"He was so curious. I told him he could look around if he wanted." Isaac watched a group of men raise a tent for a new camp. "There's plenty to see."

Demetrios frowned. His servant shouldn't have left without his permission. He had enough worries without needing to keep track of Rufus. "I'll fetch him. We need to talk."

He found Rufus among a mob of spectators observing a legal dispute. Each of the two lawyers stood atop a large, flat rock shouting out their opinions. When they pronounced something particularly clever, the crowd applauded. If the other failed to respond with a suitable retort, people jeered and mocked. Rufus hovered near the periphery of the group, his jaw slack as he listened to the speeches.

Demetrios grasped Rufus's elbow. "Did you hear me calling you?" Demetrios pulled Rufus from the crowd. "Let's go back to the camp."

"Aren't they wonderful?" Rufus pointed to a thick-bearded man with fair skin who looked like he seldom ventured out into the sunlight. "Especially that one. He talks about the grains of sand in the desert and the fish in the sea. So many fine words and such a beautiful voice. And when he was finished, everyone cheered." He shook his head in amazement. "I could listen all day to him."

The man Rufus admired played with the crowd, teasing them with silly jokes they slurped up like hungry cats. "Don't be deceived by clever words, Rufus. Look at what happened to Elazar."

"Oh!" Rufus stopped short, making Demetrios stumble. "I'm sorry, Master. Elazar . . ." He ventured a timid smile. "I'm sure Elazar will come home soon."

Elazar was not Demetrios's concern at the moment. "I need to speak with you and Isaac privately." Demetrios kept walking at a fast clip, with Rufus trailing behind. His slave seemed reluctant to leave the show. "Hurry up. Isaac's waiting for us."

The three of them gathered in an area far away from the pilgrims. Demetrios took a deep breath. He had to carry out the wishes of the gods and protect his freedom. He knew they would have questions. A caravan owner does not abandon his caravan in the middle of the journey, but he wouldn't be gone long, or so he hoped. "Isaac, you've performed your work well for me. I'm pleased."

Isaac nodded. His gaze traveled from Demetrios to Rufus and then back to Demetrios. The expression on his face revealed his confusion. Demetrios had praised him often. Why did they need to meet for this?

"And, Rufus . . ." Demetrios hesitated, knowing his servant would never understand.

"Yes?"

"Both of you are loyal. I can trust you." Demetrios paused. "I have to leave the caravan," he blurted. "Tonight."

"Why?" Isaac asked.

Demetrios didn't anticipate his authority would be challenged. "Do not question me, Isaac. I have important business, urgent business, that I must tend to in Jericho. And it cannot wait. I will leave tonight, but I'll be back tomorrow, long before we depart for Jerusalem."

"Very well, Master." Rufus turned toward their tent. "I'll gather my belongings and be with you in a moment."

"No!" Demetrios spoke more sharply than he intended. Rufus stopped midstride. "No. Rufus, I need you to stay here. Help Isaac with the caravan."

"But what about Silas?" Isaac asked. "What do we tell him?"

"Tell him nothing. Tell him I've gone to Jericho to meet someone. No more than that." They both stared at him as if he had gone mad. Everyone knew you didn't travel alone after dark; wild animals hunted, and bandits prowled for unwitting victims. But what choice did he have? He couldn't reveal his true plans to anyone. "I'll return tomorrow. You can depend on that. Rufus is to stay here. Now, see to your business." He waved his hand in dismissal. "Go."

Shortly after nightfall, Demetrios slipped out of their encampment. A pale sheen of moonlight washed over the earth's surface, lighting his way. A crisp breeze stung his cheeks. With each step he took, he felt a strengthening of resolve, a sense of rightness for what he was about to do. His destiny waited for him somewhere on the distant moonlit horizon.

He stopped near the foot of a rocky hillside. By his own reckoning, he estimated he was less than a Roman mile from the northern entrance to Jericho. Squatting behind a low stand of tamarisk, he loosed the strings of his bag. He brought out his costume—the rags of a common beggar. His dagger, safely encased in the leather sheath tied to his arm, would be invisible beneath his disguise.

Turning his wrist, Demetrios slid the iron blade free, offering it to the kiss of moonlight. Gingerly he pressed his finger down onto the pointed tip, gasping as the weapon bit into his flesh. He jerked his hand back, nearly dropping the knife. He had forgotten how quickly the blade cut. A single drop of blood beaded on his fingertip.

He cupped the dagger loosely in his palm, studying it. His finger throbbed. He turned the knife to his own chest—this time applying no pressure—and wondered what it would feel like to die.

The night was passing too quickly. He could linger no longer. He needed to be at the river before daybreak, before the crowds formed, before there were witnesses. He lowered the knife and eased it gently back into its sheath.

Demetrios stood, unfastened his woolen cloak at the left shoulder, and let it drop lightly to the ground. Cold! He had not expected the night to be so cold. More slowly, he removed his linen undergarment, his tunic, placing it with the rest of his clothes. Goosebumps prickled up and down his arms and legs. Naked and alone, Demetrios suddenly felt exposed and foolish. He could be murdered here in the wilderness and no one would ever know. He touched the sheath again to confirm his weapon was secure. He still had his knife. He would be safe.

Demetrios scooped up clods of earth and rubbed them through his closely cropped hair and over his bare skin. His hands passed over the scars at the curve of his shoulder, and he paused, feeling the familiar rage. Justice, not murder. Justice for the Roman then, justice for Jesus now. Demetrios jerked the rags of his costume down over his body, careful to conceal his weapon beneath the torn fabric.

After placing his good clothing and money into the bag, he buried it in a shallow hole. Before he covered the cache, he added his sandals—beggars must go barefoot. Then he marked the spot with a circular pile of rocks.

Still trembling from the cold, he danced across the fields like a startled rabbit. Jagged stones and hidden thorns seemed to jump out of the ground to tear at his feet, but he did not slacken his pace. Demetrios, following a path that led from the Wadi Qelt to the river, reached his destination at dawn: Jericho.

CHAPTER
TWENTY-TWO

A pink dawn striped the sky as Demetrios entered Jericho. He was disappointed by what he found in the village. According to the gossip and rumors, Jesus was in Jericho. There should be crowds, masses of people seeking the Messiah's aid, but streets were empty, quiet. Only a handful of old women gathered at the well to chat while they waited to draw their water. Keeping his head down, Demetrios sidled close to two women who perched on their upturned buckets.

"I'm so glad he's gone," one of them said. "And he's taken that rabble with him. Can you believe he even invited the prostitutes to join him?"

"The festivals always bring a motley group of strangers to town," the other woman said. "I don't feel safe at times."

At first, Demetrios was reluctant to speak to the women. What if they suspected him? What if they asked questions about his intentions? He touched his arm, feeling the silhouette of the dagger. Could they see the weapon's shadow beneath his rags? But time was fleeing. The longer it took Demetrios to find Jesus, the greater the danger.

Demetrios cleared his throat. "Greetings. I'm looking for a man named Jesus. He's supposed to be some sort of miracle worker. Do you—"

Startled, the first woman turned and rose quickly from her seat on the bucket. She took a step back, then spat on the ground three times as a gesture to ward off evil. "Who are you? What's wrong with your leg? Get away from me, beggar. I have nothing to give you."

Rage burned in Demetrios's throat. If he had been dressed as a caravan driver, she would have been fawning over him, eager to see his spices and perfumes. Instead, she treated him like he was dung from a donkey. Determined to remain calm and subservient, Demetrios said quietly, "I simply wondered if you knew where I could find a man called Jesus of Nazareth. I won't bother you anymore."

The woman frowned, hesitating, then said, "He's at the river with his crowd of beggars, thieves and prostitutes. Follow the road to the Jordan."

"My thanks."

The woman didn't answer.

Demetrios raced east, down a narrow road leading to the river. He was soon joined by hordes of people, all hurrying the same direction. They spread out along the banks of the river north of Jericho, squeezing close, a grove of trees bent in the wind at their backs and the burbling water at their feet. Demetrios scrambled up the steep, sandy slope, establishing his place on firm rock.

The relentless sun beat down; a sticky heat weighted the air, making it difficult to breathe. Sweat pooled under Demetrios's arms, streamed down his face. His own bodily stink caused him to wince.

By midmorning the people had filled every available space of level ground. They trampled the grass into a muddy soup that clung to their sandals and spattered their clothes. Exhausted and weary, they stood, watching for the Messiah, fanning their faces, leaning against one another for support. Demetrios knew he had come to the right place. Jesus was here.

But Jesus wasn't here—not yet.

A man close to the water shouted, "I see him! He's coming!" The mob surged toward the voice, straining for a better view. Pressed by this wall of human flesh, Demetrios pushed back. The group garnered new energy. Those in the back shoved up against the people in front of them, forcing everyone into a tight formation. Demetrios felt as though he was being crushed from every side. He hated the touch of their grasping hands. Their breath stank of stale onions and garlic; their bodies reeked of filth and disease. Covering his nose and mouth with his hand, he edged to the side.

"I see him now. There he is!" A man balanced on a friend's shoulders so he could scan the sea of people.

"Where is he?" the voices behind Demetrios demanded. "Is he coming this way?" More bodies pressed against his back. Determined not to lose his place, Demetrios stood firm.

"No, I was mistaken," the lookout proclaimed. "It's not the Rav at all. I think it's one of the fishermen who travel with him."

"Are you sure?" a person near Demetrios's ear called. "How can you know?"

"No, it's not Jesus. He's turned back. He's not coming here."

A collective sigh passed through the crowd. Several women standing near Demetrios dropped to the ground, gasping. A man closest to the river scooped up handfuls of water and dribbled it over their faces. Demetrios remained on his feet. He took a few cautious steps forward. Where was Jesus? Had Demetrios come all this way for nothing?

"How long have you been here?"

"What?" Demetrios said, startled by a voice beside him. He glanced at the man who had spoken to him: a fat creature with puffy bags of skin under his eyes, wisps of thinning hair, and florid cheeks. He reminded Demetrios of one of Marcus's pigs.

"I was here before dawn," the man said. "You must have come later. Can you believe there are this many people waiting to see a healer?" He shook his head and untied a goatskin bag at his waist.

Demetrios did not reply. Unnerved that someone had spoken directly to him, he tried to maintain his attitude of indifference.

"You should hear what people are saying about the Rav in the caravan camps." The man drank from his bag. The stench of fermented grapes wafted from his lips, causing Demetrios to cough. "They say that if he can bring dead people back to life, then he should be king. King of the Jews."

"He doesn't look much like a king." Immediately, Demetrios wished he had kept quiet. He looked at the river, watching the current. The water had been muddied by the crumbling bank.

"So you've seen him before?"

Demetrios was silent. A quick attack, that was what he had planned. A quick stab to the torso, drop the dagger, and disappear into the mob. He needed the stranger to leave him alone. Demetrios edged closer to the water.

The pig-faced man followed, still chatting. "I bet you're from Galilee. I can hear it in your voice. You must have seen him often."

Demetrios pulled his own tattered cloak up to his chin. "I'm not from Galilee. I've only been there once. I saw Jesus there then."

They both jumped at a shout from farther up the river: "Rav! Jesus! Over here!" Everyone began running. Clutching his wine flask, the fat man cut in front of Demetrios. "There he is." He elbowed Demetrios aside. Demetrios reached out and grabbed the man's leg, bringing him face down into the muck. Others around them scuttled across the prone figure and sprinted up the bank. Demetrios didn't hesitate any longer. He leapt over the man's sprawled body and joined the race to get to Jesus.

"Move back! Move back!"

A broad-chested man with muscular arms faced the mob, blocking their way with a skinned tree branch. "Get back." He waved the stick at them. "Make room for the Teacher." Like a wave of water parted by the wind, the people separated into two uneven lines.

Demetrios pushed through the opened space and stared in amazement as a tall, gaunt figure emerged from the confusion: Judas. Trembling, Demetrios swallowed. "Peter," Judas shouted to the man with the stick, "keep these people in line. They'll overrun the Rav if you let them. Push them back. There's not enough room for him to walk here."

The man named Peter glared at Judas. "I'm doing all that I can. How do you expect me to keep so many in order?"

"Find a way." Turning, Judas disappeared into the brush along the river.

But the people refused to wait. Breaking ranks, they dashed toward Peter, crying out, "Give us the Rav. We want to see the Teacher."

Peter whirled around, brandishing his stick like a club. The massive branch whooshed above several ducking and dodging heads. "Stay back! He'll see you in good time."

Three men lost their balance and fell, skidding down the slippery bank. Demetrios glanced nervously at the river. The current here was swift, with swirling eddies that splashed over the floundering men's faces. Demetrios moved closer to the trees. He wasn't afraid of Peter's stick, but he wouldn't risk slipping and drowning.

In any case, Jesus was not here yet. The excitement had been over nothing.

Then suddenly, Jesus was there. The Rav, as the mob called him, ascended the riverbank to an earthen mound next to Peter where he could survey the crowd. A hush descended upon the gathering. For a few moments, no one moved or spoke. Some of Jesus's disciples emerged from the bushes to stand next to the Messiah.

A shrill voice shattered the silence. "Master, speak to us." And everyone was shouting at once.

It was time. Demetrios slipped his hand inside his tunic.

His fingers shook.

His heart pounded, like a bird flapping against the bars of a cage.

Demetrios pressed his palm against his breast to quiet the rapid beating. Again, he touched the hilt of his knife. It, too, vibrated beneath his fingertips. A sting of death waiting to come to life.

So much waiting and he could not get any closer to Jesus. Peter still held them back. He had to reach Jesus, had to silence him now. Demetrios bounced on his heels, impatient to break through the barrier of shoulders and backs.

"I was here first!" a man cried as Demetrios tried to sneak around him. He jabbed a fist into Demetrios's side, a glancing blow. "Wait your turn," he said to Demetrios. But Demetrios needed to get to the front of the line. He had to find a way to go around this Peter who stood so solidly in the middle of the path. There! An opening. A woman had knelt down to pick up her basket. Demetrios darted through the gap toward the fisherman.

"Please." Demetrios touched Peter's arm. "Please. I have an urgent message for Jesus. From Jerusalem. I must speak with him."

Peter turned his sunburned face toward Demetrios, pulled his arm from Demetrios's grasp. "What? What message?" He shook his head. "Everyone's message is urgent." He peered at Demetrios. "Do I know you?" Before Demetrios could answer, Peter hefted his stick and said, "No, no. Move back now." When Demetrios did not budge, Peter pressed his stick against Demetrios's shoulder. "I told you to get back in line." Demetrios started to push back, then hesitated when he saw a movement from the corner of his eye.

Jesus, leaving his circle of disciples, approached the crowd. People rushed up the path behind Demetrios, jostling and shoving him forward. As Peter was pushed backward, he waved his arms wildly in all directions. "Get back! Get back!" Someone tripped him, and he stumbled, the branch dropping from his grasp.

"Stop!" Jesus shouted. When he held up his hand, light seemed to pass through his pale flesh. "Stop."

The rabble was silenced.

"I will come to you all." Jesus leaned forward and said something to Peter, but his words were drowned out by the resuming noise of the mob.

Taking advantage of Peter's distraction, Demetrios dashed around Peter and planted himself on the path directly in front of Jesus. Demetrios took a deep breath. Jesus was now less than ten cubits away from his own death. Demetrios touched the dagger's hilt. "Jesus," he said, struggling to keep the tremor out of his voice. "I must speak with you."

Peter glanced at Demetrios and blocked Demetrios with his hand. "The Messiah wants to see the children." He raised his voice to be heard. "Bring up the little children to Jesus."

Demetrios froze. Children? His hand was poised to grasp the knife. Ready. No, no! No children. I cannot do this in front of children. He felt the blade—still shrouded in its sheath—pulsing against his arm. It was cold, so cold. A spear of ice against his feverish skin.

Ice! Ice to chill the blood! Ice to kill the soul!

Do it now. Do it before the children come! Move quickly. Do not let them stop you.

He began to run.

Almost there.

He reached for the knife.

Just a few steps closer. Closer.

The ground thundered beneath his feet; the wind screamed in his ears. Two more steps and . . . Demetrios closed his hand about the dagger's handle.

Now!

Judas stepped out.

Demetrios reeled and teetered, his legs crumpling beneath him. His hands flailed out in front of him as he fell; the knife stayed in its sheath. Landing on his knees, he looked up into the face of a smiling Judas.

Judas reached down to help him, but Demetrios pulled away. As he rose to his feet, his knees wobbled. He lurched forward and then steadied himself.

"He wishes to see the children first," Judas said, almost kindly. He paused, staring deep into Demetrios's face. "I know you. You're—?"

"No." Demetrios shook his head, adamant in his denial. "No, no, you're mistaken."

"Take my child!" a man shouted. "She's dying."

Recognizing the voice, alarmed to hear it, Demetrios pivoted quickly.

The voice belonged to Enoch, from Demetrios's own caravan. The man who had fought over the donkey he wanted his daughter to ride pushed through the crowd, carrying his child in his arms.

Why was he here? Had Enoch followed him?

Bile rose in Demetrios's throat. His disguise had been unmasked. Peter had spoken to him. Judas had recognized him. If Enoch saw him now . . .

Enoch stumbled toward Jesus; his daughter, Rebecca, rested her head against his chest, with her eyes closed, and her mouth slightly open as she labored to breathe. Her cheeks, which had once bloomed with the red flush of fever, were now the color of sun-bleached linen. Her long brown hair fell in limp strands over Enoch's arms. Enoch glanced helplessly at the crowd. Staggering with exhaustion, he struggled to balance her weight against his body.

He stopped a few steps away from Jesus. "Please take her, Rav. You're my last hope."

Peter opened his arms. "Let me bring her to Jesus."

As if he was suddenly aware of Demetrios's presence, Jesus turned toward Demetrios and smiled.

Demetrios shivered. The man's gaze cut through him. How much did Jesus know? Was this part of a larger plan? An attempt to expose him here only to turn him over to the authorities later? Demetrios staggered back, hoping to blend into the mass of bodies gathered along the river. He had to escape. Collect himself and try again, at a better time. He wanted to slay Jesus, to keep his freedom, but he did not want to get caught and have to face what would then come.

As Demetrios spun on his heel, searching for an exit, Judas grasped his arm. "Come." He guided Demetrios to the side. "Come sit down over here."

Demetrios stared at Judas's hand on his arm. Such clean, trimmed fingernails, elegant fingers. The hands of a man who never knew physical labor or toil. His touch burned like a fire.

"No. Let go of me."

Judas glared at him, his grip tightening. "I do know you. Elazar's friend. The caravan driver. I haven't forgotten."

Demetrios ripped loose. Had Judas felt the dagger hidden beneath Demetrios's garments? "I'll find my own way."

Behind Demetrios, Judas called out to the huddled suppli-cants. "The Rav will see all of you before the day is done. You must sit down now where you are and wait while he tends to the girl."

Slipping and sliding his way through the mud, Demetrios hastened down the riverbank. Questions pelted him as he passed through the crowd. "Did you see the Messiah? What is he doing?" But all sounds were lost to Demetrios as the roaring in his ears grew louder. He held a taste so bitter in his mouth, he thought he would vomit. Demetrios careened into the brush and collapsed.

He had failed.

CHAPTER
TWENTY-THREE

Late that same afternoon, Demetrios, now dressed in his trader's cloak, returned to the caravan. As he neared the Wadi Qelt, Rufus came running up the path to meet him. "There's been trouble in the camp. A donkey has gone missing, and Enoch and Rebecca are—" He stopped midsentence and stared at Demetrios. "Master, are you ill? You're so pale."

"Why do you bother me with these things?" Demetrios slumped on a rock and rubbed his feet. He was weary to the bone. What did a donkey matter? He had failed. He had been so close, the knife within his grasp, and he had faltered, fallen to Jesus's feet, the knife undrawn. Elazar was still gone, and Jesus was still alive, still a threat. Did Jesus know what Demetrios had planned to do? And what if Judas had felt Demetrios's dagger? Would he tell Jesus? Did Enoch or Rebecca recognize the beggar in their midst? Demetrios knew he had been foolish to think he could kill Jesus in a crowd. So many people, so many things to go wrong. Demetrios had failed. How would the gods punish him now?

"Master," Rufus said, "what should we do about the missing pilgrims? Isaac wants to—"

"The loss of one donkey means nothing."

"What?" Rufus stared for a moment, waited, then turned and left.

Demetrios shook his head, gazing at a point on the horizon beyond the retreating Rufus. Would Jesus stay in Jericho much longer? He could leave for Jerusalem any day. Demetrios wondered how much time he had, how long he could delay his caravan's departure, what excuses he could use.

Moments later, Rufus came running toward Demetrios again. "Please, Master, you need to come. Isaac found the donkey wandering untended near the road, but Enoch and Rebecca—"

"Enoch?" Demetrios turned to face his servant. "What about Enoch?"

"Enoch and Rebecca are gone. And Menachem is furious. He says the caravan is unsafe, and he wants to post his own guards tonight. Isaac tried to talk to him, but he won't listen. He insists something bad happened to them."

"Enoch and his daughter are fine. I've seen them. They won't be returning to the camp." Demetrios rose unsteadily to his feet. "We need to go back now. I want to rest."

Leaning forward, Rufus brushed his fingers across Demetrios's forehead. "Your skin's so gray. The sun has made you sick. Just wait here. I'll get Isaac and—"

"No." He pushed Rufus away. "I'm not sick. I'm going back to my tent."

The two of them walked back to the camp in silence. As Demetrios pulled back the tent flap to enter, Rufus stopped him. His servant's face creased with worry. "Master, please let me bring you something to eat."

Demetrios didn't answer.

"At least let me get you some fresh water. Please?"

Demetrios looked at Rufus and sighed. The effort left him dizzy. "Yes . . . I'm thirsty." He stepped inside without waiting for his servant to follow.

The interior was cool and dark, a welcome change from his earlier sojourn along the river. Stepping around the bags piled on the floor, he fell onto his sleeping pallet. He did not speak when Rufus tiptoed in with a bucket of water.

Watching his master, Rufus waited for a moment. Then he dipped a cup into the bucket. "I've brought you something to drink. I'll place it by the bed so you can reach it without getting up."

"Tell Isaac I'll speak to him later. You can go now." The golden slanting rays of the setting sun flashed across Rufus's face as the slave exited. Then the door flap dropped, sealing him in darkness. He lay back on his pallet and closed his eyes, thinking about his futile quest. Hours of waiting by that river. For what? A single chance. Lost.

A group of women strode past his tent. Their high-pitched chatter sounded like shrieking gulls.

"There's plenty of deadwood near the river," one woman said. "We could use that for the fire."

"No, no, that's too far," the other argued. "Let's look over there."

A baby began to cry, and someone murmured, "Hush, hush now." The women moved on, and the voices faded away.

The river. All of those people. Pushing and crushing up against him. He could still feel their body heat; the rank odor of their poverty clung to his clothing. And then Enoch with his dying daughter. Demetrios had not expected that. He tried to imagine his fate after Jesus came to power as king. Would he resurrect the Roman to exact revenge? Or would he simply order Demetrios's

228

execution? He should leave tonight, abandon his caravan, run away. He touched the dagger still strapped to his body, stroking the smooth curves of the handle.

Laughter reverberated in the distance. Children at play. Their unabashed pleasure mocked him, showed him the fool he had become. But it couldn't end here, not in this way. Demetrios vowed he would try again—when Jesus was alone.

Suddenly, a man's voice sang out, "Happy are they who dwell in your house!"

Demetrios sat up, listening. Others were laughing, running toward the man's call. Someone jingled a string of brass bells.

A chorus of voices burst into song: "They will always be praising you."

A crowd had gathered outside. Traditional with every pilgrimage to the Holy City, the Jews celebrated their forthcoming entry into Jerusalem. They would sing tonight, on the road, and as they passed through the city gates. Again, the man's solo call, "Happy are the people whose strength is in you!"

And the pilgrims replied, "Whose hearts are set upon the pilgrims' way."

Demetrios struggled to his feet. What right do these Jews have to sing of happiness? He stumbled over the bags that blocked his path. The Romans occupy their homeland; their wealth is limited to the food in their house; and their invisible god ignores their cries for deliverance. Why should they sing now? Pulling back his tent flap, he stepped out into the night.

The Jews had stoked their fire high, bright yellow flames leaping into the black sky. All of the Jewish men, including Isaac and Silas, had joined arms to dance in a circle around the blaze. Behind them, outside of the ring of dancers and off to one side, the women clapped hands in time to the music. Someone produced a single-reed pipe and began to echo the central melody. The piper was soon joined by several women pounding upon timbrels.

Dark, elongated shadows—of dancers and spectators alike—floated like huge, faceless giants across the rocks behind the gathering. The lead singer, Menachem of Cana, called out the next verse, and when the people looked up at him, the flames of a hundred fires were reflected in their deep-brown eyes. They answered with a single voice of joy, their faces glowing with an incandescent light. Almost against his will, Demetrios walked toward the Jews.

It was neither the dancers nor the fire that attracted him so; it was the music. The sweet, lyrical descant of the pipe, accompanied by the throbbing beat of the timbrels, seemed to swell into an intoxicating cloud, enveloping him in a powerful embrace. He felt in their haunting duet the secret song of a man and a woman, of two lovers communicating in a language that surpassed words.

Demetrios closed his eyes. He had not forgotten her. She resided in his thoughts, like a sweet taste on the back of the tongue to be savored during times of hunger. And how he longed for her, for someone.

He did not hear Menachem sing, "They will climb from height to—" But he did hear the silence. Suddenly, everything stopped.

Demetrios eased open his eyes.

What had happened to the music?

Menachem stepped forward, his presence forbidding further progress. "Yes? Is something wrong?"

Demetrios realized then he was only steps away from the circle of dancing men. The circle, however, had broken, the women retreating quickly into the darkness. Even the glorious blaze had died down to a few flames. As he and Menachem stood there face-to-face, a cool wind swept through the brush, swirling the sand up around their feet.

"What do you want?" Menachem asked with rising irritation.

"No, nothing is wrong." Demetrios answered the man's first question. "I—" For a moment, he was transfixed by the deserted fire. Rufus touched him on the shoulder at the same time that Isaac said, "Demetrios—" He turned around. They were all staring at him, looking at him as if he were an intruder. "I need to speak with Isaac," Demetrios said. "And you, too, Rufus. Come with me." He strode off without another word.

"I'm returning to Jericho," he told them when they were out of the hearing of the others. "Tonight."

Both Isaac and Rufus began to protest at once. "Master—" Rufus said, as Isaac interrupted, "But what about the caravan? We're scheduled to leave for Jerusalem tomorrow!"

"You will take the caravan to Jerusalem without me," Demetrios told Isaac.

Isaac stepped back, shaking his head. "Without you? You're not going to Jerusalem? Why? What has happened? Who will lead the caravan?"

"You will lead the caravan. Silas will help you. I have urgent business in Jericho, and I must go." He paused, then with increasing confidence, said, "Now, listen closely. When you get to Jerusalem, find a place to stay in the Upper City. And set up your booth in the Upper Agora. I've reserved a space there with a man called Nicolaus. Ask for him. You know what price to set for the spices. We've already discussed that. As for the camels and donkeys, quarter them in any pen on the north side of the city. Just give the stableman my name. All of them know me." He paused. "And they know Elazar. Use his name if you think it will help you."

"But Demetrios—" Isaac began.

Demetrios held up his hand. "You can do this. You must do

this. I cannot go with you to Jerusalem. Wait for me at the Upper Agora. I will be there soon—" He took a deep breath. What if he did not make it to Jerusalem? "Rufus," he said quickly, "you'll come with me. You'll be my messenger. If—for some reason—I don't get to Jerusalem, you must find Isaac and tell him what to do."

"What do you mean, Master? What would keep you from going to Jerusalem?"

Demetrios shook his head. "That's not for you to know. I'll be in Jerusalem in three days at the latest."

"And if you don't come in three days?" Isaac asked. "What then?"

Aware that he was about to make a statement from which there was no turning back, Demetrios hesitated. "Then you and Rufus must follow the dictates of the document I have left for you in my tent."

"Master, are you in—" Rufus began.

"I'm declaring Elazar my heir. You'll find a scroll in my tent stamped with my seal. It explains all of my wishes." His voice was brusque. "And you, Rufus, are my witness. I trust that you'll be honest with Isaac—if that time should come." He placed three denarii in Rufus's palm. "Take this and follow me. If something happens to me, find a caravan going to Jerusalem. This will pay for your passage and lodging in the Holy City."

Demetrios took a breath, thought for a moment. Then, removing a brass ring from his finger, he gave it also to Rufus. "This ring will speak for me when I cannot. Isaac, if Rufus arrives in Jerusalem alone with this ring on his finger, you will know I am dead."

Isaac gasped. "What do you mean?"

Demetrios managed a wan smile. "Don't worry. I'm sure I will be fine."

Rufus kept shaking his head. "I'm sorry, Master. I can't accept this. I just can't."

"No, the ring is yours until we all meet again in Jerusalem. And I'm sure we will." He took Rufus's hand and slid the ring on his finger. "See? A good fit." He cleared his throat. "Now, gather your belongings. It's late, and we'll have trouble finding a place to sleep in Jericho tonight."

As Rufus scurried to collect his bags, Isaac touched Demetrios on the shoulder. "Are you certain you have to go to Jericho tonight? Can your business wait until we pass by here again?"

"If I wait, I'll have no business." Demetrios shifted his weight, squared his shoulders, assuming an air of authority. "Tend to the caravan. You must be ready for the ascent to Jerusalem." He clasped Isaac's arm. "I'll see you soon."

Demetrios watched Isaac trod back to the camp. So much he could not say. How could he explain to Isaac what he needed to do? He was not a monster, not like the Roman. He could be kind. He could even love another, but he could not let Jesus talk to the authorities. The risk was too great. He had to go back to Jericho and find Jesus—alone, away from the crowds—and this time, he would succeed. And the gods would be appeased.

"I'm ready," Rufus said, bringing Demetrios out of his reverie.

"You have your things?"

Rufus nodded.

"Good. Come then, let us find an inn." They started down the road to Jericho—a road swallowed by the same darkness that soon swallowed them as well.

CHAPTER
TWENTY-FOUR

After visiting several places that turned Demetrios and Rufus away, Demetrios found a dilapidated inn located just off the road north of Jericho. Tryphon's Inn was a mean, dirty establishment, with a front and side courtyard reserved for animals. A high wall protected the courtyards and main building from thieves and intruders, but the place was also legendary for harboring bandits. Experienced travelers knew they should always sleep with one eye open at Tryphon's establishment. Tonight, however, this inn would have to do.

Instructing Rufus to hold the torch high, Demetrios led the way up the worn path to the inn's entrance. Behind him, Rufus kept up a steady stream of questions and concerns. "Master, are you positive this is the right place? Perhaps we should go back to the camp?"

"Be quiet, Rufus." Demetrios rapped loudly on the wooden gate. From deep inside the courtyard, a donkey brayed nervously.

"I don't think anyone is home," Rufus said.

"They're here." Demetrios scooped up a rock, weighed it in his hand. For a moment, he recalled another stone, a stone he had held as a slave. The Roman's crushed skull flared in his memory. He thumped the gate again, making the hinges rattle.

"I'm coming," someone shouted. "You don't have to wake the household." There was the sound of a bolt being lifted, and then the gate opened just a crack. A red-faced watchman peered out. "What do you want?"

"Beds for the two of us," Demetrios said.

"Sorry. No room. You'll have to go somewhere else."

"I was told you still have space available." Extracting a coin from his purse, Demetrios rolled it around his palm and held it out between two fingers. The watchman reached for it, but Demetrios pulled his hand back. "Are you sure," he asked, waving the coin so the man could see the flash of silver, "that you don't have a place for us to stay?"

The watchman stared at Demetrios's hand. "Wait here." He closed the gate.

Almost immediately, Rufus began to protest. "I think that man was drunk. And, Master, did you smell the courtyard? This place smells of beastly animals and dung."

"Rufus—"

"Well, well, another desperate traveler darkens our door," a deep voice said as the gate swung open wide. "So you think my inn stinks?"

Both Demetrios and Rufus turned to face a bulky, heavyset man who blocked the entrance. An infection fused his left eye shut, while the right eye wept continuously. The watchman stood behind the giant, nervously picking at a boil on his own neck.

"You must be Tryphon." Demetrios smiled and nodded. "We need a place to sleep for the next three nights. I'll pay—"

"Three nights!" Rufus exclaimed. "I thought we were spending just one night here."

"I'll pay in advance." Demetrios reached for his purse.

"Aren't you with one of the caravans? If so, why aren't you sleeping in your camp?" Tryphon shook his head and laughed. Mucus dripped from his nose, but he didn't seem to notice. "Never mind. Don't ask questions you don't want answered. So, you need a bed? You're certainly small enough. And he's not much bigger." He studied Rufus carefully with his functioning eye. "Does he eat much?"

"We've brought our own food. Do you have beds for us?"

"I have one place on the roof, if you don't mind sharing."

"How much?"

Tryphon grinned. "It's a busy season, but for the right price, I can make arrangements. One sestertius a night. That includes one bed and bread and water in the morning. But no other food. Fair enough?"

Demetrios nodded slowly and with purpose.

As he accepted the money, Tryphon said, "I believe you promised my servant something." He pushed the watchman forward. The man extended his hand, grinning foolishly. Once everyone had been paid, Tryphon lifted a lamp from a hook on the wall and motioned for Demetrios and Rufus to enter. "This way then. And tell your servant to give his torch to my watchman. I don't need a fire in here."

The group stepped around sleeping animals, piles of straw, and a couple of wheeled carts. "Oh!" Rufus cried out. "I have donkey droppings stuck to my toes."

"Rufus," Demetrios said sharply.

Tryphon merely laughed.

The innkeeper escorted them up a narrow outside staircase to a sleeping roof that was partially sheltered by a goat-hide tarp. Other travelers slept near the top of the stairwell, creating a treacherous path to the single empty pallet near the edge of the roof. "This is it." Tryphon held the lamp aloft so they could see.

Demetrios knelt by the straw pallet and turned over a few strands. Mildew. He slapped at the straw, stirring up a horde of tiny black crawling spots. Behind him, Rufus gasped.

"Quiet," Demetrios ordered. He sighed. They would be eaten alive by fleas. But they could not sleep by the road. Or in the wilderness. Much too dangerous. "We need a blanket to cover the straw. A clean blanket," he added.

Tryphon nodded. "I'll have my servant bring you one."

After the innkeeper had departed, Rufus complained again. "Are we really to sleep here? This place is so dirty. You saw the animal droppings in the courtyard. And the smell. Are you sure about this, Master?"

"That is enough, Rufus. We cannot sleep anywhere else." He held out a handful of straw. "Here. Help me shake some of this stuff out so we'll be more comfortable."

Tryphon's servant brought them a threadbare blanket a few moments later. Demetrios held it up, disgusted by the numerous holes and tears. He feared it would provide little protection from flea bites.

Despite the poor quality blanket and Rufus's grievances about the inn, Rufus fell asleep almost as soon his head rested on the pallet. Although Demetrios was equally exhausted, he was not so relaxed. He tossed and turned, shifting his weight, searching for a good position. Rufus had sprawled across the small bed, pushing Demetrios almost off the edge. Demetrios pressed close to his servant, and Rufus rolled over to his back. His loud snoring reverberated in Demetrios's ears like a rumbling thunderstorm. He poked Rufus in the ribs; the snoring stopped. Rufus snorted once and then began mumbling unintelligible sounds. His fingers twitched, but his eyes remained closed. Demetrios watched him for a few moments, wondering what troubles disturbed his servant's dreams. Finally, unable to sleep, he rose from the pallet and crept to the roof's edge.

The courtyard below was flanked with a handful of flickering torches. A full moon glowed like a nighttime sun, illuminating every corner. Quavering shadows danced across the trampled ground, but there was no sign of human activity. Even the animals were quiet. Aware of movement over his head, Demetrios looked up.

The predawn sky vibrated with life. Hundreds of birds soared through the heavens in great spiraling arcs, their wings suspended in effortless flight. They circled the rooftop, glided from the window ledges to the courtyard walls, and floated on the wind currents like misty clouds. Their silhouettes defined in the moonlight, Demetrios identified them by their size and shape: swallows, cranes, even a flock of white storks, all on their spring migrations north.

Suddenly, the smaller birds broke rank, scattering in multiple directions. If Demetrios had not turned his head at the whoosh of air racing past his face, he never would have seen the owl plummeting into their midst. The great silvery bird dominated the sky, and the night seemed to stop still with fright. From somewhere off to the right came the sound of desperate scrabbling, tiny feet running. A terrified squeak was cut short as the owl swooped silently down and snatched up its prey. The bird alighted briefly on the far edge of the rooftop, the rat gripped in its talons. Golden orange eyes blinked, staring at Demetrios. The owl opened its beak and emitted a deep *hoo-uk hooo,* like the tones of a low-pitched flute. Then the bird spread its wings and took flight. *I-am! I-am!* it screamed. *I-am!* As the owl flew off into the night, the eerie voice faded to a distant keening.

An omen. The owl's cry foretold an imminent death.

Demetrios was sure of that. He pressed his hand against his arm, closed his fingers about the ivory handle. As if of its own volition, the knife slid from its casing. Demetrios turned the dagger over in his palm, feeling its weight. The weapon comforted him, gave him strength.

He had just replaced the dagger in its sheath when he was startled by the strange sound of a sharp *cack-cack,* then silence. It sounded like the call of a partridge, but there was something very odd about it, as though the bird had been choked in midcry. Why would a partridge appear so soon after the attack of the owl? Demetrios gazed down into the courtyard, but he couldn't see the bird.

Again, *cack-cack. Cack-cack.* The cry was louder and more confident—and definitely human. A shepherd's whistle answered, singing two notes. Below, the door of the inn opened and a cloaked figure—a man, by his walk—stepped into the courtyard. The stranger moved swiftly, navigating the obstacles of beasts and baggage with ease. He called out once more, *cack-cack.* He was answered by the whistle. Then he opened the gate to the court-yard. A second man stepped through the gate.

"I've been waiting," the cloaked figure said.

"What do you want? Why did you send for me?"

Demetrios tensed. He recognized the second voice instantly, Judas. The key to locating Jesus had just entered the courtyard.

The cloaked man coughed. "The Council grows impatient. They asked me to speak to you. We need a date, a specific place."

"I can't give you that. Not yet. Trust me. It will be done."

The other man moved closer to Judas, who backed away. "When? When will it be done?"

Judas's voice betrayed his fear. "Not here. The crowds are too large."

"Before Passover?" the stranger said, his voice rising. "Before he arrives in Jerusalem? It can't be done in Jerusalem. We don't want to start an uprising."

"Quiet," Judas warned. "You'll awake the watchman." He turned from the man, studying the courtyard.

"But we have your word?"

Judas faced his companion. "You have my word. It will be done, but sometimes I—" He paused.

"Yes? What is this hesitation I hear? Do you doubt?"

"Not doubt. But you don't walk with him. He's sincere. And the good that he does for the people. The wisdom that comes from his lips . . ."

A brief silence before the cloaked man answered. "The false prophet shall be silenced. He blasphemes every day. You should know that well."

"How can you be so certain? What if—" Judas stopped abruptly. "Shh! Did you hear that? Someone's coming."

"The night watchman. Go!" He pushed Judas out the gate. "Go quickly. We'll talk again. Soon." The man closed the gate and slid the bolt into place. His feet whispered over the ground as he darted across the courtyard to slip silently through the inn's doorway.

Demetrios hesitated only for a moment. Judas had already started down the road. Judas—and the light of the moon—would guide him to Jesus. Gathering up his cloak and staff, he tiptoed down the outside staircase into the night. Demetrios didn't think to reflect on the darker purpose of the conversation he'd overheard from the rooftop, so excited was he at the prospect of things to come. The owl's prophecy was about to be fulfilled.

CHAPTER
TWENTY-FIVE

Demetrios followed behind Judas at what he hoped was a safe distance. The moon was high in the sky, making the man's form clearly visible on the horizon. Although Judas carried no torch or lamp, he jogged at a rapid pace, showing a comfortable familiarity with the route.

Judas made an abrupt turn to the right, leaving the main road to cross into a lush valley. As Demetrios followed him, he thought Judas had detected his presence. He let out his breath slowly, though, when he saw that Judas only paused to drink at a flowing spring and wash his hands. Judas then started toward the cluster of mud-brick houses that rimmed the oasis. This was an older section of Jericho. Herod had erected his palaces along the Wadi Qelt, but other, less wealthy settlers built here, making good use of the rubble of stones to fashion a solid village of small, dusty houses among the palm trees.

Demetrios stood at the crossroads, watching as Judas cast a wary glance to his left and right, but he didn't look behind him. Emboldened, Demetrios moved in closer, trailing behind Judas on a twisting, winding road into a neighborhood where the houses were pushed close together with high courtyard walls that created narrow passageways sprouting off in all directions. Demetrios shivered as he passed under a low-hanging arch. The buildings tilted and pitched, bearing down upon him with a fearful presence.

At that hour of the morning, the streets were deserted, but Demetrios couldn't escape the feeling he was being observed by the village. Several times, he caught glimpses of shadowed movements: a hand quickly dropping a curtain into place, a face peering at him suspiciously from a cracked open door. As he followed Judas through the ramshackle neighborhoods, he felt as though he were descending into the bowels of the underworld where the dead never rested. He was entering a dark place, a place that suffered not only the absence of natural light but a darkness of the spirit as well. He kept close to the high courtyard walls so he couldn't be so easily watched.

Judas turned right again, passed under a rectangular-shaped arch, and ducked into a blind alley. Demetrios followed for a few steps, then stopped. A trap? He couldn't see into the dim passageway. Did Judas wait for him at the dead end? Taking a deep breath, he eased past the arch into an open space bathed in the faint glow of moonlight. The alley split at a square angle, with an open doorway leading to a courtyard on his left and a long, narrow corridor extending straight ahead. The corridor was lined on both sides with high walls. Other than the doorway on his left, there was no exit. Far down the corridor, attached to the courtyard wall, also on his left, an incomplete staircase ascended toward the sky: six broken steps leading to nowhere. Judas had disappeared. Demetrios edged toward the stairs.

Hearing footsteps, Demetrios stopped. Was he being followed? The mysterious person kept walking, pacing on the other side of the doorway Demetrios had slipped past. Judas? Had he seen

Demetrios? Why hadn't Judas entered the courtyard? Ducking behind the broken staircase, Demetrios leaned against the wall.

The stairs had pulled away from the foundation, creating a fissure the width of three fingers and the length of a man's arm. Demetrios peeked through the crack and saw a cramped courtyard in front of a two-room, mud-brick house. A lamp hung on a hook in the front window, but the rest of the house was dark. The courtyard was empty.

Demetrios felt the wall shift under his fingertips before he heard it. A shower of pebbles rained down the broken staircase into the alley. Had anyone else heard? The sound of pacing footsteps by the doorway ceased.

The silhouette of a large man blocked the window of the house, and the light in the doorway suddenly grew brighter. The occupant had set the lamp on a shelf near the entrance. "Is someone there?" the man called.

He received a surprising response. *Cack-cack.* A pause and then again, *cack-cack.* A warning. But to whom? Did Judas believe the man at the inn had followed him? Demetrios held his breath and waited.

The door to the house opened. "Who is it?" The man with the lamp stepped into the courtyard. "I know you're there. Who is out there?" He raised the light to his face, bringing his features into sharp focus: Peter, the fisherman from Galilee, the one who protected Jesus so fiercely at the river. Peter moved warily across the courtyard.

"Master," a voice said quietly in Demetrios's ear. Demetrios whirled around to come face-to-face with his servant, Rufus.

Without a word, Demetrios grabbed Rufus by the shoulders and pressed him against the wall. Demetrios clamped a hand tight over his servant's mouth and shook his head, indicating—he hoped—for Rufus to stay silent. Rufus's shoulders tensed, but he didn't struggle. Demetrios leaned close to the staircase, holding Rufus tight. He breathed lightly into Rufus's ear.

"Who is out there?" Peter called. "I can hear you. You might as well be seen." The steady crunch of Peter's footsteps advanced toward them. As he approached, the light of the lamp pooled through the cracks in the wall. Demetrios's hands slipped with sweat, but he didn't release his grip on Rufus. Demetrios looked up, watching the moon fade into a lightening sky. The wall next to them shook as Peter leaned against it.

"Peter," Judas called from the doorway. "Is that you? Why are you out here?"

Peter hesitated, as though unwilling to quit his search. Then he turned toward the entrance to the courtyard. "Oh, it is you, Judas. I thought—" He paused. "I should ask you the same thing. What are you doing out here? Are you alone?"

The gate squeaked as Judas pulled it shut behind him and stepped into the circle of light from the lamp. "What a ridiculous question." He spoke quickly, the pitch of his voice rising. "I came outside to tend to a problem."

"That's what the pot is for."

"I didn't want to wake anyone." Leaning forward, he took Peter by the elbow. "Come. Let's go inside. I want to talk to you." He guided Peter back to the house.

Breathing a little easier, Demetrios removed his hand from Rufus's mouth. However, he laid a finger over his servant's lips as a warning. Then he pressed his eye to the fissure in the wall and peeked again through the space.

Demetrios had missed part of the conversation. Peter was angry about something Judas said. Judas took a firmer grip on Peter's arm, and his tone became pleading, insistent. "I've been thinking about this. You must speak with him. Convince him of the danger. He'll listen to you."

"We've had this discussion before." Peter eased his arm from Judas's grip. "You know the answer. He wants to pray."

"But now? Before the full light of day? Alone out there in the wilderness?" Judas's tone grew impatient. "No, it's too foolish. We've too many enemies. The authorities suspect him. It would be so easy for him to be arrested. And for what? For nothing. Jerusalem will still be enslaved."

"We're not slaves, Judas." Peter turned to enter the house, but Judas blocked his path.

"You must listen to me!" Judas demanded so loudly that Demetrios flinched. "You don't understand. Jerusalem must be free, free of the Roman boot. This land is ours. It was promised." He leaned forward, nose to nose with Peter. "I beg of you to tell him. Tell him it's time for him to take possession of his throne."

"Take your hand off my shoulder, and let me pass," Peter ordered, staring at Judas's hand.

A brief silence punctuated the night. Demetrios was certain the two men would come to blows. But when Judas finally stepped back, he seemed to have changed. Before, he had been humble, almost obsequious. Now, his voice turned cold, sinister. Judas's malevolence pierced the morning light. "Now I understand." Judas's voice dripped with venom. "You are Simon, the fisherman, the one he named Peter. His rock. His foundation. Peter!" He spat, and the name was like a curse. "Peter who follows his master around like a little lamb and does whatever his master tells him to do. And for this devotion, Peter, does he love you enough?"

"Judas, you know that he loves us equally." He sighed. "And we love you as well. Haven't we trusted you with all of our wealth? You alone carry the purse."

"Pah!" Judas screamed, flinging the bag at his waist to the ground. "This is what I think of your purse. Your money is a cheap substitute for love."

Peter stooped and picked up the purse. He handed it to Judas. "Come, my friend. No more harsh words." He glanced over Judas's shoulder. "Let's go. He is inside, waiting."

After they had entered the house, Demetrios turned to Rufus. "Why are you here?" He kept his voice low. "You should have waited for me at the inn."

"I'm sorry." Rufus's words came out in a breathless whisper. "I saw you leave so abruptly, and I was worried."

"You should have stayed at the inn."

"Who are these people? Do you know them? Have you found Elazar?"

Demetrios flinched, but he did not answer Rufus's question. "Go back," he ordered his servant. "Go back to Tryphon's."

"Yes, Master, I will, but—"

Suddenly, Demetrios rushed at Rufus and slapped a restraining hand over his mouth. "Hush! Someone is coming." He pushed Rufus back against the staircase. "Do not make a sound. Do not move. Do you understand?"

Rufus nodded.

Releasing his servant, Demetrios crept over to the crack in the wall and waited.

Jesus appeared first. He advanced into the courtyard slowly, with a deliberate, ponderous step, and he carried a thick wooden staff for support. Demetrios was impressed by his quiet composure. In contrast to Peter and Judas, Jesus ventured fearlessly into the wilderness.

The three men huddled close, arguing softly. Judas seemed to be encouraging Jesus to return to the safety of the house. But Jesus refused. He raised his arm with a commanding sweep and pointed toward the street. "We'll take the road to Jerusalem. When we reach the wilderness, you must leave me. I have much to pray about, and I choose to do this in solitude."

Demetrios sucked in a quiet breath. At last, he would find Jesus alone.

Judas shuffled his feet, looked down at his hands. "Surely, Rav, you can pray here in the safety of the house. Peter and I will see that the crowds stay away."

"No, Judas, today I go into the wilderness. Alone."

"Rav—"

"Judas—" Peter interrupted. He shook his head, warning Judas not to argue further. They fell silent. Jesus stepped into the alley, and his two disciples followed. The courtyard gate closed quietly behind them.

Pulling his servant back behind the staircase, Demetrios motioned for Rufus to keep his head down. Demetrios could hear them walking through the passageway now. But he couldn't see them. If he couldn't see them, he reasoned, then they couldn't see him. He pressed flat against the wall, listening.

The sound of their footsteps faded. Demetrios crept forward and peered around the staircase. Gone. He straightened up, shaking the tension out of his arms and legs. He had to move quickly now, or he would lose them.

"Master?"

Startled, Demetrios looked back at his servant. He had forgotten Rufus. He cast a worried glance toward the passageway, and then turned to face Rufus. "Go back to the inn. Wait for me there. Remember what I told you and Isaac. You know what to do if I don't return."

"Are you in danger, Master?"

Jesus would be out of his reach soon; he could not delay. "Just go." Without waiting to confirm that Rufus would obey, Demetrios dashed under the archway and into the village streets.

CHAPTER
TWENTY-SIX

The dawn burned off in a crimson flame, slashing the pale blue heavens with streaks of red. A thin sheen of sweat shimmered on Demetrios's face. As Demetrios followed the men out of the lush Jericho valley, the terrain became barren and lifeless. Dun-colored hills rose up on either side of the road, their surface scarred with crumbling caves and outcroppings of rock. Demetrios had traveled this road to Jerusalem with his caravans before, but he had never taken this journey alone. And never for a purpose such as this. He waited for the moment he and Jesus would be alone.

But Peter and Judas were reluctant to leave. Whenever Jesus paused and pointed at the hills, the two argued with him, refusing to turn back to Jericho without him. Worried they would see him, Demetrios lagged farther and farther behind. Now he struggled to keep them in his line of sight.

Jesus slowed, brought his group to a halt. Demetrios backed into the shadows. Peter, Judas, and Jesus resumed their debate, but Demetrios couldn't hear their words. Jesus gestured to his left. Peter stomped his foot and shook his head. Peter started to say something, but Jesus cut him off with a wave of his hand. Then, without another word, Jesus abandoned the road and started up into the hills. Judas and Peter followed.

The steep goat path Jesus had selected twisted in and out of the ridges of rock like a spiraling serpent. Jesus tackled the trail with a light, quick step, hurrying into the wilderness as though he were meeting a lover. Peter and Judas stumbled behind him, grasping for the nearest handhold or foothold. Judas lost his footing once and fell, catching himself with the branches of a bush. Demetrios stayed close behind them and out of sight.

Judas grasped Peter's arm. "A moment. I need to rest."

While Peter waited for Judas to catch his breath, he turned and glanced behind him. Demetrios ducked behind a rock. Had Peter seen him? If so, he said nothing.

Jesus called out, "Shall we continue?" They resumed their climb.

Demetrios peeked out cautiously. Jesus and his two disciples crossed over the crest and disappeared.

Demetrios panicked. What if they continued into the wilderness and he lost them altogether? What if they returned to the road at a different point? What if they knew he had been following them and were waiting for him on the other side?

He should go after them, but he dreaded the climb. Hesitating, Demetrios turned and looked back toward Jericho. There was not another living being anywhere. A fitful gust of wind snaked across the road, trailing a funnel of dust. He was alone here. And vulnerable. He could be preyed upon by wild animals or robbed by thieves, and no one would ever know. He faced the hill again. He had no choice but to continue his pursuit.

Pain shot down Demetrios's twisted leg as he ascended the hill. He jabbed his walking staff into the gritty soil to gain better purchase, but the treacherous, skittery rocks slid and slipped under him with each step. Small thickets of bramble bush carpeted the more stable ground. As Demetrios staggered up the final grade, slapping at the brush with his staff, he wondered if they'd heard him.

At the top, he eased to his knees and crawled to a large, smooth shelf of rock. Leaning over the edge while gripping the rock shelf with his bare hands, he watched Jesus and the two disciples walk across an open flat valley that was at least twenty-five cubits beneath him. The vertical drop made him dizzy. The thought of falling frightened Demetrios, but the possibility of discovery terrified him. What if they looked up, caught the spy in their midst? He had nowhere to hide, and he desperately needed to get closer to them, to hear what they were saying. Using his staff as a wedge, he scooted across the rock, his heels pressing against the hard surface. A chunk of the boulder broke loose, and he was sliding down the hillside, tiny fragments of stone and earth pinging to the valley below.

Demetrios flipped onto his stomach and grabbed at the brush, the dirt—anything to break his fall. He finally thudded to a stop against the base of a huge, round stone formation that jutted out from the earth like a bulbous growth. His staff jabbed into his ribs, snagging in the bushes. Demetrios took a breath, strained not to cough. He wrenched the staff loose, sliding it quietly across the ground. The skin on his hands felt raw, shredded. Silencing the pain, he closed his eyes, waiting beneath the overhang of this rough shelter.

"What was that?" Judas said.

Judas's voice was so loud. How close were they? Did they see him?

"Calm yourself, Judas," Jesus said. "Just a wild goat or a deer.

There are many in these hills."

When Demetrios peeked around the side of the boulder, he was surprised to discover that he had fallen only about halfway. Jesus's close proximity was an illusion, a trick of sound echoing from below. The valley was framed on three sides by sheer, perpendicular cliffs, forming a tomb-like chamber in which even the slightest noise reverberated through the stillness with shocking clarity. Whispers were magnified to resonate like normal speech. When Jesus turned to address his companions, Demetrios could understand every word.

"I want you to leave now," Jesus ordered. "Return to Jericho and wait for me there."

"But, Rav," Judas argued, "you know it's not safe here. This is foolish. You should—"

With an insistent gesture, Jesus brushed his hand across Judas's cloak. "My friend, unstop your ears. You do not listen. You do not hear. I tell you again that the time has not come for the Son of Man. Go back to Jericho and wait for me there. This is not your place."

Judas shook his head and backed away. Peter placed a restraining hand on his arm. He turned to Jesus. "Rav, we'll do as you say. We'll go back to the house."

"If you do not return by dark," Judas added, "I'll search for you."

"No," Jesus said.

Peter tugged at Judas's arm. "Come, let us go that way." He pointed to a rugged path a few cubits from where Demetrios hid.

Terrified of being discovered, Demetrios ducked behind the boulder. He could hear Judas grumbling. More rocks tumbled into the valley when Judas slipped and shouted to Peter for help. "Give me your hand." Peter laughed, dragging Judas to his feet.

Demetrios waited for them to find him. How would he answer their questions? What reason could he give for being in this place?

They reached the top of the hill. Then their voices and steps trailed away as they started down the other side to the road.

Demetrios released a long, labored sigh and emerged from his hiding place. He crept across the hillside to the path and looked down. Jesus stood immobile and silent in the valley below, with his back to Demetrios, staring at something only he could see.

Demetrios took a single step. Then another. Jesus remained still, imprisoned in thought. His courage growing, Demetrios scrambled down to the valley floor. He stopped less than ten cubits from Jesus's back. He slid the dagger from its casing with a slithering, hungry hiss. Now.

Jesus moved. He jerked his head back. Uttering a violent, unintelligible cry, he grabbed the shoulders of his robe, ripped it from his back, and pitched face forward into the dust.

The wind gusted, whistling through the valley, cold and chilling. Demetrios shivered but Jesus, his back now laid bare to the sun, was soaked with his own perspiration. Jesus's shoulder blades writhed and jerked beneath his dark brown skin. Several times he cried out. No words. A loud, guttural moan. Like a wounded animal, he clawed at the earth, tearing out large clods of soil with his long fingers.

Demetrios froze, the blade in his hand poised. It would be so easy to plunge his knife into the hollow of Jesus's back. But that wasn't what Demetrios wanted. He planned to whisper in Jesus's ear the last words he would ever hear: "The Roman shall remain dead. My secrets will remain secret." Demetrios held his knife high, determined to wait until Jesus rose and faced him.

Jesus did not rise, but he spoke, "Abba."

So unexpected. Not a cry for mercy, but an endearment.

Demetrios stepped back.

Jesus recited the first words of a prayer. "Abba, Abba." He pressed his hands together in front of his face. "My father, my dear father." His voice choked with swallowed tears.

My dear father? What did he mean? Demetrios cast an uneasy glance to his left. No one was on the hill. He looked at the cliffs. They were too steep, too sheer to hide anyone. Had Jesus planned to meet someone here? His father? And what was a father? Nothing but a man who beat you daily—who crippled you without a thought, who sold you into slavery for a pair of donkeys and a few coins. Father! The very word was poison in Demetrios's mouth. Demetrios spat.

Jesus continued to cry out, a pitiful weeping lament that rose and fell in pitch with each sweeping gust of wind. "Father, my fa-a-ther-r!"

Demetrios stood as rooted as a tree. More than anything, he wanted Jesus to shut up, to stop screaming that infernal word.

Jesus's fevered chanting accelerated in tempo, growing louder and louder until miraculously, he was quiet.

Demetrios watched him, waiting. He repositioned the knife in his grip. Now was the time. Now. He raised his weapon.

A twig snapped nearby and sent a flock of birds whirling into the sky. A woman emerged from a cleft in the cliffs. Stone brought to life. Demetrios blinked. Had she been there all along? It didn't matter. Demetrios and Jesus were no longer the only two human beings in the valley.

The knife still clutched in his hand, Demetrios backed away. He turned the dagger over in his palm, running his finger across the flat of the finely honed blade. Too late. He had delayed too long. He slipped the knife back into its sheath and fastened the hasp. Later. After she left. He sat down in the dust to watch, wondering what she would do when she saw him. Would she run?

Her attention focused on the motionless form of Jesus, the woman took no notice of Demetrios. She tiptoed toward Jesus with short mincing steps, moving forward and then to the side. A heavy veil covered her hair and most of her face; her patched woolen cloak, woven with silken threads, draped over her arms down to her fingertips. Demetrios leaned forward, stunned. He was gazing upon the woman from Capernaum, the woman who had haunted his dreams.

Jesus pushed back to his knees, his head still bowed. When he spoke, his voice was firm. "My daughter, what is it you wish from me?" He didn't look at her.

The woman stilled. Then, like a moth that beats its wings against the sticky chains of a spider's web, she flailed out her arms and spun on her heel, darting away. She had nearly reached the seclusion of the cliffs when Jesus called out to her. "Wait!" He sat upright and crooked his finger at her. "Come."

His gentle tone had the desired effect. Pausing, she looked back. He nodded. "Come here, my daughter." His words were so soft they were nearly drowned out by the moaning wind. "Closer. Where I can see you."

The woman obeyed.

When she was less than an arm's length away from him, Jesus stood and faced her. Demetrios, an unwilling participant in the events that were unfolding, rose also. His fascination drew him to her in a manner he couldn't explain. She was a delicate creature, with the ethereal quality of a jewel of sunlight trapped in the sparkling drops of early morning dew. Like the glittering beads of moisture—which were doomed to disappear with the first heat of the day—she could vanish in an instant. She danced from side to side, swaying slightly with the effort.

Pushing back her sleeve, she extended a bandaged stump to Jesus.

Demetrios drew in a sharp breath and stumbled, his legs wobbling.

He shook his head in disbelief, but he couldn't deny what he saw. This enchanting, mercurial lady had no fingers, no hands. She had nothing but useless stumps of flesh bound in filthy cotton wrappings, which were streaked and stained with blood and dirt. When the heavy folds of her cloak fell away from her arms, what should have been strong, healthy limbs were also revealed as dying appendages, scabbed and peeling from disease. She was a leper.

Oblivious to her deformity, Jesus never even glanced at her stumps but reached out instead for the veil that shrouded her features. Gently sliding his palms over the top of her head, he pushed the covering back from her face and neck and let it drop to her shoulders. He then gripped her by her upper arms and examined her closely, looking at her as if he had met her once before and could not recall her name.

She stood perfectly quiet, her head tilted toward Jesus. Tragically, her face, too, had been ravaged. Her skin was pitted and marked by former scars, like a sloping pasture eroded by rainfall. Her lips, disfigured by a missing flap of flesh, were twisted into a perpetual snarl. When she attempted to smile, she exposed decaying teeth set in putrid, infected gums.

His breath escaping in rapid gasps, Demetrios rubbed his hands against his beggar's cloak; he needed water and salt to clean his body, sour wine to purify his skin and clothing. Had he touched her in Capernaum? He had wanted to. He couldn't remember.

An odor of rotting flesh rolled on the breeze, like the smell of the garbage in Marcus's refuse trench.

"No," Demetrios moaned.

She heard him. Her head turned toward him, her face registering shock at Demetrios's presence. A tear slid down her scarred cheek.

Demetrios knew she had seen his disgust, his horror. Yet, he was drawn to her. When Jesus removed her veil, her glossy, ebony tresses flowed over her shoulders and down her back like a shimmering curtain. She raised her head, and that same shining hair reflected thousands of pinpoints of light, brilliant hues of blue and gold that whirled around her like sparks from a fire.

Demetrios held out his hand, his fingertips aching with desire; she was both hideous and glorious to behold. He closed his eyes, the memory of the woman who haunted his dreams, returning unbidden: Soft, sensuous hair. Black as obsidian. Teasing his sleep, whispering against his skin. The hushed tread of her footstep upon the earthen floor, the tantalizing scent of her perfume. Nardinum. Traces of it wafted in the biting wind.

"Rav," she said softly.

The sound of her voice made Demetrios open his eyes.

Ignoring Demetrios, the leper woman gazed at Jesus. "Heal me." She bowed to him. "Help me."

That voice, calling out to Demetrios in his dreams, Demetrios, Demetrios. Help me. The woman from Capernaum was a leper. Was this his fate? Was he so repulsive that only a leper—someone more ugly than he—would find him desirable?

Demetrios dropped to his knees. A burning pain shot through his chest; the violent pounding of his heart would not stop. She was beautiful. He wanted her to be whole. "Save her," he croaked as he pressed his hands against his aching ribs. "Please." He blinked; he loved her.

Jesus pulled the woman closer. Then, still holding her pitiful, bound stumps within his grip, he brought them to his lips and graced the dirty wrappings with a tender kiss.

Pushing to his feet, Demetrios grasped his staff and edged closer to them. Did she know Demetrios loved her? He had thought of her so often. But what could this charlatan offer? So many wild claims about his powers: bringing the dead to life, becoming king of the Jews, miraculous healings of the maimed and diseased. Was any of it true? And why did she come here? Why now? Demetrios's mind reeled with desire, loss, fear, anger.

They stood a short distance from Demetrios, studying one another with an intensity that made Demetrios tremble. Jesus released her. "Undo your bindings so that I may see."

The leper woman made no reply, but when Jesus took hold of the cloths that covered her wrists, she shook her head and tried to back away. Demetrios understood. He knew she was afraid. She didn't want him—or anyone—to see the magnitude of her deformities.

Jesus, undaunted by her refusal, peeled back the top layer of fabric, patiently unwinding each dirty, gray piece of cloth, strip by strip. The tattered cotton bands dropped to her feet in large, twisting coils.

The woman stared at her feet in shame. Jesus nodded, smiled. His fingers trailed down her arms, lingering at each sore. She gasped. He turned her stumps over, enclosed the damaged flesh in his hands, squeezing tight, the blue veins in her skin pulsing. She looked at him, her eyes wide, frightened. "Rav?"

Again, the reassuring smile.

Demetrios moaned, his knees weak, his stomach churning.

The leper woman screamed, and Demetrios fumbled for his dagger.

Not a scream of terror but of amazement. She pushed Jesus from her and screamed again with joy, the sound trilling like a ringing bell. Clutching her veil, she pulled it over her head, masking all but her eyes. Then she snatched it away, twirling it in the air as she danced around Jesus. Finally, she stopped and collapsed at his feet. She wept, drying her tears with the hem of his robe.

Demetrios was stunned. What had happened?

She raised her arms up to Jesus and touched his cloak with long, tapered fingers. The flesh on her palms was pink and raw, with the mottled flush of a newborn babe. Demetrios rubbed his eyes. Healthy new skin did not grow from oozing sores; hands did not appear where there had been nothing but stumps. Who was this Jesus? Had Demetrios witnessed a miracle or an illusion? Where did Jesus find the power to heal a leper? Demetrios shook his head, still disbelieving. It had to be a trick. Demetrios stared at her more closely. Why did she look so familiar?

Jesus stroked her hair, his touch tentative, halting. He seemed embarrassed by this outpouring of affection. "Stand up." He coaxed her to her feet. "No, do not thank me." He held her at a distance as she struggled to embrace him.

Jesus gave her a slight shake and forced her to face him. "No," he repeated, a harsh edge coming into his voice. "I've done nothing. I am unworthy of such praise." He paused for a moment, his head bowed. Then, looking directly into her eyes, he said, "If you must give thanks, then give it to the One who truly deserves your gratitude and praise. Give your thanks to my father."

Again, that intimate term—Abba. My father, my dear father. But there was no father here. The three of them were alone. Unless . . . Demetrios glanced uneasily at the cliff walls that surrounded them. He felt plagued by doubts; his fingers tightened around the handle of his walking staff.

He placed his hands on both sides of her face and pulled her close, studying her. "What is your name, my child?"

"Tabitha."

The word swept Demetrios's breath away. Tabitha? His Tabitha? The shining black hair, her dancing walk, the scent of nardinum on the breeze. Could it be? And then he knew: Tabitha of the oasis, the woman at Capernaum, the leper woman here— they were all the same. Demetrios extended his hand toward her. Tabitha, oh, Tabitha! I've always loved you. I've called out for you in my dreams. Tabitha. Even now, my voice is silent, but I still cry for you. Will you not come to me? Swift and fleet of foot as your namesake, the gazelle, you run from me. Tabitha, come to me.

"Tabitha," Jesus said, repeating her name aloud.

Demetrios startled, surprised to hear his own thoughts spoken by another. He glared at Jesus and Tabitha, jealous of their intimacy.

Jesus placed his palm on his chest. "I've done nothing but look into your heart. The beauty I saw there is now revealed for all the world to cherish." He smiled. Suddenly, he turned away. "Go now." He jerked his head to one side. "Your future awaits you."

Tabitha hesitated, a bewildered expression on her face. She stepped toward Jesus, stopped, turned halfway around, and paused, surprised to see Demetrios so close.

In that instant, time was suspended. Jesus started to walk away and did not look back to acknowledge Tabitha or Demetrios. Tabitha watched Demetrios, saying nothing. Demetrios remained quiet, afraid she would bolt. He wanted her to come to him; he wanted to hold her, to touch her, so that he could know the truth for himself. She recognized him; he could see it in her eyes. Why didn't she speak?

Tabitha cast a quick glance at Jesus. Then, without another word, she darted for the cliffs behind her, disappearing as suddenly and as swiftly as a puff of smoke.

At the same time, Jesus started up the hill, taking the same path Peter and Judas had chosen earlier.

Demetrios started after him. "Wait!" He stopped, whirled around to face the far cliffs. Tabitha was gone. He spun back toward the hill just in time to see Jesus ascending the final rise. His voice dropped to a whisper. "Wait."

Jesus crossed the summit and vanished.

CHAPTER
TWENTY-SEVEN

Demetrios could have followed Jesus over the hill. He could have turned and pursued Tabitha, exploring the cliff walls for the crevice that swallowed her. But he remained alone in the canyon, his confusion whirling like the dusty wind. What was real and what had been an illusion? He had no answer.

When Demetrios finally ascended the path Peter and Judas had taken, the sun was high above him, burning down on his head with a fierce light. Demetrios slipped and skidded down the final steps of the trail to the Jerusalem road and stopped in a sheltered overhang of rock at the base of the hill. Tired and thirsty, he paused to tip his waterskin to his mouth.

A solitary figure ran toward him, waving. Had Jesus come back? But then the man called out, "Master, Master!" Demetrios lowered his waterskin and waited.

"I thought I told you to go back to the inn." Demetrios didn't speak too harshly, for he was relieved his servant had disobeyed him. They could walk back together. With both Tabitha and Jesus gone, there was nothing else Demetrios could do today.

Rufus flushed and ducked his head. "I'm sorry. I know I was supposed to go back to the inn, but I thought those men might hurt you, so I followed you. But then all of you went up into the hills, and I—I didn't." He stared pensively at the imposing hills. "I should have gone after you, but I was afraid, so I hid until I saw you come back. I prayed to Mercury for your safety. But still, I shouldn't have let my fear keep me from my duty. I should have protected you." He held out his hands, palms up. "I've done many wrong things. You can punish me now."

Demetrios shook his head. "You know I don't hit you." Taking his servant by the arm, he said, "Walk with me and be quiet. I have much . . . to think about." He had gone only a short distance when he stopped short. "Wait." Demetrios turned Rufus to face him. "Did you say you hid?"

Rufus nodded.

"Where? Where did you hide?"

Rufus pointed to a gully running parallel to the road and choked with brush and the rubble from rains. "There. I followed you all the way from Jericho, but I was careful to stay out of sight." He glanced at Demetrios. "When you climbed the hill, I waited here along the road. Then I heard voices, and I ran and crouched down in the ditch." His gaze flickered over the shadows that closed in on them from the hills above. "I don't like this place."

Demetrios gripped Rufus's shoulders. "Voices? Whose? Tell me exactly what you saw."

"Just those two men, Master. I swear. The big one, the man they called Peter, and that other one. I don't remember his name, but he got angry at Peter in Jericho, and he made those funny sounds. He came to the house that time with Elazar, remember?"

Demetrios nodded. "Yes, Judas. After those two men came

263

back, you didn't see the third man? The one they called Jesus of Nazareth?"

"No, just those two. And then when you didn't return, I knew something bad had happened." He looked down at his feet, refusing to face Demetrios. "I'm sorry. I should have followed you up that path."

"Why didn't you?"

"I was too scared."

Demetrios smiled. "Well, as you can see, nothing happened to me. But you're certain that Jesus never came back to the road? And what about a woman? Did you see a woman come out of the hills?"

"What? Why would a woman—" He stopped midsentence, his eyes focused on something behind Demetrios. "Run!" He pulled Demetrios forward.

Demetrios stumbled, caught his balance. He whirled around. Three men—strangers—rushed at them.

"Bandits!" Rufus pushed Demetrios again. Hard. "Run, Master. Run."

Demetrios ran. Something—a rock, a foot?—snagged at his ankle and sent him sprawling face forward. He hit the ground with a thump, and his staff flew from his hands. He lay still for a moment, stunned and breathless. Before he could push himself upright, a pair of knees ground into his back, pressing his face into the dirt. He coughed and strained to throw off his attacker. His dagger. He had to get to his dagger.

"Give me your purse," a voice said into Demetrios's ear. The man's weight pressed Demetrios down. Two hands closed about his throat. Squeezing. Black spots danced before Demetrios's eyes. He couldn't breathe. Then the pressure eased slightly, and the voice said, "If you fight me, I'll kill you. Do you understand? Speak."

"Yes." The single word rasped from Demetrios's lips. He swallowed, tasting the grit of the road in his mouth.

Still keeping his weight on Demetrios's back, the bandit removed his hands from Demetrios's throat and began fumbling with Demetrios's clothes, pulling and probing, searching for the cord that bound the purse to Demetrios's body. Demetrios was vaguely aware of activity behind them, shuffling, stomping feet. Grunts and groans. The sounds of a fight, a battle fought without words. Suddenly, he heard Rufus's voice rise above the melee. "Get off. Get off of him."

The bandit on Demetrios's back grasped the cord of Demetrios's purse and tugged, snapping it free. "I've got it!" he shouted, sitting back on Demetrios's legs. "I've got the purse."

Demetrios struggled to roll the man off of him, but someone did the work for him, grabbing the bandit and pulling him back. Demetrios staggered to his feet. Behind him, Rufus called out his name. There was a thud, the sound of a body falling to the ground, but Demetrios did not look back. He reached for his knife.

Demetrios slashed at the figure moving in front of him, the blade whistling through empty air. Nothing. He turned and struck again. Blood spurted over his hand. His fingers gripping the slippery handle tight, Demetrios lashed out again. Missed. The man closest to him cried, "Why you dirty—you cut me!" The bandit lunged toward him.

Demetrios saw the kick coming but couldn't dodge quickly enough. The wounded bandit struck Demetrios's wrist, sending the dagger spiraling into the air. Demetrios jumped to the side, teetered off-balance. The bandit's second kick hit Demetrios in the knee, and his legs gave way. Demetrios dropped to the ground, pain erupting in his leg, his hands partially breaking his fall. The third kick caught him in the ribs. He heard the crack before he felt the new explosion of pain. He doubled over, curled up into a ball.

"Where is that knife?" the bandit said. "I'll kill him."

Two pairs of feet passed in front of Demetrios's face. "It's nothing," one of them said. "Just a small cut. Forget it." Coins jingled. "I have the purse. Let's go."

Sensing another kick, Demetrios jerked back, still pressing his hand against his injured ribs. He rolled over, sliding off the road, down a rocky slope choked with thick, thorny bushes. He was falling, falling, descending into a void.

Buzzing. Demetrios awoke to the sound: a low hum that droned in his ears with incessant monotony. It made him sleepy. He closed his eyes, listening to the drone fade away.

When Demetrios opened his eyes again, the buzzing was still there, but louder, much closer to him than before. He squinted at the sky. Demetrios passed his hand across his eyes and realized he was staring at the blinding sun. How much time had passed? Where was Jesus? The woman? Rufus?

Then it all came back to him, and he wondered again where everyone had gone. Demetrios rolled onto his side, pressing his fingers against each sore rib. The bruises were deep and tender. He couldn't tell if any bones were broken. He sucked in a ragged breath, grateful the pain didn't completely cripple him. He could move. Determined not to die here, alone, in this hostile wilderness, he pushed to his knees.

The buzzing called to Demetrios. Dragging himself forward with raw and bruised hands, Demetrios crawled toward the sound. He pressed the bushes down flat and stared at the scene before him. Great black flies swarmed over a man lying on his side in the ditch. The man's head was twisted at an odd angle, as though he were gazing at something far off in the distance, and his chin rested in a pool of mud. The cloud of flies hovered over the mud.

Demetrios didn't speak or call out. If this was one of the bandits, it could be a trap. He touched the man's foot.

He was answered by a soft groan.

Demetrios had seen that sandal before, in his own courtyard. "Rufus, are you hurt?"

Rufus didn't answer.

"Never mind," Demetrios told him. "Don't speak. I'll help you. Just rest quietly."

Rufus opened his eyes. His right eye, swollen to a narrow slit, squinted at the afternoon light. The left eye, wide open and clear, gazed at Demetrios and yet, did not see him. When Demetrios leaned close, he noticed the pupil was dilated; the eye focused on a place high above Demetrios's shoulder. Demetrios waved the flies away from his servant's face. A large purple bruise swelled across Rufus's right cheek. Clots of dried blood blackened the flesh around his nose. If it had not been for the familiar shock of tangled reddish-brown hair curling over Rufus's brow, Demetrios wouldn't have recognized him. "Rufus, can you hear me? I'm here," Demetrios said, panicked, worried for Rufus's life.

Rufus blinked.

"Water. You need water. My water bag is lost. Where is yours?" Demetrios parted the bushes and spotted the bag caught on a thorny branch near his servant's extended hand. "Never mind. I found it."

The bag had been punctured by the branch and was drained nearly dry, but there was still a small amount of liquid in the bottom. Demetrios tilted the waterskin carefully and squeezed a few drops onto his servant's lips, watching in dismay as the water beaded up on Rufus's closed mouth.

"Can you drink? Just a little. Here. Let me raise your head, and we will try again."

Demetrios bit his lip to keep from crying out when he cradled Rufus's head in his arm. The back of his servant's skull was soft, pulpy, and his blood soaked through Demetrios's clothes. "Good." He struggled to keep his voice calm and held the waterskin closer to Rufus's mouth. "Just a small sip. You can do it."

Rufus licked at the water trickling over his lips. Then he closed his one good eye.

Demetrios eased Rufus's head back to the ground and rested his ear on his servant's chest. Beneath the wheeze of Rufus's lungs, he heard a soft, muted thump. The beat of a heart too large for its owner. Rufus was brave back there, braver than anyone Demetrios had known, and Demetrios was as determined as that heartbeat. He would not let his servant die. Not here. Not now.

Demetrios stripped off his clothes and ripped up his cloak to make bandages for Rufus. He set aside some of the rags to tie around his ribs; the rest he planned to use to bind up Rufus's wounds. "You just rest. I'll take care of you." He laid out the pieces of cloth. "You can even have my walking staff. I haven't found it, but it's here somewhere. And if you can't walk, then I'll carry you." He had to keep talking. As long as Rufus listened to him, Demetrios could keep him alive. "I'll take you back to the inn. I'm sure we can find a physician in Jericho."

Now dressed in only his loincloth, Demetrios stared at his own naked body. He had always been ashamed of his appearance, but Rufus had treated him with dignity and kindness. He had never questioned the scars on Demetrios's body. Demetrios touched the new bruises that blanketed his torso. These scars—unlike those from his life as a slave—were earned.

Raising his servant's head, Demetrios placed a pad of cloth

against the wound. The gash spanned the width of two fingers; the bandage flooded quickly with fresh blood. As he worked to bind the pad in place, he felt bits of bone and tissue sliding beneath his fingertips. He glanced at Rufus, wondering how the man could endure such pain without crying out. "I'm trying to be gentle, Rufus. Tell me if I'm hurting you, and I'll stop."

Demetrios looked at the sky; the sun had begun to drop. Darkness was coming soon. How could he take Rufus to safety then? He wondered if he could carry Rufus in his arms. Gently, Demetrios brushed the matted hair from his servant's face. Before Demetrios could move him, he had to tie up Rufus's wounds more securely.

The bleeding had slowed, but the pad kept slipping. Demetrios wrapped a second piece of cloth around Rufus's brow, and then another and another, until he had swaddled him with a thick layer. When he was finished, he laid Rufus's head in his own lap. His servant's face had taken on a gray pallor, and he had been quiet for far too long. Demetrios stroked his cheek. "A few more drops of water." He raised the waterskin and dribbled the liquid onto Rufus's lips. Much to his surprise, Rufus opened his one good eye.

Demetrios tried to smile. He didn't want Rufus to be afraid. "Don't talk. But if you can hear me, blink."

Rufus blinked.

This time, Demetrios's smile was genuine. "Good, now listen to me. I'm going to carry you to Jericho. We'll find help there. I don't want to drop you, so I'll need your belt to bind you to my body. Will you let me do that?"

As Demetrios reached to untie the rope belt, Rufus groaned and blinked more rapidly. Demetrios's hands hovered over his servant's waist as he hesitated. "What is it? Do you want to tell me something?"

269

Rufus blinked quickly several times, closed his eye for a long moment, and then began blinking it again.

"I see. Just a word or two. You need your rest."

Demetrios placed his ear close to his servant's mouth. He was startled to hear Rufus's rapid and shallow breaths. It sounded like an animal panting in fear, but he knew Rufus was not afraid. Rufus was brave. "Yes," Demetrios said softly. "I'm here."

For a long time, Rufus made no sound other than that strange chuffing. Then he spoke. "S-Sorry."

A flutter of air whispered across Demetrios's cheek, and Rufus was silent again.

Demetrios waited, his tears falling freely on Rufus's face. But there were no more words. No more breaths.

Chapter
Twenty-Eight

Demetrios lay next to Rufus's body until evening, reluctant to leave his servant, reluctant to give him up to a grave. Finally, under the cold glitter of starlight, Demetrios embraced Rufus one final time. The heat had slowly receded from the tender-hearted Rufus he loved. Demetrios kissed his forehead—cold now—and flopped back into the dirt. He wanted to sleep next to his servant, to rest there until Rufus could walk by his side again.

The sound of breaking branches and low grunts in the brush near the ditch brought Demetrios back, made him aware he and Rufus were still in danger. The scavengers that roamed these hills had caught the scent of death on the air, and they were hungry. Demetrios sat up, peering into the growing darkness of the wilderness.

The light of the full moon floated over the hills. The rocks stood out in bas relief, but there were also unrecognizable shadows, shapes that shifted and changed form with the breath of the light breeze. When Demetrios heard the creature rummaging nearby, he gathered up a handful of rocks and sat back, listening.

The animal circled around him, panting softly. As it sidled closer, it rumbled a low growl. Demetrios guessed it was a jackal or a wild dog, a nocturnal beast that preyed upon the weak and the injured. He scraped his feet in the dirt, hoping to scare the animal away. The tops of the bushes swayed as the jackal backed off and deflected to the left. Then the animal paused, and the bushes were still. The eerie hush of the night was broken by the jackal's wild howl, a high-pitched wail that made Demetrios tremble. The creature was cautious but not afraid.

"Get out of here!" Demetrios pitched his handful of stones in the general direction of the jackal. He hit his target. Yelping, the beast darted off into the brush. Demetrios waited, listening to the animal's retreat. Balance unsteady, he pushed to his feet. Every joint in his body ached. The trail of bruises across his side and chest made it difficult to take a deep breath. He wanted to fall down into the ditch, but he had a duty to perform, a debt to repay. He needed to bury Rufus.

A proper burial dictated that Rufus's body be washed and wrapped in a shroud. Demetrios gazed helplessly at the torn sections of his cloak scattered at his feet. Rufus's own clothes were soiled with blood and dirt. Laying the strips of fabric out side by side, he arranged them like the pieces of a large puzzle. Some sections were long enough to tie around the body, but he would have to place the other pieces on top of Rufus. A primitive solution, but it was the best he could do.

Grasping Rufus under the arms, Demetrios dragged him across the ground to the shroud. He tried not to look at Rufus's feet as they bounced and scraped over the rocky terrain. The dead felt no pain, but Demetrios regretted the injuries all the same.

Once Demetrios had Rufus positioned on the mosaic of fabric, he crossed Rufus's arms and folded his servant's hands together. For the first time, Demetrios noticed the broken and blood-caked finger on Rufus's right hand. One of the bandits had ripped the ring Demetrios had given to Rufus from his servant's finger. Demetrios draped the broken finger with a piece of cloth. "You should have given the ring to them. Perhaps they would have spared you." Even as he spoke the words, he knew they were a lie. Rufus hadn't died for a ring; he had died trying to save his master.

Tugging the cloth strips around Rufus's body, Demetrios tied them in a knot to hold them in place. He then bound the smaller pieces of fabric he had laid on top of Rufus with the length of rope his servant had used for a belt. The substitute shroud fell short, as it failed to cover Rufus's face and lower legs.

Demetrios straightened out Rufus's bent knees and pushed the legs together, running his hands over the battered and bruised feet. If Rufus had died in Tiberias, Demetrios would have ordered that his body be placed in a tomb, a shelter of rock with Rufus's name inscribed above the entrance: "Rufus, good and faithful servant to Demetrios of Tiberias." Rufus deserved more than to be left in a shallow ditch by the roadside. Demetrios patted his servant's feet again, knowing that he had nothing more to offer now.

He crawled up to Rufus's head. The clotted blood had left a black stain on Rufus's scalp. Under the luminescent reflection of the moon, it looked like dried mud. Rufus's face was shrunken, smaller, caved in on itself. His good eye remained open, staring at the full moon. Carefully, Demetrios pressed his finger over Rufus's open eye and eased the lid closed. "If I had a silver coin, even a single denarius, I would place it between your lips to pay Charon for your passage. But I have no money, Rufus. They took my purse."

He spied a gleam of shine in the dirt and pried out a bent metal ring. After wiping it clean on his own loincloth, Demetrios whispered, "Tabitha's earring."

Wiping his eyes with the back of his hand, he placed it inside Rufus's mouth, under his tongue. "Charon." He paused, looking down at the ground. "I know this has no value to you, but please accept this as my token payment for my servant, Rufus. When I return to Tiberias, I will—" He choked, the words lost to him.

Blinking rapidly, Demetrios fought back the tears. He had no time to grieve. Not now. He had failed Rufus in life; he would not fail him in death. He wiped the dirt from Rufus's face and set to work.

The ditch they had been thrown into was fed by runoff from the winter rains, providing a fertile home for weeds and brush. Thickets of scrub acacia clogged the shallow wash. Clumps of thistle and thorny lyceum flourished beneath the branches of the stunted trees, the ideal setting for animals and people alike to become lost in, but not a good place to dig a grave.

Ignoring the press of the needle-thorns into his flesh, Demetrios leaned against the acacia trees and broke off as many branches as he could. He needed to clear enough space to lay Rufus out flat so he could hide the body from scavengers. The smaller thistles ripped out easily from the soft soil beneath the trees. Demetrios set these aside in a pile.

Dry leaves crackled. A low growl rumbled in the brush. The jackal had returned. Demetrios grasped a broken acacia branch and slapped it against the trunk of the tree. "Go away!" He struck the tree again, the crack reverberating in the night. "Go away . . ." His voice trailed off into the darkness. He heard the jackal pause, turn and ease back, but sensing Demetrios's weakness, the beast continued to circle at a distance. Waiting.

Demetrios gathered another armload of brush. He would bury Rufus so completely the jackal would never find the body.

"I was always fair to you, Rufus, wasn't I?" Demetrios said as he carried more of the acacia branches to the pile. "And I saved you from being sent to the slave market, took you into my home." He plucked a thorn from his palm. "Rufus, do you remember how I told you to buy our bread from Elisheba? I wanted you to be with her. I know how much you loved her. You had the love I've always wished for, did you know that? When I return to Tiberias . . ." he choked out, wondering if he would return. "When I return, I will tell Elisheba you loved her unto death." He ripped out another bunch of thistles, set them aside. Demetrios sighed, thinking about Rufus's objections to taking this journey. The soothsayer had predicted the truth. It was too late now. All he could do now was honor Rufus's life with a decent burial.

Demetrios clawed at more hidden clumps of brush, then paused, breathing hard from his labor. One of the bushes oozed sap that made his skin itch, and although his sweat stung his eyes, he was reluctant to wipe his face. He stepped back to survey his work.

The grave was not as deep as he would have liked, but he had scraped the earth away to a layer of solid rock. He could dig no deeper. Although he had cleared most of the ground, some stubby growth remained, rooted deeply in the stone. Rufus would just have to rest on top of the flattened weeds.

He turned to tend to the body. When he took hold of his servant's ankles, he discovered that the body had begun to stiffen, making it much more difficult to drag Rufus back to the ditch than it had been to lay him out. Demetrios maneuvered his servant to the edge of the ditch and knelt beside him. "Forgive me, Rufus, for this rough treatment." Wheezing with the effort, he pushed Rufus into the shallow grave.

The body slid sideways into the trench where it snagged on the clumps of undergrowth. Demetrios stepped into the grave to straddle Rufus's waist; shooting pains in his legs and ribs reminded Demetrios he had not escaped this encounter without injury. Ignoring his own discomfort, Demetrios wrapped his arms around Rufus's shoulders and grasped him in a tight hug so he could reposition Rufus properly. Demetrios tried not to look at Rufus's face, for he couldn't bear anymore to see the beating his servant had suffered. This time, the body slipped easily into place.

Demetrios climbed out of the grave and returned to the brush pile. He had cleared enough thistles and acacia limbs to cover Rufus for his eternal sleep. Slowly, carefully, he placed the broken branches and weeds over his servant, arranging them so that not even a fingertip was exposed. When he took a step back and glanced up at the road, he was pleased to see how well he had concealed Rufus's presence. A chance passerby would have to look for the grave to know that it was there. With the first part of his work finished, he began the next step: piling on the rocks that would protect Rufus from the vultures and jackals.

It had been easier when he could still see Rufus's body, when he knew that his servant was still beside him. Demetrios looked at the pile of branches and felt even more alone.

Would he ever return to the safety of Tiberias? He was naked and carried no purse, no coin, no weapon for protection.

He glanced uneasily at the sky, watching the moon. Already it seemed to have moved to the west. He picked up a couple of fist-sized rocks and laid them on the grave.

Without explanation and without Rufus, he could not go back to his caravan in this condition. He decided to return to the inn and ask Tryphon, the innkeeper, for help. The man kept a mean establishment, but Demetrios had paid him well for their bed. The least Tryphon could do would be to give Demetrios a cloak and a couple of denarii. Then Demetrios could find his caravan, or another, and continue the journey to Jerusalem. After Jerusalem? He didn't know.

Reluctant to leave Rufus alone so soon, Demetrios gathered more stones and gravel and tossed them haphazardly toward the grave. Whenever he paused to catch his breath, the muscles in his legs spasmed. Several times, he stopped and stomped his feet and slapped his thighs and calves. But he never paused for long. The moon glided slowly across the sky, moving ever closer to dawn, and Demetrios pushed onward. At last, the grave was ready for a marker, for a single slab of stone that would help him find this place when he returned.

Using a flat spade-shaped chunk of rock, he chipped away at the dirt around a chunk of granite. The crystal flecks would sparkle in the sunlight, making this slab a fine choice for Rufus's headstone. As Demetrios dug into the earth, something flipped up and struck him in the knee. He picked it up and turned it over in his hand. His dagger.

Demetrios's first impulse was to throw it back into the brush—the dagger had failed to protect him and Rufus—but he paused. The knife was still beautiful, and it could be useful. Demetrios swiped the weapon on his loincloth. The blade was undamaged. He rubbed the handle until it was clean. Lapis lazuli eyes stared back at him. Demetrios slid the dagger into the sheath still strapped to his arm.

Once the rough grave marker was wedged in place, Demetrios pushed to his feet and climbed out of the ditch. From his vantage point on the road, he could see nothing but a small mound of freshly turned dirt. He started toward the inn and froze, aware that something had moved with him in the same direction. Two pairs of golden eyes blinked in the darkness. The jackals watched.

"Go!" Demetrios shouted, waving his arms.

He turned back for one last look at Rufus's grave. "Good-bye Rufus. I will come back for you."

The jackals howled.

CHAPTER
TWENTY-NINE

"Open the door!" Demetrios pounded again on the wooden gate to Tryphon's Inn. The watchman was either ignoring him or asleep. Demetrios had no intention of staying at the place another night, but he wanted food and water and something to wear before leaving for Jerusalem. Tryphon owed him that much.

Demetrios pressed his face against the cracks between the slats; the torches around the perimeter had burned out, and he could see nothing but the hulking shapes of a couple of dozing donkeys. One of them turned its head toward him as he rattled the handle. "Open the gate!" His voice trailed off into a moan. "I know you're in there, Tryphon." A donkey trotted close to the gate and peered at him through the gaps, curious about the man on the other side.

Assaulting the gate with a final kick, Demetrios muttered a curse and skulked around to the backside of the courtyard. The walls of the inn were too high for him to scale—unless he could find something, anything, to use for a step. He poked aimlessly through the litter of broken pottery, rotting pieces of rope, and scraps of tent cloth. The stench of emptied slop basins wafted from a deep trench a few cubits behind the buildings. Tryphon had deposited his garbage in a pile near the back wall, in front of the slop trench.

Covering his mouth with his hand, Demetrios clambered over the trash heap where he found a cracked wooden bucket. The leather strap broke when he lifted the vessel, but the bucket itself was solid enough for his purposes. He flipped the bucket over and placed it next to the wall of the courtyard. Then he heard a noise. Someone had opened the gate. The watchman?

Demetrios tiptoed around the corner to see.

A figure stepped outside, singing, "Lydia kissed my tree and fell in love with me . . ." The man stumbled into the gate and laughed. "Oh, Lydia, you wicked creature, you've given me a spear to carry . . ." He turned the corner, coming directly toward Demetrios, who flattened himself against the wall. The round moon shone down on him like a white light. How could the stranger not see him?

The man ambled alongside the wall, his gait unsteady as he mumbled the lyrics to his song. Suddenly, he stopped short and faced the inn. "You old brigand," he said, slurring his words. "Too lazy to empty the pish . . . the piss pot. Well, Tryphon, this is what I think of you." He jerked up his robe, and his fingers tugged clumsily at his loincloth. "Stupid knot." He pulled the cloth down, giggling. "I pish . . . I water your garden, Tryphon." He took a step back, caught his balance, and urinated on the wall.

Demetrios's plan had been to charge past the stranger into the courtyard, but now he hesitated. The man was a worthless drunk, not fit to lick Rufus's feet. Demetrios seethed. He had lost his caravan and his money; he had lost Rufus. Demetrios clenched the handle of his dagger. Why not take what he needed from this piece of trash? Demetrios lunged toward the drunk and slammed his face into the wall.

Groaning, the man writhed under Demetrios's tight grip. His loincloth fell to the ground.

"Don't move. Don't speak." Demetrios pressed the flat of his blade against the man's throat. His other hand kept the stranger's torso pushed against the wall. The stink of urine and fear rolled into Demetrios's nostrils, and he suppressed the urge to cough. "Do what I tell you, and I'll let you live. I just want your money and your clothes." He jabbed the point of the dagger lightly into the man's chin. "My knife is sharp. Do you feel it?"

"Mmm . . ." The sustained pressure against the wall kept the man from answering, but it was clear he understood.

"Good. Untie your purse from your girdle. Slowly." Demetrios eased his hold on the man's back. "Don't forget my dagger is still at your throat."

The stranger played with the cord for a moment. "I can't," he said, just before he grabbed for Demetrios's knife. Startled, Demetrios jerked his arm away. The man turned, but Demetrios struck him in the side of the face; the stranger's head bounced against the wall. There was a sharp cracking sound, as if the wall had split open, and Demetrios jumped back. Time and place blurred in that moment, throwing Demetrios into the memory of a stable in a villa long ago, of a desperate struggle between Master and slave. The stone. Where was the stone? Demetrios looked at his own hands. He held no stone, but he did hold a dagger.

Demetrios stared at the stranger who had slumped to the ground, arms and legs askew. The man's head flopped to one side. His eyelids fluttered once and then closed. A thin trickle of blood burbled from a cut above his brow.

Careful to avoid the puddle of urine around the man's body, Demetrios knelt over him and pressed his ear close to the stranger's lips. A faint breath warmed Demetrios's cheek. He was still alive. After taking a quick look around, he ripped the stranger's purse from his belt and tipped its contents into his palm. Four denarii. Not much but enough to provide food and water. After another glance at his surroundings, he untied the girdle around the man's waist and stripped off his clothes.

Food stains crusted the front of the man's cloak, and a hole under the armpit had been unevenly patched. Demetrios pulled the garment up over his shoulders, feeling the coarse texture of the fabric scrape against the abrasions on his own body. Cut for a taller man, the robe hung down almost to his ankles, making him feel awkward and ungainly. He folded the girdle, wrapped it twice around his waist and tucked the extra layers of the cloak into his makeshift belt. Then he hid the purse in one of the deep pockets he had created.

The man hadn't moved. How could someone this poor afford to stay at an inn? Demetrios fingered the purse again. Only four coins. Nothing more. There was something he had missed, something he had overlooked. Jewelry.

Wealth came in many forms, and this creature, though he may be a drunkard, was not a complete fool. His right hand was adorned with four heavy golden rings, each impressed with a single precious stone. Careful not to disturb the man's repose, Demetrios lifted his hand and slipped off the rings one by one. The first ring was decorated with lapis lazuli, the next with a pearl, the third with white striped onyx, and the final one with topaz. The man had turned the rings on his fingers so that only the gold bands were visible. Demetrios felt a slight chill as he balanced their weight in his palm. If the stranger had been alert, the rings could have taken out Demetrios's eye with a single punch. He reached for the left hand.

There was only one ring on the left hand, made of brass, not gold, and it carried a seal: a carving of winged sandals inside the letter Δ for Demetrios. He yanked the ring from the man's finger.

He grabbed a handful of the stranger's hair and jerked his head around, slapping him lightly on the cheek to wake him.

"What?" The man blinked. His skin looked raw and red where he had been struck.

"Where did you get this?" Demetrios waved the seal across the stranger's line of sight.

The man stared at the ring and then at Demetrios. A slow expression of recognition passed across his face. "You. I thought you were dead." He grinned crookedly. "Go away, ghost."

Demetrios had his answer.

He pushed the point of the dagger against the bandit's throat. A bubble of blood beaded around the tip. An aroma of fear roiled from the man's sweaty body, a scent acrid and sharp that made Demetrios want to gag. The bandit's left eyelid twitched, but he didn't speak.

"You don't deserve to live," Demetrios said. He teased the dagger into the folds of flesh under the man's chin, relishing in the terror on the bandit's face. Then Demetrios lifted the dagger and stepped back. Demetrios could kill this man, but he wouldn't. He was not Marcus. The bandit moaned, rolled to his side.

Muttering an oath, Demetrios kicked the man once in the ribs. "You shouldn't have killed Rufus."

Demetrios was interrupted by the sound of the front gate opening and a voice shouting. "Who is out there?"

Demetrios whirled around. Tryphon!

Tryphon stepped out of his courtyard and raised his torch. "Who is it? What are you doing out here?" He blinked his good eye, straining to see clearly in the darkness.

Demetrios rushed toward Tryphon to intercept him near the

gate. "I came to tell you I'm not staying here," Demetrios said as he approached.

"Oh, it's you."

"Something happened. My servant and I . . ." He paused. "I want my money back."

Tryphon frowned. "You and your slave slept in the bed I provided. I don't owe you a single denarius." He stared at Demetrios. "Why are you wearing those clothes?" Leaning to one side, he tilted his torch toward the back wall. "Is that . . . ? What happened to him?"

"Drunk," Demetrios said hastily. "He's still alive, and I needed—"

"Thief!" Careful to balance the torch in his right hand, Tryphon raised his left fist. "Just like your friend. I should summon the magistrate!"

Demetrios backed away. "No, no, I—" He stopped. Was Elazar in trouble? Had something happened to Isaac? "What? My friend? Who?"

Slowly, Tryphon lowered his fist. "You don't know?" Without waiting for Demetrios to answer, he said, "A young man named Caleb. He came here earlier today looking for you, said he had visited every camp and inn around Jericho trying to find you. I told him you had left, that I didn't know where you were. He begged me to let him stay and wait for you, but he had no money. I was about to have my guard throw him out when Roman soldiers arrived and arrested him for stealing."

"Arrested him? Where did they take him?"

Tryphon shrugged. "Jerusalem, I guess."

Demetrios felt sick; he needed to find Caleb, to talk to the authorities. Demetrios had to get to Jerusalem quickly. If Tryphon would lend him a donkey . . ." Can you help me? I—"

"Help you do what? Rob someone else? You befriend a thief, you become a thief. I don't think so." He nodded at the prone figure near the wall. "You stole his cloak. Who knows what else you and Caleb have taken. Get out before I have you arrested, too!" Turning, he entered the courtyard and slammed the gate shut.

CHAPTER
THIRTY

Demetrios fled the inn. Rufus dead, Caleb arrested? How could so many things have gone wrong? Roman justice was efficient, swift. How much time did Caleb have? Rather than go back through Jericho and waste hours navigating the winding and confusing streets and alleyways, Demetrios decided he would cut through the hills and join the main road at a later point.

But daylight found Demetrios deep in the woods near the river. He had taken a wrong turn in the darkness, and now he was lost. The trail curved in and out of a wooded copse that framed the riverbank. Tall, crooked oaks arched over his head, their muscled branches locked together like the bars of a cage. The air was thick and still, the heat rising from the path like a miniature steam cloud. Demetrios pushed through the heavy brush. If he could find an open space near the water, he could determine whether he was going the right way.

The dense undergrowth blocked most of Demetrios's view of the river, but he could hear the wavelets splashing against the stones along the bank. In the areas where the brush and trees thinned, long reeds tipped into the water, their green leaves swimming in the fast-flowing current. He turned toward the Jordan and bent back the graceful reed stalks.

The bank was too steep for him to approach. The swirling water frothed against the jutting rocks. He kept walking at a fast pace, following the narrow track farther into the trees.

Gnats hummed around his ears. He swatted at the air. Perspiration dripped off the end of his nose; the wool cloak adhered to his back like a sticky sap. With each step he took, the leafy canopy over his head stirred and rustled. When he looked up, he saw dark, beady eyes hidden in the branches watching him. Once or twice, he caught the flash of a wing as sparrows and bulbuls darted through the trees. Their shrill voices twittered at him incessantly. Jeering, mocking. *You failed Rufus. Will you fail Caleb as well?*

Demetrios heard then another sound, a faint trill that emanated from a far distance, like the shrill whistle of the wind in the Jerusalem hills. The antiphonic call tugged at his senses, challenging him to recognize its source. He paused, listening. What was it? His memory failed to provide the answer.

Demetrios ripped at the low-hanging branches, shoved them away from his face. He was trapped in this forest while Caleb languished in prison, awaiting his sentence. Demetrios had to find his way back to the Jerusalem road. He needed to find the caravan and Isaac. Demetrios's desperation made him reckless. He charged down the twisting path.

Knobs of roots reached out to trip him, but he kept his balance, kept running. The matted growth of grass, reed, and thorn impeded every step, but he stamped the underbrush down and kept running, falling into an uneven, jerky stride. He sprinted toward the river and then into the trees, never quite knowing how near he was to the water. And as he fought his way through the brush, he heard that melodic trill grow ever louder, a siren song calling him to come closer.

The bough of a wild oleander swooped across his path, lashed his face, the pain sudden and intense, like the sting of a whip. Shocked by the assault, Demetrios stopped short. When he touched his brow, his fingertips came away wet, coated with the deep, purple-red of his own blood. Every part of the plant was poisonous: the flowers, the leaves, even the sap, harbored a toxin that could sicken a grown man. Already he could feel his wound burning, itching beneath the skin.

He heard the sound again then. Laughter. Pilgrims in a caravan? Surely, they would be able to take him to Jerusalem.

Demetrios pushed aside the branches of the oleander and stepped out into a large, grassy clearing. The sudden brightness blinded him, and he blinked as he took in the scene. Three adolescent girls, their skirts tied about their waists, waded knee-deep through a chain of pools formed by a dam of stones. Various articles of their clothing—striped scarves and tunics—were spread out on the rocks to dry. Another slightly older woman floated quietly in the river, her long black hair fanning out in the rolling current as the green water washed over her shoulders. All of them had their backs to Demetrios; neither the girls nor the woman had seen him.

Demetrios cleared his throat. Raising his voice above the noise of their play, he called out to them, "Greetings!"

The woman in the river heard him first. She turned toward him, her eyes widening at the sudden appearance of a man in their midst, but she didn't cry out. At that same instant, the three girls screamed and snatched at their skirts, running for cover into the trees.

The woman ignored them. Her body still submerged, she raised her arms from the deep water and coiled her hair on top of her head, securing it with a stick. She faced Demetrios. Glistening drops of moisture beaded on her bare arms; her lips parted as though she were about to speak, but she made no sound. She remained in that pose, silent and still as a marble statue. But this woman was no stone goddess, no lifeless object of desire.

Demetrios lifted his hand and called her name, "Tabitha."

"What do you want?" a female voice behind Demetrios asked.

Demetrios turned to face an old woman who had appeared from the brush. She glared at him. Her wet, stringy, gray hair clung to her scalp. Water dripped from the fringe of the blanket wrapped around her body.

The woman looked pointedly at the ribbon of blood on his forehead. "Are you in trouble?"

Demetrios didn't answer. He stared at the old woman. She was ugly. A disgusting hag with a drooping chin and wrinkles around her bony neck. Her brown eyes blazed with anger, and when he glanced down, he saw that she carried a thick branch solid enough to use as a club. She moved defiantly in front of him, blocking his path.

A burst of derisive laughter cut through the silence. The girls were hiding in the bushes, giggling. He shifted his feet and squirmed under the heat of the old woman's hostile stare. In an attempt to mask his discomfiture, he stooped to the ground and picked up a small, round stone. It felt smooth and cool against his sweaty palm, a protective charm against the threatening forces in this unfriendly environment. He rolled the rock slowly around his fingers, keeping his eyes focused on the river. He wanted Tabitha to speak, to call out to him and ask him to stay. He heard a splash. When he peered over the old woman's shoulder, he saw Tabitha swimming upstream, away from them.

The old woman pounded the stick against a rock. The sharp crack made him flinch. She raised the splintered limb and aimed the point at his face. "Go away."

Demetrios squeezed the stone in his hand. "I want nothing."

As he plunged back into the thickets of trees and undergrowth, toward the trail he had abandoned, the adolescent girls tossed handfuls of pebbles at him, shouting, "Away, you nosy man. Martha will beat you."

Demetrios stumbled upriver through the brush. The grass thinned to a muddy slime as the path turned back toward the water. When his sandal became trapped in the muck, Demetrios jerked his foot loose, breaking the thin strap around his ankle. He removed both sandals and dropped to the ground. He breathed in and out as if it was his last breath. He had to keep going. Caleb had been arrested, and he had no idea if Isaac and the caravan were safe.

What could he do?

More than anything, he wanted to undo what had been done. Oh, he wished he had never killed Marcus. He wished he and Elazar could have secured their freedom some other way. Then Elazar would still be with him, Rufus would still be alive, and Caleb would be safe in Tiberias. Demetrios would be simply Demetrios of Tiberias, a caravan driver and trader. And Tabitha? Yes, he and Tabitha would be together. Truth was an elusive dream. And if he'd not killed Marcus that day, how long before Marcus would have killed him?

Demetrios rolled over and gazed into the water.

The face that looked back at him was blurred, its contours lost in the depths. He dipped his hand into the river, watching the image as it fragmented in the flowing current. A cloud passed overhead, blotting out the sun's hot rays, and the white soil of the Jordan's banks faded to a dull gray. His reflection vanished in the subdued light. He twirled his fingers in the water, waiting.

Demetrios had not looked at his reflection for a long time, for he often despised what he saw—a man with a crooked leg who could never rise to his full stature, a man whose body was marked with the scars of beatings, the whip, and a slave's brand cut by a knife. Tabitha had rejected him. What did Tabitha see when she looked at him? Did she see the ugliness, the pain? Did she see his love for her?

The clouds shifted and the sun stepped out from behind its curtain, its bright yellow beams of light striking the water with full force. And the face reflected in the water—sharp and radiant now—looked back at him. The long, angular jaw, the piercing eyes, the familiar haunting smile. He was staring at the countenance of Jesus of Nazareth.

Demetrios gasped and jerked his hand from the river. A fine spray of droplets rained down, but the image remained solid. That couldn't be.

He pushed back from the riverbank, stood, and spun around on his heels, fully expecting to see Jesus standing over him, but the bushes near the river were empty. Demetrios was alone. Was Jesus hiding deep in thickets of trees, beyond his reach? Demetrios touched the dagger strapped to his body, lowered his hand, leaving the dagger in its sheath. "Jesus?"

Jesus didn't answer.

Insects buzzed through the blanket of flowers under the trees near Demetrios, and he thought of the flies that had swarmed around Rufus's face. He stared at his hands, prepared to see them coated in blood, but his palms were caked with the white mud of the Jordan. In his right hand, he still clutched the smooth stone he had picked up near the bathing women. The stone felt warm, fired by the heat of his flesh. As he rolled it between his fingers, it throbbed with a vibrating energy. Stones can build or destroy.

Demetrios edged closer to the river. Below, the image of Jesus wavered on the current, the man's lips set in a firm line, his expression grim, judging. "No," Demetrios said. "I did what I had to do." Demetrios flung the stone at Jesus's face.

Instantly, Jesus's image disappeared, dissolving into concentric ripples that spread out over the river's surface. Demetrios sighed. There was no Messiah, no face in the water, no judgment for Demetrios. The quiet water closest to the bank shuddered. Then all was calm. The formerly dark surface of the river developed a glossy sheen. As smooth and white as polished silver, it sparkled in the afternoon sunlight, within the very circle where Demetrios had thrown his stone.

"Jesus," Demetrios said, "they claim you resurrected a dead man. If that is true, then you can do it again. Give Rufus his life. Bring him back." Now he knew what he had to do.

He would go to Jerusalem, ask Jesus to raise Rufus, and free Caleb.

Demetrios stood as the full glare of the sun beat down upon his head and shoulders. Sweat trickled down into the small of his back. He hesitated for only a moment. Then he dove into the river, welcoming the cool relief of its swift currents.

Glass. Demetrios was looking through a thin sheen of glass, colored by green wavery light. When he reached out with his hands, bubbles arced from his fingertips like sparks from a fire. Below him, dark streamers—the long, thin leaves of rushes and water plants—swirled around his feet. In places where the water was clear and he could see the bottom of the river, tiny pebbles gleamed like silver coins in the light. It was all so beautiful and so quiet.

Demetrios didn't panic when he dropped into the river. He floated face down just beneath the surface of the water, drifting farther and farther out to the middle of the Jordan, beyond the comfortable reach of either bank. But then his heavy woolen cloak folded and twisted around his legs, the sodden weight of it pulling him down, down, deep into the dark chambers of the river.

Terrified, Demetrios kicked against the constraints of his cloak, pushed with his feet. With a mighty heave, he bobbed to the surface, but the current pulled him back, and he went under again, the weight of his clothing dragging him to the bottom.

Demetrios pounded the water with his hands, fought his way back to the top, bouncing with the fast-moving force of the river. Weak and exhausted, he gasped for breath, struggled to keep his head up. A hidden, submerged rock snagged his cloak, and he was yanked back, twisting and turning, sinking quickly. This time, his clothes were caught on something that held him fast. Demetrios knew then he was drowning.

The pain in his chest was intense. An invisible rope tightened around Demetrios, pressing his spine against his ribs. He whirled in a circle, feet flailing against the current, stirring the mud from the river bottom. Blinded by darkness and confusion, Demetrios gripped his cloak. If he could tug it over his head, he would be free. The water roared in his ears; his eyes felt as though they would burst from the pressure. He risked a small breath and sucked in water, coughed, and clamped his mouth shut tight. The desire to take a breath was so strong that he feared he would swallow more water without thinking. Demetrios wrenched the cloak from his body, and in that moment, he broke loose.

Demetrios kicked hard and shot to the surface. Coughing and choking, he fought for air, but the river kept splashing into his mouth. He had no strength to cry out, to call for help, and if he did, who would hear him? The forceful drift tilted him backward, bumping him against the swirling debris. He pounded his hands futilely against the surface, but managed only to spin in a circle. When his head struck a floating log, he screamed for the first time, ingesting more water, and burst into a spasm of coughing.

Demetrios reached out, searching for something to grasp. He strained for the first thing that appeared before him—no more than a shadow in his line of sight—and his hands closed upon nothing. The river refused to release him.

His vision blurred and distorted, Demetrios pawed at the air again, searching for something or someone to grab. He heaved and twisted against the power of the surging river. Demetrios kicked his legs, struggling to swim, but his weak attempt offered little. Then it took hold of him; with a single mighty yank, Demetrios was thrust upon solid ground. Wheezing and gasping like a speared fish, Demetrios rolled over onto his side and vomited up what felt like an amphora of muddy, green water. He opened his eyes once and then closed them again, too exhausted to express his gratitude or understand what had just happened.

CHAPTER
THIRTY-ONE

Demetrios did not know how long he'd slept. He did recall awakening once to cough and spit out more water. It hurt him to breathe deeply, but he hungered for it. Demetrios gulped the air, tasting the honeyed sweetness on his tongue. Then he spat out more water and dropped off into a troubled sleep.

As Demetrios groaned and tossed and turned, he heard a voice speaking to him. "Shh," it said. "Quiet now. You're safe." The pungent aroma of nardinum caressed his face. Soft, gentle hands stroked his cheek, and a cool unguent was laid over the gash on his brow. If this was a dream, he hoped never to awake; if this was death, then he was content.

Demetrios was slow to return to full consciousness. His feet were cold and bare, and he wore nothing but his tunic. He lifted his hand, languidly, brushing his fingers against the dagger. Still there.

The voice spoke to him again. "Oh, you're awake."

He turned over and looked up into the face of the being who had haunted his dreams and knew this time that she was real.

"Tabitha," he said to the woman kneeling beside him. "You've come."

She smiled. "Demetrios. I've never forgotten you." She smoothed the unguent over his forehead; her fingers cooled the heat of his skin.

He blinked. "How did—" His words were cut off as he coughed.

She brushed mud from his cheeks. "You're ill. Rest now." Behind her, the slanting sun cast the mist from the river into a golden haze.

"No." Demetrios clasped her wrist. To his horror, he was seized by a paroxysm of violent shivering. His teeth chattered so hard he couldn't speak. Tremors rolled down his limbs. His hand slid over her wrist and fell limply to his side. He glanced at her open hand. Clean. No scabs. He looked at her arm. She was whole.

Tabitha's expression was tender. Without another word, she unfastened the clasp on her mantle, slipped it over her shoulders, and spread the garment over him like a blanket. She wore nothing under her cloak but a plain, woolen tunic.

Demetrios, his hand trembling, reached out for her. He wanted to touch her face, to bury his fingers in her hair, but if he did so, would she think he'd violated her trust?

Tabitha answered the question for him. Taking his hand between her own, she puffed warm breaths into the space between their palms. "You have a fever." She released him and stretched out on the ground next to him, pulling her mantle over the two of them so that it covered them both from their shoulders to their knees. Then she wrapped her arms around him, drawing him close, her head on his shoulder, her thin frame pressed against him. The heat of her body radiated through her tunic. "Quiet now," she said, her voice muffled in his shoulder. "I will hold you until the chills stop."

Demetrios shuddered again, fighting off a cold that penetrated his bones. The constant shivering left him drained. As Tabitha held Demetrios close, warming him with her body, Demetrios slowly calmed. He breathed in her scent and sighed. Tabitha was so still that Demetrios wondered if she had fallen asleep. Tentatively, he stroked the arm that embraced him. Her skin was smooth. Like alabaster. "Tabitha?"

Her arm tightened about him, and he felt a surge of fear, remembering the rope that had restrained him in the river. Was he still in the water? Still fighting to breathe? Were these the last thoughts of a drowning man? Crushed reeds lay beneath him; the river burbled against the rocks.

Then she answered. "Yes?"

"What did Jesus say to you?"

She pulled away from him then. Demetrios rolled over to face her. She was sitting up, her black, shining hair falling down into her face. He reached out to caress her and drew his hand back, hesitant.

When she lifted her hair up and pulled it back, the aroma of her perfume overpowered him. He felt as though he were drowning again, this time in her sweet, floral scent.

She looked down at him, her gaze dark, piercing. "Would you have me break my vow?"

A vow. Other vows had been broken. Elazar had betrayed Demetrios when he confessed to Jesus. What vow had Tabitha made with Jesus? "I was there. I saw him. What did he tell you?"

Tabitha shook her head. Demetrios wondered if he had asked too much of her.

"You're right." Her voice softened. Demetrios leaned closer to hear. "You saw everything." Tears filled her eyes, and she blinked rapidly to keep them from spilling down her cheeks. "Despite my sores, my disease, he gathered me into his arms. He kissed me on my forehead and said to me, 'Daughter, you are beautiful. Do you believe?'" She put her hands over her face and covered her eyes. "And I was afraid." Lowering her hands, Tabitha looked at Demetrios. "I was afraid to say what I believed, for I knew what I was. But he asked me again, 'Do you believe?' And I said, 'Yes.' And then you saw. Diseased skin fell away. New flesh, as smooth and pure as a newborn's appeared on my body. And I was whole. He told me then, 'Go. Tell no one what has happened here, what I did, what I said to you.' And I promised to keep his secret. But now I've told you." She stared at her perfect hands and fingers, as if she expected them to shrivel up and disappear.

Demetrios's fingers glided from her cheek to her neck and across her collarbone. "You're still clean. You won't be punished for telling me this." He wanted to say to her that he would have embraced her the way Jesus had done, but he couldn't, for it was a lie. When he had seen her as a leper, he had been afraid, too. "Your father, Shumrahu?" He tilted her chin toward him. "Does he know?"

"Demetrios, you're a curious man. You ask so many questions." Tabitha pushed him away and rose to her feet, turning her back to him. "I'm so sorry about what happened. I should have stopped him, but his rage terrified me. I didn't want him to hurt you any more than he had." She turned, glanced at him, her gaze troubled. "I saw you in Tiberias. Did you know? Before you bumped into me in Capernaum, before Jesus healed me." She lowered her head. "You were coming out of that prostitute's house."

Demetrios flushed with shame. He thought about Shappira's dirty room, the emptiness in Shappira's eyes, the rank odor of so many men, the shabbiness of it all. Tabitha was beautiful and whole, kind, unlike Shappira, who was cruel and broken.

"I am sorry," Demetrios hesitated, then asked, "How did you become a leper?"

"We went to Petra after we left the oasis. A few weeks later, the first marks appeared on my cheeks. I tried to hide them with clay powder, but my father saw the white patches anyway. He dragged me out in front of the slaves and everyone, made me wash my face clean with cold water."

Tabitha paced restlessly in front of Demetrios. The thin reeds along the riverbank bowed down under her sandaled feet. "My father told me I was being punished for bringing shame to our family." She whirled around to face Demetrios. Her voice was soft, almost a whisper, "Then he ordered me to leave and to never return."

"Where did you go?"

Tabitha resumed her pacing. "There was a leper colony in the caves outside of our town. They took me in. When we heard about the prophet Jesus, a group of us left for Galilee, hoping he would cure us. But I got separated from them in the crowds at Capernaum. The others went home. I decided to follow Jesus until he would see me and help me."

"You followed Jesus all the way to Jericho? Alone?" Demetrios was astonished by her courage; few women would travel outside of their village alone.

Tabitha tossed her head, strands of black hair flying over her shoulders. "No one touches a leper." She was quiet for a moment. "Jesus said something else when he healed me. He told me to forgive him."

For a terrifying moment, Demetrios wondered if Tabitha was talking about himself, but that was impossible. Tabitha knew nothing about his past. "Forgive who?"

"My father."

"You would do that? Forgive him for throwing you out of the house?"

She shrugged. "Since Jesus asked me to, yes. My father was afraid. I know that. If I carry the bitterness in my heart," she said, tapping her chest, "it gives me nothing but pain. So I have forgiven him." She smiled at Demetrios.

Demetrios was silent. He studied his hands, looking at the cuts from his adventure in the river. Tabitha made forgiveness sound easy, simple. Demetrios knew otherwise. There were some acts you could never forgive.

Tabitha dropped to the ground next to Demetrios and took his hand in her own. The scent of her perfume trailed her every movement. Her gaze traveled over his shoulders, down his back. "Your scars, the twisted leg. Did you want him to heal you, too? Is that why you were in the wilderness with him? Jesus could take them away, if that's what you want."

Demetrios recoiled and pulled his hand out of her grip. Did she see him as ugly? Find him repulsive? But she had not looked away. "Not me. I want to ask Jesus to help a friend." Before he could say more, his teeth began to chatter again. He lay back down on the ground and closed his eyes, willing himself to stop shaking.

Tabitha responded immediately. She pulled her cloak over him and tucked it tightly around his legs and arms. "Shh," she said. "I'm sorry. You're tired and ill, and we've talked too long." Her cool hand rested on his forehead, but Demetrios didn't open his eyes. So weary. To feel her touch, to breathe in the sweet aroma of her presence. But for how long? How long before she left him, before she learned of his crimes?

Her lips brushed against his ear, whispering, "Listen, I'll sing you a song my mother taught me. A song of a magical bird that grants your every wish. Listen. And sleep."

"I wish . . ." Demetrios's voice trailed off with the deep tug of exhaustion. The last sound Demetrios remembered hearing was the melody of Tabitha's song as it blended with the murmur of the rushing river.

Fish steamed on a rack over the brazier in the courtyard. Demetrios thought it needed more spices, perhaps a little garlic. A cup of wine to drink with his meal would be nice. "Rufus," he murmured, "bring the jug from the storeroom." A plate was set before him, bearing a severed head with tangled hair and swollen, blackened eyes. A bloody knife lay on the plate. The head looked at him and said, "Yes, Master?"

Demetrios moaned.

"Please wake up," a woman's voice said. "You're safe. Just a dream."

"Tabitha," he said.

"Yes." She stood. "Rest. I need to finish cooking our breakfast."

Demetrios watched Tabitha while she stirred a small fire ringed by stones. Then she sat by the sputtering flames, sewing a garment she held in her lap. The food—a fish?—over the cook fire popped and steamed. She speared it with a pointed stick and flipped it over. A puff of white smoke floated in the air.

Demetrios realized he had slept through the night, and despite the bad dream, the rest had given him strength. He no longer felt feverish. Sliding Tabitha's cloak off his shoulders, he pushed to his feet. The sky above him was the color of sea-washed pearls—thin marbled clouds imbued with soft gray light. Pink glowed on the horizon.

"The fish is almost ready," she said as he approached. "I caught it with the net Martha left me."

Demetrios sat down next to Tabitha, his legs stretched out awkwardly in front of him. "Martha?"

Tabitha laughed. Her voice was light, playful. "The woman who threatened you with her club." She peeked at him with lowered lashes, like a young girl flirting with her suitor, the Tabitha whom Demetrios remembered from the oasis. "You should have seen your face," she said, grinning. "You looked like a boy whose hand had been slapped for stealing his mother's fresh bread. Martha is a close friend of Jesus. She and her sister, Mary, and some of the other women took me." Tabitha's face darkened for a moment. "I had nowhere else to go." A shake of her head wiped away the sadness. Taking her sewing project from her lap, she held up Demetrios's cloak. "Try it on. I found it on the rocks by the river. I washed it for you. There were some rips, but I did my best to stitch them up."

Demetrios slipped the cloak over his shoulders and wrapped his girdle around his waist.

"Your sandals are over there," she added, pointing to her left.

Demetrios smiled. "I thought the river had stripped me, but you've recovered everything." He picked up his sandals and slid them onto his feet. One strap was much shorter than the other, but he could wrap it tight around the ankle to hold the sandal in place. He handed Tabitha her mantle. "I guess I don't need this anymore. You should wear it."

"Yes, I should." Laughing, Tabitha tugged the blue woolen garment over her head. Demetrios was surprised by how well it fit her body, giving her more substance and health. At the oasis, she had seemed so confident, less vulnerable. Her bent gold hoop earring was with Rufus, but he had Tabitha with him now, whole and beautiful.

"The fish!" Tabitha cried, running toward the cook fire. "It's burning." Hooking the steaming fish with her twig, she laid it out on a flat piece of bark between them. "I'm sorry I don't have anything else. No wine or bread. I haven't filled my waterskin, so we'll have to drink from the river."

Tabitha had cooked a small silurus, a river fish with catlike whiskers. Careful not to cut himself on the sharp fins, Demetrios peeled away a chunk of the white flesh and ate. "It's good." It was bony and not as sweet as a tilapia from the Sea of Galilee but still tasty. He sucked the meat between his teeth. The fish carried the heat from the fire and threatened to burn the roof of his mouth. Rufus would have sprinkled vinegar and water on the meal to cool it before he served it. Rufus. What a fool Demetrios had been to insist Rufus travel with him on this perilous quest. If Demetrios had listened to his servant's concerns, Rufus would still be alive. Demetrios took another bite, but the food stuck in his throat. "I need some water." He started for the river.

Demetrios spat his food into the shallows near the bank. The morsels swirled around in the current and then were swept out into the water's depths, perhaps to be eaten by another, living fish. Although he was thirsty, Demetrios stared hard at the dark, green river, searching for the face, for the image of Jesus. Nothing. Just shadows and light. Demetrios heard a movement behind him, but he didn't turn. He continued peering into the water, wondering. What had happened to him in this place?

"Are you all right?" Tabitha squatted next to him, her hand on his shoulder.

He looked at her. "Was Jesus still here when you pulled me out of the water?"

She drew back in surprise. "I didn't pull you out of the river. I found you." She gestured at the bank. "Over there. Soaking wet and almost dead."

"But Jesus was here . . ." Suddenly aware that Tabitha must believe he was still feverish, Demetrios stopped. "Never mind. It's not important."

Demetrios glanced at Tabitha. Someone had pulled him from the water, and she had been there when he came back to life. But who? Tabitha dipped her fingers casually into the river. He could not stop looking at her. She had a natural grace, a way of moving through space that seemed ethereal, a gentleness that reached out to Demetrios. In that moment, Demetrios knew he wanted Tabitha to become his wife, to be with him always. He would keep her safe and love her. He could never tell her the truth about himself. How could he?

Tabitha shook the water from her hands, laughing at the drops that sprayed over the two of them as she leaned against him. "Would you like more to eat?"

A bee zipped past Demetrios's nose, and he swatted at it, making her laugh again. Tabitha rested her head on Demetrios's shoulder. He breathed in her perfumed scent. His fingers slipping through her silky hair, Demetrios closed his eyes, for the moment, content. A light breeze ruffled the reeds next to him. Above his head, birds twittered in the trees, but they no longer spoke to him or mocked him. They were just birds. The morning sun warmed his face. Morning. How many days had passed since Rufus was killed? Two, three? And Caleb was still in danger. Sitting up, Demetrios opened his eyes, turned toward Tabitha. "What day is it?"

"It's the twelfth day of Nisan."

"The twelfth day! Passover is in two days." Demetrios turned toward her, his gaze searching her face. "And Jesus is gone from here?"

"Jesus left for Jerusalem right after I was healed. Some of the women who feed the disciples and follow Him live in Jericho and Bethany. They were kind to me. They took care of me after I was whole, and later, they brought me down to the river to bathe and to celebrate. That's where you found us. The women left for Jerusalem yesterday. They invited me to come with them, but I wanted to stay." She smiled at him. "I was worried about you. I wondered where you had gone."

"And then you found me."

"Yes."

"Jesus was not at the river yesterday?"

"No."

"I need to go to Jerusalem. Now."

"Today? You want to leave today?"

Demetrios nodded. "A friend of mine, Caleb, is in trouble. He's been arrested. It's my fault. I have to help him."

Tabitha's face clouded with doubt. "How is that possible? Did you falsely accuse him?"

"No, I didn't help him when he needed it, so I must help him now." Demetrios rose and held out his hand to her. "Come with me. We'll go to Jerusalem together."

But Tabitha hesitated. "Alone? Just the two of us?"

"We have to find Jesus, too."

"To help your friend?"

"I will tell you later."

Demetrios drew his dagger, holding it up for her inspection. The lapis lazuli eyes gleamed.

Tabitha stared at the weapon. "I saw this earlier. When you slept." She reached for it, her hand hovering uncertainly over the blade. She didn't touch. "It looks cruel."

"It'll protect us. Will you go with me?"

Tabitha didn't answer him but strode back to the river. Her back to him, she gazed at the far bank, a fuzzy green line on the horizon. "There will be thousands of people in Jerusalem for

305

Passover." Her voice was hushed. "What if someone remembers me? From before?"

Demetrios sheathed the dagger and walked over to her. He took both of her hands in his own. "How? They will not recognize you." Rufus had been reluctant to go to Jerusalem, too. The dagger had failed Demetrios once; it would not fail him again. He would let nothing hurt Tabitha. But first, he must earn her love. "I will protect you." He tilted her chin so that she looked up at him. "Will you go with me?"

She sighed. "I don't know. The road is dangerous."

"Nothing will happen to you," he replied.

"What if something happens to you?" she retorted.

Smiling, Demetrios said, "I know how to protect us both."

Tabitha stood on her toes, kissed him on the cheek, and turned away.

Demetrios waited impatiently while Tabitha filled her waterskin and extinguished the fire. She tossed the remnants of the cooked fish into the river, for it would spoil in the heat of the day. Water would have to sustain them until they reached Jerusalem. Demetrios realized he still had no idea of how to find the road to Jerusalem, but Tabitha knew the way. She pointed to a break in the trees. "Over there, the trail turns toward the road."

They passed under the arching branches, beneath trees that no longer menaced but waved farewell. The rushing river was far behind them. Beyond the trees, the landscape opened up to a brilliant blue sky, so vast that when Demetrios gazed up at the heavenly vault, he felt as though he were floating. To the east, the morning sun. They turned toward the west, toward Jerusalem, their shadows, small and insignificant, leading them on.

CHAPTER
THIRTY-TWO

Demetrios paused to scan the sky and gauge the angle of the sun. He wished that they had left sooner. They faced a long, steep climb, a journey that began in a village near the Sea of Salt and ended in a city perched on the mountains of Judea. The hills, washed in forbidding gray shadows, rose up on the horizon as Demetrios and Tabitha left the Jordan Valley. Herod's small fortress loomed above on the highest peak, guarding the entrance to the Jerusalem road.

It would take a full day to reach Jerusalem. Demetrios hoped to arrive in the Holy City before dark. It was never wise to travel after sundown. Although he presented an air of confidence to Tabitha, he knew too well just how vulnerable the two of them were.

He turned to her. "Have you been to Jerusalem?" The twisting road presented a treacherous course. The Wadi Qelt dropped off into a deep gorge at the next turn where the path pushed over the crest of the eroded hills. He still felt weak from his experience in the river; she had just recovered from the ravages of leprosy. He wondered if either of them was strong enough to make the climb.

Tabitha shook her head. "I was in the wilderness—you know that—but never in Jerusalem. Is it far?"

"Far enough. We should keep a brisk pace. Do you think you can do that?"

She nodded, and they began to walk faster. Demetrios kept his eyes on the hills, searching for any suspicious movement, and he kept his hand close to his dagger. He would not be taken unawares again.

As they passed the last portal of Herod's aqueduct, they saw two shepherds leading their herd of goats through stands of bamboo in a shallow furrow that ran parallel to the watercourse. After that, they were alone. Most of the pilgrims were already in Jerusalem. The wind whistled between the rocks and the cliffs, sending showers of pebbles tumbling down the slopes. When the air was still, they could hear the scuff of their footsteps and the rasp of their breathing.

Rufus was out there in a ditch among the scraggly acacias and thorny bushes. Demetrios thought about the marker he had built, the pile of stones he had stacked to denote Rufus's burial place. Had he done enough to protect his servant's body? There were two jackals circling when he left, but more may have been waiting. By now, they could have torn Rufus's body apart and carried off the pieces.

Tabitha touched his arm, drawing him to a stop. "Up there." She pointed to a narrow trail cutting through the outcroppings of rock and crumbling caves on their left. "That will take you to the place."

"What place?"

"Where I was healed."

"How do you know?"

She flicked a glance at him, her eyes narrowing. "I remember every step I took to find Jesus."

The caves were like the pocks of leprosy: dark-brown scars on the dusty face of the rocks above them. "How could you survive in this wilderness?" He admired her courage. Or had it been desperation?

"Lepers look after each other. When I followed Jesus to Jericho, I stayed with a leper family who lived in one of those caves."

"A family?" he asked, trying to imagine an entire household afflicted with such a horrible disease.

"Yes, can you imagine? A husband and his wife and their two small children." Sighing, she lowered her eyes. "So sad."

"But they didn't come with you to see Jesus?"

"They feared the crowds. They're still up there." She jutted her chin toward the rocks. "The lepers. Not just one family but dozens of people living like animals in the caves. They're watching us now. They know everything that happens on this road." She paused and looked again to the caves. "I hope they find healing."

Following her gaze, he saw no people up there, just dark, empty hollows in the hillside. He took her arm. "We should keep moving."

They had just reached the Pass of Adummin when they stopped to share a drink of water and to rest. The hills were no longer brown, but stained red, the color of rust. Some said the color came from elements in the rock; others claimed it was the spilled blood of unwary travelers. The gritty sand left red streaks on their sandals and clothes.

Tabitha brushed the dirt from her cloak. "I'll scrub our clothes when we get to Jerusalem." She reached for the waterskin.

Demetrios nodded, thinking about what he needed to do when they arrived. If he could find Isaac quickly, Tabitha could stay with the caravan while Demetrios spoke to the authorities about Caleb. She would be safe there. What about Jesus? And Rufus? But what if his caravan had been attacked by bandits, too?

What if something had happened to Isaac? Where would he and Tabitha go then? Then he heard the clop of donkeys' hooves coming up the road behind them. He held up his hand. "Listen."

"What is it?"

He motioned for her to stay near the rocks. "A caravan, I think. Let me talk to them."

The caravan was small and shabby with three skinny donkeys and no camels. The animals were accompanied by a couple of women and four young boys. An old man, his back bent and stooped, tugged at the lead donkey.

The man drew his group to a halt when he saw the two of them. At the same moment, Tabitha edged behind Demetrios, standing close to him.

"Greetings," the old man said, looking them over. "Which way do you go?"

"To Jerusalem," Demetrios said. Tabitha touched his shoulder. He could feel her trembling.

"Just the two of you?" Before Demetrios could answer, he added, "You're welcome to join us if you'd like. Since you've traveled more than halfway, I wouldn't charge you the full price." His head wobbled on his scrawny neck like a vulture ogling its meal. His watery eyes watched them hopefully.

Demetrios glanced at Tabitha. With an almost imperceptible shake of her head, she mouthed her answer, No.

"Thank you," Demetrios said, "but we're waiting for our friends. They should be here soon."

The man clucked his tongue and signaled the donkey. "As you wish then." The caravan moved on past them, trailing clouds of red dust. They were left alone at the entrance to the "Blood Ascent." Demetrios hoped it wasn't their own blood that would be left behind.

Tabitha became more talkative as they hiked their way through the pass, peppering him with questions about his life in Tiberias.

"My home is at the top of a hill in Tiberias," Demetrios told her. "You can see all of the Sea of Galilee from my courtyard."

"And your family?" Tabitha asked. "Your uncle Elazar? Is he in Tiberias?"

Demetrios looked at her, stung by his thoughts of their broken friendship. "Elazar and I have parted. I have no other family. My mother died when I was born. And my father didn't want to keep me."

Tabitha touched his arm. "I'm sorry."

Tabitha said something about how much she missed her sisters and her mother, but Demetrios was only half-listening. For some time, he had been aware of a small party traveling on the road ahead of them. From his quick glimpses, he guessed it to be two people and an animal. Whoever they were, their pace had been growing steadily slower. They should have crossed over the next rise by now. He took a step, moaned softly, and exaggerated his limp.

Tabitha noticed immediately. "Is your leg hurt?"

Demetrios grimaced. "Perhaps we can rest for a short while?"

"Of course."

Stooping to massage his leg, Demetrios scanned the winding road. Still no sign of them. Where were they? Two people waiting up the road, or more? Why didn't they move on? They faced too many choices and none of them good. Go back to Jericho? They were less than five miles from Jerusalem. If they turned back, they wouldn't reach the Jordan Valley until well after dark. But what was waiting on the road ahead? They could stay here and hope the group would leave, but the last thing he wanted to do was spend the night on this road. If something happened to Tabitha now . . . Demetrios knelt and picked up a large stone.

Tabitha stared at him. "What are you going to do with that?"

"Listen to me." He handed her the rock. "Wrap this in your cloak and hold it tight."

"Why?"

"There are people ahead of us, either in trouble or waiting for something. I don't know. But I've been watching them, and they should have crossed on the switchback in the road by now. They haven't."

Shielding her eyes, she squinted at the hill. "On the next turn? I don't see anything. But," she added doubtfully, "I don't know if I can carry this stone. What do you want to do?"

"We're going to walk together up the hill. Slowly. Keep watch to both sides of the road. If you see something out of place, tell me. Hold that stone close and use it to protect yourself if you need to. And if we're attacked and I'm hurt, you run. Go to the lepers in the caves."

She set the stone down and stepped in front of him, planting her feet solidly on the ground, her hands on her hips. "No." She bit her lip, lowered her eyes. "I won't leave you."

"What?" Demetrios was taken aback by her defiance. There was no time for this argument. He grasped her elbow. "Come on, then."

They had just reached the top of the next rise when a man bounded out into the middle of the road. He was huge, a colossus, with arms as thick as stone columns and a chest as massive as the walls of the Temple in Jerusalem. He assumed the fighting stance of a gladiatorial bear as they approached, fully blocking the path. His clenched fists brandished the brute force of a battering ram. He did not speak.

"He's big," Tabitha said into Demetrios's ear.

"True." Sliding his hand under his cloak, Demetrios touched

312

the handle of his dagger for reassurance. He might not be able to kill this giant with such a small weapon, but it was enough to give them time to escape.

They were too close to him to run, separated by less than three long cubits between them. With a single leap, the man could crush them both. He glared at Demetrios and Tabitha for a moment and then seemed to relax. Although his suspicious frown had cracked into a cautious smile, there was a note of forced civility in his voice. "Greetings," he said. "Have you lost your caravan?"

Demetrios blinked, confused by the question.

When Demetrios didn't immediately reply, the man added, "They passed by here a short while ago, but the old fellow didn't mention he was missing another man and woman."

"We're not with them," Demetrios said.

"Alone? Just the two of you?" He broke into booming laughter. He shook his head. "Such worry over so little." Then he put his fingers to his lips and whistled. "You can come out now, my sweet. It's safe."

"We'll just go then," Demetrios began, but the man stopped him with a heavy hand on his shoulder; his fingers bore into Demetrios's bones with the force of a hawk's talons.

"My friend," the man said, pulling Demetrios toward him. "You and your woman appear to be honest folk. But the journey is long, and the road is pitted with hazards. Not a good time to travel alone. You should join us." Demetrios stumbled as he was pushed forward. He cast a quick look over his shoulder. Tabitha followed closely behind.

The man's companion—a young woman, it turned out— was waiting for them as they came down the far side of the hill. Dressed in a gray woolen cloak that fanned out around her broad hips, the woman rested in the sparse shade of a scrub oak that grew horizontally from the rocks above. A donkey, laden with two large baskets, nibbled on the dry grass at her feet. When the woman turned toward them, Tabitha gasped. "She's pregnant!" Then she blushed.

The big man chuckled. "Yes, my Sara is expecting her first child. A boy from the way he sets." He waved his hand in a gesture of welcome. "Come, come, join us. Sara," he ordered, "bring out the wineskin for our guests. They're thirsty."

Sara was quite young, only a few years into her womanhood. As she set out loaves of bread, olives preserved in salt and oil, and the wineskin, she walked with her weight bearing down on her heels, her hips swaying heavily from side to side. Although Demetrios knew little about pregnant women, he guessed she was in the final weeks. Why were they traveling so close to her time?

The big man ripped off a chunk of bread and handed it to Demetrios. "They call me B'ar," he said, his mouth full of bread and olives. "Because I'm large." Juice dribbled down his chin, and he swiped at it with the back of his hand.

Breaking the bread into equal servings for himself and Tabitha, Demetrios nodded. B'ar. The name had two meanings: to open the mouth wide, or to make a lowing sound like an oxen. It was a name well chosen, for the man was built like a bull with a voice to match.

B'ar grabbed Sara as she walked past and pulled her close to him. "My favorite wife. There are two more at home like her but not half so pretty. Isn't that so, my sweet?" Sara blushed and giggled. He turned toward Demetrios. "Well, then. You know our names. Now you must tell us yours."

Demetrios handed the last piece of his bread to Tabitha and swallowed. "I am Demetrios of Tiberias, and this is Tabitha." Demetrios reached for Tabitha's hand.

314

Gently, Tabitha placed her fingers loosely in Demetrios's grip. "Sara," Tabitha said, keeping her eyes on B'ar. "A Jewish name?"

B'ar burst into raucous laughter. "Your woman is a clever one, I see." He looked at Sara. "Shall I tell them our story, my sweet?"

Sara dipped her head in acknowledgment. "As you wish." Sara patted his beard affectionately and whispered into his ear.

B'ar chuckled. "I'm a Gentile. When her father learned of our union, he ripped his clothes and poured ashes over his head and declared his only daughter was dead." B'ar shook his head, disbelieving. "Dead? Does she look dead to you? Why, here she sits, alive and well and filled with the life of another. Pah!" He spat on the ground, showing his contempt. He helped his wife to her feet and glanced at the sky. "The daylight is fading. We should be going soon." He handed the wineskin to her. "Tuck this deep into one of the baskets. It'll stay cooler that way."

"I'll help you," Tabitha said. She glanced at Demetrios, her expression unreadable to him, and then began gathering up the remains of their meal.

A stark hiss was their only warning. The donkey screamed and reared back, his flailing legs kicking up clouds of ochre-colored dirt. A shower of grit pummeled Demetrios's face; he was suddenly immersed in a dust storm that made the air thick and dark with blood-red sand.

"Watch the hooves!" Tabitha shouted.

Tabitha. Where was she? Demetrios spun around, seeing nothing but flashes of disconnected movement: the gray flanks of the animal bucking from side to side, the women straining against the beast's ropes, B'ar backing away on his right, and a fat black and gold ribbon flying through the air. "Viper!" Demetrios cried. "In front of you."

Another fearsome scream, louder than the first. Olive-colored whips swirled over his head. A second snake? He ducked but was struck in the head by the broken rope. Baskets and their contents spilled over the ground at his feet. The donkey fled, the sound of his terrified braying following him like a fading echo.

As the dust settled, Demetrios thought he saw Tabitha's silhouette against the rocks. "Tabitha?" Something moved near his feet. He froze.

"I'm safe," she said.

The viper slithered across the road, between Demetrios and the women. Demetrios estimated it to be two cubits in length—twice as long as his forearm. The triangular head rose, twisting, turning, split black tongue testing the air. The dark patches on its back glittered like onyx beads. Beautiful and deadly. Demetrios slid his hand into his cloak, reaching quietly for his dagger. One slash. That's all he needed. But he had to be faster than the snake.

"Be still," B'ar said next to him, his words almost a whisper. "Sara," he called out, "are you safe?"

"I have her in my arms," Tabitha answered. Her voice shook. "She's fine."

"Husband," Sara began, "our donkey—"

"We'll find him later, sweet," B'ar answered. "Right now, stay where you are." He touched Demetrios lightly on the shoulder, showing him the large rock he held in his hand.

The viper sensed the movement. It paused, then drew tightly into a coil, hissing. No time, Demetrios thought, his hands closing around the dagger's grip. One of us will be bitten. But B'ar lunged before the snake did. With a mighty shout, he heaved the stone at his target and crushed the creature's head.

No one spoke for several long moments. Demetrios's hand slid from the dagger's hilt. Blood seeped out from under the stone. The viper's body twitched and jerked as though it were still alive.

"Blood," he murmured. The earth was stained with it.

"It's just the snake's," B'ar said as he grasped Demetrios by the elbow.

Demetrios stared at the dead viper. "We should pick up your things." The large baskets that had been on the donkey's back had been upended, the purses, sandals, and small leather boxes scattered across the road.

B'ar nodded, already tossing purses into one of the baskets as he moved along the path. Demetrios started to follow and then turned back. Carefully, he lifted the stone. The snake's eyes—flat and shining—gazed back at him. Accusing. They had not forgotten. Or forgiven. He shuddered and reached for the leather box nearest his feet.

CHAPTER
THIRTY-THREE

They found the donkey a short distance up the road. It lay on its side, its bloated legs trembling in uncontrolled spasms. Black pus oozed from the three puncture wounds that spanned the hindquarters. Death was imminent. The animal stretched out its neck, groaning, the swollen tongue lolling from its open, yearning mouth. A thin line of blood—as red as the sand—burbled from its nostrils.

Demetrios stood next to Tabitha, watching the donkey take its final breath. This could have been any one of them. It could have been Tabitha. His dagger? No protection at all. Nothing but a curse of bad luck. If B'ar had not heaved that stone . . . He tightened his grip about Tabitha's waist. Her body was rigid. "More snakes come out in the evening," he said, "when it's cooler. We need to be more careful now."

"Can't we do something to help it?" she asked. "To stop its suffering?"

Demetrios shook his head. He knew the creature was already dead.

B'ar set his baskets down and strode in a slow circle around the corpse. "A shame." He nudged the donkey with his foot. "He was a good, hardworking beast."

"No, no!" Sara's face turned pale when she saw the animal, and she panted with short, quick gasps. She tipped backward, Tabitha catching her by the arm. "Oh!"

"The baby!" B'ar cried. "It's too soon!"

"It's not the baby," Tabitha said, her voice firm. She wiped the girl's face with her mantle and glared at the two men. "She's sick from the excitement. Get some water." She guided Sara to a large boulder across from them and helped her sit down.

As B'ar brought out his waterskin, Tabitha quickly took charge. She directed B'ar to prepare a shade for Sara and told the girl to breathe in deeply and slowly. Demetrios knew nothing about pregnant women, but Tabitha seemed confident. Sara would be well cared for.

He watched them for a moment and then wandered down the road, far away from the donkey's body. Demetrios paced back and forth across the road, impatient to reach their destination. The setting sun painted the heavens with streaks of orange and rose, the brilliant colors seeping so fully into the red hills that sky and land merged to one piece. They were close to Jerusalem now—less than two miles from the turnoff to Bethany—but it would be dark before they reached the safety of town.

A sudden movement on the horizon caught his eye. Another traveler? He looked back at the others. B'ar had placed a blanket under Sara's head and elevated her feet with one of the baskets. Tabitha was patting the girl's face with a cloth. None of them had noticed anything.

Demetrios was determined to protect them. Fingers twitching, he rested his hand over the hilt of the dagger. He grimaced.

The dagger had been useless against the bandits and the serpent. He walked farther down the road and stopped. Whatever it was, it had vanished.

Tabitha caught up to Demetrios. "What are you looking for?" she asked.

He took her arm to walk back to B'ar and Sara. "I thought someone was coming this way. I was wrong."

Sara was on her feet when they returned, and B'ar, with all the baskets strapped around his neck and shoulders and hanging down his back, looked like a human pack animal.

"Would you like me to help you carry some of that?" Demetrios asked.

B'ar shrugged. "I haven't been given this name for nothing. We're close to Bethany. I can manage the burden that far. Thank you."

"Sara," Tabitha said, "you can lean on me while we walk."

The young girl nodded and smiled, taking Tabitha's offered arm. B'ar said to Demetrios, "Tabitha is a good woman."

Demetrios swallowed. "I know." Demetrios turned his attention to the sky, uneasy about the rapidly approaching darkness. They had neither lamps nor torches to guide them, and it would be hours before they could depend on the light of the full moon. Aside from the threat of wildlife, the road was a dangerous place during the twilight hours. "We should go now."

As they ascended the next hill, they could see the sun, hanging like a molten golden stone on the mountain's apex but disappearing when the road dipped down again. To the east, the heavens were fading into a soft gray, but the western firmament was streaked with blue and violet. Dark purple shadows stretched out on both sides of them to lengthen every fissure and crack in the ground, presenting unknown hazards to their journey. A single misstep into a hole or rut in the path, and any one of them could end up with a broken foot or ankle. They had to walk carefully but quickly.

The trail narrowed and when they moved through the final pass, they came upon the crossroad to Bethany. B'ar brought the party to a halt. "We must part here." He swiped the sweat from his face with a dirty hand. "Sara and I will go to Bethany tonight. But before we go, I have something for you." He eased the baskets from his shoulders, setting them both down near his feet. "I think I put it in here," he said, digging deep into the largest one. "I was reserving this for some poor fool whose shekels were too heavy to hold on to, but I want to give it to you, Tabitha." With a flourish, he brought forth a rabbit-skin purse. "Feel how soft."

Tabitha took the purse from him, turning it over in her hands. It was gray, with tight stitching on both sides and a long leather loop attached to the top. The animal's front legs—minus the paws—were folded over the front to make a neat closing flap. "For me?" she asked, stroking the fur.

B'ar nodded. "My thanks for saving my sweet Sara from the donkey's hooves."

Impulsively, Tabitha brought the purse up to her face. "Such a strange scent." She rubbed the fur against her cheek. "It smells like . . ." She sniffed it again. "Lime?"

B'ar grinned. "I knew she was a clever one," he said to Demetrios. "A tool of the tanner's trade," he told Tabitha. "The lime cleans the fleshy matter and extra hair from the skin."

"It's an odd odor but not unpleasant," Tabitha said.

B'ar spit on the ground. "Pah! Tell that to my village. The elders claimed my vats stunk and forced me to move outside the walls closer to the Sea of Salt. But that doesn't stop them from coming to buy my wares." He opened the purse for her. "Feel the inside. The skin is almost as soft as the fur. In the dark, you could mistake it for a baby's bottom. Isn't that right, my sweet?" He poked Sara gently in the ribs. She giggled.

"Isn't it lovely?" Tabitha asked, holding the purse out to Demetrios.

The purse was beautiful, but Demetrios had nothing to offer in exchange. After handing the purse back to Tabitha, Demetrios slid his hand under his cloak. He could feel the blade's rage pulsing beneath his fingertips. "I can see you are a man who appreciates fine craftsmanship," Demetrios said carefully. He eased the dagger from its sheath and held it up. "Perhaps you would be interested in this?"

At the sight of the weapon, B'ar pushed Sara behind him and raised his fists. "So," he said, sneering. "This is what it comes to. I feed you and give you wine and gifts, and now you want to rob me." He took a menacing step forward. "So be it. You may cut me, but you'll die trying. I can promise that."

Demetrios backed away and laughed nervously. "No, no. I mean you no harm. I just wanted to show it to you. Here." He presented the dagger to B'ar, handle first.

B'ar hesitated briefly and then reached for the knife. "Ivory!" He stroked the hilt. "A fine piece of work. And shaped like a woman." He laughed. "That makes it easier to hold, eh?" His fingers moved rapidly over the carving, exploring the intricate details of the design. His touch was gentle, respectful. Grasping the handle with both hands, he raised his arms and offered the knife to the slanted beams of the setting sun. The needle-sharp point caught a golden ray of light, glinting at them like a vicious star.

Demetrios blinked. He hadn't remembered the blade appearing so savage. As B'ar twirled it in his hands, the dagger assumed a powerful force, already searching for a new victim. It would not be satisfied until its hilt was tainted the color of rust, until the blade had been blunted and dulled so that it could murder no more.

Turning his gaze from the fearsome image of the dagger, Demetrios fumbled with the sheath.

"A marvelous tool," B'ar murmured, "but is it as sharp as it looks?"

Demetrios glanced at B'ar and froze.

A scarlet thread rose up on B'ar's palm, the mark of the blade's kiss. "Sharper than a serpent's bite," B'ar said as he wiped the dagger on his cloak. "I fear our good Caesar's nights would not be so peaceful if he knew such a treasure wandered through Palestine." B'ar chuckled. "Take good care of this, my friend." Reaching for the sheath in Demetrios's hand, he prepared to hand the dagger back to him.

Demetrios shook his head. "No, I don't want it. You keep it." He slid the dagger into its casing and tied the clasp. Was it a mistake to give it away? Did the possessor become the possessed? He sensed that B'ar admired the dagger only for its fine craftsmanship, not for its lust for destruction. He held the weapon out to the tanner. "Take it."

"Demetrios, are you sure—" Tabitha began.

"The dagger belongs to B'ar now," Demetrios interrupted, passing it to him. As he did so, he felt his hand grow lighter; he stood a little taller. No one knew what he had done; no one knew what he had planned to do. With the dagger released from his possession, no one—not even Tabitha—ever needed to know.

B'ar smiled. "You really don't want it?" Again, Demetrios shook his head. The tanner's eyes narrowed. "How much?"

"Nothing," Demetrios answered. "I want nothing for it." He hesitated, knowing it was wrong to pass the dagger to B'ar without a fair warning. "The knife is my gift to you, but it may have a hidden price."

"Price?"

"There may be a curse upon the dagger and its owner." His words were almost a whisper.

B'ar burst into loud laughter. "Oh ho, my friend! A curse, you say? I fear you're as superstitious as the Jews. I'll take it then. I don't believe in curses or bad luck, despite the trouble with the viper back there." He tied the sheath to his belt. "But I fear Tabitha's purse isn't of equal value to your offering. And I don't accept charity." He pointed to the large basket. "Sara, get me those sandals, the ones I made for that young man who died." Sara handed him a pair bound with a leather cord. "No offense, my friend, but you're on the small side, and I think these boy's sandals will fit you."

They were made in the Greek style with solid thongs at the heel and ankle and a leather ring at the front for the big toe to pass through. After kicking off his own battered sandals, Demetrios slid his feet into them and tied the straps. The soles were thick and sturdy; until now he hadn't noticed how much the rocks hurt his feet. He wiggled his toes, appreciative of the near perfect fit.

"It's agreed then," B'ar said quickly, taking note of Demetrios's obvious satisfaction. "We have an even exchange. My fine sandals and rabbit purse for your dagger."

Demetrios nodded. "Agreed." He felt he could walk to Jerusalem and back a hundred times in these sandals. He grabbed Tabitha's hand. "It's almost dark. We shouldn't delay here any longer. A safe journey to you both."

B'ar had already strapped the baskets to his back. "I hope you don't regret your decision. Without any protection, you need safe wishes more than I do."

Demetrios shrugged. "I'm not afraid." He felt safer now than any time since he had first picked up the dagger.

B'ar nodded. "Well then, as they say in my village, 'May the gods of good fortune watch your shadow.' Perhaps we'll meet again in Jerusalem."

Tabitha leaned her head on his shoulder as they both watched B'ar and Sara trudge down the hill to Bethany. Demetrios treasured this brief moment of intimacy, wishing it would never end, but night came upon them too quickly, the sun disappearing behind the last hill and sending the road into blackness. It was time for them to go.

Before them lay the Valley of Kidron, lush with the groves of olive trees that now waved quietly in the early evening breeze. A cool mist, like a whispering fog, hugged the hills of the city to drape the entire valley with a luminescent veil. As the moon rose over the mountains, the towers of Fortress Antonia peeped through the clouds. Tonight they would find his caravan and a safe refuge. And tomorrow? Tomorrow, Demetrios would speak to the authorities about Caleb. He would find Jesus and ask him to bring Rufus back to life. Afterward, he would ask Tabitha to be his wife.

"Come," he said to Tabitha. "Jerusalem awaits."

CHAPTER
THIRTY-FOUR

As Demetrios and Tabitha approached the city, Demetrios thought of the refrain he had heard the pilgrims sing on earlier caravan journeys to Jerusalem. "If I forget you, O Jerusalem, let my right hand forget her cunning. Let my tongue cleave to the roof of my mouth, if I remember you not; if I do not set Jerusalem above my chiefest joy."

The Jews loved Jerusalem above all other cities, believing it to be a holy site. The city was renowned for its beautiful architecture, but Demetrios had become indifferent to its splendor. He much preferred Tiberias where every structure was new and clean. The palaces and public buildings of Jerusalem, constructed of huge blocks of white meleke limestone, sparkled in the daylight like glittering jewels, and were, indeed, spectacular. But to the south, in the Lower City, the streets were narrow and twisting, bordered by tiny, dirty limestone hovels stacked atop one another.

Filth and garbage spewed out into the terraced streets, and the alleyways that crisscrossed between the houses were thick and close with the odor of cooked food and crowded quarters. At night, though, all they could see was the glory of Jerusalem: the imposing towers of Fortress Antonia rising above the massive walls of the Temple itself.

Tabitha murmured an "Ooh" of admiration, and Demetrios smiled. It was a wonder to see the city through her eyes.

They entered by way of the Gate of Waters, a double-walled passageway connected by storage rooms on both sides. Torches flanked the opening, and guards stood watch on the towers above. There were few people passing through the gate; most of the pilgrims had already found lodging in the city or were camped on the hills nearby. A publican stopped them as they crossed.

"Do you bring goods to sell?" he asked Demetrios. "If so, you pay the tax here."

"No."

"Then what is your business in the city?"

"We come to see friends." Demetrios disliked tax collectors, as most of them were corrupt. When challenged by one, he provided no more information than necessary.

The publican gave Demetrios a dubious look but then waved his hand for them to pass.

The gates were quiet, but the Lower City bustled. Every house seemed to be lit with lanterns and lamps; groups of pilgrims flowed through the narrow streets, singing songs of praise and triumph; fragments of laughter and loud conversation burst from the opened doors of the homes. Several lambs, still awaiting purchase, were tethered in a small courtyard off to their left. By morning, they would be taken to the Temple for sacrifice.

"So many people," Tabitha said quietly. She seemed intimidated by the crowds, pulling her shoulders inward, huddling within herself.

Demetrios pulled her into the shadow of an archway to allow a pair of Roman troops to pass. The Roman soldiers in Jerusalem were often bored and had a reputation for public drunkenness. It was best to avoid any encounter.

The legionaries' hobnailed sandals thumped the pavement stones as they strode toward a narrow alleyway. Demetrios stopped. The soldiers were talking about arresting someone tonight. He tried to catch the details, but they moved past the archway too quickly.

"The city swells to five times its normal size during Passover," Demetrios told Tabitha when he was certain the soldiers were gone. "It's not always like this."

"But how will we ever find your caravan?"

She posed a question Demetrios had been worrying about as well. If Isaac had followed his instructions and come to Jerusalem on schedule, he should be settled near the Upper Agora close to Herod's palace. That was the best location for upscale trade. However, if something had gone wrong, the caravan could be relegated to the outskirts of the New City or even camped in Bethany or Bethpage. Search for the caravan in the wrong place, and they could spend the night roaming the streets of Jerusalem. Demetrios took her arm. "Don't worry. You'll have a tent and warm blankets tonight." He guided her down the steps toward the Tyropoeon Valley.

The valley was a deep ravine that cut through the heart of Jerusalem. On the eve of Passover, dozens of tents and small fires dotted the trails and ridges. People had settled wherever the land was level enough to lay out a bed. Of all the places to stay in Jerusalem during the festival, this was the least expensive and the most congested. But Isaac could be here. Demetrios and Tabitha wound their way down one of the steep paths.

"Over there." Demetrios pointed to a large goat-hair tent sporting a familiar brown-and-white-striped flag. With only the light of the campfires and the full moon to guide them, they traipsed along a course that paralleled a shallow stream.

"Is that your caravan?"

"No, but someone there can help us." Sensing her hesitation, he squeezed her hand. "We'll stop here only long enough to ask about my caravan and my friend Caleb. I promise."

A guard with massive shoulders and stumpy legs patrolled the camp's boundaries. The fierce expression on his face brooked no challenges to his authority.

"Sorry," he said when they approached. "But you can't stay here. We have no room." He grasped a wooden staff in his fist, swinging it as though he were eager to strike anyone who disagreed.

"I have no interest in camping here," Demetrios snapped and then held his temper. It was not the time to engage in an argument. He needed to find his own caravan. "Is your master here?"

The guard glared at him. "I told you we have no room."

Demetrios had four denarii, the sum total of the money he had found in the bandit's purse at Tryphon's Inn. And now he would have to sacrifice one of his precious coins to this lout. He sighed and extracted a single denarius. "Tell your master," he said, dropping the bribe into the guard's waiting palm, "that Demetrios of Tiberias wishes to see him. He'll know my name."

The guard examined the coin and then slipped it into the bag tucked in his girdle. "Wait here."

Romulus himself came out to greet them. "So, it is true." Grinning, he shook his head. "We all thought you were dead, but here you are, my old friend, alive and well." His crafty eyes gleamed in the firelight as he peered at Demetrios and Tabitha. He picked at the knots in his beard. "And I see you're not alone. Who is your lovely companion?"

Demetrios curled his arm about Tabitha's waist, holding her close. Romulus gazed upon every woman as though she were his new possession. "This is Tabitha. My . . ." He hesitated, wondering what he should call her. "My friend."

Romulus looked first at Demetrios and then at Tabitha. "You've been missing for days with no word, no sign you were still alive. And now you appear in the middle of the night with . . . What did you say her name is? Tabitha?" He chuckled. "Incredible. And when my poor servant told me your name, I was expecting to see a ghost."

"No ghosts," Demetrios said. "Just two weary travelers." He wanted to ask about Caleb, but he decided not to say anything, not yet. Romulus would lie if he thought it would give him the advantage. Negotiations with this old crook were always difficult.

Romulus tugged at his cloak. "Well then, why do we stand out here in the cold? You two weary travelers must join me in my tent." He turned toward Tabitha and offered his arm, but she shied away, still clinging to Demetrios.

Demetrios patted her hand, assuring her he would keep her safe. She had pulled her scarf around her face so that only her eyes were fully exposed. "We can't stay," he said to Romulus. "It's been a long journey, and Tabitha is exhausted."

"But you must have a cup of wine and something to eat," Romulus insisted. "I would be offended if you refused." Sweeping his arm toward his tent, he motioned for them to enter. "Come, come. Just for a little while. Tell me news of your travels." He hurried ahead of them to pull back the opening flap.

The floor of the tent had been carpeted with heavy rugs and layered with overstuffed cushions stacked on top of one another to form a curved couch around a low table. Several clay lamps hung from iron stands in the corners, casting a soft yellow glow against the tent walls. The faint scent of perfume greeted them as they reclined on the cushions.

Romulus clapped his hands. "Bring us a jug of wine, bread,

and a jar of that fine honey," he said to the slave who poked his head into the tent. "Tonight we feast."

If Demetrios hoped to learn anything from Romulus about Caleb's fate, he would have to keep a sharp mind and a quick wit. Demetrios glanced at Tabitha, who lay wearily back against the cushions. Her eyes were glazed with fatigue. "Your trading goes well?" Demetrios asked Romulus politely as Tabitha sat up to accept a cup of wine. He held out his own cup to be filled.

Romulus made a sound that resembled more of a cough than a chuckle. His mouth curled up in the semblance of a smile, but his eyes were cold. "Not so well as yours, I would think." He held his cup out in an ironic toast to Demetrios. "I must say, my old friend, that Isaac of yours is smart. Not only does he secure a booth in the Upper Agora, but he sets up shop in one of the best stations on the Cardo, fourth from the left of the main entrance to Herod's palace." He took a sip of his wine, watching Demetrios carefully. "You must know some important people."

Demetrios nodded, relieved to have located Isaac—and that he had managed to make it to the Upper Agora. "I trained him well." It was all he could do to keep from grinning. His caravan was safe. Demetrios broke the loaf of bread in two pieces and handed one to Tabitha.

"Indeed," Romulus replied. He faced Tabitha. "Did you know, Tabitha, that your friend is a cheat?"

"A cheat?" Demetrios pushed upright, glaring at Romulus. "I've never taken a single denarius from you." He had to watch his temper. Romulus was trying to trick him, to draw him out. What was the jackal up to? "You shouldn't frighten Tabitha with such wild accusations, Romulus."

Next to Demetrios, Tabitha stirred. "Demetrios has been very kind to me."

Romulus dipped his bread into the jar. Honey dripped from his fingers as he gallantly offered the treat to Tabitha. "Some sweets for your beautiful friend," Romulus said, leering at Tabitha.

Tabitha pulled back, shaking her head. Demetrios drew her closer to him and glared at Romulus.

Shrugging, Romulus stuffed the sticky bread into his own mouth. Beads of honey stuck to his beard. "Oh, I never said you cheated me. You misunderstand. I said you were a cheat." He smacked his lips. "You misled me, Demetrios. You told me Caleb was a good and honest worker."

"That's true. He was always honest with me." Demetrios paused, taking another drink of wine. "Of course, I never hired thugs to beat my caravan drivers."

"Nor do I, Demetrios. Except when I have cause. Your Caleb thought he was a smart one, too, but he's not so smart. You know about that incident then? The first time I caught him stealing?"

"I heard something about it."

"Then you know he was warned."

The game was becoming tiresome. Romulus intended to tell Demetrios nothing useful. "Did you have Caleb arrested?" Demetrios blurted. "Caleb has made mistakes, but he didn't deserve this. Where is he?"

Suddenly, Romulus stood, waving his cup in the air, the wine sloshing over his hand. "What do you know of it? Your goods are in a shop on the Upper Agora while I'm stuck down in the Small Market with the poor who don't have a shekel to spend. And you sent Caleb to betray me, to steal from me, and destroy me. But you failed." He drained his cup and sat back down. "You failed," he repeated, slurring his words slightly. "Where is that slave? We need more wine."

Demetrios reached for the wine jug on the floor. "There is still some here." He offered it to Romulus. Perhaps the drink would loosen Romulus's tongue. And then they could leave.

"I told you I warned him," Romulus continued after he took another swallow from his cup. "He tried to steal from me twice, you know. No, three times. The first time he suffered a beating by brigands. You know about that because you sent him back to me, my old friend. The second time was just before we reached Jericho. That road is dangerous." Romulus paused, coddling the cup of wine in his hands. "Someone caught him and cut off two of his fingers. Then he ran away."

Two fingers! Poor Caleb. What would become of him? "He ran away? But you said he stole from you three times."

"Ah, that." Romulus nodded. "He came back to the caravan in Jericho. But you know about that, don't you? Isn't that why you're here? To find out if he was successful? He claimed he was hungry, that he knew nothing about where you were. But he was lying. He has always lied." Romulus narrowed his eyes as he leaned closer. "Since you sent him to steal from me, perhaps I should have you arrested as well."

Demetrios shook his head. "No, no you're mistaken. Ask Tabitha. We just arrived this evening. I didn't know he was in Jericho." He hated to bring Tabitha into the discussion, but he worried that Romulus could become violent. Perhaps the gentle voice of a woman would change his tone. "Isn't that true?"

She looked confused and a little frightened. It was clear she didn't understand their disagreement. "We entered Jerusalem a few hours ago," she said slowly.

"Indeed?" Romulus glanced at Demetrios, seeking confirmation. "Well, it doesn't matter anymore, does it?" He poured out the last of the wine. "If you want to see Caleb, you'll have to go to the Fortress Antonia."

The bite of stale bread clung to the roof of Demetrios's mouth. He thought he would choke. He could no longer stay here, not another moment. Rising abruptly, he pulled Tabitha to her feet. "Thank you for the food and drink." He dropped his cup. It rolled across the carpet, leaving a dark stain. "But we must be going. Tabitha is exhausted, and Isaac is waiting."

Romulus stood to escort them outside. He touched Demetrios on the shoulder as he and Tabitha started to pass under the tent flap. "You didn't send him, did you?"

Demetrios shook his head. "No."

Romulus lowered his eyes, his swagger and arrogance gone. "Do not blame me then, Demetrios. He did this to himself."

Demetrios could do nothing for Caleb tonight. No one would see him at this late hour. But tomorrow, he vowed, he would go to the Fortress Antonia to see how he could help. Caleb might be a liar and a petty thief, but he deserved better. "Goodnight," Demetrios said. "Perhaps I'll see you in the markets."

When they were outside the camp, Tabitha sank against Demetrios. She was trembling. "That man. He hates you. The way he looked at me scared me."

Demetrios gripped her by the shoulders and turned her to face him. "Can you walk a bit farther? Isaac will have a room for us in the Upper Agora."

"Yes, I want to stay with you."

"Come, then. The steps at the top of the ravine will take us to the Upper City."

Torches, set strategically in niches of the walls along the road to the Upper City, illumed their way. Demetrios and Tabitha had just turned toward Herod's palace when a familiar voice called out to him. "Demetrios, is it you?"

"Is that your uncle?" Tabitha asked, "Elazar?"

"Yes." Taking her arm, Demetrios led her to an archway off the road. "Wait here," he said. "I'll talk to him, and then we can go."

She shook her head. "I want to stay with you."

"Very well then." He took her arm. "Come."

Elazar waited near one of the torches. He drew back in surprise when he saw Tabitha. "Is that—?"

"It is Tabitha from the oasis," Demetrios said, holding her close. "We are in Jerusalem together. What do you want?"

Elazar stiffened. "I see Isaac brought the caravan safely to Jerusalem." He picked at the fringe on his scarf, looked at Demetrios. "At our last meeting, I told you I would see you again in the Upper Agora, remember?"

"You betrayed me. I have no interest in speaking to you." Demetrios started to leave, then stopped midstride. "Is Jesus near here?" he asked, facing Elazar again. "I want to see him." The flame in the torch flared, and for the first time, Demetrios was aware of how much Elazar had changed. He looked much older, his wrinkles more pronounced. His gray beard looked white. "I have questions for Jesus," Demetrios added. "Can you take me to him?"

Elazar's shoulders sagged. "I don't know where Jesus is. I've left him and his followers."

"Why?"

"He's not the promised one. I know that now."

Stunned, Demetrios stared at Elazar. "Jesus is . . ." He stopped, unable to put his feelings into words. Demetrios pulled Tabitha forward to stand under the torchlight. "Look at her. She was a leper, but Jesus took away her sores and scabs and disease, and now she's whole, healthy. I witnessed it myself." Demetrios turned toward Tabitha, the woman he loved. "Tell him."

Throughout their conversation, she had kept her head down, as though she was embarrassed, but now she held it high and faced Elazar. "Jesus healed me. It was a miracle."

Demetrios nodded. "A miracle. And I want to ask him to perform another. Rufus is dead, murdered by bandits on the Jerusalem road. I want to ask Jesus to bring him back to life." Still standing close to Demetrios, Tabitha gasped.

"A miracle." Elazar spat on the ground. When he spoke again, his voice dripped with disdain. "You believe in miracles, magic tricks for the gullible. And yet, you still walk with a limp. No, Jesus is not the Messiah. Jesus consorts with ruffians, tax collectors, prostitutes, even Gentiles. The true Messiah would not waste his time with such people."

"Gentiles? Like me?" Demetrios swallowed his bitterness. He and Elazar were partners in a crime, partners in a caravan business, but as Jew and Gentile, they remained divided. "Your commitment is shallow, Elazar, but I should know that well. You abandoned me, you abandoned the caravan, and now you abandon your beloved Messiah."

Elazar stood up straight, his eyes flashing with anger. His shadow danced against the wall as he jabbed his finger at Demetrios. "What do you know of faith? You pray to statues. Yahweh promised a Messiah to our people. The One True God will cast off the shackles of Rome, liberate the tribes of Israel, and restore the rightful kingdom. Jesus has done none of this. He's a fine teacher, but he's not the Messiah. I made a mistake. I placed my belief in the wrong person." He sighed loudly. "I'm sorry, Demetrios, but Jesus can't resurrect Rufus. It's all a lie, a hopeless wish."

"Elazar, he is the Messiah. I saw him heal Tabitha. She was once a leper, now she is clean. Look at her!"

"After Passover, I am going south to En-gedi to live with the Essenes."

"You can't go. You should come back to Tiberias with us."

"I don't want my money from the business. I want nothing, only peace."

Elazar slumped against the wall, his eyes wet with tears, but Demetrios resisted the urge to comfort him. He did not know why. Demetrios glanced at Tabitha, aware of her anxiety, her fear of waiting along this lonely road. They should go, find Isaac's booth, and tomorrow, they would try to free Caleb. He would seek Jesus and ask for his own miracle.

"I will find the answers I seek there," Elazar said. "In my study with the Essenes."

Elazar's misery tugged at Demetrios. He struggled to find the right words. "I owe you much. I will share the profits from the caravan with you. Talk to Isaac after Passover. He'll give you your portion."

"Thank you." Elazar's voice was barely a whisper. Wrapping himself tight in his cloak, he said, "Good-bye, Demetrios, my good friend."

Demetrios didn't reply but turned and guided Tabitha toward the booths in the Upper Agora.

The square in the Upper Agora was empty, the vendors' booths locked down for the night. Demetrios guided Tabitha quickly across the paving stones, counting the stalls. Fourth from the left of the main entrance to the palace. Each shop looked exactly like the other. He hoped Romulus had not been mistaken. He knocked at the fourth door, the sound reverberating through the deserted market like a pounding drum.

"We'll wake the whole square," Tabitha said nervously. She glanced behind her, looking at the walls of the palace. "Is Herod there now?"

"Isaac is the only one I care about. And he should be here." He knocked again, this time a little more softly. When he paused to listen, he heard the shuffle of footsteps from within punctuated by the grumble of an irritated voice. Isaac. He had come to the right booth.

"We don't open until daylight," Isaac said as he flung open the door. "You'll have to—" He stopped, his mouth hanging open. "Demetrios?" Rubbing his eyes, he stared at Demetrios. "Am I dreaming? Is it really you?"

Demetrios smiled. "You're not dreaming. I'm here."

"I was so worried about you. When you didn't return and Rufus never sent word. Have you been hurt?" He pointed at the scab on Demetrios's face. He cast a curious glance at Tabitha, but he didn't ask her name.

"A small accident." Taking Tabitha's hand, Demetrios guided her into the booth. He breathed deep, taking in the comforting surroundings of the marketplace. Isaac had chosen a shop with two rectangular windows in the front, a solid stone floor, and enough space for customers to examine the merchandise. A narrow table with a stool behind it divided the front from the back. At the rear a door appeared to lead to another room. "Did the caravan arrive without any problems? Is everything well?"

"Oh, oh, yes. I've done everything you told me to. See?" Waving his hand over the displays, he narrated the arrangement. "Fine fabrics in front. Perfumes, spices, and jewelry in locked boxes on the table. And over there, in the corner, what is left of the wine we brought from Galilee. Only two amphorae. Everything else sold yesterday as soon as we opened the shop. The fruit of Galilean vines is quite popular here. Silas is with the animals, all safely boarded in the stables you requested." He paused. "I think you'll be pleased."

Demetrios nodded. He was pleased. Isaac had done well. "This is Tabitha." Demetrios brought her forward. "We are both very tired from our journey. Do you have a place for us to sleep?"

"Both of you?" Isaac blushed.

"It doesn't have to be a bed. Just a place for us to rest."

"There's a small room at the back. I'll show you."

The three of them crossed under a low threshold into a narrow, windowless space with a sleeping mat in one corner. They lined up single file to keep from bumping one another. When Demetrios extended his arms, he could touch the walls on both sides.

Isaac coughed. "I was sleeping in here, but I guess it's too cramped for three. I'll make a bed in the front room."

"Thank you, Isaac. That would be fine."

As Isaac gathered up his blankets, he paused. "Demetrios, where is Rufus? He didn't come with you?"

Demetrios turned. He had been waiting for the question, but what answer could he give? "No, he's not with me." He sighed. "Tabitha needs to rest, Isaac. We'll talk more in the morning."

"Of course." He pulled the door shut behind him.

Sliding next to Demetrios on the thin sleeping mat, Tabitha dropped almost instantly into a deep and even sleep. Her sweet perfume filled the warmth of the room, summoning memories long forgotten. Memories of a vial of nardinum mysteriously returned to him. Memories of an impulsive young man giving a bracelet to a dying child. Demetrios did not deny that Caleb was a thief, but to turn him over to the Roman authorities was a terrible thing. With his mangled hand, he had little value as a slave. Would they put him on the ships? If not, what would be his sentence? Every guard had his price, but how much for a young Jewish man with eight fingers? Tomorrow Demetrios would find out.

Demetrios had never been punished for his crime of murder,

but Caleb, who had been simply foolish and impulsive, now suffered mutilation and imprisonment and perhaps faced a worse fate. Where was the justice in that? Demetrios closed his eyes, listening to Tabitha's steady, slow breathing. But sleep did not come.

When Demetrios first heard the shouting, he thought he was dreaming, that he had slept after all. "Isaac, open up," a man cried from the square as he banged on the wooden door, rattling the hinges. "You've got to let me in. I need your help. Please. Open the door."

Isaac was still crawling out of his bed on the floor when Demetrios climbed over him and rushed to the door and jerked it open. The eastern sun had just risen above the Judean hills, bathing the walls of Herod's palace in a brilliant light. Demetrios peered at Elazar. "I thought you were leaving."

Elazar stumbled into the booth, shoving past Demetrios. His face was streaked with tears, and his eyes were bloodshot. He whirled around the room, tearing at his clothes, which were stained and dirty. "Quick, Isaac, close the door. Lock it. Oh, I cannot believe this has happened." Twining his fingers into his thinning hair, he pulled out tufts. "Lock the door. They're coming."

"What are you talking about?" Isaac asked, grasping him by the arms to calm him.

Elazar pulled away. His hip hit the table of perfumes and spice, making the boxes rattle ominously. "No, no. There's no time. They will be after all of us soon. You must lock and secure the door. Hide me, hide me until we can escape."

"Demetrios," Tabitha said, "what is happening?" She stood in the doorway to the back room, her black hair falling loosely over her shoulders.

Elazar looked directly at Demetrios. "You never did understand. But now you have to listen to me. They've arrested him!

We're all in danger."

"I know about Caleb," Demetrios said. "I'm going to Antonia today."

"No, not Caleb!" Elazar moaned, his voice a pitiful weeping lament. "They've arrested Jesus!"

Chapter

Thirty-Five

They huddled inside the shop near the back room, the oil lamps barely burning, the front door locked. Elazar had collapsed in the corner.

"Why would they arrest Jesus?" Demetrios asked. "What has he done? Did he say anything against Rome?"

Elazar looked up at him, his face blotched and flushed. "Blasphemy. The Sanhedrin charged him with blasphemy."

Blasphemy? In Capernaum the Pharisees said they threw Jesus out of the synagogue for blaspheming, but what would the Sanhedrin do? Expel him from Jerusalem? Stone him? The Jews had so many rules. Sorting them out was like tying down a whirling wind.

"We're all doomed," Elazar groaned.

"Don't be a fool," Demetrios snapped. Seeing the terror on Elazar's face, Demetrios began to think. Elazar had been good to him in the past. He had cared for Demetrios after Marcus beat Demetrios and branded him. And when Demetrios murdered Marcus, it was Elazar who had planned their escape. It was time for Demetrios to help Elazar. "We'll go to the Sanhedrin together. If they want Jesus to leave Jerusalem, then he can come back to Tiberias with us."

"Demetrios," Isaac said. "Elazar's really upset. Perhaps he should stay here."

"The sentence is death," Elazar said.

Demetrios spun around, staring at Elazar. "They can't do that. Only Rome has the authority to carry out an execution."

"Do you understand nothing?" Elazar rose. "The Sanhedrin despise him. Any excuse. That's all they need. They'll tell Pilate he's plotting against Caesar, and Rome will carry out the sentence. And the rest of us? We'll be accused of treason, too."

"Demetrios," Tabitha said. "What are we going to do?"

Demetrios held up a hand, motioning for them all to be quiet so he could hear the activity outside. The marketplace had opened for business. Merchants shouted from their stalls, "I have wine. Over here! The best perfume in Jerusalem. Come see my jewelry." All things that were in this room. But the booth for Demetrios's caravan remained closed. No one was searching for Elazar. The people out there were seeking merchandise for a good price. He turned toward Isaac. "Open the door."

"No," Elazar protested.

"Perhaps just a crack at first," Isaac said. "We'll see if it's safe."

Demetrios pushed past Isaac and flung the door wide. To his astonishment, a large group of men suddenly started running across the square toward Herod's palace. They crashed into the shoppers, shouting curses and ordering them to move out of the way, crushing people against the booths in the center of the marketplace.

Donkeys brayed in fear, their loads spilling into the street. One kicked against the wall of the booth next to them, and an amphora of olive oil toppled to the ground with a violent crash. The slippery liquid oozed over the cobblestones; an elderly Jew, struggling to escape the mob, slipped and fell to the ground. He screamed as he was trampled underfoot; the merchant in the booth pleaded vainly for order. Any moment now, the soldiers would come, swinging their swords. Demetrios held fast to the door.

When Tabitha touched his shoulder, he jumped and then clasped her hand. "What is happening?" she asked.

"Go back inside," Demetrios demanded as a cacophony of horns blared near the Praetorium.

"Trumpets," Elazar said. "Do you hear them? Pilate has arrived. The Sanhedrin will take Jesus to him to carry out their sentence."

"Then we will go to the Praetorium," Demetrios said.

Elazar backed away from the door. "I can't."

Tabitha clutched Demetrios's arm. "I'm going with you."

Demetrios hesitated. The need to help those he cared for weighed on his shoulders like a bucket of stones. What could he say to the Council of the Sanhedrin? They would rebuff him, call him a "dirty Gentile," send him on his way. Was it even possible to seek an audience with Pilate? Demetrios had no power. Nothing. And he had made promises he wasn't sure he could keep. He stroked Tabitha's cheek. "No, you can't come with me. It may be dangerous." That was not true for Elazar, though. Demetrios turned away from Tabitha and grabbed Elazar. "Isaac," he shouted over his shoulder as he dragged Elazar into the street with him, "close the door and keep it shut until we return."

Elazar's words of protest were lost in the noise of the crowd. Bodies bumped against them from all sides, forcing Demetrios and Elazar to walk close together. Everyone seemed to be moving toward the Praetorium near Herod's palace. Demetrios expected

Elazar to flee, but his old friend remained by his side, sullen and silent.

When they reached the Praetorium, Roman soldiers lined the steps, their helmets gleaming in the morning light. The brazen reflections bounced off the limestone walls of Herod's palace behind them like blinding suns. Leaning close to Elazar, Demetrios squinted against the glare and struggled to find a place for them near the front of the mob. The soldiers guarded two men: Jesus and another Demetrios did not recognize. The excited chatter of the people settled to a quiet murmur, as they waited for Pilate to make his decree.

Pilate, a small, mean man with a tight pinched expression, sat on the curule chair, the seat of justice. With a disdainful look at the people assembled before him, Pilate said to the soldiers, "Release Barabbas. And scourge the other one. Perhaps that will be enough." He swept down the stairs and into Herod's palace.

The soldiers had barely removed Barabbas's bindings when he leaped to the ground, growling like a wild bear. His friends swarmed around him. "We want Barabbas," they said as they laughed and pounded him on the back. With Barabbas in the lead, the group left the square. Others in the crowd lingered briefly to watch Jesus being taken away to the courtyard next to the palace.

Demetrios started to follow Pilate into the palace but was stopped by the soldiers. "I must speak with the prefect."

"Not today," a legionary answered, blocking the way. "He's busy."

Elazar took Demetrios's arm. "Wait until after the scourging and after everyone has left. Perhaps he will be more receptive then."

The scourging. The halfway death. How could Jesus survive such a punishment? Demetrios glanced around the square, suddenly aware of who was missing. Where were Jesus's loyal followers? The men who had surrounded him at Capernaum and Jericho? Where was Peter? And Judas? Had they all fled? Or were they awaiting execution as well? "Where are his disciples?" Demetrios said to Elazar.

Elazar shook his head. "I don't know."

The silence and the absence were all wrong. Someone had to speak for Jesus. If he could not talk to Pilate now, then Demetrios would attend the scourging. He would be there for Jesus, an advocate without a voice. He turned to Elazar. "We're going to the courtyard."

Elazar hung back. "It's not clean. I can't defile myself so close to the Shabbat."

Stunned, Demetrios stared at his friend. "What are you talking about?"

Elazar looked like he wanted to weep. "If I enter a Gentile's house now, I'll have to purify myself again before the Shabbat, before going to the Temple for Passover." He swallowed. "There isn't enough time."

Demetrios clenched his fists, opened his hands again. He looked at Elazar. "You may not believe he is your Messiah, but he has done nothing to deserve this punishment. You won't even stand with him when he suffers." He spat on the ground, waiting. "Come, then," Demetrios said when Elazar made no comment. "You'll join me in the courtyard."

Demetrios and Elazar passed through the courtyard gate without restraint, ignoring the insulting looks of the pious Jews who stood outside. A small group of weeping women watched from just inside the walls. "The one in the middle," Elazar said. "I think that's his mother."

Demetrios nodded. He was grateful he had insisted Tabitha

remain at the booth. This wasn't something she should see.

The scourging had not yet begun, but the preparations were already in place. As they stationed themselves close to the entrance, a drum began to beat, and another cohort of legionaries marched out to line three walls of the yard. Witnesses for Rome.

Jesus, under guard, knelt in the middle of the floor. Like Barabbas, he had been stripped down to his loincloth. Two soldiers emerged from the palace and dragged him to his feet. They led him to a thick stone pillar that was about two cubits high. Bending him forward over the pillar, they pulled his bound hands down over the far side of the pillar and secured them to a large iron ring so that his bare back was fully exposed.

The Tribune circled Jesus, confirming all was ready.

The lictor, dressed in his traditional brown cloak, set aside his fasces: a tightly wound bundle of wooden rods with an axe head protruding. He grasped the proffered flagellum.

The Tribune declared, "The punishment is forty minus one."

A snap, a crack in the air. A whistle on the breeze.

The count began. One . . . Two . . . Three . . .

At first touch, Demetrios knew, the flagellum was a tender, stinging kiss. Swift as a scorpion's strike. Marcus's whip, which had been a single leather strip, cut into Demetrios's skin like a flashing blade. The flagellum contained multiple thongs, each end tied off with pieces of metal and bone. How much greater the agony!

With each snap, Demetrios jerked back, trapped once again in the terrible sense of anticipation, the knowing of what was to come. On three, fire blooms beneath the skin, searing the aching bone. Flesh rises up to meet the burning lips. A gasp as the scorching heat soaks deep, arches away. White-hot fingers curl around the body, embracing, tearing flesh. By ten, the inferno burns from within and without. The air is a cauldron of flame. The light golden, the floor red. But fire consumes all. On thirteen, the body seeks incineration, to become one with the conflagration. A sun fallen from the heavens. Seventeen. Embers smolder and glow, settling into ashes still burning beneath the rubble.

The lictor stopped.

The Tribune walked over to Jesus to examine him. With a wave of his hand, he ordered a soldier to dump a bucket of water over Jesus's head. The Messiah sputtered and coughed. Another bucket was poured over him; the streaming red liquid sluiced across the cobblestone floor toward Demetrios's feet.

Demetrios jumped back.

The Tribune said, "He is alive. Finish your work."

Elazar cried out, "I cannot watch!" Shoving his way past the spectators standing at the gate, he dashed into the street.

"Elazar!" Demetrios shouted, running after him.

CHAPTER
THIRTY-SIX

Demetrios plunged into the throng that milled around the upper market. The morning commerce had reached its peak, and the square echoed with the shouts of merchants and their customers. He experienced a strange sense of unreality. People shopped just outside the walls of torture? He paused, scanning the bobbing heads for his old friend. Off to Demetrios's left, a white-haired man ducked and darted through the crowd. "Elazar," Demetrios cried. "Come back."

Elazar stopped and turned around. A brief moment of recognition flashed across his face. Then he slumped, and the muscles in his face went slack. He said nothing to Demetrios, but the meaning was clear: despair.

"Elazar!" Demetrios shouted.

"No, go back. It's finished," Elazar cried. Pushing his way past a group of pilgrims leading a donkey, he careened through the narrow streets.

Demetrios followed, jogging in his awkward, ungainly stride, a gait that threw him off-balance, causing him to collide with angry passersby. More than once, he was slowed as he stumbled over a spilled basket or dropped bundle. More than once he was cursed when he didn't stop to help. He kept running.

Elazar turned to the right and crossed into an alleyway off the main square. Demetrios had hoped he would go back to their booth, but he was headed south and west, toward the Gate of the Essenes that opened to the Hinnom Valley. Perhaps sensing that his white hair made him more visible, Elazar slowed briefly to pull up the back of his mantle to cover his head. Then he made a dash for the gates. The last glimpse Demetrios had was of that blue-and-white-striped mantle passing through the opening in the stone walls.

Except for a few travelers on their way to the Sea of Salt, the road beyond the Gate of the Essenes was quiet. Demetrios walked a short distance in the same direction he thought Elazar had gone and then turned back. Had he been mistaken? Was Elazar still in the city? There were so many blue-and-white-striped mantles in the upper marketplace. It seemed every Jew from Galilee wore a blue-and-white cloak. He could have followed the wrong person through the gates. But if Elazar had not come this way, where had he gone? His parting words to Demetrios, "It's finished." An uneasy feeling nagged at Demetrios. Finished for whom?

The Hinnom Valley was a deep ravine that curved around the wall of Jerusalem. Once used as a site for human sacrifice, the valley was held in such abhorrence by the Jews that it had become a dumping ground for human sewage and animal carcasses. Flames sparked unbidden from the refuse, then subsided, leaving a foul stench of putrefying flesh that hung over the valley like an evil presence. The Jews called the valley the "lake of unquenchable fire." The Greek name for the place was "Gehenna," or hell. What if Elazar had not taken the road at all but had gone down into the ravine?

Rubbing the blister that had formed on his big toe—B'ar's new sandals were too tight—Demetrios leaned over the low wall that guarded the entrance to the Hinnom. Several shadowy figures picked through the piles of trash below, moving like ghosts through the haze of smoke. Was one of them Elazar? He could call out to them, but he realized that they would never hear him from the road.

He faced north, taking deep gulping breaths of the fresh air that drifted down from the hills. He was so weary. When he closed his eyes, he saw the flagellum fly through the air, the spray of blood from Jesus's back. And below this road, a pit of horror waited. No, he could not leave Elazar. If he was down there, in that ghastly hole, Demetrios would bring him back. Opening his eyes, Demetrios adjusted the strap on his sandal and climbed over the wall to the steep path that descended into the ravine.

The interior of the Hinnom Valley was even worse than it appeared from the road. Bloated animal corpses lay atop heaps of smoldering rubbish; the air reeked with the odor of decay and rot. Black vultures swarmed overhead, their hungry screeches punctuating the murk like the screams of tortured souls. Had Jesus cried out when the flagellum cut his flesh? Demetrios could not remember.

His eyes stinging, Demetrios pulled his cloak up over his mouth and plunged into the burning fog. He approached a scrawny old man who was poking a stick in a pile of ash. "I'm looking for a friend. A man called—"

"He's not here," the old man answered.

Demetrios stared at the man and shuddered. The poor creature had wrapped his feet in rags, and his skin was coated with so many layers of grime that it had turned the color of charred wood. Demetrios wanted to feel pity for him, but his disgust overpowered his sympathy. Why would anyone live like this? "I never told you his name." His voice was harsh, angry.

"Doesn't matter. This is the home of the dead." He looked up at Demetrios with rheumy eyes that had been blinded with a white, milky film. "Is your friend dead?"

Demetrios didn't answer.

"Then he's not here," the man said, as he returned to digging through the trash. He picked up a small, black lump about the size of a seed and popped it into his mouth. "Bone," he said, spitting it out. "Hoped it might be a pearl." He wandered away.

How foolish to think that Elazar would come here. Elazar was a stronger man than these desperate half-dead beings who roamed over the mounds of smoldering garbage. Demetrios knew he would never find Elazar in this doomed place. Perhaps Elazar had left, after all, to be with the Essenes. Tabitha and Isaac were waiting for Demetrios at the booth. He should go back.

Demetrios had climbed less than halfway up the trail to the road when he heard a snap of a tree branch and a terrified scream from above. The scream was followed by the crash of more broken branches and the sound of something, or someone, tumbling down the hillside. It fell over the rocks to land on the ridge below. Demetrios heard a faint groan—human—and then silence.

When Demetrios reached the lower portion of the path, he saw a man sprawled on his back on the ground, his head cocked at an odd angle. His eyes were closed. Alive or dead?

It was Judas.

Demetrios knelt beside him, and Judas's eyes fluttered. Alive then. Judas licked the trickle of blood on his lips, mumbling. His fingers fumbled for something at his waist.

Judas's own waterskin had been split open in the fall. Demetrios raised the bag Tabitha had given him and dribbled a few drops into the man's mouth. Judas struggled to swallow the water, then took another sip and seemed to grow a little stronger.

For the first time, Demetrios noticed the cord wrapped around Judas's neck. A hemp rope of the same kind used to secure goods on an animal's back, it had been looped around Judas's throat and tied in a knot, leaving deep abrasions in his skin where it had pulled taut. A single long piece trailed off from the knot like a forgotten tail. Perhaps Elazar was right. The friends of Jesus were in danger.

Judas held out his hand and spoke, but Demetrios couldn't understand him. The rope had damaged his voice so that every word was a raspy croak. Judas pushed down against the ground with his hands, groaning with the effort.

Grasping him under the arms, Demetrios eased the man into an upright position and Judas's words came more easily, although they still had that strange hoarse quality. When he looked at Demetrios, his gaze was startlingly direct. "I know you. The caravan driver."

"Yes."

"Why do you follow me?" Judas asked. "I know. I saw you. In Capernaum and Jericho. And now, here."

"I wasn't following you. I—" He stopped. What could he tell him?

Judas gestured toward the waterskin. He took a deep drink and then spat out a bloody tooth.

"Is it finished?" he asked Demetrios.

The same words Elazar had used. "Is what finished?"

"I forgot," Judas said. "You're a Gentile. You know nothing."

Demetrios flinched.

Judas laid his head back against a rock and closed his eyes. "The chosen one," he said softly. "That's what he told me. That I had been chosen." He laughed, a sound so bitter Demetrios could taste salt on his own tongue.

Uncertain of what Judas meant, Demetrios merely nodded. Judas didn't seem to notice that he was bleeding from the nose and the mouth.

Judas reached out and grabbed Demetrios's wrist. "Are you real?" he asked. He squeezed his arm with surprising strength. "No, not a ghost after all. I still live. The rope failed."

"The rope? You tried to hang yourself?"

Judas released him, his arm falling back to his side. "When they first came to me, I told them, 'No, I won't do it.' Threw the money back in their faces. Keeper of the purse!" He was quiet for a moment. "He was supposed to be a king, you know. Prophecy. Were the prophets wrong?"

"I don't know what you're talking about."

"How far is it to the road?" Judas asked.

"A good distance. The trail is steep."

Judas nodded. "Too far then." He wiped his mouth with his hand and looked at his fingers, stained with his own blood. He began fumbling with his girdle. "Is it still here?"

"What?" Was he looking for his waterskin? It had been drained away on the rocks. "I have more water here if you want some."

"No," he said, shaking his head. "Not water this time." He reached into his girdle and drew out a double-edged dagger. Holding the dagger in front of his face, he turned it around in his hands, admiring its beauty. "Yes."

An ivory handle shaped like a woman with lapis lazuli eyes. A blade so finely honed that its point gleamed like a malignant star. Backing slowly away, Demetrios asked, "Where did you get that?"

Judas stroked the handle. His fingers left dark red smears over the white curves. "Lovely thing, isn't it? What do you think the maker dreamed about when he created this?"

"No good dreams have ever come from that."

Judas grinned, exposing his chipped and broken teeth. His skin had developed a gray cast, and his eyes seemed to lose their focus. "Early this morning. The tanner said he needed money for a new donkey. I thought I might need the protection. But they all ran away." He slid his finger along the blade, oblivious to the new cuts opening up. "The woman. A pagan idol. Unclean. I shouldn't handle it at all." And he laughed his grotesque laugh again.

Demetrios picked up the waterskin and moved closer to Judas. "Why don't I hold the dagger while you have a drink of water?"

Silence. Judas's breath was more labored now. When he turned to face Demetrios, a fever burned in his eyes, bright and glittering.

"Jesus is in trouble," Demetrios said. "He was arrested early this morning. I was there when he was whipped by the lictor. Where were you? You and the others? He needed you."

Taking short, quick breaths, Judas pushed himself up. "Gentile, do you understand nothing?" he raged. "I killed Jesus."

"What?"

"I brought the Roman soldiers to him. I betrayed him with a kiss." He raised the knife to the heavens. "Jesus, I forgive you." And before Demetrios could stop him, Judas shoved the dagger deep into his own belly. A single stab on the left and then a quick motion to the right. Blood streamed through his clasped hands, and the dagger slipped from his grip. He tilted to one side, his mouth fixed in a smile as blood spilled out of his abdomen. "Hurts," he whispered as he fell over.

Demetrios reached out, his hand hovering over the man's shoulder. He did not touch him. "It is finished," Demetrios said. The dagger lay under Judas's body where it belonged.

CHAPTER
THIRTY-SEVEN

Isaac answered at the sound of Demetrios's first knock. He swung the door wide, welcoming Demetrios into the protection of the booth. Tabitha sat in the corner, her hands busy refolding lengths of wool. She jumped to her feet as soon as she saw him come through the door. "You've come back." She pulled him into the room. Her face was pale and her eyes red from weeping.

"Is Elazar here?" he asked as Tabitha guided him to a stool, where he sat down heavily.

Isaac shook his head. "But Elazar sent word. He's gone to En-gedi."

Relieved, Demetrios sank down on the stool, his back braced against the wall. Elazar was safe. "Good." He glanced around the stall, struck by the simplicity of the familiar. This was what he did. He owned a caravan, and he transported people and goods across the roads of Palestine. During any normal Passover festival, he would be here, in this booth or another one like it, Elazar at his side, selling his merchandise to the wealthy Jews and Gentiles who frequented the Upper Agora. That was how it should be.

But that world outside this door—the very marketplace where he had collected money and exchanged gossip in the past—had been transformed into a nightmare of misery and death. He wanted to close the door now and forget. He addressed Isaac. "Do you have a basin of water?" He looked at his hands. Dirty. Stained with blood and guilt and a terrifying confession. Why had Judas told him those things?

"There isn't time," Tabitha exclaimed. "They've taken him away."

"What are you talking about?"

"I know you told us to stay inside," Isaac answered, "but Tabitha insisted. We went out to watch the procession."

Demetrios stared at him, still not comprehending. "What procession?"

"Jesus," Tabitha said. "They've taken him to be crucified."

"Tabitha asked someone in the marketplace," Isaac added. "They said it will be on the hill called Golgotha."

"No!" Demetrios slammed his hand down, striking a table, making them all jump. Too late then. Nothing he could say to Pilate to change things now. And what of Caleb? Was he still languishing in a prison cell? He couldn't save Jesus, but perhaps he could help Caleb. He stood abruptly. "I have to go to Antonia. Wait here. I'll be back soon."

Tabitha gripped his arm. "I want to go to Golgotha."

Demetrios turned to her. "A crucifixion is not something you should see."

"I've lived in the caves with lepers. Do you think I fear watching a crucifixion?" In the gloom of the booth, Tabitha's eyes blazed. Demetrios thought he had never seen her so determined. "Jesus gave me back my life. He should not have to die alone. I want to be there."

Isaac gasped. "Lepers? You lived with lepers?"

Neither Demetrios nor Tabitha answered him. Demetrios looked at the woman who stood so resolutely before him. She carried a strength he had not imagined. And a loyalty not easily challenged. "Very well," he said slowly. "We'll go first to Golgotha." He turned to Isaac. "Stay here." He nodded at the goods stacked in the room. "I think it's safe to open the booth now."

Tabitha was silent as the two of them pushed their way out into the still-busy marketplace. She walked close to him, holding tight to his elbow, her head down. Demetrios wondered if she was thinking about what she would see at Golgotha.

Located just outside the city walls, the site was near the crossroads for Samaria to the north and Joppa to the west. The Romans preferred their executions to be public and visible, as a lesson for others. Golgotha, The Hill of the Skull, named for the bones of the men who died there. In his travels with his caravan, Demetrios had passed by Golgotha several times, but had never lingered long enough to gaze upon the bodies left to rot in the sun. It was said that when the wind blew from the northeast, the citizens of the Lower City could hear the cries of the dying.

As Demetrios and Tabitha exited through the Garden Gate, he glanced at the horizon: three uprights on the ridge above, three vertical silhouettes against a sky so brilliantly blue that it hurt the eyes to look upon it. Not one, but three men were scheduled to die this day.

Several priests and members of the Sanhedrin stood at the top of the hill waiting impatiently for the soldiers to begin the executions. Demetrios and Tabitha eased around them across the rocky ground to stand in front of the vertical posts.

Tabitha turned to Demetrios. "Where should we go?"

"Somewhere near the center. They won't let us get too close."

Jesus and the other two prisoners were being held off to the side, behind the posts. Flanked by at least a dozen soldiers, they could barely be seen through the barrier of shields and armor. Demetrios wondered if Pilate feared an uprising or an attempted escape. Aside from the soldiers and the priests, not many had come up the road to watch the condemned men die. The festivities and celebrations in the city held a greater appeal than the agony of a crucifixion. There were a few people Demetrios recognized, though. To the far left, five women and a young man talked softly amongst themselves. Jesus' mother was with them but no longer weeping. Quiet and composed, she faced the posts, her eyes focused on some distant point in the sky.

Demetrios blinked, studying the lone male who accompanied the women. He had seen him before in the wadi at Capernaum. Demetrios touched Tabitha's shoulder and jerked his chin toward the young man. "Who is that? Do you know?"

"John. He's one of Jesus's disciples."

Demetrios nodded. But where were the others? Where were Peter and the other men who had been so devoted to Jesus? Was this the only friend who had come?

Demetrios pulled Tabitha closer to him, thinking that he would shield her view. He had not forgotten the horror in the courtyard. "Are you prepared for this?"

Her answer was a whisper: "Yes."

But how could she be prepared to see the destruction of the flagellum? The pieces of skin ripped from the body in bloody strips? The deep chunks of flesh gouged out by the bite of the whip's metal tips? She would still be thinking of the man who had healed her in the wilderness; she wouldn't recognize the Jesus who had survived the scourging. And a crucifixion was even worse than a beating. It was an excruciating way to die.

One of the priests approached the centurion who was inspecting the site. "You need to get this done quickly," he said. "Before the Shabbat."

The centurion's face flushed, and he nodded curtly to the priest. Jews did not give orders to Roman soldiers. Turning toward his men, he began barking out commands. "Secure those uprights. Bring the prisoners forward. One at a time."

Four soldiers half-dragged, half-carried Jesus out toward the center upright. A circlet of jujube branches had been pressed onto his head, their long thorns cutting so deep into his scalp that dark streaks of blood still flowed down the sides of his face.

Tabitha uttered a small exclamation of surprise and horror, but she didn't flinch. She didn't turn away. "Jesus," she said, speaking to no one in particular, "why have they done this?"

Demetrios gripped her hand.

Jesus was immediately followed by a large man who shouldered the patibulum, the crossbar that would be affixed to the upright. The centurion directed him to set the heavy beam down behind Jesus. Then he turned to the soldier who held the titulus. "Read the prisoner's crime, so that others will know."

Black letters had been painted on a placard coated in white gypsum, a denouncement in three languages: Hebrew, Latin, and Greek. The soldier raised the sign and recited loudly in Latin, "Jesus the Nazarene, King of the Jews."

The priest who had urged the centurion to hurry stepped forward and protested. "The wording is incorrect. He said, 'I am King of the Jews.'"

The centurion glared at him. "Do you challenge the knowledge of the prefect? It is read as it is written. Move back and let us do our work."

Still grumbling, the priest stepped to one side.

The soldiers brought out the second prisoner and read the charge against him: thievery. He hadn't been scourged but beaten with a cane that left deep welts across his back. Even with his injuries, he managed to carry the patibulum easily. Unlike Jesus, who was quiet, this man railed and cursed at both the soldiers and the spectators. He shouted that he had been unfairly persecuted, that the witnesses had lied. "I was never on the Jericho road. I've been in Jerusalem the whole time."

"Quiet, you!" the centurion ordered.

As a legionary shoved the thief toward the post on Jesus's left, the man aimed a final insult. "You're nothing but stinking camel dung! Pah!" Dropping the crossbeam where he stood, he turned his head and spat on the soldier. It was an unfortunate mode of insult he chose, for those who died on the cross often suffered from extreme thirst. The centurion laughed and dragged him to his place.

The third man was silent as he shuffled across the stony ground with his head lowered, his face turned away from the spectators, as if his shame was too great to see reflected in the eyes of the indifferent crowd. He dragged the patibulum behind him with one arm. The other arm hung limply at his side, the hand bound in a bloody bandage. He had two fingers missing. Demetrios cried out before he could stop himself, "Caleb!"

Caleb released the crossbeam and looked up, searching for the familiar voice. "Demetrios?" he croaked.

Pulling Tabitha with him, Demetrios started running toward his former caravan driver. He was blocked by the centurion.

"You can't touch the prisoner." He drew his sword. "It's forbidden."

Demetrios stopped just in time, and Tabitha squeezed his arm, reminding him that he shouldn't argue with Rome. "Caleb."

Demetrios struggled to keep his voice calm. "I'm here. Be brave. I will stay with you until the end."

Caleb glanced at the centurion, his eyes questioning.

"Say what you need to say now," the centurion told him. "We'll put you up last." He sheathed his sword.

Demetrios sighed. The centurion wasn't completely unkind. "Caleb, I'm so sorry. I should have taken you back."

"I didn't do what they say. I never took anything for myself. I gave the bracelet to that poor girl who was dying, Rebecca. Romulus . . ." He stopped. He had started to cry. "Romulus is a wicked man. He cheats everyone."

Such a foolish, impetuous young man. He had no real malice in him, but this is what it had come to. To be crucified for such an insignificant act. What would they do if they knew a murderer stood before them? Demetrios glanced at the centurion, his fear choking back the truth. "I know about Romulus." Demetrios paused. "I will do what is right for you." He swallowed. "Afterward."

They were interrupted by the high keening of a group of women ascending the hill. The Charitable Daughters of Jerusalem had arrived. As they climbed up the path to Golgotha, they crooned a mournful dirge. "We weep for you, our sons. Our prayers plead mercy for your spirit. Our tears water your grave. We weep, we weep." They assembled in front of the condemned men, still singing softly.

Caleb began to sob uncontrollably.

The woman in the lead carried a jar of wine seasoned with myrrh. She faced the centurion.

"You may approach the prisoners," he said.

She poured some of the concoction into a cup and held it up to the thief who had cursed everyone. He drank it greedily, held his hand out for more.

"Be grateful for what you were given!" the centurion snapped, shoving the thief along.

When the woman offered the cup to Jesus, he shook his head, refusing even a taste. The condemned seldom rejected this comfort. Her confusion apparent, the woman glanced at the centurion, who shrugged his shoulders. "Perhaps this one will be more appreciative." He directed her toward Caleb.

Caleb was watching Jesus. "Why did you not drink?"

Jesus didn't answer.

Demetrios spoke up. "Caleb, take the wine. It will dull the pain."

Slowly, Caleb held out his good hand. He drank.

As soon as the Charitable Daughters had departed, the centurion raised his arm high and dropped it, giving the signal for them to begin. Four soldiers stripped each prisoner down to his loincloth and set the clothing in neat piles next to their respective uprights. The garments were an extra payment to the legionaries for their work today. The assigned executioner walked behind Jesus and straightened the crossbeam. Grasping Jesus under both arms, he pulled him quickly backward to the ground. As soon as Jesus fell, the patibulum was fitted under the back of his neck. Then a soldier knelt on either side of him, their knees pressing Jesus's elbows into the beam. Two more soldiers pulled his arms out straight and roped his wrists to the wood.

"No," Caleb cried. He turned his face away.

The executioner walked around the condemned man, surveying the work so far. Jesus had not made a sound, but his chest heaved with rapid, shallow breaths.

Tabitha rested her head on Demetrios's shoulder. He could feel her tears wet his skin. She wept a cold stream of sorrow.

The wind gusted over the hills, stirring up little puffs of dust. Caleb continued to murmur, "No, no," while the other thief moaned softly. Jesus remained silent.

The executioner knelt by Jesus's left arm and reached deep into the apron around his waist. He pulled out an iron nail about the length of a man's hand, positioned it over Jesus's palm, and raised his hammer.

With the first bang, Demetrios startled, remembering a stone, a stone pounding flesh and bone, Marcus's skull crushed beneath the blows, his blood spattering Demetrios's face. Demetrios looked at his hands. Clean.

He heard a woman cry out to his left. Turning, he saw Mary, the mother of Jesus, drop to the ground, the depth of her grief sweeping over her.

How terrible to witness the death of your child. She had carried Jesus in her womb, nursed him as a baby, and now she fell before him, unable to comfort him while he suffered.

Then, with mighty shouts and grunts, the soldiers completed their work, and heaved the three prisoners, all nailed to their respective crossbeams, into position.

Demetrios tried to shut out the noise, but he still heard the horror.

Now fully suspended on the cross, with his lungs inflated with air he could not expel, Jesus pushed up on his feet, the weight pressing against the nails piercing his heels. He remained balanced on his heels until the pain defeated him. Then he began to sag, sliding slowly down the vertical post until his arms were pulled taut against the patibulum.

The curious passersby who had joined the crowd gathered in front of Jesus and watched his struggles with feigned interest. "A miracle worker," one of them said, shaking his head and laughing. "Make a miracle for us now. Come down from there and heal yourself."

Another one scooped up a handful of pebbles. "You said you could tear down the Temple in three days and raise it up again." He threw the rocks at Jesus's head. "Well, here are your building blocks."

Demetrios lowered his hands, clenching his fists. He wanted to strike them. "Have you nothing better to do than mock the dying?"

One of the men turned toward him, his lips curled into a sneer. "Gentile, this is none of your concern. Go home."

Demetrios glared at the man, and the man glared back, unmoved, his derision searing the space that separated them.

Taking Tabitha by the arm, Demetrios moved away from the man to stand closer to Caleb, who was fighting for breath. A shudder passed over Caleb's body each time he gasped for air. "Caleb," Demetrios said. "Be strong. I'm here."

Caleb didn't respond.

Tabitha asked Demetrios, "Why is it getting so dark?"

Over two hours had passed since the men had been placed on the crosses, and the sky had deepened from crystal blue to the darker shadowed hues of twilight. When Demetrios gazed up into the heavens, he saw a crescent of gold disappearing behind a perfect black orb. No clouds. No approaching storm. The world had transformed to night in the middle of the day. "Something is happening to the sun."

"What does it mean?" Tabitha asked.

Demetrios shook his head. "I don't know."

Behind them, one of the women who waited with Mary said, "We're all being punished for our crimes."

Demetrios looked at her. What crimes have these two men

committed? One heals the leper; the other bestows gifts upon dying children. Demetrios turned back toward the Messiah, watching, waiting. How much longer could he and the others endure?

Jesus's arms and shoulders writhed in pain, contorting like twisted ropes, as he wrenched his body upward to prevent suffocation; to halt the process of drowning in his own breath. Beads of sweat mixed with blood rolled down his brow and dripped into the corners of his eyes. Flies crawled across Jesus's open wounds, making his flesh twitch. When he pressed down on his heels, sucking hungrily for air, his head, still crowned with jujube thorns, bumped against the base of the titulus, opening new cuts in his scalp. Jesus stayed upright for long moments, panting and wheezing until, crushed by the weight of his own body, he sank back down onto the nails in his feet.

The soldiers had sorted out the clothing of the condemned men and were making their claims. The centurion held Jesus's tunic up to the fading light. The fabric had once been the color of milk, but now it was stained black with layers of caked blood. "Who wants this?" he asked his men. Several soldiers spoke up at once.

Demetrios was surprised by the quality of the garment. He had always assumed that Jesus came from a poor family, but this tunic was seamless, something rare and of great value.

One of the legionaries reached for the tunic, but the centurion snatched it away. He threw a pair of knucklebones at his men. "Winner takes it."

Jesus appeared to be near death but when he heard the soldiers gambling for his clothes, he opened his eyes. His lips, parched and cracked, moved. At first, no sound came forth. Then he said suddenly, startling everyone, "Abba, forgive them. They do not know what they have done."

Shocked by Jesus's request, Demetrios gazed up at him. *Is this what you ask, Jesus? My father, the Roman . . . can I forgive them for what they've done? What can be forgiven? Are all things forgivable?* He remembered the crowd's thirst for blood, and now, as he was dying on the cross, Jesus's last breaths, forgiving them.

Jesus's outcry had stirred the thief on his left to a new energy. He pressed down on his feet, straightened his torso, and shouted, "If you're the Messiah, then do what is right. Save yourself and save us." He fell back then, easing down the post, groaning in anguish.

Tabitha jerked out of Demetrios's arms and buried her face in her hands.

Demetrios stared at her. He wanted to go to her, to comfort her, but he could not move. *Abba. My father, my dear father. Forgive them.* The words Jesus had spoken in the wilderness. Demetrios thought of all the injustices he had suffered and of all the injustices he had committed. Was one more forgivable than another? He looked at Jesus. How could Jesus find the courage to forgive the soldiers who whipped him, or the followers who had abandoned him? How could Jesus forgive his own executioner?

Caleb said then, "Jesus, do you hear me?"

"I hear."

Caleb's speech was labored. "I've stolen and taken . . . what is not mine." He paused, struggling to pull himself upright. "My punishment is . . . just. But you . . . you are innocent. I know." Another long silence passed while he slipped down and then pushed up. Demetrios fought the desire to rush over and help him. "Will you," Caleb asked at last, "remember me when you come into your kingdom?"

Jesus's voice was surprisingly strong. "I promise you that today you'll be with me in paradise."

Caleb smiled a small smile and sank lower. The centurion, seeing that the end was near for him, raised a club and smashed it into Caleb's lower legs, breaking the long bones with two resounding cracks. A familiar pain shot through Demetrios's leg, and he moaned. But Caleb's agony was over.

Tabitha wept. Demetrios walked over to her and embraced her.

Jesus drew himself again up on the cross, so that he could speak. "Mother," he called, and the woman named Mary stepped closer. "Mother, behold your son." Jesus nodded to John. "Son, behold your mother." Then Jesus closed his eyes and slid back down the upright. John wrapped his arm around Mary, taking her off to the side while she wept.

It was nearing the ninth hour; the sky had turned so dark Demetrios thought he could see stars. The soldiers who had been left to guard the condemned men watched the heavens with growing unease. Several commented that this was an "evil omen."

Night never descended upon the world of the Hinnom Valley, the most evil of all places. There, eternal fires suspended time in eternal twilight. Demetrios wondered if Judas had found the peace he sought. Demetrios patted Tabitha's shoulder, and she leaned heavily against him, her body as limp as if she were sleeping. "Do you want to go?" he whispered. It seemed inappropriate to speak in a normal voice.

She shook her head. "Not until it's over."

Demetrios looked at the men on the crosses. Caleb had died, and the other thief breathed his final moments. He hadn't moved for some time. Jesus still shifted his weight, pushing up to exhale short breaths. The first to be crucified and the last to die. "It won't be long," Demetrios said.

The muscles in his legs and arms quivering with the effort, Jesus pressed his full weight on his heels and levered his body up so that it was even with the top of the patibulum. "Eli, Eli, lama sabachthani?" he cried in a voice so terrible and vibrant that every-one jumped. "My God, my God, why have you deserted me?"

Two of the spectators ran toward Jesus, their faces blanched with fear. No man who expired on the cross had ever shown so much force at the end. One of the men said, "He calls for Elijah. Watch to see if Elijah comes to help him."

"In trailing flames of glory," another person murmured. He looked at the sky as though he expected the firmament to rain fire.

Several of the soldiers spit three times on their hands.

"What does it mean?" Tabitha asked.

Demetrios shook his head and said nothing. So much lost, so much sacrificed. Out there, in the wilderness, buried under a mound of acacia branches and rock, Rufus watched for his Master to return. "Wait for me, Rufus," Demetrios whispered. "I will come back for you."

Tabitha did not stir.

The thief on Jesus' left was dead. His body hung limp from the crossbeam, his mouth open and slack. The centurion ordered one of the legionaries to club the man's legs, just to be certain. Then he sat down. Only one remained.

"I thirst!" Jesus shouted.

Sighing, the centurion rose. He took a hyssop from one of his legionaries, speared a sponge, and dipped the sponge into a jar of vinegar. The centurion smeared the dripping sponge over Jesus's cracked dry lips, but Jesus did not drink. The liquid ran freely down his chin, mixing with the dried blood on his shoulders. The centurion doused the sponge a second time and held it up. Jesus turned his face away.

"Abba," Jesus said, "into your hands I commend my spirit!" He moaned, a deep sighing cry that made the air shimmer. "It is finished!"

Demetrios sensed it before he felt it. A huge flock of birds careened into the darkened sky, screeching in alarm. Donkeys brayed in the distance, their cries hysterical with fear. Doors slammed open and shut; people ran from the hillside and into the streets, screaming; pottery crashed and shattered. A slow rumble rolled beneath Demetrios's feet, increasing to a roar. "Get down," Demetrios shouted, pulling Tabitha to the ground. "Away from the crosses. It's an earthquake."

He pressed his palms flat against the soil; the earth trembled like a frightened horse. Voices cried out around him: "Save us, save us! It's the end of the world!"

The ground shifted and pitched beneath them, and Demetrios held fast to Tabitha, as his mouth filled with dirt. Another slight tremor beneath Demetrios's fingertips, and it was over. Demetrios and Tabitha lay quietly for a moment, but others were already up and moving. A blur of bare legs and bright colored clothing flashed across Demetrios's line of sight. Staggering to his feet, he helped Tabitha stand. They were both covered in dust and grit but otherwise unhurt.

At the first tremor, the priests and Sanhedrin had fled, scurrying back to the safety of the city. Jesus's mother and the crying women waited for a moment but soon followed down the hill with John, the disciple.

All was still.

Demetrios stepped to the center cross and knelt down.

He placed his hand on Jesus's foot, feeling no life under his skin, and looked up. "Tell me who I should forgive," Demetrios said, but Jesus didn't answer. "What about Rufus? You were supposed to raise him up." Pools of water began to form in his eyes. "You could have saved Caleb's life. Why do you remain silent?"

Jesus's head was drooped to the side. A single drop of Jesus's blood fell on the back of Demetrios's hand. The blood was warm and soft. Demetrios did not touch it; he did not move. Another drop fell, landing close to the first. He leaned in and kissed Jesus's foot. And then a third drop struck Demetrios's head. His body shuddered, and he thought he would fall, but his hand seized the Messiah's foot harder. Demetrios closed his eyes. He received his answer; Jesus spoke—words heard only by Demetrios.

The quietude was interrupted by the flock of birds circling overhead.

Demetrios stepped back at last. He felt the peace he had yearned for his whole life. All of his guilt and sorrow and rage had been taken away. Breathing easier, he turned to Tabitha.

She touched his cheek; her palm was soft, smooth. He stood still.

Demetrios cupped his hand over hers; he wanted to hold this moment in time forever. "Yes. I understand, and I believe."

Tabitha nodded. The valley below was awash in a sea of brilliant red anemones.

"Lilies of the field," Tabitha murmured. "That's what Jesus called them." Her dark-brown eyes, flecked with golden sparks of light, were shining. "There's still beauty, isn't there?"

"Yes," Demetrios said. Forgiveness. Demetrios could forgive his father, Marcus, and perhaps, even himself. Forgiveness.

Demetrios squeezed Tabitha's hand, his voice shaking when he spoke, "Tabitha, I have much to tell you and something to ask." The secrets that had imprisoned him for so long would be secrets no more. "You need to know my past. I will tell you everything."

Demetrios sensed she was about to walk away. Instead, she took his arm. "Then tell me," she said. "Tell me everything."

Discussion Questions for Blood of a Stone

1. When Demetrios's father sells him to Marcus, Demetrios is stunned. To what extent does Demetrios blame his father for this turn of events, and to what extent does he blame himself? Do you think Demetrios and his father loved each other? Why or why not?

2. From their first meeting, Demetrios and Elazar are bound together, first by their situation as slaves to Marcus, and later as partners in crime and a business. Does this bond evolve into a close friendship between them? Does one of them need to maintain the bond more than the other?

3. When Elazar and Demtrios discover the dagger hidden among Marcus's belongings, Demetrios declares the dagger is "a gift from the gods." But Elazar warns him, "Beware of divine gifts. They may carry a price you don't want to pay." What do you think Elazar meant by this statement? Later, when Demetrios

gives the dagger to B'ar, he tells B'ar: "There may be a curse upon the dagger and its owner." How does this statement relate to Elazar's warning about "divine gifts"?

4. Despite his misgivings, Demetrios purchases Rufus to be his slave at Elazar's insistence. How does Demetrios's relationship with Rufus differ from the relationship he and Elazar had with Marcus? Does Demetrios's relationship with Rufus change during the course of the story?

5. When Demetrios catches Caleb stealing a hair pin from a shop in the marketplace in Sepphoris, Demetrios makes Caleb return the pin. But he agrees not to tell Elazar about the theft. Why do you think he decides to keep Caleb's theft a secret?

6. A theme that threads through the story is that Demetrios is an outsider. How does Demetrios's desire for family and love affect his feelings about Elazar's confession to Jesus?

7. In the scene with the Sorceress of Galilee, Endorah employs all sorts of tricks to deceive Demetrios. Do you believe she is dangerous or simply a charlatan? Why do you think she told Demetrios he should kill Jesus?

8. Tabitha is a character who brings hope into the story and into Demetrios's life. How does the fact that Jesus heals her leprosy alter Demetrios's worldview?

9. Rufus's death is a turning point in the story. How do we know Demetrios has been changed by this experience? How do the circumstances of Rufus's death connect Demetrios to his past crimes?

10. Demetrios feels profoundly betrayed by Elazar's confession to Jesus and by his own father. After being betrayed by the two people he loves the most, what enables Demetrios to place his trust in Tabitha?

11. B'ar and Sara seem to represent everything Demetrios desires. They have a happy marriage and a comfortable, settled life. What lessons does Demetrios learn from B'ar during their time together? Why does Demetrios give the dagger to B'ar?

12. Romulus is responsible for turning Caleb over to the authorities, which results in Caleb's crucifixion. Do you believe Romulus's actions were unjust, or do you believe Caleb brought his troubles upon himself?

13. After Jesus's death on the cross, Demetrios says to Tabitha: "I have much to tell you and something to ask." But his question is never broached. What do you think Demetrios is going to ask Tabitha?

Author
Interview

Q: What inspired you to write this book? Why this era?

A: My original idea was to write a book about a man who plots to assassinate Christ. But, as the book matured, I realized the plot was too simple. I came to believe the more interesting story for the readers was what would it be like to live on the edge of the Jesus movement and the Roman Empire? I think readers wonder what they would have done at that time period. Also, the story can be seen as a struggle between the temporal and the divine; we all can relate to those struggles.

Q: How did your main character, Demetrios, come to be? How unusual was it for a slave to rebel against his master?

A: Demetrios evolved out of the idea that I wanted a main character who was an outsider, someone unfamiliar with the beliefs of the Jews or the Romans. I also wanted a character who needed to overcome a troubled past, and thus, Demetrios became a slave with a terrible secret. We do not know how Roman masters treated their slaves. I believe some were harsh, like Marcus, and others treated them with dignity.

Q: How did you come up with the character Tabitha?

A: As you may know, Tabitha appears once in the Bible in Acts where she is raised from the dead by the Apostle Peter. I always had an affinity for her and wondered why Peter chose her to be raised from the dead. What was her story before she was resurrected? Had she ever met Jesus? Tabitha's mysterious history piqued my writer's imagination, and I began to craft a life for her. Over time, she evolved into a female companion for Demetrios, someone who could understand what it's like to be rejected and outcast. Also, if I should decide to write a sequel to *Blood of a Stone*, I want to write Tabitha's story. Imagine what a story it would be for a woman to be healed by Jesus, die, and then be raised from the dead by Peter—quite a beginning and a story.

Q: Which, of all of your characters, was the most satisfying to write about? Which character was the most difficult? How did your choice of point of view help or hinder the process?

A: The most satisfying character was Rufus. He never wavers in his devotion, and I confess that I cried when he died. We all need a Rufus in our lives, someone who loves us no matter what we do. The most difficult character had to be Elazar because of his complex relationship with Demetrios. They are friends, bound by their crimes and a business, but they are not necessarily close. Demetrios was written from what is known as a close-in, deep third person point of view. As the author, this meant that I was living inside Demetrios's head, and Demetrios was not always pleasant. But it also meant I was limited by what Demetrios knew and understood.

Q: Demetrios is beaten, betrayed, and abandoned by the father figures in the novel. Other father-child relationships depicted in *Blood of a Stone* are also negative (e.g., the relationship between Tabitha and Shumrahu). Could you elaborate on this?

A: One major theme in the book is the need for love and family. When families are broken by abandonment or betrayal, the members often create a new family from their larger community. This was certainly true for Demetrios and Tabitha.

Q: Demetrios commits murder in what some may call an act of self-defense. Can a murderer be forgiven? Why or why not?

A: Wow, tough question! I hope Jesus forgave Demetrios because Demetrios repented and changed, but whether murder in general can be forgiven I will leave up to God and the reader to decide.

Q: From the scorpion to the knife that Demetrios takes from Marcus, the novel is full of symbols and images. How did you come up with these? Why are they important to the novel?

A: We are taught in school to look for symbols in literature. But as an author, I don't intentionally place symbols into the story. Rather, these images are organic to the story and plot, arising somewhere from an author's subconscious. Only after the book is completed do these images take on a greater significance. Perhaps symbols encourage the reader to ponder the deeper meanings embedded in the story.

Q: What is the significance of the title?

A: The title refers to more than one bloodied stone. The first stone, of course, is the one Demetrios uses against Marcus. But there are other bloodied stones in the story as well. The story moves from the blood of a murder to the blood of Jesus's sacrifice, by which we are redeemed.

Q: How long did it take you to write the novel?

A: Too long! From the original concept to completion of the novel, it took about six years. During that period, the characters and story underwent significant transformations.

Q: Who are some of your influences?

A: Whew, so many, many influences, but if I had to narrow the list, I would say: Flannery O'Connor, William Styron, Feodor Dostoevsky, John Milton, and Thomas Mann. All of these authors write with an intensity and passion I admire, and they aren't afraid to take risks.

Q: Are you planning on writing a sequel? If not, would you write another book of historical fiction in the same or a different era?

A: Again, possibly, but not immediately. My current novel-in-progress is set in the mid–twentieth century during the height of the Cold War. And I'm working on a collection of short stories, so I would need to finish those projects before I could tackle a sequel. If I do, it will be Tabitha's story.

AUTHOR BIOGRAPHY

Jeanne Lyet Gassman lives in Arizona where the desert landscape inspires much of her fiction. She holds an MFA in Writing from Vermont College of Fine Arts and has received fellowships from Ragdale and the Arizona Commission on the Arts.

In addition to writing, Jeanne teaches creative writing workshops in the Phoenix, Arizona metropolitan area. Her work has appeared in Hermeneutic Chaos Literary Journal, Red Savina Review, The Museum of Americana, Assisi: An Online Journal of Arts & Letters, Switchback, Literary Mama, and *Barrelhouse*, among many others. *Blood of a Stone* is her debut novel.

Find Jeanne online at: www.jeannelyetgassman.com

TUSCANY PRESS TITLES

The Book of Jotham
By Arthur Powers

Eyes That Pour Forth and Other Stories
Editor Joseph O'Brien

The Cana Mystery
By David Beckett

A Hunger in the Heart
By Kaye Park Hinckley

What World Is This? and Other Stories
Editor Joseph O'Brien

Wild Spirits
Pita Okute